Linda Fairstein, America's foremost prosecutor of crimes of sexual assault and domestic violence, has run the Sex Crimes Unit of the District Attorney's Office in Manhattan for almost three decades. She is the author of three earlier internationally bestselling Alexandra Cooper novels, *Final Jeopardy*, *Likely to Die* and *Cold Hit*. She lives with her husband in New York and on Martha's Vineyard.

THE
DEADHOUSE

Linda Fairstein

LITTLE, BROWN AND COMPANY

A *Little, Brown* Book

First published in the United States in 2001 by Scribner

First published in Great Britain in 2001 by Little, Brown and Company

Copyright © 2001 by Linda Fairstein

Map of Roosevelt Island by Paul Woodward, © 2001 by
The Countryman Press. Excerpted from *The Other Islands of
New York City* by Sharon Seitz and Stuart Miller.
Reprinted with permission of the publisher,
The Countryman Press/W.W. Norton & Company, Inc.

The moral right of the author has been asserted.

A CIP catalogue record for this book is
available from the British Library.

Hardback ISBN 0 316 64628 8
C format ISBN 0 316 85751 3

Printed and bound in Great Britain by
Clays Ltd, St Ives plc

Little, Brown and Company (UK)
Brettenham House
Lancaster Place
London WC2E 7EN

www.littlebrown.co.uk

For
ALEXANDER COOPER
and
KAREN COOPER

Who steals my purse steals trash,
But he that filches from me my good name . . .
—Shakespeare

Best man, brilliant architect

with gratitude for the loving loan
of your good name

Acknowledgments

I never asked permission of Alex Cooper—the real one—when I purloined his name for my heroine several years ago. He and Karen have been dearest friends, perfect traveling companions, great readers, and part of the family since Justin and I first met. I treasure their friendship.

A very special credit is due to Judy Berdy, who shares my passion for Renwick's stunning skeleton, and who helped enormously with my research about Blackwells Island. To Judy and the Roosevelt Island Historical Society, I am enormously grateful.

I was fortunate to find a wealth of material, in the form of old institutional records and reports, at the superb library of the New York Historical Society. My thanks to Betsy Gotbaum, and the librarians who take such fine care of the antique documents.

The archives of *The New York Times* and the microfiche files of the New York *Herald Tribune* were also invaluable. And two books, *Gotham* by Edwin Burrows and Mike Wallace, and *The Other Islands of New York City* by Sharon Seitz and Stuart Miller, provided wonderful vignettes of the crime scene.

Several characters take their names from real individuals. That is because a number of very generous people contributed to a variety of charitable causes and public service auctions in exchange for the opportunity to have a figure named for them in an Alexandra Cooper novel. Some are good guys, some are suspects, some are perps—that's the chance they take. They all have my thanks for their good cheer and benevolence.

Robert Morgenthau remains the professional patron saint of prosecutors, and I am always mindful of my great fortune in working for him for a quarter of a century. My friends in the New York County District Attorney's Office Sex Crimes Prosecution Unit are the very best in the business. They prove it every day of the year. The men and women of the NYPD who risk their lives for all of us on a daily basis have my most sincere gratitude, and our colleagues at the Office of the Chief Medical Examiner continue to amaze me, giving us cold hits and solutions to major cases with increasing frequency.

Everyone at Scribner has made this experience a real joy. That starts at the top, with the generous support of Susan Moldow, which I appreciate tremendously. Giulia Melucci is the best publicist in a tough business and a delightful friend.

Susanne Kirk, my beloved editor, started me on this path a few books back. She has been with me every step of the way, and her reputation as the finest in this field is well deserved. Her heart is in these books, along with my own, and that means the world to me. Thanks, also, to her assistant, Erik Wasson, for his good cheer and attention to detail.

My agent and pal, Esther Newberg, is beyond simple acknowledgments. She has changed my life. How did I ever get so lucky?

Family and friends make all this possible. My incredible mother, Alice—and all the Fairsteins, Feldmans, and Zavislans— continue to give me joy and encouragement.

And most of all, my husband, Justin Feldman, remains my devoted coach, most loyal fan, and constant inspiration.

Roosevelt Island

MANHATTAN

QUEENS

EAST 86 STREET

EAST RIVER — West Channel

EAST RIVER — East Channel

Island

MAIN STREET

Roosevelt

ROOSEVELT ISLAND BRIDGE

AERIAL TRAMWAY

EAST 59 STREET BRIDGE

QUEENSBORO BRIDGE

1. United Nations building
2. Smallpox Hospital ruins
3. Strecker Laboratory ruins
4. Pepsi-Cola Factory sign
5. Tram dock
6. Subway station Q & B
7. Meditation Steps
8. Blackwell farmhouse
9. Chapel of the Good Shepherd
10. Octagon Park
11. Octagon
12. Lighthouse Park
13. Lighthouse
14. Gracie Mansion

0   miles   1/2

Paul Woodward, © The Countryman Press

1

It was hard not to smile as I watched Lola Dakota die.

I clicked the remote control button and listened to the commentary again on another network.

"New Jersey police officers have released a portion of these dramatic videotapes to the media this evening. We're going to play for you the actual recordings the three hit men hired by her husband to kill Ms. Dakota made to prove to him that they had accomplished their mission."

The local reporter was posed in front of a large mansion in the town of Summit, less than an hour's drive from where I was sitting, in the video technicians' office of the New York County District Attorney. Snowflakes drifted and swirled around her head as she pointed a gloved hand at the darkened facade of a house, ringed with strands of tiny white Christmas lights that outlined the roof, the windows, and the enormous wreath on the front door.

"Earlier this afternoon, before the sun went down, Hugh," the woman addressed the news channel's anchorman, "those of us who gathered here for word of Ms. Dakota's condition could see pools of blood, left in the snow during the early morning shooting. It will be a grim holiday season for this forty-two-year-old university professor's family. Let's take you back over the story that led to this morning's tragic events."

Mike Chapman grabbed the clicker from my hand and pressed the mute button, then jabbed at my back with it. "How come the Jersey prosecutors got to do this caper? Too big for you to handle, blondie?"

As the bureau chief in charge of sex crimes for the New York County District Attorney's Office for more than a decade, sexual assault cases—as well as domestic violence and stalking crimes—fell under my jurisdiction. The district attorney, Paul Battaglia, ran an office with a legal staff of more than six hundred lawyers, but he had taken a particular interest in the investigation of the professor's perilous marital entanglement.

"Battaglia didn't like the whole idea—the risk, the melo-drama, and . . . well, the emotional instability of Lola Dakota. He probably didn't know the story would look this good on the late news broadcast or he might have reconsidered."

Chapman lifted his foot to the edge of my chair and swiveled it around so that I faced him. "Had you worked with Lola for a long time?"

"I guess it's been almost two years since the first day I met her. Someone called Battaglia from the president's office at Columbia University. Said there was a matter that needed to be handled dis-creetly." I reached for a cup of coffee. "One of their professors had split from her husband, and he was stalking her. The usual domestic. She didn't want to have him arrested, didn't want any publicity that would embarrass the administration—just wanted him to leave her alone. The DA kicked it over to me to try to make it happen. That's how I met Lola Dakota. And became aware of her miserable husband."

"What'd you do for her?"

Chapman worked homicides, most of the time relying on sophisticated forensic technology and reliable medical evidence to solve his cases. He rarely dealt with breathing witnesses, and although he was the best detective in the Manhattan North Squad when he came face-to-face with a corpse, Chapman was always intrigued by how the rest of us in law enforcement managed to untangle and resolve the delicate problems of the living.

"Met with her several times, trying to convince her that we could make a prosecution stick and gain her trust to let me bring charges. I explained that filing a criminal complaint was the only way I could get a judge to put some muscle behind our actions." Lola was like most of our victims. She wanted the violence to stop, but she did not want to face her spouse in a court of law.

"It worked?"

"No better than usual. When reasoning with her failed, we relocated her to a temporary apartment, arranged for counseling, and sent a couple of our detectives to talk to her husband informally and explain that Lola was giving him a break."

"Happy to see the local constables, was he?"

"Elated. They told him that she didn't want us to lock him up, but if he kept harassing her, that wasn't a choice I would allow her to make the next time he darkened her doorway. So he behaved . . . for a while."

"Until she moved back in with him?"

"Right. Just in time for Valentine's Day."

"Hearts and flowers, happily ever after?"

"Eight months." I turned back to glance at the screen, motioning to Mike to give us sound again. Flakes were caking up on the reporter's eyelids as she continued to tell her story, reminding me that undoubtedly snow was piling up on my Jeep as well, which was parked in front of the building. A picture of Ivan Kralovic, Lola's husband, appeared as an insert on the bottom right corner of the screen.

"We've got to take a short break," the reporter said, repeating the euphemistic phrase that signaled a commercial interruption, "then we'll show you the dramatic footage that led to Mr. Kralovic's arrest today."

Mike got rid of the noise. "And at the end of those eight months, what happened? Did you lock him up the second time?"

"No. She wouldn't even give me a clue about what he had done. Called me that October to ask how to get an order of protection. After I greased the wheels to expedite it for her in family court, she told me she had rented an apartment on Riverside Drive, moved to a new office away from the campus, and settled her problems with Ivan the Terrible."

"Don't disappoint me, Coop. Tell me he lived up to his name."

"Predictably. It was in January of this year that he cut her with a corkscrew, while they were enjoying a quiet dinner for two. Must have mistaken her for a good Burgundy. Sliced open her forearm. He raced her to St. Luke's and it took twenty-seven stitches to close her up."

"They were together for just that one evening?"

"No, he had coaxed her back for the holidays a month earlier. A seasonal reconciliation."

Chapman shook his head. "Yeah, I guess most accidents happen close to home. You nail his ass for that one?"

"Once again, Lola refused to prosecute. Told the doctors in the ER—while Ivan was standing at her bedside—that she'd done it herself. By the time I heard about it through the university and got her down to my office, she was completely uncooperative. Said that if I had Ivan locked up, she would never tell the true story in a courtroom. She had learned her lesson by trying to reunite with

4

him, she assured me, and wasn't going to have anything further to do with him."

"Guess he didn't get the picture."

"He stalked Lola on and off. That's what led her to hide out in New Jersey, at her sister's house, sometime in the spring. She called me every now and then, after Ivan threatened her or when she thought she was being followed. But her sister got spooked—worried about her own safety—and brought Lola to the local prosecutors over there."

"Let's go to the videotape," Mike said, spinning my chair back to the television screen and hitting the sound button on the clicker. The film was rolling and the reporter's voice-over was providing the narrative. The scene appeared to be the same large suburban house, earlier in the day.

"... and you can see the white delivery van parked at the side of the road. The two men walked up the steps in front of the home, which is owned by Ms. Dakota's sister, carrying the cases of wine. When the professor opened the door and came outside to accept the gift bottles, both men put their packages on the ground. The one on the left presented a receipt that Dakota leaned over to sign, while the man on the right—there he goes now—pulled a revolver from beneath his jacket and fired five times, at point-blank range."

I leaned forward and watched again as Lola clutched at her chest, her body pushed backward by the force of the impact. Her eyes opened wide for an instant, seeming to stare directly at the lens of the camera, before they closed, as she fell to the ground, blood oozing from her clothing onto the clean white cover provided by the preceding day's dusting of snow.

Then, the camera, held by a third accomplice in the van, zoomed in for a close-up, and the man seemed to lose control of the equipment as it apparently dropped from his fingers.

"When the killers played their tape for Ivan Kralovic in his office at noon today, after the Summit Police Department released the news of Ms. Dakota's death to the wire services, they were rewarded with a payment of one hundred thousand dollars in cash."

Back to a live shot of the chilled reporter, wrapping up her story for the night. "Unfortunately for Kralovic, the gunmen he had hired to kill his estranged wife were actually undercover detectives from the county sheriff's office here in New Jersey, who staged the shooting with the enthusiastic participation of the intended victim."

The tape rolled again and showed the supposedly deceased Dakota now sitting upright against the front door of the house and smiling for the camera as she removed the outer jacket that had concealed the packets of "blood" that had spurted and flowed so convincingly moments before.

"We've been waiting here, Hugh, hoping this brave woman would tell us how she feels now that she has taken such dramatic steps to end years of spousal abuse and bring to justice the man who wanted to kill her. But sources tell us that she left the house here this afternoon, after Kralovic's arrest, and has not yet returned." The reporter glanced down at her notes to read a comment from the local prosecutor. "The district attorney, however, wants us to express his gratitude to the county sheriff for this 'innovative plan that put an end to Ivan's reign of terror, something that prosecutors from Paul Battaglia's office and the New York Police Department across the Hudson River have been unable to do for two years.' Back to the studio—"

I pulled the remote away from Chapman and slammed it onto the desktop after shutting off the set. "Let's go back to my office and close up for the night."

"Temper, temper, Ms. Cooper. Dakota's not likely to win the Oscar for her performance. You peeved 'cause you didn't get a chance to do the film direction?"

I turned off the light and closed the door behind us. "I don't begrudge her anything. But why did the Jersey DA have to take a shot at us? He knows it hasn't been our choice to let this thing drag on as long as it did." There wasn't a seasoned prosecutor anywhere who didn't know that the most frustrating dynamic in an abusive marriage was the love-hate relationship that persisted between victim and offender, even after the violence escalated.

My heels clicked on the tiles of the quiet corridor as we snaked our way down the long, dark hallway from Video to my eighth-floor office. It was almost eleven-thirty at night, and the tapping of an occasional computer keyboard was the only noise I heard to suggest that any of my colleagues were still at their desks.

Only a handful of cases went to trial this time of year, in the middle of December, with lawyers, judges, and jurors all anticipating the two-week court hiatus for the holiday season. I had been working late—reviewing indictments for the end-of-the-term filing deadline, and preparing to conduct a sex offender registration hearing after the weekend—when Detective Michael Chapman came over to tell me the eleven o'clock news was leading with the Dakota story. He had been down the street at headquarters to drop off some evidence at the Property Clerk's Office and called to see if I wanted a drink before knocking off for the night.

"C'mon, I'll buy you dinner," he now said. "Can't expect me to last the midnight shift on an empty stomach. Not with all the dead bodies I'm likely to encounter."

"It's too late to eat."

"That means you got a better offer. Jake must be home, cooking up some exotic—"

"Wrong. He's in Washington. Got the assignment on that story of the ambassador who was assassinated in Uganda, at the economic conference." I'd been dating an NBC News correspondent since early summer, and the rare nights he was free in time for dinner took me away from my usual haunts and habits.

"How come they keep giving him all that Third World stuff to cover when he seems like such a First World guy?"

The phone was ringing as I opened the door to my office.

"Alex?" Jake's voice sounded brusque and businesslike. "I'm at the NBC studio in D.C."

"How's your story coming?"

"Lola Dakota is dead."

"I know," I said, sitting down in my chair and turning away from Chapman for some privacy. "Mike and I just watched the whole bit on the local news. I think she's got a real future on the stage. Hard to believe she went for all that phony ketchup and—"

"Listen to me, Alex. She was killed tonight."

I turned back to look at Mike, rolling my eyes to suggest that Jake clearly had not seen the entire story yet and didn't understand that the shooting was a setup. "We know all that, and we also know that Paul Battaglia is not going to be thrilled when the tabloids point the finger at me for not putting this mess to bed a couple of—"

"This isn't about *you*, Alex. I've heard the whole story with the Jersey prosecutors and their sting operation. But there's a later headline that just came over the newsroom wires a few minutes ago, probably while you and Mike were watching the story run on the air. Some kids found Lola Dakota's body tonight—her dead body—in the basement of an apartment building in Manhattan, crushed to death at the bottom of an elevator shaft."

My eyes shut tight and I rested my head on the back of my chair as Jake lowered his voice to make his point. "Trust me, darling. Lola Dakota is dead."

2

"I'm sorry, Miss Cooper, but Lily doesn't want to talk with you just now. It's almost midnight, and our doctor is about to sedate her to let her get some rest. She thinks Lola would still be alive if you prosecutors hadn't talked her into this ridiculous scheme and exposed her to so much risk by faking her death."

My first impulse had been to call the victim's family, despite the late hour, to offer our assistance in the aftermath of this tragic turn of events. I knew they were unlikely to accept my help. It was her brother-in-law who answered the call. "I'm sure you must be aware that my office didn't think it was wise to—"

"It's all the same to us. None of you was able to protect Lola from this insanity of Ivan's."

Chapman had taken over my phone and I had moved to the alcove to use the one on my secretary's desk. My conversation ended abruptly and I stared at the calendar hanging on the wall in front of me.

"Snuggle into your snowsuit and mittens, kid. We're going to the two-six." He hung up the receiver and called out to me as I tried again to get through to the sheriff's office in New Jersey. The line was still busy, so I put on my coat, gloves, and boots and followed Mike to the elevator. "Leave your car here. I'll drop you at home when we're done."

The snow had tapered off to a flurry as we walked around to the rear of the courthouse and got into the black Crown Vic that was Mike's duty car. "Body's already been taken down to the morgue. Thought you'd like to grab a look at the scene with me."

"Why didn't Peterson beep me about Lola? Nobody reached out for me . . ."

"Don't take it personally, Coop. The lieutenant didn't even get this one till an hour ago. Seems that as soon as Dakota heard the ex had been arrested, she told her sister she needed a break. She'd been cooped up in the burbs for three weeks and wanted to go home for a few hours. Nothing to worry about with Ivan in custody, so those schmucks from the Jersey office let her drive off into the sunset. Alone. Four seventeen Riverside Drive—must be somewhere near 116th Street. Peterson says it's one of those old prewar apartment houses, in the process of going co-op. Scaffolding out in front 'cause they're repointing the building, and lots of repairs under way inside, too."

"Jake said some kids found her. Did the lieutenant mention anything about that?"

"Yep. Just around dinnertime, some of the boys from the 'hood came into the basement from Riverside Park to hang out. Get warm and get high, probably in reverse order. When they pressed for the elevator to come down, the doors didn't open completely, since the cab couldn't get all the way even on the bottom."

Mike was driving north to Canal Street, then heading over to the West Side Highway for the ride uptown. Tacky aluminum holiday decorations bordered the closed stalls on this dismal downtown shopping strip, where every kind of counterfeit designer product would be back on sale, out on the crowded sidewalks, by daybreak.

"The super heard a commotion and started to chase the kids outside. He thought they'd screwed up the equipment by playing around with it. So they offered to help him raise the cab a few feet to see whether something was stuck beneath it. When they looked into the shaft, they saw the body."

"Did they know—?"

"Whether she was dead? Fuggedaboutit."

"No, did they know that it was Lola?"

"You know what happens when you step on a cockroach? Any idea if it was Willie or Milton? The one that was crawling on your desk, or the one that was living in your file cabinet? The super hadn't even seen her in the building for months. Emergency Services responded to help get the remains up, and she was carted off to the ME's office."

"But they didn't treat it as a homicide?"

"Everyone involved assumed, up to that point, that it was all an accident. The elevator's been on the fritz, stopping between floors when it wasn't quitting altogether. The super told the first cops on the scene that some broad—probably just visiting in the building—must have stepped off into the black hole without even noticing that the elevator wasn't there."

"No one had any reason to know what she had been going through," I mumbled aloud as I struggled to recall whether I could have pushed Lola any harder when I had wanted her to press charges.

"Hell, it wasn't till one of the morgue attendants found a few papers in the pocket of her blouse that anyone even knew the identity of the deceased. Called back up to the Twenty-sixth

Precinct, and they passed the news on to the lieutenant. Could still easily be an accident, according to what the super's been telling the cops. But then, in light of all the other bad news in her life, I'd have to think Ms. Dakota had outlived her string of lousy luck and was due to win the lottery."

Mike hit the brakes and I jerked forward, restrained by the seat belt. He had tried to pass a Yellow Cab at the entrance to the highway, and the turbaned driver gestured obscenely and cursed at us as he fishtailed on an icy patch of road.

"Move it, Mohammed!" Chapman yelled back, blasting the words into my ear as he aimed them across me toward the cabbie. "Those camel-humpers can guide a herd across the burning sands of the Sahara, but there oughtta be a law to keep them off the snow."

"I thought we had a deal for the new year?"

"I got a couple of weeks to go, kid. Don't expect any mouthpiece miracles overnight."

The New York City skyline glittered against the cobalt ceiling stretched out above and beyond it. From the Chelsea Piers, outlined against the water off to our left, to the red-and-green-lighted spire of the Empire State Building, across the middle of town in the distance, everything was gaily dressed for Christmas. I stared out at the assortment of blinking lights while Mike dialed up the numbers on his cell phone to check the whereabouts of his team.

I had known Chapman for more than ten years, and accepted the fact that he was no more likely to change his ways than I was able to explain the nature of our friendship, intensely close and completely trusting, despite the vast differences in our backgrounds. It had been almost twelve years since I joined Battaglia's office, and I smiled, remembering my father's prophecy that I wouldn't last there much past the three-year commitment required by the district attorney when I signed on. No one in my family believed that my training at Wellesley College and the University of Virginia School of Law would prepare me for the grim realities of life in an urban prosecutor's office.

My father, Benjamin Cooper, was a cardiologist who had revolutionized surgical procedures when he and his partner invented a plastic valve that was used in virtually every heart operation in the country for more than fifteen years following its introduction to the field. To this day, he and my mother, while aware of the great personal satisfaction I derive from my work, worry about my ability to separate myself from its constant emotional drain—and its occasional dangers.

"Tell Peterson I'm on the way." Chapman turned to me and winked. "I'm bringing the lieutenant a little surprise." He clicked off the phone and was quiet for a few minutes. "I just assumed you'd want to come with me tonight. If I'm wrong, I can cross over to the East Side and drop you at your apartment."

Mike knew me well enough to know that I wouldn't have missed the opportunity to go with him to Lola Dakota's home and see for myself, firsthand, what the police were about to learn. It was logical for onlookers to presume some kind of freak accident, but the odds should truly have been in Lola's favor at this point, and the lieutenant was not going to let go of someone who had met an unnatural death on what he would consider his watch.

"Did you like this Dakota dame, blondie?"

I rolled my head back away from Mike, staring at the vista as we drove up onto the elevated portion of the highway.

"She was a tough character to like. Admire, maybe, but hard to warm up to. Very smart. And even more arrogant than brilliant. But she was willful and shrill, rode herself really hard, and from what I understood, rode her students even harder."

"And the husband? What made him so irresistible?"

"Who knows what goes on inside anyone else's marriage? I'll pull my files together in the morning and check my notes. I've got all kinds of details from our conversations and meetings about the case." I remembered again the many hours I had spent with

Lola throughout the past two years, trying to convince her that we could make the criminal justice system work for her, and to let me take Ivan to trial for assault.

Chapman came from another direction altogether. His father, Brian, had been a second-generation Irish immigrant, who worked as a cop for twenty-six years and then died of a massive coronary two days after turning in his gun and shield. Mike was in his third year at Fordham when he lost his father, and although he completed his degree the following spring, he immediately took the exam and enrolled at the police academy, in honor of the man he most admired and respected. He was half a year older than I, and had recently celebrated his thirty-sixth birthday. Mike was one of the few people I knew who was thoroughly comfortable in his own skin, doing exactly what he most wanted to do in the world. That was simply to come to work every day at the Manhattan North Homicide Squad, with the best detectives in the city of New York, and spend all his waking hours restoring some dignity and a bit of justice to victims who had been murdered on what he liked to think of as his half of the island.

"Maybe we can stop by Mercer's house over the weekend. He's got some case folders on this one, too," I added. "And probably some good insight about Lola."

We had both been counting the days until Mercer Wallace would come off sick leave and back to the department on limited duty. Four months had passed since the attack that had almost taken his life, and it still took my breath away to think how close I had come to losing one of my dearest friends. Mike and Mercer had been partners in Homicide for several years, until Mercer was transferred to the Special Victims Unit, where he carried the lead role in some of the most complex rape investigations in the city.

Grand old apartment houses lined up along Riverside Drive, to our east, and Mike took the Ninety-sixth Street exit to wind his way up the quiet streets till we saw the array of NYPD cars and trucks that blanketed the intersection and rested on the snowy slopes of the park entrance opposite Lola's building. "Must be the place, kid."

Two uniformed cops were stationed on either side of the front door, and one nodded at Mike as he flashed his badge and asked the way down to the basement. "Press hasn't crawled all over this yet?" he asked, puzzled by the lack of interest from the media.

"Been and gone," the younger guy answered, jiggling one foot at a time and flexing his fingers, trying to keep warm. "They pulled out after a few shots of the body bag."

"Is there a doorman?"

"Not all day. Just came on at midnight. The entrance is only covered from twelve till eight A.M. And I think we're cramping this guy's style already. He likes to hang on to his flask pretty tight, and he's really spooked out by this. You gotta use the stairs or the north elevator to get down to where they found her. The south car has been shut off altogether. That's where the body was."

A couple in formal dress glanced at the police officers and brushed past Chapman on their way inside. They were still in the rear of the lobby as we entered, standing in the recessed area off to the right, by the mailboxes, trying to find out from the confused doorman what the commotion was about. Two elderly women in flannel bathrobes and one grad student type with purple-streaked hair had beaten them to the old guy for a chat, and I expected that by dawn, most of the tenants would have some version of a rumor from one of these sources.

Chapman pulled open the heavy service door that led to the fire stairs. There was no lightbulb at the top of the landing, and I followed him slowly down the two flights of steps.

Lieutenant Peterson was sitting at a bare desk in what I assumed was the super's office at the foot of the staircase. His cigarette dangled from his lips as he clutched the phone receiver with one hand and held up his other in our direction, palm outward, signaling Chapman to be quiet.

When he finished the conversation, he rose to his feet to greet us. "Alexandra, how've you been? That was the deputy commissioner, Mike. Can I talk to you alone for a minute?"

"Jeez, and I brought Sonja Henie all the way up here just to see you, Loo."

Peterson wasn't amused. He motioned Mike into the small room and closed the door. I turned the corner and said hello to the rest of the team from the Homicide Squad. Four of them were standing in front of the open space of the elevator shaft, and the bottom of the deadly cab was posed eerily above their heads and behind them, like a huge weight ready to drop again. They were talking about the squad's Christmas party, planned for the next evening, with no mention of the gruesome death that had brought them to this filthy room.

"You in on the pool?" Hector Corrado asked me.

"Only if you make sure I don't win. Battaglia thinks it's in such bad taste that we shouldn't humor you guys by chipping in."

"Pick a number, Alex. It'll only run you twenty bucks, and it's a big pot this year. You wanna lose, go low. Man, things always get crazy around the holidays, and this one's starting off wild. You're too young to remember, but it's beginning to look like the eighties around here."

Homicide cops had a tradition of betting on the number of murder cases they expected to occur before the end of the year. Hector kept track of the field, since choices had to be made by late summer. If there were open slots left, prosecutors were invited to kick in before the night of the party.

"So far, we've only had three hundred sixty-two in Manhattan this year. I just missed by six bodies back in eighty-eight. Total was seven sixty-four, can you believe it? And these wimps think they're overworked now when they're carrying a handful of investigations."

Chapman had left his overcoat in the super's office and emerged holding an oversize flashlight. He held out his right hand to Hector and asked the guys if the Crime Scene Unit had finished its work.

"Hard to make this a crime scene. Super was selling it to the first guys who responded as an accident. Peterson pulled in every chit he could think of to get Crime Scene to come over and give it a look, sort of unofficially. They're treating it as a suspicious death, not a homicide yet. Not every day you get a broad who lays down and rolls out her front door into an elevator shaft just hours after somebody else paid a lot of money to have her knocked off," Hector opined. "They took some photos of the body before she was scooped out. You could look. All you're gonna see is some dark stains."

Lieutenant Peterson, the veteran detective who ran the Homicide Squad, could get the Crime Scene Unit to do almost anything he requested. He had the best instincts in the business when it came to death investigation, and the finest track record in the department for solving cases. When he asked for backup, men knew he wouldn't be wasting their efforts.

Mike squatted and pointed the beam into the dark shaft. I rested one hand on his shoulder and looked in over his head. "You want to step aside, blondie? I know you think you give off quite a glow yourself, but you're blocking the little bit of help that seventy-five-watter is shining down at me from over your head."

I straightened up and stepped back.

"Hector, anybody get down here and scrape some of this crap up? It's impossible to tell what's blood and what's oil from the works, just by looking." Mike was standing, too.

"Yeah, that's all been done."

"They dust for prints?" I asked.

"Nobody even knew what parts of the building to include in the scene, Alex. We don't know if she had been dead for one hour or four by the time she was found. In the meantime, one super, two handymen, and a bunch of teenagers had been all over this area. They didn't know who she was, so they couldn't figure out which floor she'd dropped from or which elevator button she'd pushed. Sure, they went up and down all twenty-two landings, dusting for latents, looking for signs of a struggle, canvassing to see if anyone was at home who heard any noise. Pretty futile runaround so far. You go try that other elevator bank. It's not impossible that she just missed her footing and went off into a swan dive. You'll see, these things are on their last legs."

"Anyone been inside her apartment yet?"

"Waiting on that now. Peterson sent someone down to the morgue to get the keys they found on the body. Emergency Services is on their way back with a ram. Whoever gets here first, that's how we're going in."

"Super doesn't have a key?"

"Nope. She didn't trust nobody with nothin', is what he says."

That would be Lola. Chapman motioned to me to follow him back up the staircase to the lobby. There was a pair of stuffed armchairs against the wall, covered in a dreary tapestry fabric, sorely in need of reupholstering, and we sat opposite each other in them while he told me about his conversation with the lieutenant.

"Loo's really ripped. The commissioner's sticking with the accident story. It certainly can't be Ivan who had anything to do with this, they figure, since he was already under. That's what Peterson took me inside to tell me. That, and to get you off the premises pronto. If the mayor says this is an accident, then there's no need to have an assistant district attorney meddling in it."

For the moment, we both ignored that point. "They never heard of backup? What if Kralovic didn't trust the guys he hired in Jersey and wanted a little security, some extra insurance, to make sure his plan to kill Lola worked?"

"I don't need convincing. City Hall does. The first day of Christmas my true love gave to me, a shove in the back and a trip to the morgue, right? The mayor doesn't want to add to the murder tally for the end of the year. And he's getting additional pressure from the powers that be at Columbia University."

"But Lola didn't even work there anymore."

"They farmed her out to a new, experimental school—King's College. It's got an entirely separate administration, but it bought some of the old Columbia buildings, so it's adjacent to the Columbia-Barnard campus. Somebody up there's got a direct pipeline to the mayor's office. The school officials don't want to open the whole can of worms about the history of their own tortured relationship with Lola Dakota, so they'd like this shoved under the carpet as well."

"They're leaving out a great big stumbling block, in the oversize form of the rotund, thick-skulled, and honorable Vinny Sinnelesi, the Jersey prosecutor who put together this clever sting operation. Battaglia thinks the entire plan was to snag some visibility to launch Sinnelesi's bid for the gubernatorial race next year. Vinny had no qualms about getting attention on the back of Ms. Dakota while she was alive, so I doubt he'll lose a minute's sleep about doing it over her dead body."

Mike laughed at my description of Sinnelesi, and at my obvious state of agitation. "Calm it, Coop."

I was too wound up to stop. "Easy for him to sit tight in his own little fiefdom and point his fat finger at us, calling this a murder—whether it is or isn't—knowing he can't screw up *this* investigation 'cause it will be in Battaglia's jurisdiction."

The front door of the building opened and, with the frigid air, in walked Lieutenant Peterson. Chapman got up and his trademark grin vanished in a flash. "I thought you'd gone home, Loo."

Without breaking stride as he moved toward the elevator, Peterson barked back, "I told you to get Ms. Cooper out of this building, Chapman. She's got nothing further to do with this matter. This, this, . . . accident."

3

I sat in Chapman's car, shivering against the chill of the night air, which kept me wide-awake despite the late hour. Peterson's unexpected reappearance in the lobby had been due to the arrival of the detective who had been sent to the morgue to fetch Dakota's keys. The two had crossed paths as Peterson was about to close his car door, so the lieutenant doubled back to see whether they could gain entry to Lola's fifteenth-floor apartment.

Chapman knew that it wasn't Peterson's style to examine the woman's home himself. He wasn't a micromanager in that sense, and would rely on the intelligence of his men—and the photographs they would bring back—to highlight any information of significance. "Loo'll give it a once-over just to satisfy himself, somebody'll snap some pictures, and then I'll come down to get you," he said as he led me to his car and unlocked the door. "Just slink down in the seat so he doesn't see you when he's leaving—no heater, no radio. He'll be gone in twenty minutes."

"You know he'll kill us if we get caught."

"Can't happen, kid. It'll just be you, me, and George Zotos. Who's gonna squeal?"

Zotos was one of the guys on Mike's team in the squad, and I had worked well with him over the years. "There's no downside to this for you. Battaglia doesn't even know you're here, and Peterson gave orders to me, not to you."

Shortly before one-thirty in the morning, Peterson walked out on the sidewalk and his driver swung around in front of the building to pick him up. Ten minutes later, Chapman came out the same way, said something to the uniformed cops still posted next to the entrance, and crossed the street to the car to help me maneuver the icy road. We walked down to 115th Street and into the alley that led to the rear of the building. The heavy iron door was wedged ajar by the flashlight that Chapman had been holding earlier. He picked it up from the ground as he pulled open the door and took me inside through the basement. We rode to the fifteenth floor on the one elevator that was still in service, which creaked its way upward, slowly and noisily, then crossed over to the south side of the building to get to 15A. When Chapman tapped lightly on the door, Zotos opened it immediately and we joined him inside the apartment.

Mike passed me a pair of rubber gloves, in exchange for the black leather pair I'd been wearing all evening. "Don't touch anything without showing it to me first. Just poke around and see what strikes you as interesting."

"Some kind of slob, eh?" George was shaking his head, not knowing where to begin. "You think it was ransacked, or she just liked to live this way?"

I had been to Lola's office several times to discuss her case and to try to pressure her supervisors into supporting her during the process. "I think this is her natural habitat. It's pretty consistent with what I saw on campus."

We were standing in the living room, which appeared to have been decorated with the remains of a Salvation Army used-furniture sale. The classic bones of a prewar six-room apartment were practically obscured by the bizarre accumulation of odd-shaped chairs, a pair of Victorian love seats covered in faded burgundy velvet, a beige Naugahyde lounger, and cardboard boxes piled everywhere, with strapping tape still in place. Whenever she had moved them in, Lola had not yet opened or unpacked them.

I walked through the other rooms to get a sense of the layout. The small kitchen, still decorated in the drab avocado tones of the sixties, was quite bare, which fit with the fact that she had been living in New Jersey for almost a month. The dining room featured an old oak table, pushed up against the window, overlooking a glorious view of the park and river. It, too, was stacked with boxes, with the word BOOKS scrawled on the sides of almost every one.

The master bedroom had the same view, outside and within. Here, some of the cartons had been opened and the volumes were spread around the floor and partially scattered on shelves.

"What'd she teach?" Mike asked, moving into the room with me.

"Political science. When I first got the case and met her, she was still on the faculty at Columbia. Had a spectacular reputation as a scholar and a teacher. Lola was a brilliant lecturer."

I glanced at a small stack of books on her nightstand. They were all novels rather than textbooks. I wondered whether they were favorites she kept at hand to reread. A bookmark stuck out from the pages of the one on top of the pile—an early Le Carré, one that Lola would never finish.

"Students loved her because she brought the classroom alive. I remember one day last winter, I was going up to the school for a meeting with her. She said I could catch part of her class. Municipal institutions in the early part of the twentieth century—the mayoralty, the corrupt officials of Tammany Hall, the city jails and courthouses. Of course I was intrigued, so I made a point of getting there in time to walk in and sit in the back of the classroom."

"Busman's holiday," Mike said, opening drawers and examining their contents.

"Lola lured me right into that one." I smiled, remembering the day. "She'd spent the week on the politics of Gentleman Jimmy Walker, the mayor of New York City in the late 1920s. But she had a unique method of showing the students the tone of the period. She was parading around the podium, doing a perfect imitation of Mae West, describing the actress's arrest and prosecution for the stage performance of her play—called *Sex*—in 1926. She was reading from West's autobiography, describing the condition of the prison cell in the Tombs, and how the confused, diseased women were herded inside like animals."

"A bleeding heart, under all that flesh, you're gonna tell me."

I ran my finger across the spines of a row of books, checking the titles and noting that most in that section were treatises about nineteenth- and twentieth-century government in New York City, which was her specialty. "She ended by describing how the jail system was run by greedy and stupid civil servants, worse than the prisoners. She looked over the heads of her students and quoted West right to me. 'Humanity had parked its ideals outside.'"

"Staged just for you?"

"I was there to make her understand how important it was to prosecute Ivan, and she wanted me to know that she wasn't about to see him stuck in a jail cell. The typical ambivalence of a survivor of domestic abuse."

Chapman lifted the dust ruffle to look under the bed and continued to poke around the room.

"Doesn't sound like scholarship to me. Sounds like two-bit, second-class theatrics. Same kind she went for with those Jersey jerk-off prosecutors yesterday."

"She was capable of both. I'll give you some of her published articles to read. You'll like her writings about the Civil War period and the Draft Riots." Mike knew more about military history than anyone I had ever met and read extensively on the subject.

"Save 1863 for another day and transport yourself back to the twenty-first century."

Mike was impatient with my diversion, with good reason, and I turned away from the bookshelves and moved on to the desk. "The computer?"

"Leave it alone. Jimmy Boyle's coming to pick it up tomorrow."

Boyle headed our cybercop squad and was a genius at retrieving files and information that literally, to my view, were lost in space.

The rest of the desktop was a maze of spiral notepads, computer disks, phone messages dated three and four months earlier, which detectives would scour in the days to come, and small framed photographs. I recognized a young Lola in her cap and gown, at what must have been her graduation from Barnard, and then a Dakota family shot of more current vintage, taken in front of her sister Lily's home in Summit.

There was a black knit cardigan sweater over the back of the desk chair. "Any idea what she was wearing today?" I asked.

Mike called to George, but he hadn't seen the body either, so Mike added that question to the list he had started in the memo pad he kept inside his blazer. "They'll have it inventoried at the ME's office in the morning. Then I've got to check with the sister to see if the clothes she had on when she died are the same ones she left Jersey with."

I used my forefinger to pull at the pocket on the chest of the sweater. "Hey, Mike, want to take out this piece of paper?"

I didn't want to be responsible for touching anything that might raise an issue of chain of custody. For all intents and purposes, I wasn't there tonight. He slid his gloved fingers in and came up with a folded page from a telephone pad printed with the words KING'S COLLEGE at the top, and beneath that, the single handwritten notation, in bold print:

THE DEADHOUSE

Below the words was a list of four numbers: 14 46 63 85.

Mike read the words aloud. "Mean anything to you? A person? A place?"

I shook my head.

"Probably what the other tenants will start calling this building," George said.

"Is that her writing?"

I had seen enough of her correspondence to recognize it at once. "Yes. Any date on it?"

"Nah. I'll voucher the note and the clothing. When we go to Jersey, remember to ask the sister if she can tell us whether Lola had this sweater there with her yesterday."

I opened the closet door and we poked around the contents. An ordinary mix of skirts and slacks, dresses and blouses, sizes consistent with Lola's large chest and slim hips.

"What do you know about a boyfriend?" George called out to me from the second bedroom.

"News to me." I closed the closet and went into the smaller room.

There was a couch and a chair, and George was standing in front of a chest of drawers, having pulled open each of the three levels. He was dangling a pair of Jockey shorts on the end of his pen. "Get me some bags from the kitchen. Let's see if we can find out who Mr. Size 40, Briefs-Not-Boxers, might be."

Mike noticed the end of a striped sheet sticking out below the edge of the couch. He threw the cushions onto the floor and rolled out the metal frame of the sleep sofa. He stripped the sheets off the narrow mattress and folded the top and bottom ones separately. "Let's see if the lab comes up with any love juice." He wrapped each one in an ordinary brown paper bag, to avoid contamination from one surface to another, and because sealing damp materials in plastic could cause them to deteriorate.

George chuckled. "So much for the mayor's theory that she threw herself in the elevator shaft 'cause she was so despondent about having Ivan arrested. Peterson told me the first thing I had to look for in here was a suicide note. Damn, seems like she squeezed in one last fling before it was lights out."

"Let's just leave this all here and send a team in for the morning with an Evidence Recovery Unit. Someone needs to go through this stuff," Chapman said, waving his hand at the several pieces of men's clothing hanging in this room's closet. "Got to check the labels, look for ID. It'll take hours. We'll just seal off the apartment now and have them put a uniformed post outside the door for the night."

"Any mail here?" I was taking one more look around as I put on my coat.

"No. The brother-in-law said all her mail was being forwarded to her office at school, then she went through it there. We'll have to pick it up tomorrow."

"Fat chance. I've had dealings with the legal departments, both at Columbia and at King's. I can only tell you that if Sylvia Foote gets to Lola's office first, everything will be so sanitized that you'll think it had been swept by a CIA operative. Never a trace of Professor Dakota."

Foote was the general counsel of King's College, having served in the same post at Columbia for more than a quarter of a century. She would opt for protecting the institution every chance she had.

"You know her personally?"

"Yeah. And she's like fingernails on a chalkboard. 'Don't disturb the students' is her mantra, but what she really means is that the university's golden rule is not to scare the parents. Nobody paying those tuition rates wants his kids to go to a school where there might be a hint of scandal. We'd better try to get in there as fast as we can."

Chapman called the two-six and asked the desk sergeant for an extra body to sit on the door of 15A. Then we said good night to George and retraced our steps downstairs and out the rear door of the building, around to Riverside Drive, where the car was parked.

As we let the engine warm up, I reached for the radio and moved the dial to 1010 WINS, the all-news station, to see when this arctic front would pass through the city. I caught the tail end of the traffic cycle, warning about icy patches on the bridges leading in and out of town, and shivered again at the top of the early morning news.

"This just in: the body of a Yale University senior, missing from her New Haven dormitory since the day after Thanksgiving, was found shortly after midnight, floating in the Hudson River, near the promenade off Battery Park City. The content of the letters left behind by Gina Norton have not been released to the press, but police sources say that there are no signs of foul play."

"So much for my mother's theory that the school yard was a safer place to be than the streets—one more corpse tonight, we'll have a hat trick. And how handy for Hizzoner. No foul play declared before she's even been dried off, thawed out, and taken apart by the medical examiner," said Chapman, flipping off the radio, turning on the headlights, and easing out of the parking space to take me home.

4

I heard *The New York Times* slam against my apartment door at six-thirty, flung there by the porter who distributed the papers throughout the building every morning. Drops of water from my hair, still wet from the shower, dripped onto the front page as I leaned over to pick it up and check the headlines for the story of Lola Dakota's death.

Three pages back in the Metro section was a photo of Lola, standing at a lectern in full academic dress, mortarboard atop her head. The caption read "University Professor Dies in Bizarre Accident," above a subheading printed in smaller type describing her as a "Witness for the Prosecution." The reporter had managed to incorporate every stereotypical expression of reaction into his brief story. The administration was shocked and saddened by news of the beloved professor's death, students were puzzled by the ironic twists of fate in Dakota's final days, and her husband's family was outraged at charges that he was alleged to have been involved in the thwarted plot to kill her.

The phone rang and Chapman gave me the morning weather report. "You're gonna need a dogsled to get downtown this morning. The streets are coated with ice and the windchill brings it down to about five degrees. I'm on my way home to catch a few hours' sleep."

"Anything develop during the rest of the tour?"

"Nope. Made the usual notifications, took care of all the paperwork, got the preliminary reports down on the chief of detectives' desk so he's in the know first thing he walks in. Subway's the only way to go today, kid, much as you hate it. The driving is treacherous. See you around lunchtime."

I finished dressing and reluctantly headed for the Sixty-eighth Street Lexington Avenue station, anxious to beat the rush hour crowds. Once settled into my seat, I scoped out the other passengers and sat back to read the rest of the newspaper. It was early enough so that most of my companions appeared to be people going to their jobs and offices. A bit later and too many of the riders who stayed on board south of Forty-second Street would also be on their way to the courthouse, to make appearances for their criminal cases. On those occasional days that I got on the train at nine o'clock, it was an eerie feeling as we looked each other over for the last ten minutes of the ride, knowing at a glance—the closer we all got to the Canal Street station—that we were combatants on opposite sides of the battle. Usually, I preferred to drive to work.

The cold air bit at my cheeks as I reached the top step of the subway exit and turned south for the short walk to Hogan Place, fighting the strong wind as I walked carefully around icy patches on the sidewalk. The guy inside the small pushcart on the corner closest to the office saw me coming and readied a bag with two large black coffees.

I scanned my identification tag into the turnstile, greeted the uniformed cop who sat at the security desk, and got on the elevator with a few other lawyers from the staff. I stuck my head in at the press office around the corner from my own desk to remind the assistant to include Dakota's story and obituary in the clips she was preparing for the district attorney to read. Each morning, Brenda Whitney's aides combed the *Times* and the tabloids, the local and national papers, cutting and compiling all the stories related to our cases or to crime stories that might be of interest to Paul Battaglia and his executive staff.

Before I could remove my coat and boots, Pat McKinney stood in the doorway, resting a hand on the back of my secretary's, Laura's, empty chair. "Lost a big one last night, huh?"

I tried not to let my intense dislike for McKinney, who was deputy chief of the trial division and one of the supervisors to whom I answered, affect my response. "After all that woman had been through, you might think about putting it in terms of *her* life, not mine."

"Lucky for us it didn't happen on *your* turf. Pretty clever sting they pulled off in New Jersey with the fake hit. How come you weren't so creative with the case?"

"It was Paul's decision not to be involved in such a risky plan, and I think he was entirely right about it."

"That's what you get for not going up the chain of command, Alex. I would have backed you on that one. Our squad wouldn't have let her walk away yesterday afternoon without taking better care of her, tucking her in at home, making sure she was safe and sound. Next time, check with me first. I can often be more flexible than Battaglia. And Lola Dakota would be alive." He slapped his hand against the back of Laura's chair and walked away toward his office at the end of the hall.

The phone rang and I picked it up as I sat down to turn on my computer. Rose Malone, Battaglia's executive assistant, was calling to tell me that he was on his way downtown and wanted to see me as soon as he got in. That gave me half an hour to try to get the Jersey prosecutors to bring me up to speed on what they had learned during the night. The one answer Battaglia didn't like getting too often was "I don't know, boss."

I dialed the number for my counterpart in Sinnelesi's office and left a message in his voice mail to call me back as soon as possible. How did the case against Kralovic look? Exactly what time did Dakota leave her sister's home? How did she travel into Manhattan? What kind of mood was she in? Who saw her last? Battaglia was likely to ask me what she'd had for breakfast, too, and whether or not she had cleaned her plate. There wasn't anything about her last days on earth that he wouldn't expect me to detail for him as soon as he got into the office.

"Have a minute for me?" Jody Soellner was standing tentatively in my doorway, and I waved her in. Her arms were loaded with notepads, a copy of the penal law, and what looked like an NYPD evidence envelope. "I'm on my way to the grand jury to put in that case I picked up last weekend. The guy who broke into the apartment on West Twenty-third Street and raped the babysitter who was watching the three kids. Remember the facts?"

I told her I did.

"The victim just showed me two of her fingers. When the perp put down his knife on the bed, she tried to roll off, away from him. But he pulled her by the arm and bit down hard." Jody held up her left hand and grabbed her own middle and ring fingers. "She was back at Roosevelt Hospital for her follow-up yesterday and the doctor confirmed that she had two severed nerves. Can I charge an extra assault count—you know, that the perp's teeth are a dangerous instrument?"

"Good try. Unfortunately, the court of appeals disagrees with you. I think the case is *People* versus *Owusu*, a couple of years back. The distinguished jurists said it's different from upping the ante by bringing a weapon along to assist the bad guy in his criminal endeavor. His teeth come with him naturally—they're not 'dangerous instruments' and you can't get the extra charge, even though I like your creative thinking. What's in the brown folder?"

Jody unclasped the catch and withdrew a plastic package covered in black ink with a voucher number and case identification. When she flipped it over to the clear side and held it up to show me, I could see the carving knife with the ten-inch blade. This victim was lucky. The jurors wouldn't even need to wait to hear the definition of forcible compulsion before they voted a true bill.

"Be sure and give Laura a copy of the indictment as soon as you file it."

I e-mailed instructions to Maxine, my paralegal, to pull the Dakota papers as soon as she got in. Reporters would soon be calling to get whichever facts about the case history were public record in order to reconstruct the story behind yesterday's events. I pushed aside the notes on the hearing for which I was trying to prepare, jotting down a Post-it reminder to take the whole file home for the weekend and work on it there, when I could better concentrate on the issues.

Battaglia had a speed-dial number that rang directly on my console, bypassing both of our secretaries. Usually, I jumped out of my seat when I heard its distinctive ring, but this morning Rose had helped me with an estimate of his arrival time. I greeted him and told him that I would be in immediately to brief him on the Dakota case.

"Save it till this afternoon. The governor just called. He's on his way to the Mayor's office and wants to stop in to talk about the DAs' Association proposed legislation package for the January session. You got anything that can't wait, or is it as straightforward as the papers make it appear?"

"I've made all the calls to get details on what happened during the last twenty-four hours, and I'm waiting for Jersey to get back to me. Chapman and I were both pretty skeptical about the accidental death theory last night, but I've got nothing unusual to give you yet."

"Keep it that way, if you can. The last thing I want for Christmas is a high-profile case that sets me up as Sinnelesi's whipping boy."

"No problem," I promised him, and kept my word for almost two hours.

Chapman sounded groggy when Laura put through his eleven o'clock phone call. "The news from both ends is bad."

"Hey, you're supposed to be sleeping. How can anything bad have happened?"

"Peterson just woke me up with the results of the inventory that some of the guys have been doing. You know all those shoe boxes in Lola's apartment? Well, she didn't share your fetish for high heels, slinky sandals, and velvet slippers. A few of those cardboards have some worn-down leather pumps, most are crammed with index cards that look like notes or research for a project, and two tired old boxes are stuffed full of cash."

"Like savings for a rainy day?"

"Like a stash for the monsoon season, Coop. Not kosher."

"Glad I wasn't on the scene for that discovery. What else?"

"And then there's the latest word from the ME's office. Autopsy won't happen until the end of the day, but Dr. Kestenbaum has already noted a few things that don't make him happy. Like some hairs—not Lola's—that she had gripped in her tight little fist, and, more to the point, lots of petechial hemorrhages in her eyes."

I knew the significance of the findings before Chapman went on. The tiny red pinpoints were the classic forensic hallmarks of strangulation.

"Kestenbaum thinks she actually struggled with her attacker while he choked her to death. Then he rolled her into the elevator shaft to make it look accidental. Fasten your seat belt, Coop, while he takes a close look at Lola's innards. He's just getting ready to declare this case a homicide."

5

I called Sylvia Foote. She was not an easy person to reach.

"She'll be in meetings all afternoon," her secretary said. "I don't think she'll be returning any calls until the beginning of the week."

"Tell her it's about Lola Dakota. About the murder of Lola Dakota."

"Murder?" she asked, taking down my number.

By the time I had left a similar message with Rose Malone for Battaglia, Sylvia Foote was on the line.

"Miss Cooper, my secretary just repeated your conversation to me." Foote was in her late sixties—humorless, rigid, and entirely protective of the administration's concerns. "I need to tell my president about this immediately. I'd like you to answer some questions for me."

"And I'd like *you* to answer some questions for us."

"Perhaps we can schedule an appointment for the end of next week."

I knew that the Jersey prosecutors would move in as quickly as possible, looking for clues that would connect Ivan Kralovic to Lola's death. If, in fact, Dakota had been murdered in Manhattan, then Sinnelesi would have no jurisdiction here. But if he wanted to keep his name in the headlines, as Battaglia figured, Sinnelesi would argue that he had a duty to investigate whether Lola had been kidnapped from his side of the river and follow the trail to our doorstep.

By Monday, New Jersey police might already be swarming around the King's College campus and Lola's apartment building, scouring students and neighbors for information, gossip, and potential witnesses.

"I think we need to talk this afternoon. One of the detectives can bring me up to your office."

"I simply don't have time to do that."

"Don't have time?" A prominent member of the university family was dead, and I was only hours away from formal confirmation that we were dealing with a homicide, but Sylvia Foote was stonewalling me already. "I'll be up at your office by two o'clock."

"I'm sorry I won't be here to discuss this with you today."

"In that case, I'll start with the students over in the political—"

"We'd prefer that the students are not involved in this."

Where was Chapman when I needed him? He'd be telling Foote that either she could play hardball with him or do this the nice way. He'd be up there with grand jury subpoenas that she could ignore at her own risk, or she could cooperate and be treated like a lady. And the first time she looked down her long crooked nose at him and attempted to dismiss him with an arrogant order to leave, he'd stick out the subpoena and tell the sour old bag to take it.

"Not involved? It would be lovely if nobody had to be involved, and even nicer if Lola Dakota was alive. That's simply not one of your choices. We're going to have to sit down with you and go over everything that will need to be done, identify every individual we'll need to interview and each document we'll need to access."

Laura walked into my office and placed a slip of paper on my desk as I listened to Foote drone on: *Mickey Diamond is on your other line. He's looking for confirmation that Dakota's death has been declared a homicide by the ME.* I shook my head in the negative and mouthed back to her to get rid of him.

"I've already got the *Post* calling me," I tell Sylvia. "Somebody's leaked the story to the press and the autopsy hasn't even been started yet. You'd better give some thought to how the students— and their parents back home in Missouri and Montana—are going to react to news of a murder in your comfortable little community. It's going to get their attention a lot more quickly than the obituary page did." How would Chapman punctuate that point? "Especially if word gets out that the president's office is stalling our investigation."

Foote was silent. I expected that she was balancing the reality of what I was saying against the bet that her old friend Paul Battaglia would not approve of my heavy-handed style. But she was also smart enough to know that he would back me in my effort to get to the campus before Sinnelesi's troops arrived on the scene.

"My office is in the new King's College building on Claremont Avenue, half a block in from 116th Street. Did you say you could be here by two?"

I phoned Chapman and told him that since I'd left my Jeep at the office the night before, I would swing by to get him in front of his place and head uptown to interview Foote. I told Laura to beep me if any urgent calls came in, and that I would check with her for messages when the meeting was over. The ice was still caked thick on the windshield, and I struggled with the scraper as the defroster worked slowly to melt it.

Chapman was standing in front of the coffee shop next to his apartment building on First Avenue. His only concession to the bitter cold was the fact that he wore a trench coat over the navy blazer that he had adopted as his uniform once he had been assigned to the detective bureau. His black hair was blowing wildly in the wind, and he kept reaching up with his hand to chase it. He opened the passenger door and got in. "So what else do I need to know about Columbia beside the fact that its football team sucks?"

"You'll drive Foote crazy if you don't keep it straight that Dakota was teaching at King's College when she died, not at Columbia. They'll be very jumpy about that. They use some of the same facilities, and students enrolled in either school can take courses at the other, but they are entirely separate institutions."

I had spent a lot of time in Manhattan during my undergraduate years. My best friend and roommate at Wellesley, Nina Baum, met her husband, Gabe, when we were sophomores. He was a junior at Columbia, and I had often accompanied Nina when she came to the city to spend a weekend with Gabe.

As we drove uptown, I tried to fill Mike in on the bits of college history that I remembered. Columbia was founded in 1754, by royal charter of King George II of England, and its original name was King's College—the name recently adopted by the experimental school that carved out a piece of the neighborhood for itself at the start of the new millennium. The university's first building was situated adjacent to Trinity Church on lower Broadway, and some of its earliest students included the first chief justice of the United States, John Jay, and the first secretary of the treasury, Alexander Hamilton. The institution closed down during the American Revolution, and when it reopened eight years later, it had shed its imperial name in favor of "Columbia," the personification of the American determination for independence.

By 1850, the college had moved to Madison Avenue at Forty-ninth Street, shaping itself into a modern university by the addition of a law school to its undergraduate and medical faculties. In 1897, the campus was moved to its current site in Morningside Heights at Broadway and 116th Street; this academic village—modeled on the idea of an Athenian agora—represented the largest single collection of buildings designed by the great architectural firm of McKim, Mead and White.

"What's with this experimental school thing?"

"I only know what I've read in the news. King's is an effort to set up an alternative educational model, drawing from a few of the stars of the Columbia teaching staff, but trying to structure a fresh view of the process. It borrows some of the stature of the Ivy League reputation, but it's been spun off on its own, free and clear of the mother university."

"Who's in charge?"

"We're about to find out. Foote said she'd have the acting president at the meeting."

"Wanna take Third Avenue uptown? Stop for a minute at the corner of Seventieth Street."

I pulled up in front of P. J. Bernstein's.

"Hungry?"

"No, thanks. Had a salad at my desk."

Chapman got out of the car while I double-parked and waited for him. In a slight nod to Christmas, Bernstein's window displayed a few large smiling Santa faces. But there was also a huge menorah with electric candles on the countertop, while blue, gold, and white-fringed streamers declared a Happy Hanukkah to the deli's customers.

Mike returned in a few minutes with two hot dogs wrapped in a napkin, overflowing with sauerkraut and relish, and a can of root beer. "I know the rules. No droppings on the floor mat. No sucking the sauerkraut out of my teeth in public." He chewed on his lunch as I continued driving and cut through Central Park at

Ninety-seventh Street, taking Amsterdam Avenue the rest of the way north to the campus.

"Had any cases out of King's College yet?" Mike asked, licking the mustard off his fingers and swigging from the can of root beer.

"Not one."

"Must be the only school in the country with no reported crimes. Wait till these kids find Cannon's and the West End." Those two bars were magnets for the collegiate community and havens for the binge-drinking students who found their way to our offices with every kind of problem that alcohol abuse created.

Mike displayed his badge to the expressionless, square-tinned security guard who sat inside the small gatehouse at the entrance to College Walk on 116th Street, barely looking up from the skin magazine he was holding in his bony hand. "Okay if we park this inside for a couple of hours? I'm taking my niece here for an interview, see if I can get her back into school. A mind is a terrible thing to waste."

The guard waved us in without looking up. I found a space in front of the Graduate School of Journalism, on the corner of Broadway, and Chapman locked his arm in mine as I lowered myself out of the Jeep; we jogged together across the double-wide street and headed down to Claremont, fighting against the strong wind as we ran.

Sylvia Foote's secretary was expecting us. She took our coats and led us into Foote's small office, which overlooked the avenue and Barnard Hall directly opposite. Foote extended a hand to both of us, and made the introductions to Paolo Recantati, explaining that he was the acting president of King's College, and formerly a history professor at Princeton.

Recantati invited us to sit in a pair of black leather seats with our backs against the large bay window, while he moved across from us to a straight-backed wooden armchair and Foote remained behind her desk. They offered nothing, and waited for me to speak.

"As you know, Sylvia, I'd been working with Lola Dakota on the case against Ivan for almost two years. And I'm sure she made you aware of what the New Jersey prosecutors were doing. Despite their best efforts, it's doubtful that Lola's death was an accident after all. Detective Chapman and I are here to try to get your help in finding out what was going on in her life and who else, besides Ivan, might have wanted her dead."

Recantati spoke to me before Foote even opened her lips to form a response. "I know what your area of expertise is, Miss Cooper. Are you telling me that someone sexually assaulted Lola and then killed her?"

"There's no reason to believe that at—"

"Then exactly why are you involved? Shouldn't we be working with Mr. Sinnelesi's office on this? Lola's case was being handled by his people."

"The Dakota matter has been my investigation for close to two years. I supervise the domestic abuse cases as well as sex crimes. The issues, the sensitivity concerns, the needs of survivors going through the system—many of the problems overlap in these situations. I know the background of Lola and Ivan's relationship, most of her history, a lot of the intimate details of her private life. If she was the victim of an attack—a murder—in New York, I will be the person in charge of the prosecution."

Recantati pursed his lips and looked off to his left, as though to take a cue from Foote. He was tall and lean, and for a few moments, the crossing and uncrossing of his long legs was the only obvious sign of his discomfort. He'd probably never dealt with anything quite like this in his idyllic ivory tower, before coming to Manhattan.

Chapman pushed himself to the edge of his seat and eyeballed Recantati. "You think if you don't give us what we need, we'll just fold up our tents in the night and slip off to the next unsolved crime? You got how many students here?"

"Almost three thousand at King's," he said softly.

"And how many next door at Columbia?"

"Close to thirty thousand," he murmured.

"So start out with something like sixty-six thousand mothers and fathers picking this up on the evening news, half of 'em spread out around the country, who didn't want their kids coming to this city of perverts and potheads to begin with."

Foote and Recantati exchanged scowls.

"Best view of it is, you had a little marital discord that got out of hand, off campus, so nobody else here is at risk," Chapman said, brushing his hands against each other as though to wipe away the problem. "Worst view of it is that you got somebody roaming this neighborhood, making all these darling scholars and social saviors of the future vulnerable to violence. And exactly what are *you* two doing to make little Jennifer and little Jason safe at school?"

"Believe me, Detective, this is an entirely new problem for us here on campus."

"You must be frigging nuts if you think I buy that one. We're not talking 'animal house' and student pranks. This is a college in the middle of a neighborhood that used to boast one of the highest homicide rates in the city. Just look next door at Columbia— they've had students murdered in their dorm rooms and apartments, kids who've been robbed and raped by other students, as well as by strangers from the street."

Recantati opened his mouth to speak but Chapman wouldn't be interrupted. "There's been more drugs used in some of these halls than Keith Richards and Puff Daddy have seen in their combined lifetimes. This isn't the time to hide behind your cap and gown, pal."

Foote broke in to relieve the president. Chapman's directness didn't make her happy. "Alex, for the moment, since Lola had personal contact with you, can't we just discuss this one-on-one? The police don't have to be included until we get official word that this wasn't an accident. After all, that's our understanding of the findings at her apartment last night."

Chapman got up and walked to the phone on Foote's desk. "Mind if I call the morgue? I'd hate to waste your time if the docs can step away from the table in the middle of sawing Lola in half to assure you this was only a slip and fall."

Recantati's stunned gaze moved back and forth between Chapman's face and Foote's hand, which she had clamped over the telephone receiver. He seemed caught in the glare of the headlights and longing to be back in the library instead. "Have you and Ms. Cooper worked together on this kind of thing before?"

Chapman laughed. "Seventy years."

Recantati's brow furrowed more deeply. "But—?"

"I count 'em in dog years. Every one I spend with Coop feels like seven."

Recantati was responding to Mike in a way Sylvia Foote never would, looking as though he hoped the police would help him out and take the entire matter off his hands. "So, what is it you need from us?"

Foote cleared her throat. "Not that we can promise you anything before the middle of next week. We've got to clear this administratively."

"How about a command decision, Mr. President?" Chapman ignored Foote completely and spoke only to Recantati. "Next week's gonna be too late. I'd like to get into Ms. Dakota's office this weekend, start checking her files, her correspondence, her computer records. I'd like to find out who knew her best, which students were in her classes, what faculty members worked with her, who liked her and hated her, who slept with her . . ."

Recantati's face reddened at the mere thought, it seemed, that we would be exploring such intimate aspects of Dakota's life. He was silent.

"We could walk right over to her office now, with both of you. That way you can make sure that Ms. Cooper and I don't do anything to cause trouble here."

Time to soften the approach while we had him on the line.

"You understand, sir, that not everything Detective Chapman is talking about may be necessary," I said. "It's entirely possible that Lola's death will prove to be related to her husband's efforts to get rid of her, and not to the campus community at all. We're exploring that angle first, of course. Nobody wants to involve the school or the kids, except as a last resort."

Foote was harder to fool. "Suppose I can gather together some of the political science faculty for you on Monday morning. We'll make the library available to you for interviews, so our staff members don't have to be carted downtown. Then we'll move on to talk with the students, but only if we must."

Not a bad compromise. "I've got to be in court for a hearing at nine-thirty on Monday. So if we can say two o'clock for you to have some people lined up, that will give you the morning to contact whoever you haven't been able to reach over the weekend. Shall we take a look at Lola's office while we're here?"

Foote buzzed the secretary and asked her to have the head of security bring the passkey up to us as quickly as possible. Within minutes, Frankie Shayson knocked on the door and came into the room. "Hey, Mike. Alex. Haven't seen either of you guys since that racket they threw when me and Harry left the job. Never dull, is it?" The former detective from the two-six squad, the neighborhood precinct, crossed the room and grabbed Chapman's hand as he greeted us warmly. "Want me to take 'em downstairs, Ms. Foote?"

She was obviously unhappy that we had an independent connection to the college, and she wasn't about to let him take us to Dakota's office alone. "If you give me the key, I'll return it to you later today." She reached out her hand to take the ring from Shayson, motioning to Recantati to come along.

The three of us marched down the hallway behind Sylvia Foote and up two flights of stairs to a turreted corner office. On the wall next to the door, instead of a nameplate, there was an ink and pen drawing, two inches by three inches, of a small piece of the U.S.

map, with the word BADLANDS written in the middle. The Badlands of Dakota.

Foote unlocked the door and entered first, followed by Chapman.

"Jesus, the feng shui in here is for shit."

Recantati continued to look lost and overwhelmed. "Sorry, Detective?"

"Don't you know anything about the principles of negative energy? This place is a hellhole, just like her apartment. First of all," Chapman said, kicking a box of books out of his path into the room, "all entrances should be free from obstruction. You need a generous flow into the working environment. And she's got too much black fabric in here. Bad karma—symbolizes death."

Chapman worked his way around the room, looking at books and papers that were piled on the floor, careful not to touch or disturb surface items. Foote had taken Recantati aside and was whispering something to him. I took the moment to stifle a smile and ask Chapman a question. "When did you become an expert in the Chinese art of feng shui?"

"Attila's been shtupping an interior decorator for the last six months. That's all you hear about when you work a tour with him. The office is beginning to look like a Jewish princess's idea of a Chinese whorehouse. 'Don't leave your toilet seat up 'cause your fortune will flow down into the sewer.' See, dried flowers like this?" Mike pointed at the dusty arrangement on Dakota's windowsill. "Lousy idea. Represents the world of the dead. Gotta use fresh ones."

Marty Hun was one of the guys in the Homicide Squad. Mike had nicknamed him Attila.

"We'll get Crime Scene over here this afternoon. I'd like them to process the room for prints and take some pictures. Okay with you two?"

Mike moved behind Lola's desk, noting in his steno pad what lay on top of it and sketching a general outline of the office. The smile was erased from his face, and with his pen he shifted some of the papers on top of the blotter. "Who's been in here since last night?"

"No one," answered Foote.

"I'll betcha my paycheck you're wrong on that count."

Foote approached the desk from the opposite side and placed her palm on a stack of books as she leaned over to see what had caught Mike's attention.

"You wanna get your hand off there?"

She straightened up and brought her arm down to her side.

Mike pulled open the top middle desk drawer by putting his pen into the brass handle. "It's too neat. Way too shipshape, both on top of the desk and in this first drawer. Right where you'd keep whatever it was you'd been working on most recently, or something that was pretty important. Every other pile is sloppy and out of line. Even the stack of mail is too fastidious. Somebody went through some of this stuff and couldn't resist just patting these papers into order. Nothing major, but it's just not in keeping with Lola's messy style. Maybe a careful once-over can come up with a print or something. She chew gum?"

Recantati looked to Foote and then shrugged. "Not that I ever noticed."

It was Chapman's turn to whisper now, leaning over and speaking only to me. "Let's lock up the office and get Crime Scene over here immediately. There's a wad of Wrigley's in the wastebasket. It's great for getting DNA. All that juicy saliva will tell us exactly who's been messing around in here."

Mike turned back to face the others. "Ever hear Ms. Dakota talk about a deadhouse?"

Foote glanced at Recantati before both of them looked at us blankly. "Sounds more like your line of work than ours."

As Mike walked from behind the desk, he stared at a small corkboard affixed to the wall by the window. "You know who any of these people are?" he asked.

Foote moved in next to him, and Recantati looked over his shoulder. "That's a photograph of Franklin Roosevelt, of course, and this one's Mae West. I believe that woman in the corner, in period dress, is Nellie Bly. I can't place the other man."

"Charles Dickens, I think." My undergraduate major in English literature kicked in.

Foote stepped back and turned away, but continued speaking. "I'm not sure who the people are in the photos with Lola herself, but I assume they're friends and relatives. That other snapshot is one of the young women Lola taught last semester, in the spring."

Mike must have thought, as I did, that it was unusual for one student's picture to be singled out to be on the board. He asked the obvious question. "Know her name?"

Foote hesitated before she spoke. "Charlotte Voight."

"Any idea why Lola would have her picture up here?"

Dead silence.

"Can we talk to her?"

"Detective Chapman," Foote answered, sinking onto the cushion of the sofa against the far wall, "Charlotte disappeared from the school—from New York—altogether. We have no idea where she is."

Mike's anger was palpable. "When did this happen?"

"She went missing last spring. April tenth. Left her room early one evening, in the midst of a bout of depression. No one here has seen her since."

6

Chapman wanted to preserve the integrity of Dakota's office for the Crime Scene team to photograph and fingerprint, so he led the unhappy pair of administrators back down to Foote's quarters to finish the conversation.

"And now we're gonna play 'I've Got a Secret' and hope the dumb cop doesn't figure out what kind of problems we got here at school, right? Who was this Voight kid and what do you think really happened to her?"

Foote picked up the story. "Mr. Recantati wasn't appointed until this fall semester, so he's not to blame for not remembering to bring up Charlotte's disappearance." The osteoporosis that had stooped Foote's shoulders seemed even more pronounced as she sat hunched in her chair, calling up facts about the missing girl.

"Charlotte was a junior—twenty years old. Came to us with a very troubled background. She was raised in Peru, actually. Her father's American, working down there for a large corporation. Her mother was Peruvian. Died while Charlotte was finishing high school. The girl was extremely bright, but had had a long battle with depression and eating disorders."

Mike was taking notes as Sylvia Foote talked.

"We didn't know until she got here, of course, that she had a history of substance abuse as well. I doubt that she would have been better adjusted at any other college in the States. There were no relatives anywhere in this country, and when one of those black moods overtook Charlotte, she'd just disappear for days at a time."

"Surely someone found out where she'd been, once she returned?" I asked.

"She was never very open or direct about it. Freshman year she dated a Columbia student who lived in an apartment off campus, and she'd spend time with him. Then she got involved with some Latinos from the neighborhood, the source of her drug supply, we believe."

"What did her roommates think?"

"She didn't have any. Charlotte requested a single when she applied to King's, and she lived a pretty solitary existence. She didn't number many of the girls among her friends. D'you know the kind? She preferred the company of men. Not boys, and generally not other students. She was restless and isolated from most of the school social life. Thought herself much too worldly for most of the kids she met here."

"Didn't you get the police involved when she disappeared?"

"Certainly we did. You must know how it is. They won't even consider a missing person's report until forty-eight hours have elapsed. Nobody noticed Charlotte was gone for most of that time.

The girls in the dorm assumed that she'd gone off to party with her drug crowd, and the professors had grown used to her cutting classes. The Twenty-sixth Precinct has a record of the report we filed. I made the notification myself, after I called her father."

Chapman looked up. "What'd he have to say about all this?"

Foote lowered her head. "He didn't even come to New York. Not then, or later. He had just remarried, which engaged most of his emotional interest, and seemed to believe that Charlotte would show up eventually, when she needed his money or his help. He thought it was just a gimmick to get his attention."

"Anybody check out her room?"

"Yes, the detectives from the precinct. Undisturbed and unremarkable. Her credit cards were never used, her bank account was never tampered with—"

"Make a list, Coop, when you do your subpoenas for Dakota. Let's get bank records, credit card information, and phone records for Voight, too. Her computer still around?"

Foote shrugged. "I imagine when the semester ended in June that all of her belongings were shipped back to her father in Peru, but I'll check that for you."

"And line up some of her classmates for Monday, some of the kids that she lived near in the dorm or hung out with in class. The former boyfriend, too."

Recantati knew that he was in over his head. "Can we slow this down? I think you're making some quantum leaps here that will serve no good."

"Welcome to the real world, Professor. Wake up these it-can't-happen-here nerds and make them get involved in all this. You do it, or I will." Chapman slapped his steno pad against the palm of his hand to drive home his point.

The sharp buzz of the intercom startled me. Foote's secretary's voice came through the speakerphone intercom. "Professor Lockhart is here for his four o'clock meeting with you. He thinks you might want him to join you now."

"No, no. Tell him I'll leave him a message and reschedule for early next week." She turned her attention back to us. "What else do you need by Monday?"

I spoke before Mike could. "Every detail about every criminal incident that has occurred on this campus and to your students, whether here or wherever they're living in the city."

"That's hard to put together quickly. There's no, well . . ." Recantati was stammering.

"I guess you're not familiar with the Cleary Act, Professor?" I asked.

This was Sylvia Foote's territory, and she stepped in to spare Recantati the embarrassment of his ignorance about an important administrative function. "We're in the process of putting together that information now, Alex. I can certainly give you whatever reports and referrals we have."

"Then we'll see you here, on Monday. We've each got a beeper," I said, handing my business card to both Foote and Recantati. "If you need us for anything at all, or want to bring something to my attention, just give a call."

As we walked out of Foote's office, her secretary told us that Detective Sherman and his partner from the Crime Scene Unit were on their way up to Dakota's office. Mike nodded to me to follow him up the staircase to watch them get to work.

"So what's the Cleary Act?"

"About fifteen years ago, a student named Jeanne Cleary was raped and strangled to death in her dormitory at Lehigh University in Pennsylvania. The bastard who killed her was also enrolled at the school. He was a drug addict with a history of deviant behavior who had broken into her room to burglarize it while she was sleeping. Her parents fought a long, tough battle to get federal legislation to make it mandatory for every campus official to report the statistics of criminal occurrences at their schools."

"At least it gives the applicants an idea of what the problems are at each college."

"That's the point. It's got to be in all the admissions literature, so families making decisions about where they're sending their kids can assess the risks. What kind of security measures the school has, how it handles crime reporting, what kind of disciplinary measures the administration enforces—all that sort of thing."

"Does it work? Do any good?"

"It's a great idea, but I haven't seen one school anywhere near this jurisdiction that reports it accurately. Not Columbia, not NYU, not Fordham, not FIT. Do you know there are more than twenty college campuses in Manhattan alone, from those large universities down to small commercial colleges that just have a single building? I can give you ten criminal complaints a year taken from students who report to the local precinct or to my office for every one you'll see in the numbers supplied to the government—and to the parents—by the schools. They all want to fudge it."

The door to Dakota's office was open and Sherman was beginning to document everything in sight with his camera and flash.

"Get a shot of that bulletin board on the wall by the window, Hal. And watch your mouth—I got Cooper with me."

"Hey, Alex, how goes it? Understand Kestenbaum's got a hush-hush preliminary finding of a homicide on this broad. So much for the accidental death theory they were floating last night, I guess. Tough break on that verdict last week in the case from the bus station. Sorry the stuff we came up with wasn't too helpful. Helen took the loss pretty hard."

One of my assistants had just had a not guilty verdict the previous Thursday. Her victim had been beaten in the face so badly that she was unable to identify her attacker. The fact that thousands of people a day passed through the Port Authority terminal made it impossible to get a clean set of fingerprints from the corridor in which the attack occurred, and the circumstantial case had been too weak for a jury to believe in.

"Cooper trains her troops not to look at an acquittal as a loss, Hal. Just figure Helen came in second place . . . right behind the defense attorney. Most other jobs, that gets you the silver medal. No harm in that."

"What do you want me to do after I dust these surfaces?"

"I want copies of as much of the paper as you can give me. Originals if it's not worth trying to lift prints off this stuff."

Sherman removed the gum from the wastebasket with a pair of tweezers, slipping it into a small manila envelope and labeling it with the date and number of the Crime Scene run. "I'll drop the copies off at your office. Gotta get to midtown. Just had a double homicide called in. Guy in a Santa suit did a stickup at a dough-nut shop, using a ten-year-old customer as a shield. The owner had a licensed pistol. Plugged Santa and one of his aging elves before they could make it back into their getaway sleigh."

"Best of all possible dispositions, eh, blondie? Case abated by death. Perps blasted into the great hereafter—God's own Alcatraz—by a law-abiding citizen just trying to make a living. Give the doughnut man a kiss for me. You gonna make it to the party later, Hal?"

"Depends on whether the good guys or the bad guys are win-ning. Have one on me."

It was the night of the Homicide Squad's annual Christmas party, and although our moods were not festive, Chapman and I wanted to be there for a while to wish our colleagues some holi-day cheer. Darkness had enveloped the city early, and the tempera-ture had dropped substantially during our hours at Foote's office. I pulled on my long gloves and raised the collar of my coat as Chapman held open the front door of the building and we trudged uphill toward Broadway to get the car. Tiny white lights decorated the trees on College Walk and candles rested on win-dowsills in some of the dorm rooms.

As the motor idled, I watched the groups of college kids, seem-ingly oblivious to the bitter cold, making their way from class-

rooms to living halls to dining facilities. There were bunches talking on the great steps of Low Memorial Library, which was fes-
tively adorned with a giant wreath, and I imagined they were
making plans to meet at parties or nearby bars and apartments. It
wasn't much of a stretch to recall the feeling of invincibility in
that period of my life, the sense of security the academic community offered—the endless possibilities of youth, fueled by intelligence and energy.

Yet one year ago, the Columbia campus had been rocked by the
death of a talented and popular athlete, found in her dorm room
with her throat slashed, killed by another student she had been
dating, who threw himself in front of a subway car hours later.
That followed the similar killing of a brilliant law student the preceding year, also by a former boyfriend who had stabbed her
repeatedly.

I began to think of all the cases I had handled with students
from schools throughout the city and to make a mental list of
what the relationship was between victim and offender, so I could
pull the files and examine the facts. For the students at King's, the
illusion of the sanctity of the university setting was about to be
shattered.

"Want to stop by my place and relax for a bit before we head
to the soiree?" The party was held at the Park Avenue Armory, on
Sixty-sixth Street, just a few blocks from my home.

"Sure. Is Jake gonna be there tonight?"

"No. He doesn't get back to New York until Sunday." The
schedule Jake Tyler had as a political correspondent and stand-in
anchor for Brian Williams on *NBC Nightly News* made his life
even less predictable than my own. It was a pleasure, for a change,
to be involved with a lover who had no complaints about my
unavailability when I was called out on a major case.

I parked the car and we went upstairs. As soon as I put the key
in the door, I could smell the delicious scent of the Douglas fir
that I had bought two nights ago on my way home to serve as a

Christmas tree. I had been raised as a Jew and was observant in the Reform tradition, but my mother's religious upbringing was entirely different. Her ancestors were Finnish, and she had converted to Judaism when she married my father. Our family tradition combined elements from both of their backgrounds, and although I had lighted the candles on a Hanukkah menorah earlier in the month, I always looked forward to decorating a tree and rediscovering the boxes of antique ornaments that my mother had collected throughout her life.

"I'm going to freshen up. Make yourself useful. Pour us a drink."

"Mind if I use the phone? I was gonna meet some of the guys down the street at Lumi's for a drink before the party."

"Of course. Anybody I know? Invite them over here. And while you're calling, check with your office to see whether there's a final on the autopsy results. Then you can start putting some of those bulbs on the top branches of the tree that I can't reach. Don't peek at the pile of presents. I haven't finished wrapping yours yet."

I went inside to wash my face, add a colorful scarf to my black suit, slip into a pair of higher heels, and spritz some Caleche on my neck. I played back the messages on my answering machine. The usual freeway greeting from Nina Baum in L.A., a callback from one of my sisters-in-law in response to my question about what the kids wanted for Christmas, and the persistent voice of *Post* reporter Mickey Diamond begging me to give him any kind of scoop about the Dakota investigation. I held my finger down on the delete button.

Chapman had rested my Dewar's and his Ketel One on the coffee table while he hooked and hung some of the fragile old ornaments. "That one belonged to my grandmother. She landed at Ellis Island when she was an infant, just before Christmas in 1900, a century ago. It's a glass bird, hand painted, that her father bought for her that year."

"Think she'd approve of the way you make a living?"

"She would have liked me to have gotten married by the time I was twenty and had six kids in pretty short order. Made her crazy that I never learned her recipes for Finnish icebox pudding or blueberry pie."

I thought of the time I had almost made her happiest. In my grandmother's last years, when she was living as an invalid in my parents' home, I had come up from Virginia during my final semester of law school to tell my family that I was going to marry Adam Nyman, a young medical student with whom I had fallen in love. Although in her nineties and quite infirm, Idie had insisted on coming to the Vineyard to be with us at the wedding. I know it hastened her death and literally broke her heart, as it did mine, when she learned that Adam had been killed on the turnpike the night before the wedding.

"Wipe that frown off your puss and stay with me, Coop. My Granny Annie wanted me to go back to the old sod as the ambassador to Ireland. Live in Phoenix Park. Ride to the hounds. If she ever thought for a minute I'd be sniffing around dead bodies like my pop, she'd have locked up all the liquor and never let me watch *Dragnet* or read Dick Tracy in the Sunday funnies. Ready for the latest?"

I sipped at my scotch and nodded my head.

Mike glanced at his steno pad to read the notes of his conversation. "The ME spoke to Lieutenant Peterson an hour ago. Lola's death was asphyxial. No question she was strangled, probably with a ligature. Kestenbaum will do some more tests on the pattern of injury, but he thinks the killer used her own woolen scarf. Thrown overboard just for show. The elevator cab certainly crushed the body, which was designed to disguise the homicide. But somebody made sure she took that header without any air in her lungs."

"Any semen?"

"Nope. Not in the body. He hasn't checked the bed linens yet.

That takes more time. But there were two strands of hair—just loose, no roots. Kestenbaum can't say for sure that they were in her hand, like she'd grabbed at anybody. Could be they just transferred from someone's clothing earlier in the day—or from the first cops who came to the crime scene. They're not going to be of much value at the moment.

"The other news is from the building inspector, who was at Lola's apartment with Lieutenant Peterson. He's confirmed that the elevator's been out of whack for weeks. First of all, it was under repair, and wasn't even supposed to be in operation yesterday. The out-of-order sign that had been posted in the lobby had been taken down at some point, which could easily lend itself to an accident theory. Besides, people had complained that the cab was stopping between floors all the time, so it wouldn't have been tough to catch it a foot off the ground on the fifteenth floor and roll the body in."

Chapman glanced at his watch and walked into the den to click on the television. A series of commercials preceded Alex Trebek's close-up, announcing the subject of the *Final Jeopardy!* answer. Mike and I had a long-standing habit of betting on the last question. The rest of the show didn't interest us, but I had seen him ferret out a television screen at crime scenes, sports bars, and the morgue. Once, outside a concert at Madison Square Garden, he even commandeered Tina Turner's chauffeur to let him watch the end of the show in the back of her stretch limo while she was in her dressing room warming up for the big performance.

"Tonight's category is Famous Quotes," Trebek said, pointing up at the card displayed on the screen.

"Twenty bucks," Mike said, taking the bill out of his pocket and dropping it on top of the coffee table. "I'm feeling lucky. Jake's out of town, I've got a new murder on my hands, and there's no reason for Santa to put coal in my stocking this year."

I laughed and told him to make it thirty, pulling the bills from my wallet.

"Pretty cocky, blondie." He withdrew another ten and tossed it on the pile. We knew each other's strengths and weaknesses inside out after a decade of this trivia exercise. My four years of major concentration in English literature before going to law school raised my expectation of taking the evening's pot.

"Well, gentlemen," Trebek enthused, turning to the three contestants poised at their buzzers. "The answer is, the majestic leader who urged his troops to battle with the phrase: 'Soldiers, forty centuries are looking down on you.'"

Dead meat. Chapman had not only studied military history at Fordham, but the subject had become a passion for him: he read about it voraciously and visited battlefields whenever the opportunity presented itself. The butcher from Kansas City and the ophthalmologist from Louisville seemed as clueless as I was, neither one writing anything on his electronic screen.

"Belly up, blondie. What's your best guess? Double or nothing?"

"Not a prayer." I watched the pastry chef from Baltimore record his answer with furious determination, as I tried to think of a civilization with that long a heritage. "Who was . . . Genghis Khan?"

Chapman gloated as he picked up the sixty dollars, giving the correct response while Trebek was telling the chef he had guessed incorrectly. "Napoleon, 1798. Rallying his men to fight the Egyptians at the foot of the great pyramids of Giza. Enjoying a brief success, actually, like ten days, before m'man Horatio Nelson arrived in time to destroy the entire French fleet."

I sidled up next to him and reached my fingers into his pants pocket, pulling out the wad of money. "But you forgot to put it in the form of a question, so—"

As he slapped my hand away, the doorbell rang.

"And one more surprise for the night," Mike added. "Hope you don't mind, I told the doorman your guest didn't have to be announced." I walked behind him as he went to the entrance, and gasped with delight to see Mercer Wallace.

He towered over both of us, six feet six inches tall with dark black skin and a rock-solid chest that had stopped a bullet just four months ago. Mercer grabbed me in an embrace as we swayed each other back and forth. "This is the very best of Christmas presents," I said, pulling his face down to mine and planting a kiss on the top of his head.

"So this was the date you were meeting at Lumi's, huh?" I said to Mike. "And not planning to invite *me*? Santa may have to rethink whether that was naughty or nice."

"Well, if you hadn't suggested stopping here, I was going to take you there. But they don't have a TV and I didn't want to miss the chance to score a few bucks off you, Coop. You allowed to drink yet, Detective Wallace, or does it still pour out through that mean-looking exit wound in your back?" He headed back to the bar to fix a club soda for Mercer.

I had visited Mercer at his home at least once a week since the shooting last summer, and I knew his recovery from the chest wound that had threatened to rip him apart had progressed well. He was due to come back to work on modified duty early in the new year, but I thought it would take more than a holiday party to bring him to my doorstep.

Chapman was in the den pouring drinks against the background noise of *Win Ben Stein's Money* on the Comedy Central channel. The brainiac host was, as usual, about to knock off all the contestants with a string of good answers to tough questions, while I watched Mercer—still limping slightly—walk ahead of me and sit down. "Just took enough money off Coop to buy you a Kwanza present, Detective Wallace."

Mercer raised his glass and we all clinked. "To a better year for each of us. And to Lola Dakota, may she rest in peace."

"Mercer started beeping me this morning with a million things he wanted to know. Said he was coming into the office to bring his case folder and notes for us, so I figured he might as well make a guest appearance at the armory."

We spent close to an hour talking about all the facts Mercer remembered from handling the domestic assault investigation that was part of Lola's original complaint. She had loved the quiet calm and dignified manner of the detective, which had made him such an outstanding member of the Special Victims Unit, the police department's companion unit to my bureau. Lola had called him often when she was indecisive or frightened, and he had talked her through some of the toughest moments of her ordeal with Ivan. I could tell how it pained him that, in the end, nothing he could do had saved her.

"Time to bundle up and boogie." Mike was on his feet, taking our coats out of the closet and getting ready to leave. "Who gets the first dance, Chief Allee or Inspector Cutter?"

"What are you doing tomorrow night, Alex?" Mercer asked.

"No plans. I had been thinking about going to D.C. to meet Jake, just for Saturday night, until Mike got that preliminary report from the ME this morning telling him this was probably going to be declared a homicide. I called Lola's sister, Lily, right after I got the news, to see whether we could go out to her house to talk with her. It's not a very smart time for me to leave town."

"Come out to my place for dinner. Mike'll drive you. I'm having some friends over to do my tree. Seven o'clock."

"Sounds good."

"Still nice to get a crack at Miss Lonelyhearts when her own personal talking head is out of town, isn't it, Mercer? Just like old times."

I rode with Mike and Mercer to the Seventh Regimental Armory, an enormous fortress on Park Avenue, built in 1879, which took up an entire city block. The interior was a throwback to another era, its vast halls—designed by Louis Comfort Tiffany—lined with plaques honoring war dead from the last century, and its rooms decorated with moose heads and other dusty antlered animals whose glass eyes stared down at the festivities. The original function of its drill hall had given way to use as rental space for endless rounds of weekend antique shows and the occasional rubber-chicken dinner meetings of organizations too penny-wise to engage private salons at real restaurants.

As we entered the fourth-floor room in which the squad party was being held, we were swamped by detectives and cops who had not seen Mercer since the shooting. I stepped back and walked over to greet the chief of detectives before I made the rest of the rounds.

"Heard you and Chapman were up at King's College this afternoon. Any headway?"

"They're beginning to see the light."

We talked for several minutes until I felt my beeper vibrating on my waistband. There was a phone booth on the main floor and I excused myself to go downstairs to return the call. I recognized the number displayed as the main line from ECAB—the Early Case Assessment Bureau—which was the intake unit through which every arrest in Manhattan entered our office. The expediter answered.

"Hey, it's Alex Cooper. Any idea who beeped me?"

"Ryan Blackmer's looking for you, Alex. Hold on a minute."

"Sorry to bother you, but I figured you'd want a heads-up," Ryan said. He was one of the brightest and best lawyers in the division, and had drawn the Friday night supervising position in ECAB. "Uniformed guys in the Sixth Precinct just collared a mope for sex abuse tonight."

"You got the facts yet?"

"The complaining witness was walking home from a friend's house, right along Washington Square Park—on the north side near the Arch—when this clown grabbed her from behind and started to rub against her, trying to drag her into the park. She was able to break away and get home. Called nine-one-one from her apartment. Cops drove her around for almost an hour and she ID'ed him a few blocks from the square."

"Make any statements?"

"Yeah, claims he's gay. Not guilty."

"Anything I can do to be useful?"

"No. Just didn't want you to read about it in the morning papers. The victim's a graduate student at NYU. It's probably not related to what you're working on, but I thought you ought to know about it. Seems like it's open season on college campuses this week."

I hung up and took the elevator back to the fourth floor. Lieutenant Peterson had just arrived and was talking to the chief, who summoned me to them with his forefinger.

"I'm surprised you and Chapman didn't stay for the service."

"What service?"

"Peterson's just telling me that President Recantati called for a prayer session and candlelight vigil tonight, then canceled all the classes and exams next week, and dismissed the students for the Christmas recess."

I was livid. Recantati and Foote must have made those plans before we saw them in the early afternoon, and they had chosen not to tell us. I thanked Chief Allee for the news and worked my way through the crowd to find Chapman, who was in the middle of the dance floor with one of the assistant DAs from my unit, Patti Rinaldi.

"You can have the next tango with him, I just need him for a few minutes." I took Mike's hand and led him to the side of the room, explaining the news to him. "You realize that means we're not going to have any kids there to interview by Monday afternoon, and possibly not any faculty members? They'll all scatter home over the weekend."

"Relax, blondie. I'll pay Foote a visit first thing tomorrow morning and get some names and numbers. We'll do the best we can." He shuffled back to the dance floor without missing a step, calling out to Patti, to the Motown beat: *"Rescue me! Take me in your arms . . ."*

I fumed on the sidelines, annoyed that Chapman didn't seem as distressed as I was by Sylvia Foote's duplicity.

7

"Just once, I'd like to read an obituary of a murdered woman who hasn't been canonized overnight." It was Chapman, my Saturday morning 6:45 wake-up call. "Doesn't anybody wicked and ugly ever get blown away? I picked up the tabs on my way home."

Home from where? Patti's apartment? I wondered.

"'King's and Columbia Mourn Death of Beloved Professor.' Who beloved her? Mercer says she was a real ball breaker. 'Raven-haired Prof Slain After Spousal Sting.' The *Post*, of course. The broad is dead—what frigging difference does her hair color matter? D'you ever read a man's obit that says he was balding or blond? Someday I'm going to write the death notices for all of my victims. Truthfully. 'The despicable SOB, whose face could stop a clock, finally got what she deserved after years of being miserable to everyone who crossed her path.' That kind of thing. So what's the plan for the day? What time is Lola's sister expecting us?"

"When I spoke with her yesterday, she suggested one o'clock. Is that okay with you?"

"Rise and shine, twinkle toes. I'll pick you up at Fifty-seventh and Madison at noon."

Mike knew that my Saturday routine began with an eight o'clock ballet class, the one constant in an exercise schedule that had long ago been abandoned to the unforeseeable nature of the prosecutorial job. I had been studying with William for years, and relied on the stretches, pliés, and barre work of the studio to distract me from the tension of my daily dose of violent crime. From there, I was due at Elsa's, my hairdresser at the Stella salon, for a touch-up on my blonde highlights, for what I had expected to be a cheerful holiday season.

I picked up the paper from my doorstep, took the elevator down, and waited in the lobby until someone pulled up in a Yellow Cab, not anxious to stand on the corner trying to hail one in the frigid early morning air. On the ride across town, I read the *Times* coverage of the Dakota story. The reclassification of her death as a homicide bumped the news from the second section to the front page, above the fold: "Academic Community Stunned by Scholar's Death."

The piece led with the achievements, publications, and awards that the professor had garnered in her relatively short career. A second feature described the reaction of college officials. "Morningside Heights Mourns Neighbor," it began, explaining the decision of both Columbia University and King's College to suspend classes on the eve of the holiday week, while police tried to determine whether the killing was the work of someone stalking Dakota, or a threat to the schools' population at large.

Another sidebar item traced the course of the case against Ivan Kralovic, questioning the wisdom of the Jersey prosecutor's choice of techniques to cement the evidence against Lola's estranged husband. Each of the articles wove in quotes from a variety of sources close to the deceased, and referenced the eloquent words of King's chaplain, Willetta Heising, Sr., who spoke of the loss of her friend and also urged the students to remain calm in the face of this menace to their general sense of security. A photograph of the throngs pouring out of Riverside Church after the service, slim ecru tapers in every hand and a tissue dabbing the occasional eye, filled the rest of the page on which the stories concluded.

I folded the paper inside my tote, hoping to find time later to do the crossword puzzle, and paid the driver. I raced in the door and down the steps to William's studio, leaving my coat in the dressing room and joining a few other friends who were limbering up in the center of the floor. The warm smiles and routine complaints about stiff joints and unnoticeable weight gains signaled to me that none of the dancers had connected me to the bad news in today's headlines. It was a relief to be spared the questions and concerns that accompanied my involvement in the tragedies of others' lives, and I continued my stretches in silence.

Each time I picked my head up, I looked around the room to see whether Nan Rothschild had arrived. I knew that she was on the faculty at Barnard College and remembered that we had talked about Lola Dakota on several occasions a year earlier. I thought I could pick Nan's brain for some insights about how to handle her colleagues during this sensitive investigation, but there was no sign of her this morning.

I finished my knee bends as William entered the room, clapped the class to attention, and moved us to the barre to begin the session.

He started with a series of deep, measured pliés, counting for us to set a tempo. The recording, he explained, was Tchaikovsky's symphonic fantasy "The Tempest." I let my mind wander with the music, enjoying the fact that if I concentrated hard enough on holding my position correctly, I stopped thinking about the things I needed to do for the Dakota investigation.

"Head higher, Alexandra. Pull straight up when you do the relevés." He ran his pointer down the legs of the woman in front of me, showing me the perfect lines of her elevated pose. By the time we were ready for floor exercises, I had worked up a good sweat and loosened my limbs completely. I sat on the hardwood and extended my legs into a wide V-shaped wedge, my ballet shoes coming toe to toe with the elegantly arched foot of Julie Kent.

"What are you doing for Christmas? Going to the Vineyard?" she whispered.

I nodded. "A really quick trip. You and Victor?"

William put his finger to his lips and "ssshed" us to silence, tapping me on the shoulder with his wooden stick. Julie beamed at me and mouthed the word "later."

At the end of the class, we chatted about the holidays as we showered and dressed against the wintry day. I slogged for several blocks through slush made gray by traffic and filthy car exhaust without sighting a taxi, and finally reached the crosstown bus to take me to the hairdresser. My friend Elsa had read the morning paper, and we talked quietly about the bizarre events of the preceding day while she painted streaks in my pale blonde hair.

When I went down to the lobby of the building shortly before noon, Mike was parked directly in front, on Fifty-seventh Street, with his flashers blinking. We drove to the West Side and down to the Lincoln Tunnel for the ride to New Jersey. Typical for this time of year, most of the traffic was heading into Manhattan, not in our outbound direction. Suburbanites were coming to shop for Christmas, view the elaborate window displays at the Fifth Avenue department stores, skate, and enjoy the mammoth tree at the Rockefeller Center rink. We had much more sobering business before us.

Mike had called Lola's brother-in-law while I was at class in the morning to tell him and Lily that the medical examiner had officially declared Lola's death a homicide, something the morning papers had broadcast to the entire metropolitan area. Now the family seemed quite anxious to meet with us.

We pulled up in front of the house at one-thirty, and it was instantly recognizable from Thursday night's broadcast of the footage of Kralovic's hired hit. The wreath was gone now, and signs of seasonal joy were overshadowed by the gloom of the postvideo events.

As Mike lifted the brass knocker, the door swung open. A portly man in his fifties greeted us and introduced himself as Lily's husband, Neil Pompian. "My wife's in the kitchen. Why don't you come inside."

We wiped our feet on the bristled mat and followed Pompian through the entry hall and past the great room, which was dominated by a large tree surrounded by dozens of wrapped packages. Three women, who identified themselves to us as neighbors, rose from their seats around the table, took turns hugging Lily, made sure platters of pastry were fully packed for our choosing, and offered us food and drink as they let themselves out the back door.

I poured two cups of coffee and we joined Lily at the kitchen table, in a bright corner of the room, facing a large backyard with a swimming pool all covered up for winter. Lily was sitting on a window seat, her legs tucked up beneath her, and a glass of white wine in front of her.

"That bastard was determined to get Lola one way or another, wasn't he?" She lifted the drink and sipped at it as we each introduced ourselves. "I know you didn't think we were right to do what Vinny Sinnelesi suggested, Ms. Cooper. My sister told me about her conversations with you. But she was really at her wits' end, and she liked the idea of an undercover sting to get Ivan once and for all. She thought it was a much more aggressive way to keep him behind bars, once she decided that's where he belonged."

"Here's what we'd like to do, Mrs. Pompian. I'm a detective

with the Homicide Squad. I know how you feel about Ivan Kralovic, but he was in custody when Lola was mur—"

"This whole case is about control, Mr. Chapman. Ivan liked to control everything. Everybody. All the time. He needed to control Lola the way most people need to eat and sleep. That's what his fights with my sister were about. It would be an understatement to call Lola independent. Once she got it in her head to disagree with you, or to disapprove of something Ivan was doing, there was no bringing her back into the fold."

"I understand that, but I don't want to jump to—"

"I'm not jumping to any conclusions. These are facts, Detective. Ivan wanted my sister dead. He put the word out. Unfortunately for him, the cops are the ones who got the word. He paid handsomely to have these cops pretend to kill Lola."

"That's my point. That's why he's in jail."

"Yeah? Well, suppose he was smarter than they are? Suppose he didn't trust them? Let's say he caught on to their scam and just wanted to lull us all into thinking Lola would be safe the moment that Sinnelesi's cop team pretended to shoot her? Then he one-ups all of you, and sends the real killer to her apartment." She shook her head back and forth and reached for her wineglass again.

"That's one of the possibilities we're looking at, Mrs. Pompian."

"*One* of them? I suggest you look a little harder, Mr. Chapman. And faster, this time." She glanced in my direction. "Where's Ivan now? He's not loose is he, just because Lola can't testify against him?"

"He's locked up over here on the attempted murder charge. He's being held without bail." Mike had gotten through to the sheriff's office before he picked me up. "Who's the prosecutor you've been working with? We'd like to talk to him, too."

"Her name is Anne Reininger. She was very good to Lola. You think Ivan isn't capable of controlling this thing from inside the jailhouse? He's got money, he's got connections to every scumbag on both sides of the river, and he wanted Lola dead."

"Do you know why?" I asked. It was one thing to attack her himself, in the middle of a fight when they were alone together. But a hired killing, after they were separated and living out of each other's way, suggested another kind of problem. Avoidance of alimony payments? Something that Lola knew about Ivan that she threatened to expose, personally or professionally? A matter, perhaps, that was connected to the cash she kept hidden in a shoe box? I was willing to consider that it might be an issue less obvious than marital discord.

Lily Pompian thought my question was a stupid one. She had already explained why. It was becoming obvious to me that this was going to be Chapman's interview. I was being dismissed without an answer, and the repeated hits of Chablis, as Lily refilled her glass, were making Mike look like the warm and fuzzy one on our team. She shifted her weight on the bench and leaned in on her elbow to talk directly to Mike.

He took advantage of that dynamic and, armed with his most sensitive gaze, responded to her approach. "Let's start with Ivan. I think Alex knows a lot about him, from the earlier incidents, but why don't you tell me what kind of business he's involved in?"

"Yesterday or today?" Lily laughed at what she thought was her own joke. "Ivan started out with an MBA from Columbia. Worked on Wall Street for twenty years. Left his company after a merger and went out, quite comfortably, on his own. Then he got involved in all kinds of penny-stock deals. Stuff I didn't understand at all."

"Did you and your husband invest with him?"

"Not for a minute. He was always trying to get us to pour money into his deals, but we've got two kids in college and my husband wasn't falling for any of Ivan's tricks. You'll have to talk with Ms. Reininger. Maybe she can tell you who he was scamming lately."

Lily got up from her bench to open another bottle of wine. "You comfortable there?" she asked, gesturing toward the table. "Either of you want to join me in something stronger?"

We both thanked her for the offer and Mike stood to refill our coffee cups.

"Tell us about Lola. I mean, from your perspective, as family. Before Ivan. And after him."

She closed the refrigerator door and leaned her back against it, pausing before she motioned to us to follow her into the adjoining room, a wood-paneled library. Two walls were stacked with bookshelves and the one behind the sofa was lined from floor to ceiling with family photographs.

"To understand any of us, you'd probably have to start with my mother, Ceci Dakota. Ever hear of her?" Before we could answer, she went on. "That's your problem, Detective. You're too damn young." One of her hands clutched the glass firmly, while the other rested on Mike's broad shoulder. "Mother was a Broadway showgirl, a hoofer, really. Better dancer than she was a vocalist, but in the days of the great American musicals, those girls had to be able to do it all."

I moved behind Lily to examine the early black-and-white pictures. "Cecile—she hated that name—made her debut in *South Pacific*, playing one of the nurses in the chorus. April seventh, 1949, Majestic Theatre on Broadway. Ask me anything about those days, and I can tell you more than you'll ever want to know, just from listening to Ceci. That show played one thousand nine hundred twenty-five performances—five years—and she stayed with it for two full seasons. How many times do you think anybody can wash a man right out of her hair and never get beyond the chorus line? She actually understudied Mary Martin for a few weeks, but the woman was never sick a single day, so Ceci moved on.

"Bottom line was that each of us kids was named for a character from one of the shows. For some reason she got hooked on the *L*'s. I got Lily, from *Kiss Me, Kate*, which isn't at all bad. My middle sister wound up with Liat, from *South Pacific*. Bloody Mary's daughter, y'know? It's not easy to grow up Tonkinese in Totowa, New Jersey." She took another drink. "And then came Lola."

The memories had made her smile, but her own mention of Lola's name brought Lily up short. "Ceci was still dancing." She aimed her glass toward a still of her mother, dressed in a pin-striped shirt over black fishnet tights, hands on her hips and mouth wide open. "Closest she ever got to a lead. Three performances subbing for Gwen Verdon in *Damn Yankees*. Stayed with it most of the run, from opening night on May 5, 1955, through another one thousand and nineteen shows. Even got a part in the movie, in fifty-eight. Then took some time off to have another kid. That gave us my baby sister, Lola."

Mike was staring at a photo of three long-legged little girls in tutus standing around a basinet draped with blue ribbon. "A younger brother?"

"Yeah, he'll be over later, if you want to talk to him."

"Lemme guess, *Guys and Dolls*?"

"He should have been so lucky. Might have had a tough guy's name. Louie or Lefty or Lucky. Maybe missed out on a few school yard fights. But it was the sixties, and Ceci was madly in love with Robert Goulet. Try *Camelot*. Lance, she named him. Lancelot Dakota." Lily sunk down into a tapestry-covered sofa and put her feet up on the glass-topped table that faced it.

"So your mother was a Broadway gypsy, and your father?"

"Taught history at the local high school. Let Mother go her own way, take us to dance classes and sneak us into town to go to Saturday matinees if she knew some of the girls in the chorus line. Dad thoroughly immersed himself in local politics when he wasn't reading history books. Liat and I wanted to go the show biz route. Endless auditions and the deafening sound of tap shoes all over the house, day and night. Lance was my dad's clone. Very serious, very studious. His favorite place was the public library, in part to escape the constant screeching sound of Ceci making us sing 'Let Me Entertain You' to the milkman, the mailman, and anyone else who made the mistake of knocking on our door, and in part because he loved all the things he could learn from books."

"And Lola?"

"Like a perfect combination of their genes. She was smart as a whip. Couldn't keep her nose out of my father's history texts. Adored going with him to listen to the wheeling and dealing at the political clubhouses in town. But give her a sequined costume and a stage to dance on and she'd drop her schoolbooks, as long as there was an audience for her. No chorus line for Lola, and no understudy roles. She was the star or she didn't play. Being second banana to anyone wasn't acceptable to her.

"By high school, when she realized she didn't have the talent to make it to the big time, she threw herself into her studies. Got a full scholarship to Barnard. Majored in political science, with a minor in history. Got her master's and her Ph.D. at Penn. Never looked back. Liked every minute of what she was doing with her life. Her professional life, not her marriage."

Mike's wheels were turning. "Was there another woman in Ivan's life? Competition for Lola?"

"We didn't know about it if there was one. I believed my sister when she said she was rid of him for good. At this point, I think she would have welcomed the fact that he could focus his attention—and his rage—on someone else."

"How about *her* love life? Did she confide in you about that?"

"There was nothing to tell. Lola didn't have the time or the interest to get involved in a relationship at this point. She was all tied up in a new project at the college, and she had no desire to pique Ivan's anger by letting him find her with another man, until the divorce was final."

I sat in a chair opposite Lily and tried to ease my way into the conversation. "Perhaps you can take a look at some of the shirts and sweaters we found at Lola's apartment. It would help us to know how she was dressed when she left here on Thursday afternoon. And then, well, some of the things in the new place were men's clothing. You might recognize them, too."

"They must have been Ivan's. Or maybe one of her faculty

friends. Sure, you can show them to me, but it's not very likely they'll be familiar to me. I signed a power of attorney yesterday, giving Vinny's office the right to go in and take any of her property they needed to help their investigation."

I grimaced at Chapman, sorry that Lily was still in the hands of the Jersey prosecutors, and thankful that the NYPD had declared apartment 15A a crime scene. Cops guarding the door, still blocked off with bright yellow tape, would be unlikely to let anyone step into it without the express permission of the chief of detectives.

"Do you know what kind of special project Lola was working on up at King's?"

"You know, it's a bit embarrassing for me. For the last few weeks, we used to sit here most nights after dinner, long after my husband went to sleep. We'd open more wine, talk to each other about everything from our childhood to our marriages to the Broadway theater. Revivals. Ever notice that's all it is these days, revivals? We talked about how we both loved Christmas. I used to be a Rockette, did I tell you that? Did the Christmas show for six seasons, till my first kid was born. Ceci loved it, seeing her own Lily Dakota on that big stage.

"Anyhow, I just lost it when Lola started talking about her job. I couldn't tell you the first thing about New York City, its history or its politics. North, south, or east of the Great White Way just doesn't exist for me. She said something about a multidisciplinary program that she was terribly excited about—digs and dead people—"

I interrupted her. "A deadhouse? Did she talk about that?"

"I said dead *people*," she responded with a pout. "That's all that comes to mind. Maybe it's the alcohol."

Maybe it was, but she showed no signs of slowing down. I kept my fingers crossed that she wasn't going to stand up and show Mike her best kick and her great extension. Wooden soldier number forty-four. Rockette Lily Dakota.

"Lily, do you know what Lola was wearing the last time you saw her?"

"My clothes. That's mostly what she wore the whole time she was with me. Black is all I remember. She wanted to wear black, for her phony funeral. She laughed about it, too."

Mike's nose was six inches from Lily's at this point, side by side on the sofa. "On Thursday, when the cops faked the scene with Lola's shooting, were any of them here with you in the house?"

"Are you kidding? We had a basement full of them. Anne Reininger was back in this room with us, explaining things to me step by step and trying to keep me calm. There were detectives and DAs all over the place, basement to attic, making sure everything went according to plan."

"And when it was over, did any of them stay behind with you?"

She stopped to think for a minute. "I know I asked for a sedative, to take a nap. I'd been extremely worried about this, and not being able to tell the neighbors it was all a fake. Lola and I sat up practically the entire night before, just trying to reassure ourselves that if the whole thing worked, she'd be rid of Ivan forever. I remember Lola and Anne giving me something to help me sleep that afternoon, once Lola was done with the shooting, but that's about all. I don't know when any of them left here."

"And Lola," Mike asked. "Did you know she was going back to her apartment?"

"Yeah. Yeah, sure. She made me promise not to tell Anne. Anne left the room, then Lola kissed me, thanked me, and put the throw over my bedspread 'cause I was cold."

"She just told you she was going to walk out the door?"

Lily nodded.

"Did she ask to borrow your car?"

Lily's brow creased. She was working against the wine to remember what had happened. "No, of course not. She told me a car service was picking her up. At least, that's who I assumed she was talking to. She used the phone next to my bed to make a call.

Told whoever it was not to come to the front door. Lola said she'd slip out the back, cross over Tess Bolton's yard—that's one of the neighbors you met—and wait next to their garage, on Arlington Street. She told me she'd be fine. Someone was taking her home, she said, where she'd be safe."

8

An hour later I was sitting at my secretary's typewriter, pounding out subpoenas for Mike to serve as soon as possible.

"What's first?"

"Verizon telephone services in New Jersey. MUDS and LUDS. I want every outgoing call made from Lily's phone on Thursday—in fact, all of last week. I suppose you should try each of the cab companies in Summit, too, but I think there's a good chance that she reached out to someone she knew—and trusted—to drive her to Manhattan. After the emotional drain of enacting her own murder, I assume she'd pick her traveling companion carefully."

"How about phone records for the apartment and her office?"

"I'm working on them. Give me your notepad. You've got all

the relevant numbers written there, don't you?" We both knew the value of a paper trail, and started to think of any electronic or written means of communication that might have left a connection or a clue.

When I had finished looking for every possible link to Lola Dakota, I reached for another blank subpoena in my drawer. I flipped through Mike's pages until I found his references to Charlotte Voight, the student who had disappeared in April. There would be King's College records that could tell us which credit card she used at the school bookstore, and from there, we could get the company's vouchers to tell us what businesses she frequented and perhaps where she ate. As I took the subpoenas out of the typewriter, I signed them beneath the printed space with Battaglia's name in it, and passed them to Mike.

"What's this one for? King's College Student Health Services?"

"Long shot. We've got absolutely nothing to give us a control sample for Voight's DNA. None of her belongings are at school— no clothes, no toothbrush, no hairbrush. Nothing to let the lab develop a genetic fingerprint. What if we come across evidence or—worst-case scenario—a body? Once they work up a profile from that, we'd have zilch with which to compare it."

"What do you think she left at the doctor's office, a DNA sample in case of emergency?" Mike was growing impatient and was ready to leave.

"I'm willing to bet you that a sexually active college student made at least one trip to that office, had one gynecological checkup during her time at the school. Needed birth control, or maybe—with Voight's lifestyle—a test for sexually transmitted diseases or pregnancy. And if she was examined there, most doctors would have done a routine Pap smear as part of the process. The cells scraped off during that procedure are more than enough to give us a control.

"So my guess is that sitting in a lab somewhere not too far away is all we need to get started on a DNA print of Charlotte Voight."

Mike nodded his approval. "C'mon, blondie. Nothing I can do with these papers till Monday morning. None of these business offices will be open at this hour on a Saturday. I'll drop you off at home. Then I'll be back at seven tonight to drive out to Mercer's."

I stopped in the lobby to pick up my mail, an assortment of Christmas cards from friends scattered across the country mixed in with the usual bills. There were two messages on the answering machine. One was my mother, hoping I could change my schedule and join the rest of the family at their Caribbean island home for Christmas. She hadn't heard the news of my latest case, so I would plan to spend some time with her on the phone tomorrow. The other call was from Jake, and I dialed his cell phone number.

"Still at the studio?"

"Trying to wrap up the piece for tomorrow. Brian's going to lead with the Ugandan story on Sunday's *Nightly News*. We found some background information that puts a whole new spin on the assassination, and so far, it's an exclusive. How about you?"

"Wish I could say we were that far along. No spin, no leads. This is going to be a slow one. The administration closed down the school early for the holidays, so we're just treading water. Mercer's having a bunch of us over for a party tonight."

"Then you can hold out for a few more days till I get home?"

I was stretched out on the bed, phone to my ear, patting the empty space next to me. "Pretty lonely on your side of the mattress. Don't think I have any choice in the matter, do I? See if you can nab the assignment to do local traffic up here. Something unexciting that keeps you in my neighborhood all the time, okay?"

After we hung up, I called a few of my friends to say hello, wrapped some of the gifts I planned to take to the office on Monday, and dressed for the evening.

When Mike and I arrived at Mercer's house in Queens, the

door was open and there were fifteen or twenty people clustered around the bar in his den. The first person to greet us was Vickee Eaton, a second-grade detective who worked at One Police Plaza, in the office of the deputy commissioner for public information.

Mike and Vickee were the same age and had gone through the academy together. He had introduced her to Mercer when the latter's brief marriage to a girl he'd grown up with had ended. Vickee and Mercer dated for almost five years, and were married for less than two when she walked out on him without any reason that he could articulate to us. When I saw her once thereafter, at a press event the commissioner held at headquarters to which Battaglia and I had been invited, she told me she just couldn't deal with the kind of danger Mercer was exposed to in the field. Vickee's father had been a cop, and had been killed on the job when she was fifteen. He was the reason she had gone into the department, and even more, the reason she feared how being a cop could be a death warrant as well.

I thought I had masked my surprise at seeing Vickee, but she read me clearly. "You haven't heard?"

I looked at Mike, who shrugged his shoulders.

"I didn't go to visit Mercer in the hospital—too many of you guys around for me to get down on my knees and apologize for how stupid I'd been." She was talking about the shooting in August, when the three of us had been investigating the murder of an art dealer, and Mercer had almost been killed as a result. "But I went over to Spencer's house immediately and kind of sat vigil with him that whole first week."

"That old dog really kept it under his vest." Mike and I had been in constant contact with Mercer's widowed father, Spencer Wallace, who lived for his only son. He never told us Vickee had reentered their lives.

Mercer had seen us come in and was making his way across the room with two glasses of champagne in his hands. He gave one to each of us, and Mike turned to pass his off to Vickee. She waved a finger at him and picked up a soft drink she'd been working on when we came in. "No alcohol for me. Not quite my third month yet."

Mike grabbed her in a bear hug, champagne sloshing from the flute and covering his lapel. "You mean that doctor got Mercer's plumbing back in order? Damn, you *are* my idol, m'man. Here I'm thinking you need all this bed rest and you're going to get out on three-quarters 'cause some asshole disabled you, and if you can ever be lucky enough to shoot at all again you'd be shooting blanks. While the whole time you're just practicing on Vickee, making love—"

I hadn't seen Mercer this happy in more than a year. He was trying to talk over Mike and explain that he and Vickee had decided to get married. "It's just going to be my dad, and her mother and two sisters this time. And both of you. New Year's Day, in Judge Carter's chambers. Will you be there?"

"Sure, we'll be there. Long as you don't do it during any of the bowl games, okay?"

The house was filled with friends and family. Mercer's team from Special Victims had all come to celebrate, and we tried not to talk cases as we ate and danced and drank. By eleven o'clock, I could see that Vickee was tired and trying to stay off her feet. I pried the third helping of lasagna out of Mike's hand and suggested we get on the road.

"The *Final Jeopardy!* category is Astronomy. Any takers?" Silence. "Blondie, make a stab at it? Could be something in it for you." I laughed and tugged at his jacket sleeve. "What is December twenty-first?" Mike asked aloud to no one in particular as I tried to pull him toward the door. "The winter solstice, ladies and gentleman. Shortest day of the year, but the longest night. Make good use of it—*I* certainly intend to."

Mercer walked us to the door and held it open as we said good night. "If your reputation wasn't shot before, Ms. Cooper, it's gone now. What are you doing for the solstice? You need Jake up here—enough of this toughin' it out alone. We've all been doing that too long."

"If I stopped to worry about every time Mike opened his mouth, they'd have to institutionalize me. I'm so happy for both of you. What a lucky little baby that's going to be."

We walked down the path and up the street to Mike's car. For most of the ride back to the city, I was quiet. We came through the Thirty-fourth Street tunnel, then Mike swung onto the FDR Drive going uptown. The cold spell seemed to be interminable, and I stared over at the sparkling lights of the bridges crossing the East River.

Off to the right, the forbidding outline of a ruined building loomed against the dark sky, covered with frozen snow and icicles hanging from empty window frames.

"What are you thinking about? Where'd you go?"

"Just daydreaming. Thinking that's the most beautiful building in New York."

"Which one?"

"That abandoned hospital." I pointed to the southern tip of the island in the river. "It's the only landmarked ruin in the city. Built by the same guy who designed St. Patrick's Cathedral, James Renwick."

"Y'know, you can change the subject and create a distraction better than anyone on earth."

"I didn't know we had a subject. The solstice?"

"I know why you're brooding, Coop." Mike exited the Drive at Sixty-first Street and stopped at the first light. "You're thinking about Mercer and Vickee. And the baby."

"I'm not brooding."

"Makes you think about the direction of your own life, doesn't it? Family, careers, sort of what the purpose of—"

"Don't go getting all Hamlet on me tonight, Mikey. I'm thrilled for them. He's always been in love with Vickee and I think it's perfect that they've gotten back together. I really wasn't doing any heavy thinking."

"Well, you ought to do some." We were getting closer to my apartment now, and I was shifting my weight in the seat. "How much longer you gonna stay at this, Coop? Run around playing cops and robbers with us in the middle of the night? Now you've got a guy who's mad for you, plus you could name your own price at a law firm, or start one up, for that matter. Shit, you could hang it all up and have some kids. Little news jocks."

"This is all about *you*, Mr. Chapman." I tensed and fidgeted as we neared the driveway. "Sounds like Mercer's lifestyle changes appeal to you more than they do to me. He was getting anxious to settle down. I doubt he ever got over Vickee walking out the first time. Besides, he's forty—I'm only thirty-five—"

"And ticking."

"He loves kids. Always has. I watch him on the child abuse cases and he's great with kids."

"You are, too."

"Yeah, but he likes all of them. Me, I like the ones I know and love. I worship my nieces and nephews. I cherish my friends' kids. But I don't sit in an airport lounge listening to the whining toddlers, watching them wipe their noses on their sleeves, see the parents fighting with their petulant adolescents, thinking there's some great hole in my life. I'd choose a dog every time."

"People think you're nuts for staying in this job. Most of 'em think there's something screwy in your head, that you like it so much."

"I learned a long time ago not to worry about what other people think. Unless they're people I care about. You love what you do. You don't understand why I like my end of it?"

"Different thing."

"What are you talking about? You're sniffing around dead bodies day and night. I get to help people. Live ones. People who've survived the trauma, who recover from it, who get to see a bit of justice restored because we *make* the system work for them."

I realized I had raised my voice in answering Mike, so I said more calmly, "Twenty years ago, prosecutors couldn't get convictions in these cases in a court of law. Now, the guys in my unit do it every day. Different thing? According to who? To *you*? 'Cause your narrow-minded, parochial upbringing wants you to think that women shouldn't do this kind of work, right?"

My pitch had gone up again. There was no point trying to explain what he already knew.

We were stopped in the middle of the driveway at my building, the doorman standing at the passenger side to let me out, but waiting till our argument stopped before daring to approach the car. I was sure he could hear my agitated voice through the window.

Mike lowered his tone a notch and spoke to me softly. "'Cause I think you've got to start thinking about the rest of your life, Coop."

"I think about it every day. Know what my thoughts are? That if a fraction of the people I knew did something that was as emotionally rewarding as what I do, they'd be a pretty satisfied bunch. I've got loyal friends who happen to have a great time working together, with one another and with the good cops like you and Mercer."

"And you're going home, by yourself, to an empty apartment. With nothing to eat in the refrigerator, nobody to keep you warm when the heat goes off, and no way for anyone to know if you're dead or alive until it's time to show up for work on Monday. It's pathetic. You should have been on the last shuttle to Washington, slippin' into Jake's hotel room—"

I stepped out of the car and slammed the door behind me. "When you straighten out your own love life, instead of going home and playing with yourself every night, then you can start giving advice to the lovelorn."

He accelerated over the speed bumps and raced out of the driveway.

"Sorry." I nodded to the doorman. "Thanks for waiting."

"Miss Cooper? There was someone here an hour or two ago asking questions about you."

I shivered. "Do you know who he was?"

"No, it wasn't a man. It was a young woman, actually. Wanted to know if you lived here."

"What did you say?"

"Well, it was the new guy she spoke to, the one covering for the holiday break. He thought she looked harmless enough. He told her that you did live in the building before he even thought about why she might be asking."

Great security. Must be why my rent is so high. "What else did she say?"

"She wanted to know if anybody else lived with you. She wanted to know if you usually came home alone at night."

9

The light was flashing on my answering machine when I walked in my bedroom at midnight. Jake said he and the film crew had gone out for dinner, but he was back in his hotel room and would wait up awhile for my call. The second caller was an unfamiliar voice.

"Miss Cooper? Hello? This is, um, Joan Ryan. I'm one of the counselors in the Witness Aid Unit at the DA's office. We haven't met yet, and this isn't exactly the way I, uh, wanted to introduce myself. But I need to tell you about a problem on one of your cases.

"I've been counseling one of your victims, Shirley Denzig, you know the one who claims the delivery guy attacked her? She was flirting with him in the deli when she bought her dinner, and then she paid him to bring up the dessert half an hour later?" Ryan was rambling now, in that way people do on answering machines so it seems to the listener that the story will be interminable. *What's the point, Joan?*

"I, um—I probably should have given you a heads-up about this yesterday, when she showed up at my office. But then, you know, whatever she tells me is privileged, 'cause I'm a social worker and she's a victim. It was only when she showed up again tonight that the supervisor called me. She really seemed out of control, asking all kinds of questions about you. Anyway, if you want to call me at home, here's my number. You'll probably want to know what Shirley was saying. My supervisor thinks I have to tell you."

I cut off her confessional narrative and dialed the number.

"Joan? It's Alex Cooper. Sounds like I woke you up."

"That's okay. This is really my fault."

I knew who Denzig was, so there was no need to go through the story again. It was during her second interview with me a couple of weeks ago, in our discussion of her psychiatric history, that I had set her off on a tirade. While I was asking the routine pedigree questions, Denzig had told me she was a student at Columbia College. Considering the other information she had provided, I was skeptical of her claim and asked to see her identification. She had presented me with a photo ID that had expired two years earlier. It looked fairly generic, with no Columbia crest, or any of the characteristic blue-and-white university markings.

When I pressed further, Shirley admitted that she had never attended the college, and had purchased the phony card on Forty-second Street, where just about any kind of counterfeit document is available for a price. I clipped the fake ID to her case file and continued asking questions.

From then on, she avoided eye contact while staring at the file. Once the interview about the alleged attack was completed, she asked for her ID back. I refused, explaining that it was forged and had no legal validity. I had steered her down to Witness Aid, where she could get help with her counseling needs and the problems with her landlord, who was trying to evict her because she was four months in arrears in her rent. The next day I learned she was wanted for shoplifting at a store near her parents' home in Maryland.

"What stirred her up yesterday?"

"Well, when she read about the professor who was murdered—the Dakota woman—she said it made her think about you again, and how mad she was that you took her ID."

"Did she tell you what made her angry?"

"You'll think it's crazy. But then, you know she's got an extensive psych history, right? She's been on medication for two years. Says she's gained more than eighty pounds. Shirley says that ID has the only pretty picture of her that she's got, and she wants it back."

"And you didn't call to tell me that she wanted it?" It would have been easy to deal with. I could have given her the photo without the bogus identification card.

"Well, Ms. Cooper, I know I learned it in graduate school, but I forgot completely about the whole 'duty to warn' doctrine. I mean, everybody says you're so independent, it never occurred to me that poor little Shirley Denzig could really get to you."

My heart was beating faster. I was standing at the side of my bed, with my coat and gloves still on, listening to this conversation about the unhinged young woman who had apparently just shown up at my door. "Warn me about *what*?"

"The law says that it's not betraying the privilege for me to tell you if a patient threatens your—"

"I know what the case law says, Joan. The patient's privilege ends when the public peril begins. I want to know what Shirley said."

"She told me that she wanted to see you dead, just like the professor. She asked me how you got to work every day, and what time you left for home."

So far, I wasn't worried. The answers were that my travel route and hours were never the same two days in a row. This outpatient on a heavy diet of psychotropic drugs might be interested in making me unhappy, but she hadn't seemed the least bit dangerous to me.

"Actually, Ms. Cooper, I didn't know whether to believe her or not, but she told me she had a gun. Stole it from her father's house last weekend when she went home to Baltimore."

That racheted up my attention a notch. "And tonight? What happened tonight?"

"She showed up at Witness Aid. Told one of my colleagues that she was a victim in a case of yours. That you had given her your home number. That she'd been thrown out of her apartment for not paying rent, and wanted to leave a small gift for you with your doorman. They know you give witnesses your number from time to time."

Yeah, but generally not to lunatics, if I can help it.

"She acted so upset and all that they gave her the information. They didn't know how she really felt about you. I'm the only one she told that to. I just wanted to give you a little warning tonight in case she shows up. She's very, very mad at you."

"Thanks, Joan. I'm going to have one of the guys from the DA's squad make a report about this on Monday morning, okay? I'll send him down to your office. Just tell him what you told me."

I walked to the hall closet and hung up my coat and scarf. I was too wired to sleep and didn't need any more to drink, so I tried settling into bed with *The Great Gatsby*. I had embarked on a plan to reread all of Fitzgerald's novels, but this wasn't the time to begin. I went back to the living room to find my tote and fished out the crossword puzzle. The bottom left corner stumped me completely but I was determined not to go to the encyclopedia to find the four-letter name of a Tasmanian Indian tribe. I worked around the blank spaces.

At 1 A.M., I called Mike's number to apologize to him for my remarks at the end of the evening. The phone rang five times before his outgoing message kicked in. I guess he did have better things to do with himself than I had suggested.

"Just me. Sorry I snapped at you. Hope you're having a good time, wherever you are." No point telling him about my disgruntled victim. He'd hear soon enough. "And you're right about one thing. I should have taken the shuttle tonight."

I slept fitfully and got out of bed at six-thirty, when I heard the thud of the Sunday *Times* landing against my door.

I poured coffee beans into the machine and opened the paper while they ground and the brew began to drip, looking for stories about local crimes in the Metro section, before turning to the national and international news.

Mike was right about the food supply in my home, too. There were three English muffins left in my freezer, so I defrosted one and popped it into the toaster. I sat at the table and made a shopping list of groceries to order, figuring that there were some new leaves easier to turn over in my life than others. Filling the bare cupboards was one of them.

When the phone rang at seven-thirty, I was sure it was Jake, and I picked it up, eager to make our plans for the holiday week.

"Alex? It's Ned Tacchi. Sorry to hit you so early on a Sunday, but we picked one up during the night that you'll want to know about."

Tacchi and his partner, Alan Vandomir, were two of my favorite detectives at Special Victims. Smart, sensitive, and good-humored, they got victims through the investigative process with kid gloves. When they called me, I knew it was something I needed to hear.

"Sure. What did you get?"

"Push-in sodomy. East Sixty-fourth Street, right off York Avenue. Fifty-five-year-old woman coming home from a Christmas party at three this morning."

"How is she?"

"Seems to be doing okay. She's in the ER now. We'll pick her up as soon as she's released and do a more thorough interview."

"Injuries?"

"Nope. In fact, she called nine-one-one to report it, but didn't want to go to the hospital. The perp pushed in behind her when she opened the vestibule door. A bit tipsy."

"Him or her?"

"She was. A little too much holiday cheer. He knew exactly what he wanted. Told her to get down on her knees, right there in the hallway. First he lifted her sweater, opened her bra, and put his mouth on her breasts. Then he exposed himself and made her put her mouth on his penis."

"Did he ejaculate?"

"Yeah. But she went right upstairs and brushed her teeth. Doubt we'll get anything for DNA, but she still said she had an awful taste in her mouth. That's probably more psychological than anything else. We asked the nurse examiner to do the swabs anyway. We're also having them swab her breasts."

"Good thinking." Even the microscopic amounts of saliva that might be found on the victim's torso would yield enough material for the newer kind of DNA process—STR testing—in which "short tandem repeats" of the genetic fingerprint are multiplied millions of times to yield the unique, identifiable patterns.

"Get her toothbrush, too. You may get lucky. Did he take anything?"

"Yeah. Left with her pocketbook. Didn't get much. She was holding her keys in her hand the whole time. Just had thirty bucks in her purse, along with some business cards and her cell phone. Schmuck dumped the bag in a trash basket a block away. Cell phone is gone, but we've got the purse. I'm sending the cards over to latent prints, hoping they can lift something off the surfaces, if he touched them."

"Has she canceled the cell phone yet?"

"No. We told her not to for twenty-four hours."

"Great. When I get to the office in the morning, I'll fax you up a subpoena." Most of the guys who stole cell phones during robberies were stupid enough to make calls on them until the phones were cut off or the batteries went dead. With records from the companies available in three or four days, we could often track down the offenders through the calls they placed to friends or relatives.

"Thought Battaglia might want to know that the commissioner is looking over a bunch of cases in the Nineteenth Precinct. They're probably going to declare this as part of a pattern."

"I didn't know we had anything else like this going on."

"Not up at our shop. But the precinct has about four other push-in robberies between Sixtieth and Sixty-eighth Streets, Second Avenue to the river, since the beginning of November. Mostly weekends. All the victims are women. This is the first time the perp has forced a sexual assault, but the MO is pretty much the same. Then he snatches the bag every time and he always runs south."

"Same 'scrip?"

"Pretty close. Most describe him as a male black, five-ten to six feet, stocky. Well dressed, clean-cut, very articulate. Has a slight accent, but nobody can place exactly what it is. Some say islands, some say French. Hard to know."

"Can you get all the paperwork down to me in the morning so I can assign it? I'm jammed up with the Dakota case. I'll probably give it to Marisa Bourges or Catherine Dashfer, okay? But keep me posted on any developments. Are they going to beef up patrol in that area on the midnight tour, Friday to Sunday?"

"The boss in the Nineteenth wants them to saturate it, but we've still got Savino and his gang running the task force on the West Side Rapist, so we're stripped of manpower as it is." For almost three years, an attacker had been operating on the Upper West Side of Manhattan, and despite an extensive manhunt and a genetic profile that had been entered in local, state, and national data banks, he continued to elude us. "We'll call you later if we break anything else on this today."

I crunched on the cold muffin and poured a second cup of coffee. Shortly before I started at the district attorney's office more than ten years ago, not a court in the United States accepted DNA technology as a valid forensic technique. By the late eighties, as the methodology was refined in the handful of laboratories that performed the testing, Frye hearings were held in criminal courtrooms around the country. Every prosecutor, case by case and state by state, had to convince the judge—before the evidence could be used at a trial—that the kind of genetic testing at issue had been deemed reliable by the scientific community.

By the time this groundbreaking investigative tool had gained general acceptance in the criminal justice system, it roared into the headlines in the O. J. Simpson trial, and skeptics everywhere attacked the soundness of its findings. As a result, standards in lab procedures were instituted and accreditation practices were firmly established to reassure investigators of the value and accuracy of this innovative technique.

Even more important, the actual method of testing improved and changed dramatically. The original means of performing the exams was referred to as RFLP, for restriction fragment length polymorphism. It required large amounts of body fluid, in good condition, to yield a result. By the late nineties, the transfer to PCR-based technology—polymerase chain reaction—and the use of short tandem repeats, almost like photocopying the minuscule particles, expanded the horizons enormously. It is a method that requires just a minute amount of material from which to test, and is even successful with old and degraded samples. DNA technology had revolutionized the nature of our work in the short time that I had come to the practice of law, and was making possible solutions to crimes that had not been dreamed of a short decade before.

Within a week's time, the swabs taken from a victim's body

hours earlier might supply us with a secret code, unique in all the world to the man who forced himself upon her this morning. It would be analyzed and mapped, serologists detailing at least thirteen distinctive loci, or places on the assailant's genetic fingerprint that matched no other human being's on earth. They would feed it to the medical examiner's crime scene computer database to see whether this offender had committed a similar offense anywhere in New York City. Within the month, his profile would be uploaded to the state's files in Albany, and the FBI's system in Washington, in hopes that one of those sources would have this suspect on record in an unrelated arrest, and solve this latest case with a computer-generated cold hit.

The phone rang again at nine-thirty. "Only three shopping days left till Christmas. Where shall we meet? Everything in town is open late today. I need to get Jim's gift, and then pick out something for you to tell him that I want, just in case he hasn't done that yet."

One of my closest pals, Joan Stafford, was in town for the weekend, and we had planned to spend the day together finishing our lists. "He's already got it wrapped and in your stocking, kiddo. I know exactly what it is and you're going to be very happy with Santa. You've got to help me with Jake's. I've thought of almost everybody but him. I'm ready anytime you are."

"Okay. I've set an itinerary for us. Your time is too precious to screw around with. We start at James II. Best antique cuff links in town. Across the street to Turnbull. You must get Jake some more of those great striped shirts with the white collars. He'll never outdress Brian Williams, but you can keep trying." A wonderful respite from the week behind and the week ahead. Joan could make me laugh about anything. "We skim past Escada. Make sure Elaine has something in mind for Jake to take you to the Washington Press Club dinner in style. A quick peek at Asprey. Then a triumphal march up Madison Avenue, in and out of all the little boutiques. Do you have things for les deux divine detectives, messieurs Chapman and Wallace? We've got to take care of those guys—they're so good to you. Lunch at Swifty's, with a spicy Bloody Mary, and dinner at Lumi's. Dewar's for you and some kind of delicious red wine for me. You can help me concoct a menu for my New Year's Eve dinner party. Are we broke yet?"

"Credit cards will be totally maxed out and it will be a perfect diversion for me."

"And you'll turn the damn beeper off, right?"

"I"ll switch it to the vibrate mode. You'll never know it's there." Even my best friends had to deal with the fact that my days often started with an assault or were punctuated by a murder.

"Heat wave, Alex. It may actually get up to twenty-eight degrees today. See you in an hour."

The day went exactly as planned. Bundled up against the cold, we shopped ourselves into a state of exhaustion. Most of my family's gifts had been mailed out of town so they would arrive in time for the holiday. I could scatter the rest to my friends throughout the week, take a carload to the office for everyone there, and save Jake's for Christmas Eve.

We were savoring our last cup of espresso after dinner when the small device attached to my waistband began to buzz and wriggle against me. I pulled it off and saw the lighted notice declaring that I had one page. I depressed the button and it displayed Mike's home number.

"You call him back. He always asks how you are." I handed Joan the phone, knowing she would break the ice between Mike and me.

She dialed the number and spoke into the receiver, affecting her best French accent. "Can I interest you in a brandy, Detective Chapman?"

"Who's—?"

"Surely a flic as brilliant as you should be able to—"

"Mademoiselle Stafford! Your place or mine?"

"I'm afraid that I'm not alone. I've got that blonde with me.

Don't forget, I'm expecting some little Christmas trinket from you."

"Well, I've got Coop's all picked out."

"What are you getting her? I'm green with envy already."

"You know those LoJack things you install in cars so the cops can track them in case they're stolen? I'm gonna do the first human LoJack insertion. I spend more time hunting down this broad around town, trying to figure out where she is when I need her. I'm gonna stick a needle with that computer chip deep into the buttocks of her cute little right—you've probably seen 'em bare, Joanie. Which one's cuter? The right or the left cheek?"

"Neither one's that appealing, Mike. They're both a bit scrawny. Drinks on me. Please come join us. We're at—"

"No can do. Somebody beat you to it. Put blondie on."

I put the phone back to my ear. "Did you get my message?" I asked sheepishly.

"Yeah. Had to run right out and get myself a date last night. Didn't want you checking my hand for blisters."

"I'm sorry for—"

"There's more important stuff to talk about. Just got a call from the captain over in the two-six. One of the custodians was going through the dorms at King's College today. Making sure everybody was out 'cause they're closing the building down till after the first of the year.

"The guy had to break open the door to one of the bedroom suites that was locked and bolted from the inside. Found a kid from Philly, a twenty-one-year-old senior, swinging from the railing in his closet. Hung himself with the drawstring from a pair of sweatpants. Suicide."

I thought first of the boy's family, and how their lives would be shattered by this news they might not even know yet. Mike talked on.

"Criminal justice major. Julian Gariano."

"In Lola Dakota's classes?"

"No connection to her that anyone can make. Seems your office was about to bust Gariano next week. Six-month investigation with an indictment that was supposed to be unsealed for his arraignment, by the Special Narcotics Bureau. Kid and his accomplice have been importing huge quantities of Ecstasy for a couple of years. His codefendant was arrested at the airport, coming in from Amsterdam with more than a hundred thousand tablets. Rolled over and gave up Gariano in a flash."

"So what's this got to do—"

"Guess who he lived with a year ago, his main squeeze? Charlotte Voight, the girl who's been missing since April."

10

Planning anything this particular Monday morning was a futile race against time. Every agency and business from which I needed records and information would be shutting down, some for just the period surrounding Christmas, and others for more than a week until after the New Year's holiday. Lab scientists, cops, prosecutors, and witnesses would be taking days off for traditional celebrations and trips to be with family out of town. I took a cab to the office at 7 A.M. and reviewed the file for the short hearing I had to conduct at nine-thirty.

Then I blasted out a list of e-mails on the in-house network. I had to find one of my senior attorneys to handle the new pattern in the Nineteenth Precinct, and to put a rush on the subpoena for the victim's stolen cell phone records. I drafted a list of things for Laura to work on while I was in court, and wrote memos about case developments that she needed to type and get to the district attorney.

We had our own NYPD branch, a squad detail of about fifty officers, based one flight above me, so I called the voice mail of Detective Joe Roman and told him to do a complaint report with the statements Shirley Denzig had made to the Witness Aid workers. I also asked him to run a pistol permit check on Denzig's father, in Maryland, and to determine whether his gun had in fact been stolen.

Laura had just reached her desk at nine, and before she could sit down she was buzzing me on the intercom. "It's Howard Kramer."

"I'll take it. But if Chapman calls, put him right through. I thought he'd be here by now."

I picked up the phone to greet Kramer, a litigator and managing partner at one of the premier law firms in the city, Sullivan and Cromwell. Although I knew Howard through his work, we had become better acquainted after his marriage to Nan Rothschild, the Barnard professor who was also my ballet class companion.

"How've you been?"

"Fine. Everybody's well. I know how busy you are, but I thought you might want to see Nan sometime this week. She's flying in from London this afternoon, on her way back from a conference at Oxford. I read in the *Times* that you're involved in the Professor Dakota mess. Nan was working with Lola on a project that the college was sponsoring, and she may have some insights for you."

I knew that Rothschild was one of the most prominent urban anthropologists in the country. A professor at Barnard College, she has led and participated in some of the most extraordinary excavations in America, including several in the heart of New York City that had unearthed Colonial burial grounds and artifacts of early settlements.

"I was talking to Nan at class a few weeks ago and she described the dig she was supervising in Central Park. Seneca Village. Is that what Dakota was involved in?" The village was a community of several hundred people who were moved from their mid-Manhattan homes in the 1850s to make way for the creation of the Great Lawn in the park. Nan had captivated me with stories of the most current high-tech means of exploring the city's past.

"I don't think Lola had anything to do with that one. Nan was brought in as a consultant by King's College on something brand-new. The head of their anthropology department, a guy named Winston Shreve, asked her to head up a small project for them. Shreve had this idea to take a significant urban structure with an interesting architectural history, let Nan lead the excavation, and then combine the students' physical dig with courses about the political and cultural history. Lola was one of four teachers heading up the operation. It's attracted a lot of attention in academia—very substantive, but at the same time very lively for the students. You'd be amazed at some of the things they've found."

"Where are they working?"

"The Octagon Tower. Do you know it?"

"Never heard of it."

"You'll have to let Nan take you over to see it—it's quite extraordinary. It was New York's first lunatic asylum. Of course, that's what they called it then, back in the early nineteenth century. It's on Roosevelt Island, the northern end, just south of the lighthouse."

"Not part of that great-looking ruin you see from the Drive?" The one I pointed out to Chapman on Saturday night.

"No, not the hospital. You can't see the Octagon from this side of the river. Tell you what. Come over to the house for drinks tomorrow night, and Nan will tell you everything she knows about Lola. Then, when you have a chance, I want her to promise she'll take you out to the Octagon so you can watch what's going on."

We agreed to meet at seven on Tuesday just as Chapman

walked in the door, taped a sprig of green plastic mistletoe on the bookshelf overhanging Laura's chair, and kissed her on the back of the neck. "I'll be bringing a detective with me, if that's okay. See you then."

"Where are we going?" Chapman asked.

"Right now, we're going to Part Seventy-four for my hearing. Can you believe that the dig Lola was working on was an old lunatic asylum? I'm afraid if the two of us make a site visit, they're likely to keep us. My friend's wife is going to tell us what Lola was up to if we stop by their house tomorrow. This hearing will be short. As soon as I'm finished we can scoot out of here, up to the college."

Pat McKinney was standing in the doorway, mug in hand, as I gathered my papers and white legal pad. "Guess I don't need to worry about the direction of your investigation anymore, Alex. They're giving you the big guns to work the case. Detective I've-got-a-ninety-three-percent-clearance-rate-on-my-homicides himself." These two despised each other. McKinney took any shot he could at Mike, and Chapman felt a constant need to cover my back against McKinney's double dealings.

"Don't dally too long, Pat. You'll be missing your Mensa meeting," Mike said just as snidely. Over McKinney's shoulder, we could see Ellen Gunsher and Pedro de Jesus on their way down the hall to his office for their daily ritual of coffee behind closed doors.

"I want to be sure you sit down with us before I head upstate for Christmas, Alex. Pedro has some ideas about the trial you're starting in January. The blood-spatter evidence. I think it would be useful to hear him on it."

"Pedro hasn't tried a case since I was in the academy. He's giving advice to Coop? You two ought to start your own Web site. Www.I-used-to-be-a-contender dot com. Sit in your corner office telling war stories to Little Miss Gun Shy about what it was like in the days when you didn't have to turn over Rosario material, and scientific evidence meant proving someone was blood type A or O.

She probably even buys into your baloney. Thinks you were a trial dog once upon a time. Gunsher wouldn't know the difference between the inside of a courtroom and the Spring Street Bar. We got work to do, buddy. And you, Ms. Moneypenny," Mike said, winking at Laura, "I expect you to tell me whether you've been good or bad this year. Don't let McKinney under my mistletoe. His breath's funny. See you later."

We brushed past Pat and trotted down the staircase across the seventh-floor corridor to take the elevators up to the sixteenth-floor courtrooms. "How come you were late? I thought you were going to be in my office by eight o'clock."

"Forgot I had to make a stop at the hospital. See a friend."

"Sorry. Who's sick?"

"Nobody you know. Just promised to be there for some blood tests. I'll tell you later."

It was unlike Mike not to respond directly to my questions, so I left it alone for the moment. "Anything more on the student who killed himself?"

"He was one of the kids that the dean had lined up to talk to us this afternoon. So far, that's all I know about him. People are dying to get out of your way, Coop."

Truly, a sobering thought. "The narcotics assistant who has the file wasn't in yet. I left a message for him to call as soon as possible and get a copy of all the police reports over to me." I pushed through the courtroom door and walked forward into the well.

The judge, defense attorney, and court officers were all waiting for me to appear. I apologized for keeping them waiting as Judge Zavin ordered the defendant produced from the pens. Behind each courtroom was a small holding cell to which incarcerated offenders were delivered from the correction department, brought to the building from the nearby Tombs or the longer bus ride from Rikers Island.

From her desk in the far corner, the court clerk called the case for the record. "Calendar number four. People against Harold

Suggs. Indictment number 4362 of 1994. Matter is on for a hearing under the Sex Offender Registration Act. Counsel, state your appearances, please."

"For the People, Alexandra Cooper."

"Bobby Abramson for Mr. Suggs."

Since the murder of six-year-old Megan Kanka in a small New Jersey township several years earlier, every state in the country had responded with legislation mandating that convicted sex offenders be required to register their addresses upon release with a local police agency. In New York, before they could be paroled from prison, a hearing had to be held to establish a level of offender responsibility, which would determine how often that individual would have to report for monitoring of his home and work situations. It would also decide whether the public could be informed that Mr. Suggs had moved into the neighborhood.

These Megan's Laws, as they have come to be called, arose from the facts in that little girl's case. Her killer was a convicted child molester who settled in a home across the street from Megan's house, although no one in her family was aware of his background. After luring her into his yard with the promise that he would show her a puppy, the "rehabilitated" parolee molested and murdered the child.

"Ms. Cooper, Mr. Abramson—have you each had an opportunity to examine the recommendations made by the review board?"

"Yes, Your Honor," we answered at the same time.

"Do either of you wish to challenge the findings?"

Again, we each said, "Yes."

Of the three possible ratings, Suggs had been evaluated a 2 by the board. I had done a thorough background workup of him and wanted to argue that he was eligible for the most serious monitoring level, or a 3, while my adversary was fighting to reduce his exposure and take him down to a 1.

"I intend to call witnesses, Judge," Abramson said.

I glanced over to the row of benches behind him and saw a middle-aged woman with a scowl on her face, sitting beside a stack of folders. Just what I needed. An unanticipated witness for the defense to drag out the morning's proceedings.

"I'll hear Ms. Cooper first. Are you personally familiar with this matter?"

"Yes, Your Honor. I tried the case for our office in ninety-four."

"Perhaps you can give me more detail than the court file has."

It was always an odd experience to appear before Frances Zavin on a sex crime. She was a very stern jurist, nearing retirement age, who had chosen to decorate her courtroom with two oversize canvases that hung on either side of her raised chair. Both were modern paintings in bold colors, and the one situated above the witness box portrayed a large, mangy dog with an exposed, erect penis. It was our practice to warn rape victims not to look up at it as they took the stand for fear that it would unnerve them, and we often wondered what jurors thought as they listened to graphic testimony and stared at the aroused mutt.

I talked to Zavin, framed as she was by her artwork. "Mr. Suggs was fifty-eight at the time he committed these acts. He is what I would call a classic pedophile, which is the reason—"

"Objection, Judge. That's a prejudicial and conclusory—"

"Mr. Abramson, hold your objections until Ms. Cooper completes her statement. There's no jury here, so you won't impress me with your interruptions."

"In the instant case, the defendant was convicted of sexually abusing two girls, who were five and six years old at the time." The court officer standing at my back groaned softly. Score extra points for multiple victims. Score triple miles for children under the age of eleven.

"Any force?"

"Absolutely none, Your Honor," Abramson interjected. "There's no allegation of force or the use of any weapons."

Like the five-year-old was *willing* to be fondled? "Most

pedophiles don't use knives and guns, Judge. They don't need to. We never charged him under the forcible compulsion theory. These are statutory cases. Sexual abuse in the first degree, the same level of felony as if he had been armed. These babies were clearly unable to consent, in fact, and under the law."

"Oh, please," Abramson whined. "*Babies?* Can she call them something else?"

"Surely they are babies, sir. What do you think is more appropriate, 'young women'? Go on, Ms. Cooper."

I laid out the facts of the case, which involved allegations that Suggs, who was living with the mother of the children, regularly carried them into his bed when she left for work three nights a week as a nurse's aide at Metropolitan Hospital.

"Any priors?"

"Actually, yes, Judge. Although no convictions. Mr. Suggs was arrested several times throughout the eighties for similar offenses. None of those charges resulted in indictments. I pulled the papers on the cases, and because of the corroboration requirements still in place for child victims, the prosecution was not able to prove those matters at the time."

"The witness I have here today can speak to the defendant's efforts to control his own impulses." Abramson pointed at the woman seated behind him. "Dr. Hoppins with the MAC treatment program."

I turned to catch Chapman's eye. "Everybody's got a frigging acronym," he mouthed to me. We knew this one well. The Modality Alteration Center on East Ninth Street, right off Lower Broadway, a private clinic with psychologists who specialized in counseling for admitted offenders. Half of our convicted felons went to that office as a condition of their parole, and I had yet to see any of them rehabilitated. The shrinks working there were some of the same geniuses who had declared Megan's killer ready to rejoin society.

"Dr. Hoppins will tell you that Mr. Suggs was already in

therapy when he was arrested in ninety-four. He was trying to do something about his problem, without the intervention of the court."

"What Dr. Hoppins, and perhaps counsel himself, may not be aware of—since Mr. Suggs was represented by Legal Aid at that time—is that when the defendant was apprehended for these charges, he had just left Dr. Hoppins's office. Suggs was picked up for public lewdness directly across the street from the clinic, standing against the wire fence. That's the playground at the Grace Church School, where he had exposed himself while watching the kindergarten class playing kickball in the yard. Unfortunately, the center is a magnet for all sorts of sex offenders."

"Judge, my client is sixty-four years old now. He's hardly able, well—hardly likely—"

"The crimes Mr. Suggs has been charged with are not assaults that require the use of Viagra for a perpetrator to commit them. We're not claiming that he's completing sexual assaults like rape, which require penetration. No matter how old and how infirm he gets, these are acts he'll still be able to perform. This is a man who should never be allowed in the unsupervised presence of children." I knew the NYPD's monitoring unit had designated Megan-mappers, officers who worked with parole and probation to make sure pedophiles did not move out of jail and into apartments on the same blocks as elementary schools and day-care centers.

"Mr. Suggs has been a model prisoner during the term of his incarceration. No disciplinary infractions, no positive drug testing."

"I spoke with the warden at Fishkill last week, Judge. He told me that when they moved Mr. Suggs down here for this hearing on Wednesday, they conducted a routine search of his cell. There were more than five hundred photographs of naked children under the mattress of his bed.

"And one more thing on that point." Abramson and Suggs both glared at me as I spoke. "Mr. Suggs has his own Web site."

Zavin was about to turn against me. "I'm well aware, Ms. Cooper, that no prison in this country allows inmates access to the Internet. Don't undermine your entire case by making claims you can't support."

I slipped a downloaded series of papers from my folder and handed copies to the court officer to deliver to counsel and the judge. "There's a woman in Missouri who operates a third-party Internet service for prisoners. Ten dollars bought Harry Suggs his own biographical sketch, his photo, and the opportunity to have this woman forward to him—by regular U.S. mail—any responses he gets to his inquiries. I'd like to read this into the record:

> Hi, I'm Harry. I'm caring, honest, and lonely. I'm sixty-four years old, looking for a home with someone who shares my love for kids and animals. I've got a few grandchildren of my own, and there's room in my heart for you and yours. I've been traveling a lot these last few years, but I'm ready to settle down. Write anytime. Send family photos. I'm a good correspondent.

"I think this goes directly to his behavior while incarcerated." Add ten points, I thought. There aren't many other ways to act out your interest in child abuse from behind bars.

"What I would like to do, Your Honor," I went on, "is to keep this defendant in state prison for another twenty years. Unfortunately, he has served the maximum sentence that the court was able to impose for these crimes, and with his good time factored in, he will be eligible for parole by February tenth. It is imperative, I think, that he be re-rated as a Level Three offender, with all the attendant consequences."

"If you're done, Ms. Cooper, I think I would like to hear from Dr. Hoppins. Would you please call your witness to the stand, sir?"

Suggs was trying to get Abramson's attention. He was angered by my remarks and clearly agitated. Abramson ignored his client.

"I'd like a few minutes to talk with my witness." He turned and walked out of the well, as the judge announced a five-minute break and stepped off the bench to go to her robing room.

I reached for my pad to draw up a list of questions for cross-examination. With a deafening crash, Suggs lifted the massive oak counsel table off the floor in front of him and heaved it on its side. At the same time, he charged across the well and threw himself at me with outstretched arms, screaming my name and spitting as he came flying through the air. Court officers rushed from every direction to grab for a piece of the prisoner and subdue him, while the captain of the team picked me up from the floor, where I had landed when Suggs's body collided with my own.

Chapman vaulted over the railing and helped the guys lead the laughing pedophile back into the holding pens.

"You okay? Did he hit you?"

I sat at the table and tried to will myself to stop shaking. "I'm fine. He just bounced himself off me."

"And here I thought you were way too old to be *my* type, no less his. You're safer in the field with me and my murderers than with these pervs of yours. Let's go, blondie."

Mike picked up my folders and we started out of the courtroom, while Abramson and Hoppins followed us down the aisle.

"Hey, Alex. Don't hold that flying tackle against *me,*" Bobby urged. "I'll just adjourn the case till the middle of next month. Have Ryan or Rich stand up on it for you next time. They won't collapse like a house of cards."

"Thanks, Bobby, I'll be sure to do that."

"Ms. Cooper? May I have a word with you?" Hoppins asked.

"Some other time, doc," Mike said as he prodded me toward the door, away from her.

"It has to do with King's College, Detective. You both might want to hear it."

11

Hoppins followed us into the hallway to an alcove near the elevator bank.

"You handled a case several years back, Ms. Cooper. David Fillian, do you remember him?"

"Of course." Fillian was a street kid from Manhattan with a serious cocaine habit who supported himself by selling drugs to the rich prep school students of Carnegie Hill and upscale collegians. One night, after delivering a load of blow to a senior in one of the Columbia College dorms, he partied with his customer, who let him sleep over. When everyone had fallen asleep, Fillian prowled the dormitory halls, looking for things to steal. In one suite, he accidentally awakened a girl during the theft, who resisted and struggled when he tried to assault her. Fillian stabbed her in the chest, leaving her for dead. A roommate's quick response and the surgical team at St. Luke's saved her life.

"I've been doing some of the offender counseling in state prison. Fillian's in my program. You probably know that he wants to become a CI for the department."

Confidential informants—CIs—were a staple of narcotics investigations. Fillian had been hammered by the judge at his sentence, as we requested, and had been trying everything possible to reduce the time he spent in jail. I hoped no power on earth could speed his release.

"Hard to be useful to cops with current street news when you're as far north as Dannemora." He was incarcerated just miles away from the Canadian border.

"Some of the kids he ran with still keep in touch with him. He thinks he's in the know. Anyway, he's been telling me that one of the King's College professors has been selling drugs to the students—a regular candy shop. You ask for it, the prof's got it."

"Who is it? What's the guy's name?" Chapman asked.

"I don't have a name for you. There was no point in my asking him for the information, since I couldn't do anything with it professionally, and it has nothing to do with the treatment program. David was just complaining to me that nobody in the correction department seemed to be interested in the fact. I see from the papers that you've got this murder case, and also that one of the students with—shall we say, an alternative lifestyle?—disappeared last spring."

"How often do you see Fillian?"

"I'm not due to see him again until the end of January. I spend one week a month traveling around to the maximum-security jails, supervising the sex offender groups. I thought that if, perhaps, David had some valuable information to help you on the King's College cases, you could support his request for an early release to parole."

It was my devout wish that Fillian's parole officer had not yet been born. And I doubted that an occasional session, up close and personal, exchanging techniques with other convicted rapists had "cured" him of his habits. I was anxious to dismiss Hoppins and get on to our more immediate work. "We'll see if we can get him produced at a prison downstate to interview him. If he doesn't have any more details than this, he won't be much use to us."

We thanked her and walked away. I'm sure she detected the chill in my voice, as I questioned the sincerity of her patient's bona fides.

Joe Roman was waiting for us when we reached my office. "You still have that photo of the Denzig girl?" he asked.

"Sure. It's attached to her folder, on my desk."

"Talk about archaeological digs," Mike said, shaking Joe's hand. "That's what the pile on your desk looks like."

I flipped through the manila case jackets till I found Shirley Denzig's file. "What did you learn from the Baltimore cops?"

"That her papa has a licensed handgun. Kept it in a locked storage box in his garage. Sometime during the week he noticed it had been taken, so he reported it to the local detectives. I'm going to have copies of this photo made to give to Security downstairs here and to keep with the doormen at your building. Bad news is, she finally was evicted from her apartment. Captain's going to let Frankie and me work on it. See if we can find her and tell her what a lovely person you really are."

"Remember that Shirley's not wrong about herself. She doesn't look that good anymore. Tell them to add seventy or eighty pounds to that image, okay?"

"You're doing something wrong, Alex. It's supposed to be the bad guys who are after us, not the victims," Joe said, shaking his finger at me as he walked out of the room.

"Wanna fill me in?" Mike asked.

"I'll tell you later. Just an old complainant resurfacing when I need her least."

I dialed Ryan Blackmer's number. I needed more information about the assault near Washington Square Park. "Hey, I wanted to catch you before I go up to the college. Did your NYU graduate student show up for her interview?"

"Not only did she come in, but she recanted the entire story. Hope it's okay with you, but I locked her up. Filing a false report."

"What's the deal?"

"The girl was frantic when she got here. She had made the whole thing up. Her last exam was supposed to be this morning, and she had two major papers due before the winter recess. She just couldn't cope, so she figured if she told the dean she'd been accosted on the street and was too traumatized to finish the semester, she wouldn't flunk the courses. They'd let her make up the work in January."

"And for *that* she identified somebody out of the blue and actually had him locked in jail overnight?" The fabricated reports of assault were the most pernicious actions I could imagine women taking.

"Yeah. Claims she never expected the police to take her seriously, and by the time they had driven around for almost an hour, she felt like she owed it to them to pick out somebody."

"How's the poor guy doing?"

"I released him without bail the other night. The cops thought she was flaky from the get-go, and they called his employer, who backed him one hundred percent. Did I do the right thing by having her arrested?"

"You always do the right thing. See you later."

Laura buzzed me on the intercom. "There's someone named Gloria Reitman on the phone. Says to tell you she knew Professor Dakota, and she's supposed to meet with you at school."

"This is Alexandra Cooper. Ms. Reitman?"

"Thanks for taking my call. Ms. Foote asked me to talk to you. I was just wondering if you'd mind meeting with me at the law school building, over at Columbia? I'm a first-year there. But I knew Professor Dakota. I'd just be more comfortable alone, not being asked questions in front of all the administrative types at King's. Can you do that?"

"No problem. We were supposed to be in Ms. Foote's office at two."

"If you come a little earlier, I can meet you at one-thirty. I'll be in the Drapkin Lounge. We can talk privately there."

The scene on College Walk was a lot calmer now than it had been last week. The campus seemed almost deserted, emptied of the students who had moved so briskly down the library steps and between buildings the last time we were here. Mike and I entered the law school and asked the guard for the meeting room that had been named, undoubtedly, in honor of some fat-cat generous alumnus.

Gloria walked toward us and introduced herself. "We've actually met before. Not that I expect you to remember, but I heard you speak at the public service lecture you did here last year." She smiled at Mike as she shook his hand, then looked back at me, blushing slightly with embarrassment. Brunette ringlets framed her narrow face. "The reason I came to law school is because I've always wanted to be a prosecutor. In your office."

She had arranged some chairs in a corner of the room, and we sat together to talk. "The dean went through the lists of Professor Dakota's classes from the last two years and picked a few of us to talk to you. Of course, lots of the students have already gone home. I don't know how many are still here."

Gloria took a deep breath, apparently having difficulty saying what came next.

"The easiest way for me to start off is to tell you straight out that I hated Professor Dakota. Despised her. Shall I go on, or are there specific questions you want to ask me?"

I tried not to show my surprise. I didn't want to stifle what might be a candid portrait from an intelligent source. "Why don't you just tell us everything you think we should know, and we'll take it from there."

"Professor Dakota joined the faculty at King's during my junior year, from Columbia. All my friends who'd studied with her there thought the world of her. Brilliant scholar, great instructor. Told me not to miss the chance to get to know her. I even sat in the back of her classroom once or twice the first semester 'cause everyone raved about how she brought the past to life. I had a double major at King's—history and poli-sci—so it was a natural for me to sign up for her courses. It almost cost me admission to law school."

That was about the same time that I, too, had first met Lola Dakota. Maybe her domestic problems had created a change in her nature. I knew that kind of stress could alter a victim's entire personality.

"Second semester, junior year. 'Gotham Government—New York City, 1850 to 1950.' Sounded good to me, and I needed it for my major credits. I worked like a dog on my research paper. It may seem immodest, Miss Cooper, but I hadn't had a grade below A-minus since I started college. I was terrified about getting into a good law school, coming from King's, since it's so experimental, without any record of achievement by its students. All I could do was try to get as close to a four-point-oh grade average as possible, and study hard for my law boards.

"Dakota gave me a D. Only one I'd ever had in my life."

"Shit. I used to go home with one of those every semester. Stood for Damn Good, I told my old man." Chapman was giving her the full press now, putting her at ease, so he could ferret out whatever she had to tell us.

How could I measure her complaint? Every disgruntled student who'd ever fallen short wanted to blame the teacher for the grade. "Did you appeal it?"

"The dean of students almost drowned in appeals from Dakota's classes. She'd pick one or two pets for the semester—usually guys—and the rest of us would struggle to stay on board. We used to joke that she had a twenty-four-character alphabet, which began with the letter C."

Mike leaned forward, one elbow on his knee, supporting his chin in his hand. "Did you know she was in the middle of a pretty ugly marital situation at the time? That her husband had—"

"I didn't know she was still married till I read the story in the obituary. We thought she was having an affair with another faculty member."

Mike stayed focused on Gloria's face. "Who was that?"

"Oh, no one in particular. You know how college students are. Anytime we saw two of them together in the faculty lounge, or she showed up five minutes late for class, rumors would spread. Goofy stuff, and we knew it."

"Like what kind of rumors? What names do you remember?"

"One week it might have been Professor Lockhart—he teaches American history. Then it was one of the science guys—biochem, I think. I can picture his nerdy little face—wire-rimmed glasses with urine-colored lenses. When Recantati showed up this fall to take the temporary presidency, some of my friends thought she was slobbering all over him. Every now and then someone tossed a student's name into the mix."

"But did you hate her as much before you got the lousy grade?"

"There was something very mean-spirited about her. In the classroom, actually. She loved performing, so we'd be mesmerized during lectures. All the detail she had and her willingness to give it to us so openly. But then she'd snap into a rage for no reason at all, especially on the days that we had to make presentations. Maybe some of the kids weren't as smart as her students used to be at Columbia. Maybe she took out on us the fact that she'd been asked to leave that faculty and start up a program at King's.

"But there was no excuse for the way Professor Dakota made fools out of us. Made students stand up for ten or fifteen minutes at a clip, firing questions at us about obscure political events of 1893. Questions nobody could answer unless you'd gone beyond the course materials and guessed correctly which year she might focus on that particular day. She reduced a couple of my classmates to tears, and she seemed to enjoy doing that. That sign on Dakota's door—BADLANDS? She relished that reputation."

"Was Charlotte Voight one of those students? Was she in your class?"

"Who?"

"A junior, the one who disappeared from school last April."

"Never heard of her."

"What do you know about the drug scene there?"

"Like every other college campus, it was huge. Just happens not to be my thing, but you can find plenty of people to talk to about that."

"D'you have anything to do with the dig that Professor Dakota was working on, on Roosevelt Island?"

"No, but Skip knows about that. Professor Lockhart." Gloria blushed again, this time as though she had slipped in a too familiar reference.

"The one you said Dakota was rumored to be involved with?"

She twisted the ringlets behind her right ear. "Well, that's one rumor I know wasn't true. I mean, I was involved with Skip, junior year. We were sort of having an affair."

That helped account for the A in American history, I guessed. "Mind telling us about him?"

"I mean, he was single. There wasn't anything wrong with it." Gloria was looking at Mike for approval now. She seemed proud of herself, in that foolish way that girls sometimes are when they take a lover under inappropriate circumstances. "But I'd been seeing him since the summer after my sophomore year. That's why I confronted him about the stories that he and Professor Dakota were involved." She looked so earnest. "I guess I was jealous."

"What did he tell you?"

"Not to be ridiculous. Skip told me that he used to spend a lot of time with her, because their intellectual interests were the same. But he said she was a real gold digger. Not his type at all."

"What did he mean, gold digger? Was that his word for her, or yours?" From what I had learned during my initial investigation of Lola's marital situation, she seemed to have a very comfortable nest egg of her own. She had invested her money intelligently, with Ivan's professional assistance at first, through all the years of their marriage. She didn't seem to have a penchant for jewelry or fancy clothes, as I had observed in our many meetings, and it was obvious that she hadn't spent big dollars on decorating her new apartment.

"It was something like that. Treasure hunter. Gold digger. That's all I could get out of him, really. You can ask Skip yourself. I'm sure you'll be speaking with him. He's part of that multidisciplinary project they were working on at some old loony bin. Just don't tell him I told you about our relationship, okay? The administration wouldn't approve."

"So what was the buzz on campus before everyone left town? Who killed Lola Dakota?"

"I went to the service on Friday night. Not 'cause I was heartbroken about the professor. But a lot of my old friends were going to be there, so we figured we'd go out together before everybody split town.

"By midnight, after a few drinks, we all began to look guilty to each other." Gloria laughed. "A few of my friends—the ones who'd done well in class—defended her. The rest of us had gripes to air and stories to tell. A lot of guys figure it's just some bum from the neighborhood who knocked her off. Everybody worries about getting mugged up here. It's a constant problem, on campus and off. One guy was a suitemate of that kid who hanged himself the next night. Julian? You know who he is? That's how I heard about Lola and her crazy husband."

"Heard what?"

"Apparently Julian used to brag about being on Ivan Kralovic's payroll. That the husband paid him for information about Professor Dakota—what her hours were, when she was at her office, where she had moved, when she was out in the field on her new project. In fact, that's the reason some of the guys think Julian hanged himself. That he didn't realize Kralovic wanted the information so he could kill his wife. Julian just thought he was harassing her. And believe me, there were plenty of people on campus who wanted her harassed."

I was thinking out loud, directing my question to Mike. "Where in the world do you think Julian Gariano would have crossed the path of Ivan Kralovic?"

"Not hard to figure," Gloria responded. "My friend was there the day they met. Julian's dad had just hired a lawyer to handle his drug case. Turned out to be Ivan Kralovic's defense attorney, too. They met in the waiting room at the lawyer's office. Julian was wearing a King's College sweatshirt. Said Kralovic started asking him a million questions. That same night, back in the dorm room, Professor Dakota's husband called to talk to Julian again. Offered him a ton of money to rat on his wife. There was nothing Julian wouldn't do for money. He didn't think anyone would get hurt."

Mike gave Gloria his card. "Call me if you hear anything else." We thanked her and walked back across Amsterdam Avenue, passing the car and continuing on to keep our appointment with Sylvia Foote at the King's building on Claremont Avenue.

This time, she was expecting us. I suspected it gave her a good deal of pleasure to tell us that she had been unable to comply with our request to have students lined up ready to talk with us. "You know what this season means to so many families. Despite my best efforts, most of the young people from out of town wanted to keep to their plans and get home to their folks. I've got a few local students here, and you're welcome to use my deputy counsel's office now."

She smiled wanly and I guessed she had sanitized their stories pretty well.

Mike had opened his notepad and was ticking off his new requests. "We'll move on to the permanent residents, Ms. Foote, faculty and administration. Here's a list of the people I'd like to see tomorrow. At *my* office. Let's start with the acting president, Mr. Recantati. I'd like Professor Lockhart—he's the historian, right?—and Professor Shreve, from anthropology, and the heads of each department involved in the project Professor Dakota was working on. I want—"

"I'm just not certain of the availability of these people on such short notice."

"Coop, have you got any paper with you?"

I opened my folder and removed several grand jury subpoenas. Foote knew exactly what that meant. "They can be in Detective Chapman's office in the morning, or they can come directly to the courthouse at the end of the week and be questioned by me, under oath, before the grand jury. Their call, Sylvia." I scribbled in the names and dates while Chapman kept talking.

Foote ushered us into a small room adjacent to her own. For the rest of the afternoon, we saw a stream of young adults who attended King's College and lived in the five boroughs or surrounding suburbs. Most of them acted as though they would rather be boarding the *Titanic* than talking to a detective and prosecutor. Not one of them admitted to having any personal knowledge about Lola Dakota or Charlotte Voight. Drugs were everywhere on campus, they seemed to agree, but none of these kids had ever inhaled and didn't know who the dealers or steerers were.

One of the last to straggle in was a senior who had lived on the same floor as Charlotte during the spring semester. Kristin Baymer was also twenty. Her home was a Fifth Avenue apartment, where her father and stepmother were raising her infant half brother. She parked herself on the sofa opposite the desk at which I had been working and curled up with her knees underneath her, stifling a yawn as she greeted us.

"I'm not gonna get in trouble for this, am I?"

"Depends what you did," Mike said, trying to apply his charm, along with his best grin and most collegiate affect.

"Drugs. You probably know that I was on academic probation

sophomore year. Got caught with some pills. Amphetamines, tranquilizers. That kind of stuff."

"We're not here on a drug bust, Kristin. We've got a murder to solve and a girl to find. Hey, I'd like it if nobody stuck needles in their arms or snorted coke, but I'm not the Vice Squad. What you say to us about any of that stays right in this room."

Foote hadn't given us the student files, so we hadn't known Kristin's background. She looked too wasted and too tired to worry about whom she could trust. She just started talking.

"Charlotte and I had a lot in common. Both loners, both stubborn, both enjoyed getting high. My mom died a few years ago, like hers. And my father married my big brother's girlfriend. My stepmother's two years older than I am, and now I've got an eight-month-old brother. Classy, huh? And they call *me* dysfunctional."

"Did you and Charlotte spend a lot of time together?"

"Only when we were doing drugs. Otherwise, neither one of us was very sociable."

"Did she have a favorite? Not person. I mean drug of choice."

"Charlotte? She'd try almost anything. Pills were nothing for her. She'd take ups when she was depressed. Then she'd get so manic she needed something to bring her down. She liked cocaine a lot. And heroin."

Heroin had ravaged the drug users in urban America throughout the sixties and seventies. It had rarely appealed to young women, experts thought, because so many of them were averse to injecting themselves in the arm and developing track marks. The late nineties saw a surge of heroin use, with a new and potent strain that could be snorted and smoked, just like the more fashionable cocaine.

Kristin was biting at a hangnail now, twisting the torn skin between her teeth. "And Ecstasy. That girl loved her Ecstasy." She said it like an endorsement for cornflakes. Good old wholesome Ecstasy.

The pills, originally patented by the E. Merck pharmaceutical company in Germany, in 1914, were now made in Holland, Belgium, and Israel. They were being smuggled into the States in enormous quantities and had taken over the drug scene faster than any substance tracked before. The euphoric condition Ecstasy produces, along with its reputation for enhancing sexual enjoyment, made it hugely popular among young adults. The tablets stimulate the nervous system like speed, but at the same time create a sense of well-being and an almost hallucinogenic haze. So new on the scene that it wasn't even a controlled substance in New York until 1997, it was now a staple on high school and college campuses.

"Where'd you get it? The Ecstasy, I mean."

"Are you kidding? It's easier than getting a pack of Marlboros. Kids need proof of age for cigarettes these days. Ecstasy's everywhere." Kristin smiled.

"It's expensive, isn't it?" I thought the pills went for at least thirty dollars a pop. Fine for models and stockbrokers, but tough on a college allowance.

"Charlotte used to call my prep school friends 'Trustafarians.' No shortage of funds for a good time. My dad would rather send me money to keep me away from home than have me bitching about his wife all the time." She looked Mike up and down, then switched her scrutiny to me. "I don't know when either of you was last in a bar in Manhattan. But a Cosmopolitan costs nine bucks per drink. I can get the same buzz off one Ecstasy that it takes me five cocktails to match. Do the math.

"Besides, Charlotte was sleeping with Julian for the better part of a year. When you're putting out for the guy who's dealing the pills, there's an endless supply."

"Were you close to Julian, too?"

Now she was picking at her lavender nail polish. "Never slept with him. Didn't have to. Like I said, I could afford to buy most things that I wanted."

"What was he like?"

Kristin shrugged her shoulders and went on flaking off the chips. "He was an okay guy. He actually seemed to care about Charlotte. Maybe that's why she dumped him. I don't think she liked anybody getting that close to her."

"Did she leave him for someone else?" Mike asked.

"What's the difference?"

"'Cause maybe she's still alive. Maybe someone can help us find her."

"Some of us figure she doesn't want to be found. Just went off to lead her own life." Kristin's cavalier attitude about Charlotte's disappearance was disturbing.

"Did you know Professor Dakota?"

"Only by reputation."

"But Charlotte was a friend of the professor's, wasn't she?"

"No way," Kristin said, looking at me as if I were crazy.

"What makes you so sure?"

"Fall semester, last year, okay? Charlotte flunked Dakota's class. Capital F in some bullshit course about the mayoralty in New York, La Guardia to Lindsay. Set her off in a complete funk. It was one thing for her to sweet-talk a guy like Julian into feeding her pills, but if she was kicked out of King's, then she'd have no choice but to go home to South America. Tuition was the only thing her father would pay for. No frills. If she wasn't at college, hasta la vista, sweet Charlotte. You two look surprised."

"I am a bit surprised," Mike led off. "Lola Dakota kept a bulletin board behind her desk. Had some pictures of her relatives, had some snapshots of famous people. But she also had a photograph of Charlotte Voight. Like something from a freshman mug book. We just assumed it meant she took an interest in the girl. Cared about her. Missed her."

Kristin nipped at her raw skin again. "Julian would have keeled over at that one. He used to tell Charlotte that Dakota would get what was coming to her someday. I just thought he was being macho for her sake. Never thought anyone would kill the

SOB. Must be some other reason that Charlotte's picture's on her board."

"Who else can we talk to about Charlotte?" I asked. "There must have been other people she confided in about her plans. You don't just disappear into thin air."

"Can't think of a soul. I was the last person to see her alive, far as I know."

"Where was that?"

"I was coming into the lobby of the dorm about eight-thirty at night. She was on her way out, going to Julian's. She never got there. Must have changed her mind. Found another source."

"Did she seem to be in distress? Unhappy? De—"

"Nope. She seemed just fine. Cheerful almost. I asked her if she wanted to come up to my room to do a few lines with me. Charlotte laughed and said she had a better offer. She was going to the lab."

"Where's that?"

"That's what she used to call Julian's room. If he didn't have what you wanted, just wait ten minutes and he'd cook it up for you," Kristin said, obviously pleased by the memory. "He was wasting his time in the criminal justice department. He should have been a science major."

Chapman was disgusted. "Better living through chemistry," he said, looking at his watch.

"Anyway, Charlotte walked out the door and I never saw her again. I just assumed she was partying over at the lab."

12

I rang the bell at the Kramer-Rothschild town house shortly before 7:30 P.M. Nan opened the door and I introduced her to Mike Chapman.

"We might as well go upstairs to my study. All the information about our project is there. I've lost my husband to a new client this evening. He's working late." We declined her offer of a drink and followed her up to the second floor.

"Could I trouble you for a television, ma'am?"

"Let's stop in the den first, then," she said, leading us around the corner and clicking on the set. "Something breaking on the news about your case?"

"No. Alex and I have a standing bet on the *Final Jeopardy!* question. It'll only take a few minutes."

We caught up on small talk while we waited for Mike to find the station and then for the commercial to end. Trebek was reminding the three players that tonight's category was Famous Firsts.

"Twenty bucks, Coop. Could be anything."

"Be generous, in the spirit of Christmas. Make it forty."

Trebek stepped aside and the answer was revealed on the screen. "First woman in America to receive a medical degree."

"I'm toast, blondie. I can never beat her on this feminist trivia, Nan. Probably right up your alley, too."

Neither Chapman nor the flight attendant from Wisconsin even ventured a guess. "Who was Elizabeth Blackwell?" I asked, before the Maine fisherwoman or the Virginia enologist gave their wrong answers.

"Sorry, sorry, sorry, folks," Trebek said, chiding the three contestants for their failure to come up with the right answer. "Born in England, Elizabeth Blackwell immigrated to this country and in 1849, she became the first woman in the United States to get a medical degree, at Geneva Medical College in New York. So let's see how much money that leaves—"

"The Blackwell family settled on Martha's Vineyard after that. Right near my place in Chilmark."

"Not a bad lead-in to my story," Nan said, as Mike clicked off the television and we walked down the hall to her home office. "This dig we're working at is over on Roosevelt Island. But it wasn't given that name until 1973. Before that it was Welfare Island, and in the period we're studying, it was called Blackwells Island. Different Blackwells, of course. This piece of land was owned by a colonial merchant named Robert Blackwell, whose family lived there in the 1680s. Their original wooden farmhouse is still standing."

"And before that," Mike interrupted, "the Dutch called it Hog Island. It was a pig farm in the early 1600s. Covered with swine."

"You two will be light-years ahead of me," I explained to Nan. "Mike knows more about American history than anyone I've ever met. The fact that he's familiar with the island probably means it had some significance in military life. That's his real specialty."

Nan shrugged her shoulders. "Not that I'm aware of."

Mike lifted a ruler from Nan's desk and pointed to the southern tip of Manhattan on the huge map of the city she had pinned to the wall. "In 1673, when the British and Dutch were still at war, the sheriff of New York was a guy named Manning. The Brits put him in charge of the fort down at this end, the entrance to New York Harbor. The Dutch launched a naval assault to regain control of what had once been their colony, New Amsterdam. Manning surrendered without a battle. So King Charles court-martialed the disgraced commander and banished him rather than put him to death." He moved the pointer up to a place in the East River, halfway between Manhattan and Queens. "He was exiled to your little island to live the rest of his life."

Nan responded, "It's always been a place for exiles. For outcasts. That's part of its tragic background. Do you know much about it?"

"Nothing at all. I look at it just about every day, on my way up and down the Drive. It can't be more than the length of a football field away from Manhattan, and yet I've never set foot there. When you see it at night, there's a hauntingly romantic look to it."

"It's got a wonderfully romantic aura, I agree with you completely. It's a bit like the Ile de la Cité, in the heart of Paris. A sliver of land, in a river, right in the midst of a great city. And a quiet, small-town pace that makes you think you're in a private enclave, not an urban neighborhood. It's even more dramatic from the heart of the island. You get to see the magnificent skyline of Manhattan from every angle, and then off to the other side, there's the industrial backdrop of Queens that lines the river's edge—factories, smokestacks, and barges.

"Let me tell you what the project is, and what Lola Dakota's involvement was with us."

Nan took the pointer from Mike's hand and began her description of the river-bound fragment of land. "The island is two miles long and just eight hundred feet wide. See? It parallels Manhattan from Eighty-fifth Street, on its northern tip, to Forty-eighth Street in the south. That lower border of land is directly opposite the United Nations. Great views.

"Today, it's got several high-rise residential structures, parks, two hospitals for the chronically ill, a tramway that connects it to Manhattan, and a footbridge that links it to Queens. But what fascinates some of us most are its bones."

"Skeletons?" Chapman asked.

"Not human ones. The remnants of the unusual buildings that dominated the landscape here a hundred years ago—well, almost two hundred years ago. As New York grew into a metropolis, it experienced all the social problems and ills that we connect with urban America today—crime, poverty, disease, mental illness. By 1800, the city fathers came up with the idea of walled institutions to confine the sources of trouble. The compound at Bellevue housed contagious yellow-fever patients and syphilitics, and New-gate Prison, in Greenwich Village, was home to rapists and high-way robbers."

"My kind of town." Chapman was riveted.

"And did you know that 116th Street and Broadway was the original site of the Bloomingdale Asylum for the Insane?"

"A nuthouse, right where Columbia stands today?" Mike asked. "Now why doesn't *that* surprise me?"

"Then it occurred to these urban planners that they didn't need to use the valuable real estate of Manhattan to segregate their untouchables. There were a number of small islands that would relieve the growing city of its criminals and its crazies. So they looked to the river for property to acquire—to Wards and Randall Islands, to North and South Brother Islands, to Rikers

and Hart Islands"—her pointer moved across the riverscape—
"and the very first one the city purchased, in 1828, was Blackwells.

"From a bucolic family farm, the island was immediately
transformed into a village of institutions. Enormous structures,
forbidding and secure. A penitentiary, an almshouse for the poor,
a charity hospital—"

"That wonderful Gothic building that you see from Manhattan? The one that looks like a castle?"

"No, Alex. That one came a bit later, for a different purpose.
And then, of course, there's *my* pet. The Octagon—the lunatic
asylum that was built to replace Bloomingdale's."

Nan walked to her desk chair and opened a drawer, removing
from it an oversize notebook with sepia-toned blowups of old
photographs. "The asylum was designed to be the largest in the
country. It had arteries stretching out in every direction—one to
house the most violent of the patients, another for females, a third
for the foreign insane."

"Wasn't everyone a foreigner?" Mike asked.

"I think it's always the case, Detective, that some are more
alien than others. Did you know that whenever an immigrant was
found alone in the streets, unable to communicate because of the
language barrier, our benign forefathers just placed him in the
asylum until someone could make out what he was saying?

"The other discouraging thing about this place was that there
was a very small medical staff. The patients were actually cared
for by prisoners from the penitentiaries. I can only imagine the
abuses."

"Is the asylum still there?" I asked, studying the photo images
of the primitive outbuildings.

"All those wings are gone. What remains today are the ruins of
the Octagon Tower. It's a stunning rotunda, built in the Greek
Revival style, with an elegant winding staircase, all columned and
pedestaled." She showed me the interior photographs, which
looked like a shot up five spiraling flights of cast-iron steps. "It

was once considered the most elegant staircase in New York. Now that broken frame climbs up to the open sky. Completely deteriorated and neglected."

"I guess the theory of the day was to treat the inmates like animals, but do it with charm."

"Exactly. There were vegetable gardens and willow trees and an ice-skating pond so that the external appearance seemed like an oasis of calm and care. But within the walls, it was truly a madhouse."

"What interests you about it? Why the dig?"

"It's everything an urban anthropologist craves. There aren't many places to burrow into in Manhattan these days, much as I'd like to. This offers a very confined site with a fair amount of known history. We've got records of an early Indian settlement there, before the Colonials came to America. We're already finding those artifacts—tools, pottery, weapons. Then you have the agricultural community which existed there for another century.

"And, of course, the asylum years, for most of the nineteenth century. Remember, many of these patients who were not indigent went there with all their possessions. They were served on china plates, not the tin cups of their almshouse neighbors. When these buildings were all abandoned, much of this stuff got left behind, buried in place. Scores of dignitaries visited the island to see this innovative social welfare setup, and some of them, including de Tocqueville, wrote about it extensively.

"You really must—both of you—come out to see how we work and what we've found. The dig is at a bit of a standstill with this frigid weather we're having, but I can have one of the students tour you around the Octagon. The whole island, if you like."

"We'll take you up on that offer. But we'd also like to talk to you about Lola Dakota, Nan."

"I'll tell you the little that I know," she said, sitting down at her desk and motioning us to take seats opposite her. "Of course, I first met Lola when she was on the Columbia faculty. Bit of a wild card, personally, but a talented scholar."

"Did you socialize with her?"

"Not much. Without even knowing about their marital problems, Howard never trusted Ivan very much. He always seemed to be hustling people. Looking for the quick score. We were occasionally invited to the same dinner party, but the four of us never spent any time together."

There was something different about the tone of Nan's responses when she talked about Lola. She did not seem quite as open as she had when discussing the history of New York.

"Were you here for the funeral?"

"No. No, I left for London on Friday evening. That was the day she was killed, wasn't it? I didn't learn of her death until one of Howard's phone calls." She fumbled with paper clips in the top drawer of her desk.

"We've only spoken to one of her sisters and a couple of students. What was she like as a colleague or peer?"

"Well, her style was a lot flashier than my own. I wouldn't say that we had much in common." Nan was a brilliant scholar, nationally renowned in her field, and as modest as she was good. "But one-on-one, she was perfectly pleasant to work with. She never confided in me, if that's what you mean. I don't think I had seen her in more than a year after she moved to King's College. It was the Blackwells Island project that brought me into contact with her again."

"How did that get started?" Mike asked.

Nan looked at the ceiling and laughed. "Several years of wishful thinking on my part. Hard to remember which of us pushed the idea forward first. Let's see. Winston Shreve helped to organize the plan. He's the head of the anthropology department at King's."

"Have you known him long?"

"Fifteen years. Very impressive credentials, which is why they recruited him for the school. Undergrad and graduate degrees are both Ivy League, if I remember correctly. Spent some time at the

Sorbonne. Helped with the excavations at Petra. He's wanted to do something on the island for as long as I have. Like me, one of those New Yorkers in our profession who's always wanted to get his hands in some local dirt, but just keeps watching apartments and office towers get planted on top of every square inch of historical soil that we covet.

"Yes, Winston and I have been talking about digging on the island for as long as I've known him."

"And the others?"

"It was a four-department program. Multidisciplinary, as they like to call it these days. Something for everybody. We each seem to have a special place on the island that attracts us for a different reason. Winston and I run the anthropological courses. My favorite site is the northern tip, from the lighthouse to what remains of the Octagon Tower. Skip Lockhart chairs the American history segment. His heart seems to be attached to the people who passed through here, their stories and what became of them. Thomas Grenier is in charge of the biology students."

That's a name we hadn't heard yet. "Who's Grenier?" Mike asked.

"King's College. Head of the biology department there. Out of UCLA, if I remember correctly. Haven't seen him around in weeks, but I think it's because he's been on sabbatical this semester. Might not even be in town." Mike was writing the name in his notepad.

"Why biology?" I asked.

"The scientific piece is as important as all the digging we're doing. Maybe more so. By the 1870s there were almost a dozen medical facilities here. Every 'incurable' patient from the city was sent to a hospital or clinic on Blackwells. One was for scarlet fever, another for epilepsy, a separate place for cripples, for cholera and typhus sufferers. There were tuberculosis facilities, and a special building for lepers. It even had the first pathology laboratory in the country.

"Then there came your ruin, Alex. Eighteen fifty-six, to be exact. Smallpox continued to be a societal scourge throughout the nineteenth century."

"What about Jenner? I thought there was already a smallpox vaccine by that time."

"Yes, the vaccine was being used in America by then, but the constant influx of poor immigrants who had been infected in their own countries brought the disease here from all over the world. Because it was so wildly contagious, patients in New York City had always been quarantined away from the population. They were generally sent to live in wooden shacks on the banks of the two rivers, until it became even safer to ship them off to the island of undesirables."

"Blackwells?"

She nodded. "Renwick designed a stunning home for those latest outcasts. The Smallpox Hospital. You see it lighted up so dramatically at night from Manhattan, with its pointed, arched windows and crenellated roofline. A great gray monument to disease. Small wonder the biologists want to study the place."

Nan moved to the giant map and ran her finger up the narrow piece of waterway that separated Manhattan from the grim institutions of the old Blackwells Island. "How are you on Greek mythology?" she asked. "The River Styx, Lola used to say this was. Souls crossing over from the realm of the living on their way to hell. To what she called the deadhouse."

13

"What *was* the deadhouse?"

"Just Lola's name for Blackwells Island, I guess. It was a nineteenth-century expression that meant a place for dead bodies."

"Did she refer to it that way?"

"I know you had met her, Alex. She had this tremendous flair for the dramatic. Used it to great advantage in the classroom whenever things got dull. We were all brainstorming about the dig one night—I think we were downstairs in my own dining room—going through a pretty good case of red wine—and that's when I heard Lola use the expression for the first time."

"Was it an actual place on the island?"

"Not on any map that I've ever come across. Imagine the scene, as Lola used to say. There you were, raging with fever and blistering with pustulant sores, as epidemics swept through communities in the crowded city dwellings. Smallpox was spread both by direct contact and by airborne virus, as you probably know. Public-health workers separated out the ill and infected—rich and poor alike—to isolate them from the able-bodied."

The image of a plague-ridden city was chilling.

"Then, Lola would describe the bedlam on the piers in the East River as the afflicted were loaded onto boats to bring them over to the hospital. Most of them knew that for the diseased, it was a sentence of death. Some tried to escape from the officials at the docks. From time to time, one or two dared to jump in the water and brave the fierce currents of the East River rather than be ferried to hell. The once tranquil farmland had become a zone for the dead and dying. Boats went out loaded with contagious patients. As these untouchables neared the shore, their first sight was the stacks of wooden coffins piled by the edge to be loaded on for the ride home. Chances were good that if your destination was Blackwells Island, as Lola said, you were going to the deadhouse."

We were silent until Mike spoke.

"So she had the fourth piece of the project? Government, political science."

"Exactly."

"Any particular interests, like some of you others?"

"Lola had a special preoccupation, I'd say, with the prison and the madhouse. Disease and the hospital conditions revolted her, she said. But a lot of famous people passed in and out of both the asylum and the penitentiary, and she loved to learn their stories. I've never seen anyone do research about these places the way she did. Lola read all the books, she devoured letters and diaries of the time that were original source material, she even found some old survivors who had lived or worked on the island in the 1920s and thirties."

"Do you know who they were?"

"No, but surely someone in the department must have cata-logued names. I'm too busy belowground to talk to people. We left that to Lola. As long as this place was mentioned, she didn't care whether it was the notebook of a nurse or the autobiography of Mae West—"

"I saw her do that bit in her classroom once. I thought that West was locked up in Manhattan, in the Tombs."

"One night there. Then a ten-day sentence to the workhouse on the island. Mae had it pretty cushy, for a prisoner. The warden agreed that the inmate underwear was too rough for her delicate skin and let her wear her own silk teddies and white stockings. He even took her out for horse rides in the evening.

"Lola knew all their stories. Boss Tweed, Dutch Schultz, lots of corrupt New Yorkers wound up there."

"Damn, I'd love to hear some of those tales," Mike said.

"Talk to Professor Lockhart in the history department. Or even to Paolo Recantati. The historians were tracking that kind of thing. I've got my own tales of woe from the asylum."

"What kind of guy is Recantati?" I asked.

"He was new to King's this semester. Quiet, very aloof. He was a history scholar, too, so Lola tried to engage him in our cabal, get his support for continued funding. Our goal was not only to com-plete the dig, but to try to get the money needed to restore these unique buildings. She brought Recantati in on a few of our meet-ings to hear what we were up to. I've talked with him about it sev-eral times, and he seemed quite interested."

"Were you and Lola the only two women running the show?"

Nan paused for a moment. "Yes, we were."

"Any sense of Lola's personal life? Was she involved with any of these other professors?"

"I'd probably be the last one to know. The students always seemed to be more interested in that kind of information than I was."

I showed Nan a photograph of Charlotte Voight, a copy of the one on Lola's board, which Sylvia Foote had given to me earlier in the day. "Did you know this girl, one of Lola's students? Ever see her on the island?"

Nan studied the picture and handed it back. "No help to you there. I supervised the Barnard and Columbia kids. If she went to King's College, then any one of the group we've talked about would have been working with her."

"It's puzzling why Dakota would have cared about the kid enough to hang her picture in the office. Along with Franklin Roosevelt—"

"The Roosevelt piece I can answer," Nan interjected. "FDR was one of Lola's heroes, for whom Blackwells was renamed in 1973."

"Charles Dickens?"

"No idea."

"Nellie Bly?"

"She's one of *my* inmates. Your office helped, Alex."

"We did?"

"Assistant District Attorney Henry D. Macdona, 1887. Nellie Bly was a young reporter, working for *The World,* Joseph Pulitzer's scandal-loving newspaper. Some editor had a brainstorm to expose the hideous condition of the patients in Blackwells insane asylum, and Nellie Bly volunteered for the job. Undercover, you'd call it. She actually went to the district attorney for advice, and for the promise that they would begin a grand jury investigation if she found abuses.

"So Bly checked into a women's boardinghouse, claiming to be a Cuban immigrant called Nellie Moreno. Within days of her arrival, feigning insanity and babbling in an incomprehensible tongue, she was escorted to the police station and then to court. First stop was Bellevue, where doctors ruled out the delirium of belladonna, the deadly nightshade poisoning of so many nineteenth-century mysteries, and actually declared her to be insane. On to Blackwells."

"Committed to the asylum?"

"Spent ten days there, documenting everything from the filthy ferry that brought her over, to the vicious prison attendants from the penitentiary who choked and beat their patients, to the baths that consisted of buckets of ice water being thrown on her head, to the descriptions of the perfectly sane women who were just sent away because they couldn't be understood. 'Inside the Madhouse' made a pretty compelling story in the *World,* and then your office exposed the whole operation."

"Did that close the asylum down as a result?"

"Certainly helped make it happen. All the mental patients were moved away from the island at the turn of the last century. My building became the first incarnation of Metropolitan Hospital."

"The one that's now on the Upper East Side?"

"Exactly right."

Mike had checked off Bly's name from his list in the steno pad. "About Lola, would you know why someone would call her a treasure seeker or gold digger?"

"That's what we all are on this project, of course." Nan smiled. "Each of us is looking for a different kind of mother lode. For me, the treasure is as simple as a stone ax or a porcelain teacup, coal boxes or ox yokes. One of my interns actually found a handful of pearls last fall."

"Pearls?"

"In those days, men were able to discipline insubordinate wives by committing them to the asylum for a spell."

Chapman winked at me, nodding his head in approval.

"Some of the well-to-do women sewed jewels in the hems of their skirts when they were sent to Blackwells, hoping to buy favors from their keepers. Or perhaps their escape. I've got one volunteer on the project, Efrem Zavislan, who dreams of stumbling across Captain Kidd's buried gold. No one's ever found the million-dollar lode the pirate was bringing back from Madagascar to New York, before his capture. Talk to Efrem, he spent lots of time with Lola. She sure wasn't interested in my kind of booty.

"My view of it is that if all those prisoners were digging for years, and they didn't come up with any treasure, then there's none here to be found."

"What were the prisoners digging?"

"Every inch of the place. The island's bedrock is gneiss. Fordham gneiss. And there's lots of granite, too. From the time the penitentiary opened in 1835, until it was shut down a hundred years later, the healthier prisoners were forced to do hard labor. All of the stone for these many buildings on the island was quarried from its own land. No rock had to be brought in.

"The granite was used to build a seawall around the entire circumference. And the gneiss is what they mined to create the exteriors of the notorious Blackwells institutions. If there were treasure to be found, some miscreant would have dug it up long before now."

"This gives us a great head start, Nan. We're hoping to meet with some of the faculty members tomorrow. At least we'll have an idea about what has had all of you so absorbed."

Nan walked us down to the front door, retrieved my coat and gloves, and waved us off into the cold night air.

We made the short drive down Second Avenue and Mike stuck his laminated police department parking permit on top of his dashboard as he left the car illegally positioned in front of a bus stop near the corner of Sixty-fourth Street. "C'mon, Coop. There's not a brownie in town who'd brave this weather to stick a ticket on my wreck."

We weaved our way across the late-hour Christmas shopping traffic that was blocking the intersection and pressed through the crowd around the bar at Primola, hoping that Giuliano had not given away my eight-thirty reservation.

"*Buona sera*, Signorina Cooper. Your table will be ready in a minute. Have a drink on me, please. Fenton," he called over to the bartender, "a Dewar's on the rocks and a Ketel One, *subito*."

People were five-deep waiting to be seated at my favorite restaurant. Most had drinks in one hand and shopping bags in the other, adding to the volume of the pack. It was too noisy to talk murder in their midst, so we relaxed with our cocktails till the maître d', Adolfo, led us to a corner table in the front of the room.

I didn't hear the chirping sound of my cell phone ringing until I had lowered myself into the chair and hung my bag over the armrest.

"Alex, can you hear me? It's Bob Thaler." The chief serologist usually started his day in the lab at 6 A.M. That he was still working at 9 P.M. meant that he had pulled out all the stops to do the testing on the Lola Dakota case. "Am I catching you at a bad time?"

"Never. Any results?" The DNA testing that had routinely taken six months to yield information when I first submitted samples to the FBI ten years ago now came back to us from the medical examiner's office in less than seventy-two hours.

"Dr. Braun and I worked on your evidence all through the weekend. I've got some preliminary answers you might want to get going with. All I'll need from you are some suspect controls, when you come up with them."

"That's Chapman's end of the deal. He's working on it."

"Dakota's vaginal swab was negative for the presence of semen. But we did find some seminal fluid on the sheets the cops sent in for testing. From a sofa bed, is what the voucher says. I worked that up and got a profile from it for you.

"The wad of gum Chapman pulled from the wastebasket in the deceased's office? Dr. Braun handled that piece. He also got a DNA sample from it. Just thought you'd like to know as soon as we confirmed them that it's a match. Whoever was sleeping in Dakota's bed is the same guy who paid a visit to her office. Does that help you?"

14

"Anybody out there blowing bubbles?" I asked, greeting Mike at the office of the Manhattan North Homicide Squad at eight-thirty Tuesday morning. I had walked up the stairs and in the rear door, near the Special Victims Unit, to avoid any members of the King's College faculty who had responded to Sylvia Foote's directive to appear to answer questions.

"It wasn't bubble gum. It was Wrigley's Spearmint. Just keep that in mind if you see any of those jaws masticating." He motioned me to sit at the table that was back-to-back with his own.

"Won't Iggy need it when she gets in?"

"Nope. Gone to Miami for Christmas."

Ignacia Bliss was one of the only women in the squad. They

had tried to team her with Mike when she first arrived from the Career Criminal Apprehension Unit, but her humorless nature and plodding investigative technique were not suited to his style. The banner he had hung over her desk more than a year ago was still tacked to the windowsill: IGNORANCE IS BLISS.

"Who's here to chat with us?"

"Only got three. The rest of them seem to have scattered to the north and south poles." Mike's jacket was hanging from the back of his chair. He swung around and put his feet on the top of my desk, reading from his pad. "Skip Lockhart, the project's history professor, is out of town till the end of the week. Grenier's the biologist who's had the semester off. He's due back in the middle of January. May have to hunt those two down.

"Here with us for bagels and brew are Mr. Recantati, Professor Shreve, and Foote herself."

"Let's begin with Shreve. Nan puts him back at the beginning of all this. Why don't we see how helpful he is?"

Mike walked past the lieutenant's empty office and returned with a man I guessed to be in his late forties and dressed, like Mike, in jeans and a crewneck sweater, carrying a cardboard container of coffee that had been set out in the waiting area for our guests from King's College. Before we could be introduced, he reached for my hand. "Good morning. I'm Winston Shreve. You must be Ms. Cooper."

I pointed to one of the chairs usually occupied by the hapless or homeless who were being interviewed by Mike on a murder case. The stuffing was hanging out of the seat pad and two of the four rollers on the chair legs were missing, so it scraped unevenly along the floor as Shreve moved it forward to rest his folded elbows on the desk.

About all I knew was that he was an anthropologist. "Would you mind telling us a bit about yourself, Professor? We're trying to get a picture of the group of people who worked most closely with Lola Dakota."

"Anything you'd like to hear." He started with his credentials, which had been cited to us the previous evening by Nan Rothschild. His accent sounded vaguely foreign. Shreve's responses to my questions were quite direct. "No, I was born on Long Island. Oyster Bay. But you've got a good ear. My family took me abroad when I was an adolescent. I did what you would call high school in England, before coming back here for university. Harvard."

His eyes moved back and forth between us. "You seem to know some of this already. Shall I go on?"

"Till we stop you," Chapman said with a grin. "From Paris to King's College? Sounds like a downhill run to me."

"I'm young enough to take chances, Detective. There's something quite exciting about an experimental school, about the opportunity to build an entire department and all the programming from scratch. They've already attracted quite a bit of intellectual talent, wouldn't you agree?"

"Can't say I'd recognize it. I'm the beauty of this operation. Coop's the brains. If she tells me you guys are smart, I'll accept it. Talk to me about Lola."

"You knew her?" Shreve asked, surprised by the familiarity of Chapman's first-name reference.

"Coop's actually the one who worked with her. I'm in charge of the homicide investigation. How well did you know her?"

"Well enough to recruit her for King's. And to consider her a good friend. Lance and Lily, they're her—"

"Yeah, we know."

"They asked me to say a few words at the service yesterday. I guess I was as close to her as anyone at the college."

"Have you known her long?"

"I'd say almost ten years. I'm forty-six now, a few years older than Lola was. Met her the first time at the Aspen Institute. We were each delivering a paper at one of those summer panels. Seemed we had a lot of the same interests, professionally."

"How about personally?" Chapman jumped ahead, trying to speed the process of getting some body fluid to Bob Thaler's office. It wasn't subtle.

"Were we ever intimate, Detective? Yes, but it's been quite a while. The summer we first met, Lola and Ivan were separated. She had walked out on him the first time he lifted a hand to her."

I tried to recall the history of her marriage, as Lola had detailed it to me during our first few meetings. She had never mentioned any formal separation, but all the statistics about domestic violence supported the probability that several had occurred. In most abusive situations, there are seven failed elopements—seven unsuccessful efforts to split from the abuser—before a woman completes the move.

"How long did your relationship last?"

"The better part of a year. Long distance and infrequent, at that. I had returned to Paris to work on a project that just opened to the public last year. Are you familiar with it? There were extensive ruins that had been built on top of several times throughout the centuries, right at the front of the plaza where Notre Dame stands. Lutetia, it was called. The original Roman village that was settled on the Ile de la Cité in medieval times."

Interesting, I thought. Nan had likened Blackwells' midriver positioning to the Ile de la Cité, too.

"Lola was teaching at Columbia then. Used to find any excuse she could to fly over to France. Field trips, student holidays, academic seminars on international government. Boondoggles of every kind. I had a charming flat on the Left Bank, near the university, between Luxembourg Gardens and those amazing bookshops along the Seine. We spent some great weekends there."

"Ah, we'll always have Paris, right, Shreve?" Doing his best Bogie, Mike couldn't help taking a shot at the romantic reverie. The professor didn't catch the reference. "What broke it up?"

"Lola and Ivan had gotten back together. And I'd fallen madly in love with a Frenchwoman, from Toulouse. Six months later I was married. I'm a French citizen now, in fact."

"So your wife lives here with you?"

"No, she doesn't. Giselle's in France. The marriage lasted eight years. But our divorce is quite amicable, and you're very welcome to talk to her, if that's what you mean. We have two young children, whom Giselle wanted to raise in her country. And she wanted to finish her degree at the Sorbonne, too. She was my student when we married, so that meant she had to drop out of the classes. She'll finish her studies and graduate in the spring."

"But she knew Lola Dakota?"

"Certainly. Whenever Ivan and Lola traveled to Europe, the four of us spent time together. It was no problem for Giselle. I'd been single when I hooked up with Lola. But I don't think Ivan ever knew anything about our relationship. Open-mindedness is not his strong suit.

"She and I always remained close. I'm to blame, if you will, for inviting her to come to King's to teach. I assumed she would have a much greater opportunity to become a department head here. Fewer entrenched alumni to battle with over her unorthodox or, shall I say, more innovative ideas, less heritage to have to embrace than back at Columbia. Lola could rub some of the traditionalists the wrong way."

"How about you? D'you ever battle with her? Get on the receiving end of her tough streak?"

"I take it you've been talking to some of the students. Lola Dakota—the professor—was a perfectionist. If these kids weren't applying themselves according to her standards, she was ruthless." He was somber now. "My department had little to do with hers, in general. But because of the Blackwells project, many of the interns from King's worked under our joint supervision. We planned a number of courses that we cotaught, combining the anthropological features of the island with the politics of the period.

"But I can't remember fighting with Lola about anything significant. On which end of the project should the dig begin? Should a student be graded a B, or did we throw in a plus or minus? How much time should be spent talking to descendants of some of the inhabitants?"

"When's the last time you slept with her?"

"She'd admire your directness, Detective," Shreve said with some hesitation. "More than I do. Eight years ago, to be exact. In her cheap hotel room on Boulevard St-Germain-des-Prés. "And it was good for *me,* if you want to know that, too."

I tried to get us back on course. "Did you know a girl named Charlotte Voight, Professor?"

He straightened in his chair and put both hands on the back of his neck. "Sad case, Charlotte. She was in one of my classes last spring, when she suddenly walked away from all this." He looked back at me. "Now, *she* was a source of disagreement between Lola and me. I thought the girl had a lot of intelligence to be channeled, and a creative imagination."

"With or without the aid of hallucinogens?"

"Her drug use was no secret, Detective. But when she was clearheaded and engaged, as I think she was in my classwork, I thought we had a chance of saving Charlotte. Lola didn't see it that way. Came down on her hard. Some of us thought that helped drive the child off, send her over the edge, emotionally speaking."

"What do you think happened to Charlotte?"

"I just assume she went home to South America. Probably wandered around Manhattan until she ran out of contacts to keep her high, then packed her bags and went home." He brightened as he spoke his next thought. "Charlotte will come back round, Ms. Cooper. I'm sure of it. Hungry to learn, anxious to be accepted, though she didn't like to show that side to people. She's not the first college girl to take a breather."

Mike was back to Lola Dakota. "Lola must have told you what went wrong with her marriage, didn't she?"

"Ivan's right hand, so far as I know. And occasionally his left.

He beat her, Detective. And once she realized there could be life without him, and that his rages weren't confined to days of the month that she could predict and avoid, she was ready to walk away from it."

"Another man?"

"I hope so."

"Any guesses?"

"I'll let you know if I come up with any. Skip Lockhart, maybe. Lola seemed to be spending a lot of time with him. Perhaps even President Recantati," Shreve said, finishing his cup of coffee and recapping the empty container with its plastic lid. He laughed, adding, "But Lola would have been on top in that arrangement. He seems a bit passive for my old friend. She was vying for his attention from the moment he arrived, so I wouldn't put anything past her. Still waters and all that."

"What do you know about Ivan's business dealings?"

"That I wanted to be at arm's length from them, Detective. I don't know what he was up to, but Lola thought he'd end up in jail."

"Was she still getting money from him?" Chapman was thinking, like I was, of the shoe boxes full of cash that had been stashed in her closet.

"I don't think he'd give her a nickel, and I doubt she would have accepted anything from him. She wanted out. Over and out."

"What attracted you to the Blackwells Island project, Professor? Seems that some of you who were involved have favorite parts of the place that were of particular interest." I was curious about what drew Shreve to this site.

"Like Lola, I was attached to the work planned on the southern end, everything from the original mansion, which is about midpoint, down to the lower tip."

"The Smallpox Hospital, the City Penitentiary? That area?"

"Precisely. It was Lola who first brought me to the island, the same summer we met in Aspen. I was on my way back to Paris, and New York was hosting one of those parades of tall ships. The harbor was filled with magnificent old sailing vessels that evening. Lola packed a picnic and we took the tram over. She told me it would be the very best vantage point from which to see the schooners sailing up and down the East River, and the fireworks exploding above the cables of the Brooklyn Bridge. In those days, you could traipse on foot right down to the southern end.

"Do you know du Maurier, Ms. Cooper? That's how Lola introduced me to Blackwells. Ever the actress—would have made her mother proud. 'Last night I dreamt I went to Manderley again,' she said, laying a blanket below the blackened windows of the old facade."

"That's exactly what the old hospital looks like. No wonder it's always attracted me." I turned to Mike. "That's the opening line of the novel *Rebecca*."

"Same as the movie," he snapped back at me. I may not be as well read as you, he was telling me, but don't push me.

"The most startling thing that night was looking back at the incredible view of the Manhattan skyline. We were spread out on the ground, drinking warm white wine from paper cups, and staring directly across the water at River House. It's where my father lived before I was born, and I'd never seen it from that angle."

So Winston Shreve came from money. The fabled apartment building, east of First Avenue on Fifty-second Street, was constructed in 1931 as a palatial cooperative apartment, complete with squash and tennis courts, an interior swimming pool, and even a ballroom. It boasted a private dock, right on the spot where the FDR Drive was later built, at which Vincent Astor kept his famous white yacht called *Nourmahal*. Lived in then by the rich and the royal, today it was home to world-famous personalities like Henry Kissinger and the great international beauty Lady Lynn de Forrest.

"Can't you do that now? Walk down to that vista, I mean?" I asked.

"Not till we've finished our dig, Ms. Cooper. And not unless the money is raised to reconstruct Renwick's fabulous building. Now the hospital's completely in ruins, like an old Gothic castle. No floorboards to speak of, crumbling walls, falling granite blocks. That portion of the island is blocked off from public access by metal fencing across the entire plot, east to west. Topped by razor wire. It's far too dangerous to let people near it."

Chapman poked at me with his pen. "If you're nice to me, blondie, I'll get you a pass for Christmas. The 114th patrols there." Present-day Roosevelt Island had its very rare criminal statistics tallied as part of Manhattan's Nineteenth Precinct, the same Upper East Side neighborhood in which I lived. But patrol duty fell to the auto-accessible Queens cops, and I didn't know any of the guys assigned to that precinct. "I'll get you in for an up-close-and-personal."

Shreve's territorial grip took hold and he spoke, brusquely, over Mike's words. "I'll take you myself, anytime you'd like to see it."

"You got a key?"

"All of us supervising the project have access, Detective. We've got security clearance to come and go as we please for the duration of the study. The grounds are a bit more inviting in the spring, but as soon as some of this ice melts I'll take you both over."

"Did you ever hear Lola refer to 'the deadhouse,' Professor?"

"All the time, Mr. Chapman. You know the island wasn't a very inviting place, even into the twentieth century. When the city finally abandoned these properties, the officials just walked out and closed the doors behind them. Things were left exactly as they were on the last days in use. Sheets were made up on the hospital beds, stretchers stood in hallways, wheelchairs and crutches were propped in doorways and against walls. People were afraid to go there for years, frightened that some of the contagion still lurked in the empty corridors or beneath the eaves.

"Lola liked it that way. When she called the place a 'deadhouse,' it conjured up ghosts of the people who perished there. Kept the amateurs away, which suited her fine."

"I hadn't seen her in months, Professor. She had chosen to work with the prosecutors in New Jersey rather than my office, as you certainly know now. My boss thought their plan to stage her murder was absurd. Can you tell us, had she been worried about Ivan lately?"

"Constantly. Fear consumed her, wherever she was. Somehow, he seemed to know just how to spook her, whether she was walking on Broadway to meet a friend for lunch or getting off the tram when she came to the island. He always kept tabs on her whereabouts. Lola was certain that she was being followed and didn't know whom to trust. I think that's why old friends were so important to her, in the end."

"Was she afraid, even when she went to the island?" I thought immediately of Julian Gariano, and of the thought that he had been hired by Ivan Kralovic to sell information about her comings and goings.

"That's what she told me. I had no reason to disbelieve her. You see," Shreve said, his elbow resting on one knee, "she really did have a phobia that Ivan would finish her off. She was awfully prescient, Detective, wasn't she?"

"So you think that whoever killed Lola was working for Ivan?"

"As opposed to doing the job for Sylvia Foote, Ms. Cooper?" Shreve chuckled. "That's an idea I hadn't thought of until this moment. A King's College cabal? Possible, I guess, but most unlikely. You'd have to give me a pretty good reason."

"Anything else?" I said to Mike.

"I'm not going to let you go without asking a few things about Petra, Professor. D'you mind?"

Shreve rose to his feet and stretched. "If you know of it, I can only tell you that it's as spectacular as everything you've ever heard." He spoke directly to me, quoting the Burgon poem. "'A rose-red city half as old as time.' Have you ever been?"

Chapman answered in place of me. "*I'll* get there before the princess ever will. Can you still see the citadel?"

"Not much of it left. Seven centuries older than these local ruins of ours."

"Built during the Crusades. Part of Jordan now," Mike explained to me, turning to walk Shreve out toward the exit. "You still have to go into the plains over that narrow pass, on horseback? I'm definitely gonna do that someday."

As Shreve nodded his head, Mike shook his hand, continued to chat, and then took the empty coffee cup from the professor. "Thanks for coming in. I'll throw that in the trash for you."

He walked back to his desk after ushering Shreve out. "How come everyone figures right off the bat that you're so couth and cultured, and they all make me out to be such a frigging Philippine?"

"Philistine?"

"Philistine. Whatever. I know more about the Crusaders and the sack of Zara than that egghead anthropologist will figure out in six lifetimes.

"And what he was also too stupid to know was that I generously provided them with these coffee cups so that he could leave me just a little bit of saliva on the rim, in order for Bob Thaler to tell me all the unique things in his double helix that make him such a special guy." Mike was holding Shreve's container in the air, spinning it around in his hand. "Put his initials on the bottom, Coop, and stick it in this paper bag. Attila can take them down to the lab when we're done."

Pleased with his coup, he went back into the waiting area and returned with Paolo Recantati. The timid-looking historian was still clutching his cup, so Mike refilled it from the hot plate in the squad room and gave me a thumbs-up.

"Sit down and relax, sir. Might not be as bad as you think."

"I can't imagine it can get much worse, Mr. Chapman. I left Princeton to come into this nest of vipers. Whatever for? I'm an academic, you understand. Never really been involved in administrative work. The last thing I needed to end my first semester here was a murdered colleague. It's the coldest day of the year and I'm sweating as though it were the middle of July."

It always interested me how people close to murder victims put their own woes ahead of concerns about the deceased. Somehow, I expected each of these interviews to begin with some expression of solicitude about the departed soul of the late Lola Dakota.

"Had you known Ms. Dakota very long?"

"I didn't meet her until I came to the college in September. She has—had, I guess—a wonderful reputation in her field, and I was well aware of her scholarship in twentieth-century New York City government affairs long before we met. I was counting on her to continue to be one of our more productive faculty members. She didn't disappoint in that regard. Lola's next book was scheduled for publication in the spring, with a small university press. And she had already placed several articles about Blackwells, both in academic and commercial journals."

"Published *and* perished? These times are cruel."

Chapman's humor wasn't for everyone. I made a note to try to get a manuscript of Dakota's forthcoming work. Perhaps there was something in her research that would relate to the investigation. "Was she ever accused of plagiarism, or stealing another professor's intellectual property?"

"I think everyone would agree that Lola was an original. That wasn't one of her problems."

"What were they, Mr. Recantati? What were her problems?"

He stammered a bit. "Well—well, certainly, you could start with the marriage. With that crazy husband of hers. That was an issue for all of us at the college."

"How do you mean?"

"Lola brought the marriage to campus with her every day. I don't mean physically, of course. But she was always terrified that Ivan would appear at school, following an argument or after a meeting with their matrimonial attorneys. She was just as frightened for her students and for us as she was about herself. Talked about it to Sylvia and to me quite often. Afraid that Ivan would show up—or worse still, send some hired gun to the school who would kill anyone that got in the way when he targeted Lola. Thank goodness she was alone when it happened."

I winced at the man's selfishness. What must her last moments have been like? Confronted by her killer at the portal of her own home. Had he been in the apartment with her? Had he waited outside, knowing she planned to go somewhere? Or was it a chance encounter with a stranger, and were Chapman and I wasting our time talking to her cronies while a rapist or robber—an opportunist—was at large in the neighborhood?

Recantati rubbed his forefinger back and forth across his lower lip. "That sounds kind of cold, doesn't it?" His speech halted again. "And, and I—uh—we're just assuming she was alone when she was killed, I guess. Do you know anything else about it yet? How she died, I mean?"

Mike ignored the questions. He wanted answers to his own first. "You're a historian, right? Give us your background before getting to King's."

"My credentials? I did my undergraduate work at Princeton. Master's and Ph.D. at the University of Chicago. I'd been in charge of the history department at Princeton, until I came here to take the position as acting president while the search committee is finding someone for the permanent position. I'm, uh—I'll be fifty years old in March. I live just outside of Princeton, although King's has given me an apartment on campus while I'm here."

"Married?"

"Yes. My wife teaches math at a private school near our home. We've got four young—"

"She know anything about your relationship—your sexual relationship—with Lola?"

Recantati rubbed his lip furiously now. "I didn't—we didn't have any such thing."

He had hesitated a few moments too many to be credible. I had the sense that he was trying to figure out whether there was anyone who could possibly know the truth, before he had to commit himself to an honest answer.

"That's not what your colleagues tell me."

"What, Shreve? I suppose he told you that he and Lola were just friends, also. That's a laugh. Do you have any idea what it's like in a closed community like a small college? You have dinner at the faculty club with someone who's not in your department and therefore you must be in bed with her. A student stays fifteen minutes too long in your office, and you're making a pass at her. If it's a male student, you must not be out of the closet yet.

"I'll help with your investigation in any way that I can, but I won't sit here and be insulted."

Chapman leaned back and opened his desk drawer. He placed a box of Q-Tips on top of the blotter and pointed to it. "How about giving me a buccal swab, Professor?"

"What? I've never been in a station house before. I'm afraid I'm not familiar with your language, your question."

"I didn't learn the word from J. Edgar Hoover. It's science, not police lingo." Mike slowly drew open the sliding lid from the box and removed one of the cotton-tipped wooden applicators. "That's buccal—from the Latin *bucca*. Your mouth, in the old country.

"If you'd be kind enough to just run this down the inside of your cheek, then Cooper's heartthrobs, those serologists over at the lab who solve all her rape cases and make her look so damn good, they'll tell me if it matches any of the DNA we found on things in Ms. Dakota's little apartment."

"B-but you need blood, surely, or s-s-s—"

He couldn't bring himself to say the word "semen."

"I need a buccal swab, is all. The same little bit of spit that's kind of frothing on your lips, sir."

Recantati repeated his nervous habit of stroking his mouth. He stood up. "This is not what I came in here to discuss with you today. You can't make me do that."

"I got a four-year-old nephew who says that to me, too. Stamps his foot at the same time. You should add that touch, for more emphasis. *I* can't make you do it, today, is a fact. But watch out for blondie, here. She's hell with a grand jury."

"If I can be useful with serious information that might actually help your investigation, please call me. I'll be in Princeton until the beginning of next week." He walked to the exit before either of us could see him out.

Chapman smiled, picking up Recantati's relinquished coffee container and marking it with the professor's initials on the bottom. "Got him anyway."

"Well, you may have won a minor skirmish, but in my book you lost the war. Whether he's sleeping with her or not may play a role in this, but you gave up the opportunity to ask all the other questions about things I wanted to know." I tossed my pad onto the desktop.

"Look, we get these cups down to Thaler's office before three o'clock and he promised to run them for us over the holiday. By the weekend, we'll know whether or not any of these academic marvels were anywhere they shouldn't have been. I didn't mean to play with him, but it was irresistible, once he started to squirm."

"But that could be something as simple as having had a fling with Lola and being mortified that his wife will find out. Now we don't even know why she was after him for money and whether he had a hand in her project."

"You can go at him again more gently next week. I'll have other things to do. Let's get Ma Kettle in here." He bagged the empty container, separate from the one he took from Shreve, and walked to the door to bring in Sylvia Foote.

Stooped and sour-faced, Foote shuffled in behind Chapman

with a slim briefcase in one hand. He led her to the broken chair and steadied it for her as she sat. "Coffee?" he asked.

"I don't drink it."

"There's one in every crowd," Mike mumbled as he resumed his seat.

"What did you do to my president?" Sylvia glared at me. "He left in a huff. Wouldn't even tell me why."

"I think he's just rattled by all this going on during his tenure."

"I'm beginning to think my faculty shouldn't be talking to you without legal representation."

If Sylvia was looking for a signal from me that none of her employees was going to come under our microscope, I wasn't willing to give it. She realized that by my silence.

"In that case, Alex, I'll have Justin Feldman get in touch with you."

That would mean trouble for us. A friend and a brilliant litigator, Justin would brook none of Mike's tactics. They had clashed in the past. He'd be cordial but tough, and we'd be likely to lose direct access to the entire King's College academic staff.

"Why would you bring in the big guns? Coop tells me you're the legal eagle." He smiled at her. "Save those administrators some money. Feldman's hourly rates are sky-high."

"There could obviously be a conflict of interest between the college and some of the individual employees you'll be talking with. I'm sure we could get him to do this pro bono. Justin's a Columbia man—college and law school."

"Boola boola."

"That's the wrong—"

"I know that, Ms. Foote. But the only academic tunes I know the lyrics to are that one and 'Be True to Your School.'" He sang her a few bars of the Beach Boys classic while she opened her briefcase and put her glasses on, then he settled in with his notepad.

"Let's see how far we get without resorting to outside counsel, Sylvia, shall we?" I tried to keep the beginning of this conversation on course. "Why don't you tell me what concerns you have, and then we'll ask you for the things we need."

She looked over her shoulder as though Paolo Recantati would reappear at any moment.

"I didn't think it's my business to tell you what's been going on with the grant money that's been disappearing from the college, but Recantati's in charge and he has directed me to be candid with you about it."

Foote fidgeted with her papers, having mistakenly made the assumption that the subject she was about to disclose was what had rattled the acting president and caused him to storm out. "He's not responsible for this, Alex, I can assure you. We've been trying to look into this ourselves since the federal investigation started in the spring.

"Why the missing cash from the anthropology department would have anything to do with Lola Dakota's death is beyond me, but I did come prepared to discuss it with you this morning."

15

Neither Shreve nor Recantati had mentioned any financial improprieties at the college. Mike and I were both thinking of Lola's shoe boxes, and whether this would be a connection to the unexplained cash.

"Have either of you heard of Dr. Lavery? Claude Lavery?"

Neither one of us answered.

"He was thought to be a trailblazing anthropologist. We hired him away from John Jay." John Jay was New York City's college of criminal justice. "The administration convinced me, at the time, that it was quite a coup for us.

"Lavery's expertise was urban drug use." She extracted several clippings from her leather case. One of them was a John Jay alumni magazine, several years old, featuring a cover photo of Lavery and heralding an article on his inner-city work. He sported a colorful dashiki, unkempt dreadlocks, and a tangled beard. He was holding a crack pipe in his hand.

"I'm upping my contribution to the Jebbies this year. The closest this guy could get to the faculty of a Jesuit college like Fordham would be the service entrance."

Foote narrowed her eyes and examined Mike more closely. If she thought he was crossing the limits of political correctness, she hadn't seen anything yet.

"What came with Dr. Lavery to King's College was a grant of three million dollars, courtesy of the National Institute on Drug Abuse. That's a branch of the Department of Health and Human Services. It made him even more attractive to us than his résumé.

"The first problem we faced was where to put him. Winston Shreve was running the anthropology department and, quite frankly, didn't want a thing to do with Lavery's study. Shreve is a classicist, really. He has very little experience with modern urban culture and certainly not this kind of thing. He wanted us to put Lavery in the sciences, or with sociology."

"Anybody want him?"

"Actually, yes. There was a bit of competition to get him. Professor Grenier runs the biology department and was very interested in carving a position out for Lavery because of the potential for health-related studies of drug use. Long-term physical problems of heroin addicts, everything from HIV infection to dental deterioration. It fit nicely with their premed courses, overlapped with the chemistry curriculum, and linked them more tightly to the social sciences.

"And poli-sci wanted him as well. Lola staged quite a campaign to convince us. She thought it was a wonderful basis to study the city, everything from the criminal justice reaction to the drug issue, the competition for funding between prison facilities and treatment programs, and the political response to substance abuse in society."

"What was your solution?"

"It was one of the few battles that Winston Shreve has lost here. Dr. Lavery calls himself an anthropologist, and that's the department in which we saw fit to place him. Much like the Blackwells Island project—"

"Is Lavery involved in that?"

"Not that I know. But it's a similar situation in that Lavery created a multidisciplinary approach to his issue, so the other departments could each get a piece of his very large and quite delicious pie. Money for everyone."

"What's the problem, Sylvia?"

"A complaint was initiated by the government a few months ago. Not in your office, but with the feds. Southern District of New York. It seems that a substantial sum of the money he was awarded is missing and unaccounted for.

"The grant came with a discretionary fund. It made one hundred thousand dollars available annually for Lavery to use as he saw fit. Related to the research, of course." She was thumbing through documents that appeared to be spreadsheets and accounting records.

"Lavery claims that he purchased computer equipment and office supplies and gave cash to student interns who researched short-term matters for him. There don't seem to be records to support him, but most academics wouldn't be surprised by that."

"What's the theory?"

Sylvia Foote studied a point on the floor between her shoes and Mike's desk. "Drugs, Detective. Sort of everyone's worst fear about this grant from the outset. That the cash was being used to buy drugs—illegal street drugs—to keep his worker bees happy. Perhaps to use for his own pleasure. The investigation is still ongoing."

"But how—?"

"Claude Lavery is a unique character. Kind of a Pied Piper in a college setting. Smart and creative, but gave the impression of being the anti-academic at the same time. He has a very laid-back style, and early on, right out of the London School of Economics, Lavery would venture into the bleakest parts of the city. Central Harlem, Bed-Stuy, East New York, Washington Heights. He bonded with street characters, the kind who would never let outsiders into their world. That's why his research was unique.

"He wrote about phenomena that made him the darling of scholars in urban studies—both the hard government types and the more 'touchy-feely' sociologists. And then, all the major newspapers picked up his theories as though they were gospel."

"Like what?"

Foote pulled a copy of a *Washington Post* front-page story from her briefcase. "Citing data from Lavery's studies, the story backs his claim that it was the federal government's strict interdiction policies about marijuana back in the seventies and eighties that created the market for international cocaine trafficking to fill the void.

"The students were wildly enthusiastic whenever they came under his spell. They would walk into a neighborhood with Claude—the kind of place these middle-class kids wouldn't dare to go on their own—and find that he had established this wonderful rapport with the locals. That led him, and them, to the addicts and, finally, to the dealers."

"You thought maybe by bringing this guy to the college he was gonna be hanging around on Sesame Street? What's the surprise here?"

"Frankly, Detective, you're right. That's why some of my colleagues aren't the least bit shocked. They expected no less. I presume," she said with great resignation, "that some of them are the people who sparked this formal complaint. Caribbean vacations to study island sources and native drug use, major foundations pouring money in on top of the government grant—things quite likely to make other serious academics a bit envious. And then you have the real distress. What if Claude Lavery was literally putting money into the hands of these students to enable them to buy drugs themselves?"

I wondered if this could be the story that had reached David Fillian in state prison. Perhaps Lavery was the professor Dr. Hoppins was referring to when she stopped me in the courtroom to tell me the news that Fillian was trying to barter for an early release. Was he the person selling drugs to students?

"The kid who hanged himself the other day—any connection to Lavery?"

"Not that we can tell. Julian Gariano was more involved with what they call designer drugs—speed, Ecstasy, some cocaine. Claude's work was primarily with street drugs, but as you know, those lines have been increasingly blurred the last few years. They had certainly met, and Julian was in one of Lavery's classes. No one puts them together outside the lecture hall."

"The missing girl?"

"No link at all."

"Lola Dakota. Connect those dots for me."

Sylvia looked at her files. "As soon as the federal allegation was filed, we suspended Lavery. Quite frankly, we were trying to mount a case to revoke his tenure, which is not an easy thing to do. Professor Dakota led the opposition to the administration. Backed Claude with all her strength. Even turned Winston Shreve around and had him barking at us to wait and see, allow Claude the presumption of innocence."

"Why?"

"Well, we don't know exactly why. She claimed it was strictly for professional reasons. He bucked the system, just as she did. If anyone admired his unorthodox techniques, it would have been a maverick like Lola.

"Then, there's a more malevolent view. Some people were worried that there was something more in it for Lola. Money, to be exact. That she had been using some of Claude Lavery's funds for her own purposes."

"For drugs?"

Sylvia Foote frowned. "No one's ever made that claim. There's not even the hint of a rumor that Lola would have anything to do with drugs. Nor would she tolerate that in her students. But her own projects were quite costly to run. And she was dreadfully competitive. If she could buy an edge for herself, there are those on our faculty who are convinced she would have done it."

"Do you believe it?"

"Lola was a thorn in my side. Constantly. If someone could create trouble for my staff any day of the week, it would be Lola, pushing the envelope every time. I didn't like her alliance with Lavery, and the reason for it is still a mystery to me. She wasn't a particularly materialistic person, and I don't understand what she would have wanted with the money. But the fact remains that a substantial sum has vanished, and before you saw that story in the headlines or heard it from your federal counterparts, Paolo thought I ought to tell you that it was under investigation."

"But other than the fact that Lola was backing Dr. Lavery, was there anything else to suggest an attachment between them?"

Sylvia gave it a few moments' thought. "Nothing unusual. Good friends, neighbors—"

"Whaddaya mean, neighbors?" Mike asked.

"Claude lived in the same building that Lola did: 417 Riverside Drive. He lived one flight above her. Directly overhead, if I'm not mistaken."

I looked at Mike and could tell that our wheels were spinning in the same direction. I did a mental run-through of the police reports of the canvass of the apartment house that detectives had conducted the day after the body was found. I couldn't call up a memory of any particular names, but it should have been obvious that a building that close to the King's College campus would have been full of residents who were faculty members or staff. Had the cops talked to anyone named Lavery? Had they accounted for his whereabouts the afternoon Lola Dakota was killed? Had they cross-checked names of tenants with Lola's family or friends to see what her relationships were with others in the building?

Chapman's impatience was more obvious than my own. "Where's Lavery now?"

"I have no idea, Detective. The last time I saw him was at the vigil on Friday evening. So many people have gone out of—"

"Who can tell me where he is this very minute? Today." Chapman was standing now, ready to be unleashed from the polite tether of administrative interviews and get his hands into the dirt.

"He has been suspended from the college. He doesn't have to report to us or tell us his whereabouts. Dr. Lavery continues to receive a paycheck from us until this is resolved, and if the feds come down with an indictment, I assume the rules may be somewhat different for him."

"How about this other guy, the biologist?"

"Professor Grenier? What about him?"

"He's another one I'd like to talk to."

Sylvia pushed some more papers around. "Grenier's on sabbatical until the beginning of the new year. Can you be patient another week or two, Detective?"

"Frankly, Ms. Foote, I can't be patient another damn minute." He towered over her, shaking his pen in her face as he talked. "You get a forty-eight-hour reprieve 'cause Santa's coming to town and there's nothing I can do about that. These guys are on your payroll; you just said that. Lola Dakota is colder than a stone and six feet under. *Find* these guys, understand me? I want to see Skip Lockhart, Thomas Grenier, and Claude Lavery by the weekend. Move heaven, earth, and unlock your unsmiling frozen jaw to make it happen."

Sylvia's papers were sliding off her lap as she listened to Chapman's booming voice. They scattered to the floor, and I helped her organize them while he continued to list instructions. By the time she left us, she was walking so unsteadily that I had to hold her arm all the way out to the reception area.

"When are you coming back from the country?" Mike asked as I walked toward his desk. I looked at his calendar. This was Tuesday and tomorrow was Christmas Day. "I'll be back on Thursday, unless you want me to change our plans."

"Don't bother. Nobody's here to work with. Just figure we'll be scrambling all next weekend on this, if Foote rounds up her troops and if the lab is good with any test results." He picked up the phone that was ringing on his desk. "It's Laura, for you."

"The superintendent of your building just called, Alex. There's a problem."

"What kind of problem?"

"Seems like there are two workmen who were found in your apartment. The super needs you to come home right away and see if anything's missing."

I slammed down the phone and told Mike I had to go home.

"Not without me. I'm driving."

"You've got things to do. I'll grab a cab."

"Not with that chubby little whackjob whose ID you glommed running around looking for you. You live twenty floors up, with two doormen on every shift. How the hell did anyone fly into your little love nest? I can't get there on my best day, best behavior."

We drove downtown and parked in the garage in my building. The woman from the apartment below me was standing in the lobby, with her Boston terrier, when we walked in.

"The management's security guys are upstairs, along with a detective from the precinct," Jesse said, following us into the elevator.

"What happened?"

"You know the guys who've been working on the scaffolding? Well, you don't see them much, 'cause you're at work all day. But once my kids leave for school, I'm around the house in the morning, and then I'm in and out all day. It's been really creepy to have them around. They seem to be looking in the windows all the time."

For the past six weeks, scaffolding had been erected around the entire high-rise apartment building as it was undergoing repairs to the brickwork and the replacement of some of the windows. Workmen arrived early and spent most of their days hanging off the roof, being raised up and down by a series of pulleys as they went about their business.

"This morning," Jesse continued, "I left about an hour ago to do some errands. Got all the way up to the avenue and realized I had forgotten something, so I turned and went back. When I got inside, the first thing I noticed was that the windows in the living room were wide open and my dog was barking. Then I could see the scaffolding platform rising on the ropes. I grabbed the dog and ran down to the door.

"I told one of the guys on duty what had happened, and Vinny took a run up to check your apartment, since it's right above mine. He must have your passkey."

"He does."

"He opened the door, and the two workmen were standing in the middle of your living room."

We stopped on twenty and got off. My apartment door was ajar and I could hear the loud arguing between the detective and one of the workmen as the three of us walked in.

"Not the traditional way to enter someone's home, but thanks for having us, Alex." The guys from the Nineteenth greeted us as they sat in my living room, trying to talk to the two interlopers. "You heard the story?" one asked, looking over at Jesse.

"Yeah. What's their version?"

"They say the wind was so bad that they had to get inside, or they were afraid they'd be blown off." It was the first thing I had heard that seemed logical. "They kicked the window in and came through that way," Detective Powell said, pointing to the marble-topped counter on my cabinets behind the dining table. "Looks like they broke some of your china."

I glanced over to see that several of the decorative antique plates that were displayed on the sideboard had fallen to the floor, splintered into pieces.

"So how come, if they were so terrified, they broke the window downstairs but didn't go in?" Mike asked. "Doesn't make sense if all they were worried about was saving their asses."

"The story they're giving us is that when the dog started barking, they backed out."

Jesse wasn't buying it. "They were more frightened of a weeny terrier than of being blown off the side of the building? That one's hard to swallow. I think they saw me returning and just panicked. Why'd they go *up* and not down?"

Powell answered again. "Their boss says that when it's windy, it's actually more dangerous to be lowered than to go up higher. If they drop, it means they have to let out more rope, and that causes them to swing more, and that makes it riskier for them."

He put his arm around my shoulders and guided me off into the den. "I don't want to make a scene in front of your neighbor, but you gotta know that since the scaffolding went up, there have been three burglaries in the building."

I turned to look at Powell, surprised by the news. "Nobody's mentioned it to me."

"Needless to say, management would rather not have it known. There's no forced entry, so we've been looking at them as inside jobs. We actually started with the house staff as suspects—"

"Hey, I'd start with these guys on the outside. I'd go to the mat for the men who work in the building. Every single one of them."

"Well, today seems to prove the point. You want to look around for me and tell us if anything's missing? I patted them down, and they've got nothing on them. Of course, since your neighbor was so quick to act, these guys never got out of your apartment. So if they didn't drop stuff out the window, they probably didn't have a chance to take anything.

"And you might want to know, just for your comfort level, that these mopes who've been staring in everyone's window the past few weeks? They've both got sheets a mile long. The short one standing near the kitchen door, he's on parole in the Bronx for armed robbery. The taller one, who pretends he don't understand English? He's had four collars for larceny.

"One of your neighbors in the C line moved in on a Monday night, and woke up the next morning to see him standing in her bedroom doorway. She screamed her guts out."

"And he's still working here?"

"The guy backed right out. Said he thought the apartment was still empty, didn't know she'd moved in. He'd been using the bathroom as his Porta Potti all month. Apologized and left. Hard to know what to do about him."

"Would you mind getting these guys out of here while I check around for you?"

"We're taking 'em over to the precinct. Gonna print both of them, to compare against the other cases. I won't charge 'em with anything here unless you tell me something's gone, okay?"

The two detectives walked the men out of the apartment while Mike, the super, and I surveyed the damage. Broken glass was everywhere, mixed in with the shattered china.

"Is Powell locking them up?"

"I can't see it, for this. What if their lives really were at risk and they had to come inside? I'm not going to second-guess anybody on that. They don't seem to have gotten out of here with anything. All they did was make a mess." We were standing by the window, and even though there didn't seem to be much wind today, the frigid air streamed into the room.

"Yeah, well, I think it's bullshit and they're lucky they landed where they did. Nice to know you're so forgiving about guys who crash into your pad. I may bank on that. What are you gonna do about this mess?" In one corner of the room stood my cheerful little Christmas tree, while here at my feet was a pile of debris.

The super spoke. "We'll take care of it for you, Ms. Cooper. We'll clean all this up by the end of the day. Just make a list for us of the things that were broken and we'll submit it to the insurance company."

He looked at the giant hole in the glass. "I doubt I can get the window replaced before tonight. Were you planning on being here for Christmas?"

I shook my head.

"Then you'll have a new one by Thursday, I promise."

When everyone left, Mike and I knelt on the floor to pick up some of the porcelain pieces. "Now I've got something new to worry about. I can't think of many places I've felt safer than behind the doors of this apartment, once I get inside at night and turn the locks. No fire escape, no back entrance, no way in unless I open the dead bolt." I tried to laugh. "Now I've got to worry about men climbing in off scaffolding twenty stories above the street?"

"These guys were trying to give you the same message I was the other night. Time to settle down and develop a more stable lifesty—"

"Don't go there, Mr. Chapman. Get up off your knees. There's nothing to salvage in this pile. I'm just going to check with the office and then I'll take a cab out to the airport."

"But they wrecked the joint."

"Puts things in perspective, though, doesn't it? Lola Dakota is dead, and all I've got to complain about is some broken china. Want to open your Christmas present?"

"Nope. Let's celebrate when you come back. Maybe we can get Mercer in for dinner one night and have our own little holiday, okay?"

"Pick the date. That's fine with me."

I dialed my office number and checked with Laura to see if there were any messages that had come in since we last spoke. She told me no and patched my call through to Catherine Dashfer, who was supervising the unit while I was uptown. "Thanks for covering for me. Anything going on today?"

"A new case just came into the complaint room. Looks like we're going to have to do a hospital hearing at the end of the week, to hold the perp in. Do you think you can get Leemie or Maxine to cover it on Friday? Paul and I are still planning to be at my sister's house through the weekend."

"Sure. Let me make some calls. Why a hospital hearing, though?" There could be several reasons the proceeding would be held in an institution and not at the courtroom. It was frequently done when the defendant was confined with an injury or an illness, or if he had a mental condition that required detention at a long-term-care facility. In that case, the judge, lawyers for both sides, court officers, and an official stenographer trouped to the site to conduct the arraignment or probable-cause hearing. "What hospital?"

"Bird S. Coler. The one on Roosevelt Island."

"Even better. I'll do this one myself. Tell Laura to have the file messengered to Jake's doorman." That way it would be waiting for me when we came home from the Vineyard on Thursday evening. "What's the case?"

Catherine repeated the facts that the officer had told her. "Perp's name is Chester Rubiera. He's a paranoid schizophrenic with a history of substance abuse. Assaulted one of the other patients. I'll get a facilitator for her, too. The victim has a severe mental disability. You may need someone to help the court understand her testimony. Friday at ten, okay?"

I turned to Chapman and explained the situation. "How about if I ask Nan to show us around Roosevelt Island on Friday afternoon? I've never been there. The new case happened at Coler." A chronic-care facility located on the north end of the island, the hospital was home to many patients with physical ailments, and had a large psychiatric unit as well. "I can do the hearing in the morning, and you can meet me over there at lunchtime. Maybe we can get a sense of the place."

"You're living in the past, blondie. Your fascination is with

Blackwells Island. There's no such thing anymore, and there's no evidence, at the moment, to think that Lola's death is connected to what's going on over there today."

"You're right. But I'm just interested in what had Lola so engaged in that project. If there's something more important to be done on Friday, I'll skip it. If not, I'll exorcise my curiosity."

"You know what curiosity did to the cat, Coop."

"It's a perfect place to be, under those circumstances," I said, smiling. "At the deadhouse."

16

Jake Tyler was waiting for me when the shuttle landed at Logan Airport. I dropped my bags and threw my arms around his neck. "I was so afraid that something would happen to get in the way of these forty-eight hours. More murder and mayhem. Or a snowstorm."

He picked up my tote and we started walking to the Cape Air counter. "You got lucky on the first two. There's a front coming through Boston in about three hours, headed for the Cape and islands. So if we don't get out of here soon, we're likely to be stranded."

The gray sky was thick with clouds, and had dimmed to charcoal before we boarded the five o'clock flight to Martha's

Vineyard. The nine-passenger, twin-engine Cessna took off after a long runway delay, and the heavy chop in the air slowed the usual thirty-three-minute passage to almost forty-five. The wind bounced us around in our narrow seats in the rear of the plane, and we circled out over Nantucket Sound until the tower cleared us for landing. The pilot lowered us out of the fog to see the white-capped surf pounding the island's southern shore and guided us into the airport, surrounded by the tall pines of the state forest.

I had been talking throughout most of the ride about the case—Lola Dakota's life and the tragic circumstances of her death. Jake had listened carefully, and interrupted from time to time with the skilled cross-examination of a good investigative reporter. "I'm letting you get this out of your system now," he chided me. "I'm putting a two-day moratorium on all autopsy results, serological reports, and police investigations. World crises, too."

He leaned over and kissed my lips as we taxied to the small terminal, and then the pilot stepped out on the wing to come around, open the door, and lower the exit stairs. "Is that acceptable to the People, Ms. Cooper?"

"Yes, Your Honor."

I had asked my caretaker and his wife to set up the house for us—turn on heat, make up the bed, arrange flowers that were delivered a day earlier, stock the groceries that I had ordered, put champagne on ice, and lay a stack of logs in the fireplace. He had also left my car at the airport lot so that we could drive ourselves home whenever we arrived.

A thin dusting of snow coated the parked cars. We let the engine warm up and put the defroster on to melt the ice that had formed on the windshield. I had dressed warmly in slacks and a sweater, topped by my ski jacket, but the bitter cold worked at my nose and ears and within seconds gave both of our cheeks a ruddy glow. The local radio station played generous helpings of the island's musical treasures, James Taylor and Carly Simon, and I tuned in as she was singing the chorus to "Anticipation." Like Carly, I was thinking about how right tonight might be.

The twenty-minute ride up island was quick and quiet. There were no reminders of the traffic of the summer people, who poured onto the Vineyard between Memorial Day and Labor Day, renting beach houses, filling the small inns, and crowding the tiny streets in town. My old farmhouse, way out on a hilltop, overlooking an endless expanse of sea and sky, was one of the most peaceful places I had ever known. Whatever the horrors that crossed my desk every day, this was where I came to be restored.

South Road's wintry darkness gave way to the high beam of my headlights. Without the leafy fullness of the summer foliage, houses set back from the road were visible this time of year. Many were lighted for the holiday season, decorated with garlands of greens, ribbons of red and white velvet, and candles set on windowsills in the traditional New England fashion. I had bought this home with Adam, in the months before our wedding was to have been celebrated. For almost ten years thereafter, it had been impossible for me to think of it as my own. Then, with the tragic shooting of my friend Isabella Lascar, I had questioned whether I could actually come back here at all. I renovated and redecorated, knowing those changes were merely cosmetic and couldn't reach the soul of my trepidation. But since the summer, the great joy I had found with Jake had renewed my excitement and my love for this unique place.

I made the last turn at Beetlebung Corner and pulled into a parking space in front of the Chilmark Store. Nothing else was open at my end of the island, so the general store was our lifeline to all essentials. I ran up the steps, clogged in summer with beachgoers, cyclists, joggers, workmen—tourists and regulars—who sat and gossiped over morning coffee and *The New York Times*, came from miles away for a slice of Primo's pizza at lunchtime, and bought everything from iced cappuccino to batteries to fresh blueberry pie before the doors closed at sunset. A sign on the door announced that they were closed for Christmas week, so I crossed my fingers that all the supplies we needed were at the house.

My driveway was only two miles farther up the road. Wind began to howl around us as I drove up the last hill before the house. As always, my heartbeat quickened with delight at the prospect of coming home. I slowed the car as we approached the familiar stand of mailboxes on the side of the road, then drove in through the granite gateposts, startling a doe and her two fawns, who were foraging on the snowy ground for something to eat. They darted off and I drove up next to the door. Upon each arrival, I drank in the beauty of my view. Headlights off, we sat in the car without speaking as I gazed off at the dim lights in the distance, till Jake caressed my neck and again brought my mouth to his.

"C'mon, Mrs. Claus. We've got work to do. Aren't you hungry?"

I looked at my watch and saw that it was almost eight o'clock, as we took our bags from the car and went inside the house. "I've got the whole evening scheduled. You're not allowed to be hungry yet. Dinner is going to be at eleven, so that we can begin our official celebration at midnight."

"Mind if I nibble on an earlobe or a collarbone till then?" Jake was following in my footsteps as I went from room to room, turning on lamps and illuminating the scented candles. "There's got to be something unplanned, every now and then, that I can slip into your demanding schedule."

A small tree, not even two feet high, had been set up beside the stone hearth. There was a giant box, gift-wrapped and ribboned, from the great toy store FAO Schwarz. "I hope none of my wires got crossed. That's probably something that was supposed to be shipped to my niece."

"You're not the only one with a Christmas list, Goldilocks."

I unpacked two red stockings from my tote and laid them across the back of the sofa. My mother had needlepointed them for each of us, our names stitched in white and green on the cuff. "Why don't you put some music on while I clean up?"

I went into the bedroom and undressed. I stared out my window over acres of land ringed by ancient stone walls, secure that the problems against which I protected myself in the city couldn't reach me here. The fishing village of Menemsha was no longer visible across the pond through the haze as the first soft flakes of snow began to blow against the panes of the French doors and melt. This was my sanctuary.

I set the timer for the steam shower at ten minutes and the temperature to ninety-five degrees, stepped inside, and reclined on the wooden bench. The room filled with mist and I began to sweat. Memories of Lola Dakota's videoed faux shooting swirled and mixed with visions of the actual bloodstained elevator shaft. I wanted the toxins to be removed from my body and my mind to be cleared of all thoughts of death and violence. The physical cleansing worked, but the opportunity to do nothing except think made it impossible for me to erase the mental images.

After six or seven minutes, I shut off the steam and turned on the nozzle, holding my face up to the twelve-inch showerhead that cascaded hot water all over me. I washed my body and shampooed my hair. Jake was outside the steam room when I emerged, standing naked and holding a bath sheet to wrap me in. We kissed again, long this time, and tasted each other lovingly, until I rested my head against his shoulder blade. He stroked my wet curls and pressed his lips against the nape of my neck.

I led him over to the bed. "What makes you think this was *un*scheduled? You never give me credit for anything."

Jake's mouth moved along the lines of my body, kissing my arms first, and then up and down the length of my back. I rolled over to face him, bringing his face up to meet mine and inviting him to be inside me.

"Not so fast," he whispered.

"There's time for slower later. I've missed you so badly this week. I've needed you, Jake."

We both stopped talking and lost ourselves in making love to each other. When we had finished, I nestled against his lean body and rested my head on his outstretched arm. I closed my eyes, and when I opened them again I realized that I had actually fallen asleep for almost an hour.

"I'm sorry. I must—"

"You must have needed it, darling. Relax."

Jake had already showered and dressed for the evening, in jeans and a cashmere crewneck sweater. I showered again and this time when I walked into the bedroom, there was a long red shiny box wrapped with a gauzy silver ribbon on the bed.

"I'm such a baby. I'm going to wait till midnight."

"No, this one's a gift for *me,* and I want you to open it now."

I pulled at the ribbon and opened the lid. Beneath the tissue paper was a pair of lady's silk lounging pajamas in the most delicate shade of aqua. "It's the color you're wearing when I dream about you. When you have clothes on, that is." He held the top up against my skin. "Would you wear it for me, please, tonight? For dinner?"

I dressed in the pale, smooth outfit, brushed my hair, and dabbed some Caleche behind both ears, on my throat and wrists. Jake was in the living room, where he had started the fire, while Ella Fitzgerald was singing Cole Porter to him. He had poured us each a scotch and was standing by the window, watching the flakes pile up on one another.

"I understand that dinner is part of my holiday surprise, but a hungry guy tends to get nervous when the woman he loves can barely boil water. Do you need help in the kitchen?"

"The ladies who feed you so well all summer have helped me put together this wonderful feast. You'll simply have to trust them, not me. It's all island food." I disappeared into the kitchen and opened the refrigerator, where everything had been stored for my arrival, along with explicit instructions. My first task was the hardest—to open a dozen Tisbury Pond oysters.

I had learned after many summers here how to use an oyster

knife to pry the lids apart without drawing blood on both my hands. Fifteen minutes of lifting, twisting, and scooping the delicious creatures out of their shells, and I returned to the living room with one of Jake's favorite treats. The fresh, briny oysters tasted as though they had been pulled from the water just hours ago.

"You're off to a winning debut, darling. What's next?"

"You open the wine. I'll set out the first course in the dining room."

There was a smaller fireplace in my dining room, as well. And I started that, after I lighted the six candles in the chandelier above the table. Jake found a bottle of Corton Charlemagne, *grand cru,* and worked on drawing out the cork.

"The first course, Monsieur Tyler, is compliments of the Homeport." Jake loved the chowder at the lobster house in nearby Menemsha, which—like every other restaurant on our end of the island—closes in the fall. "I actually had the good sense to freeze a quart of it. Cheers!"

When we'd finished the soup and I had cleared the dishes, I sent Jake back into the living room. "The next one is trickier." There was a tiny wooden shack in Menemsha called the Bite. And for years, the Quinn sisters, who owned the business, had been cooking and selling the world's absolutely most delicious fried clams. Jake detoured to the Bite, straight from the airport, on every trip to the house. He had even convinced NBC to have the *Today* show do a summer feature on the tasty little enterprise.

Before they closed in October, I had urged Karen and Jackie Quinn to sell me a batch of the batter in which they roll the morsels before deep-frying them. I bought clams to store in the freezer, and a Fry Daddy in which to attempt to concoct their magic recipe. When I was done with the effort, I carried a trayful into the living room.

"Not even close." Jake laughed. "Tell the girls they've got nothing to worry about. Must have something to do with their shack and its ambience."

The main course was the easiest. Chris and Betsy Larsen kept one of the family fish markets open in town all year long. They had boiled two three-pound lobsters for me in the afternoon, and the caretaker had brought them up to the house. I reheated them in the oven, melted some butter, and we feasted for an hour on the meaty tails and claws.

Jake added logs to the fire, and I stretched out on the living room floor while he opened a bottle of champagne. "Merry Christmas, Alexandra," he said, joining me in front of the hearth and filling a flute for each of us. I rested my head against his knee and wished him the same. We clinked our glasses together and I watched the bubbles rise and burst before I began to sip.

"Where are you?"

"Just thinking."

"About what?"

I rolled onto my back, a pillow from the sofa beneath my head, and stared into the flames. "How much my life has changed this year. What a sense of stability you've given me, in the middle of all the turbulence I see on the professional side every day."

"Can't you look me in the eye when you tell me these things?"

I slowly turned my head to glance at Jake, smiling. "I wasn't planning on saying them. I'm not sure that I've even stopped to reflect on them before now. I just know how very differently I feel about everything I do and think. If I hadn't been able to talk to you when Mercer was shot, I can't imagine what—"

"You don't let people in easily." He was stroking my hair and placing tender kisses on my nose and forehead. "You've got to be more trusting."

"The problem is that at the beginning I trust everyone. That's what's so damn disappointing. It seems as though every time I open the door to something new, the odds are twice as likely that it will slam shut on my fingers."

"Let's try to come up with solutions. For example, darling, think about this. Here's two of us, each with a ridiculously overpriced, way too large for one person who's hardly ever home, Manhattan apartment. Same general neighborhood—same proximity to your favorite restaurants, delis, liquor store, and Grace's Marketplace. Critical factors in a relationship."

I had been drinking enough to know that whatever Jake said, I wasn't going to have the appropriate answer. I could feel my pulse quickening and knew the silken pajama top couldn't muffle the sound of my pounding heartbeat. I shifted back to watch the flames dance in the fireplace.

"I think this morning's broken window and bumbling scaffolders were an omen, Alex. Why don't you give up that place and move in with me? I'm not even in town enough to get in your way very often." Jake had rested his glass on the floor and was massaging my neck. "Imagine that every single night could be like this one."

He couldn't see the tears that had welled up in my eyes. My head was swimming with conflicted feelings. It had been so long since the heartbreak of my fiancé's death, and I had struggled for years to keep free of emotional attachments, fearing that I would lose whomever I let get close to me. For the first time, I had someone to come home to who listened to me talk about my passion for my work, the failures when I couldn't solve a victim's case and the triumphs when justice was actually achieved. Jake never carped when something kept me late at the office or when the phone rang in the middle of the night.

"I know what you're thinking now. You can't make this kind of decision yourself, without consulting your friends. This move will take a summit meeting. All the major powers have to be assembled. No problem, darling. I've covered summits for years. The Middle East, the former Soviet Union, the Pacific Rim, Camp David. How difficult can it be to move one five-foot-ten-inch, hundred-and-fifteen-pound prosecutor less than ten city blocks? Even a stubborn one? We'll bring Joan in from Washington and Nina from Los Angeles. We'll import Susan and Michael. Louise and Henry, are they on the island for the holiday? With Duane?"

I nodded my head, licking the tear that had dripped to the corner of my mouth and smiling despite myself as he ticked off the names of my friends.

"Well, I'll start with them at the crack of dawn. Take a dog sleigh up Herring Creek Road to get to them through the snow, if you insist. If I can't win you over myself, then I'll bring in all the allies I need to persuade you that it's the only sensible thing to do. Get Esther on the line. Get me Lesley Latham. Where are Ann and Vernon?"

I wanted to speak but knew that I would break the spell of the moment. Nothing Jake could say would convince me to move in with anyone, without being married. And he wasn't any closer to thinking about that permanent kind of commitment than I was. I knew him well enough to know that. I cherished my freedom and my independence. As much as I loved being with him and around him, it had only been half a year since we met, and we both had such frenetic lifestyles that it was impossible to know whether we could sustain the intensity of our relationship.

Jake put on his best anchorman's voice. "News flash. Ladies and gentlemen, this bulletin just in to our desk. Exclusive from Liz Smith. We take you live to Chilmark, on Martha's Vineyard, where former prosecutor Alexandra—"

"*Former* prosecutor?" I rose on one elbow and faced Jake, sure that the tip of my nose must be red, betraying my tears.

"—Cooper has announced that, after a conference with her college roommate and dearest friend, Nina Baum, and with the encouragement and support of a bevy of other loyal Cooperites, she is going to vacate apartment number 20A at—"

"Can we get back to this 'former' business?"

"I needed to do something to get your attention, didn't I? You seemed positively spellbound by the flames. How about it, darling? Of course you can bring your clothes. Yes, all your clothes. I'll get rid of my own, and the golf clubs and tennis rackets cluttering up the hall closet. You look bleary-eyed." He paused to kiss my damp eyelids. "I swear I'll make plenty of room for all the boxes of Stuart Weitzman shoes. What am I forgetting?"

"You're forgetting that anything I say at this glorious moment—my brain soaked in scotch and wine, topped off with a touch of champers—in the state of Massachusetts, lying off the coast of North America somewhere in the middle of the Atlantic Ocean, is not binding on me when we get back into the jurisdiction of New York. So even were I to acquiesce to your generous offer—"

"You can say anything except the word 'no.' You can tell me you're flattered, that you'll think about it, that the movers will be there on Thursday, that you had them come in earlier today because you hoped I'd ask you, or that you'll leave all your worldly goods behind and come, barefoot, with just the silk pajamas on your back. Any of those answers is fine. The only thing I want for Christmas is that you do not turn me down tonight."

"That's a deal. It's a wonderful offer and you make me very, very happy, just for wanting me to be there."

Jake took a minute to reflect. "Didn't you always hate it when you were a kid and you asked your parents if you could do something wonderful or exciting the next weekend—go to the fair or get a new bicycle or buy a puppy—and they answered, 'Maybe'? I think that's what I just got. A big, fat 'maybe.' Think about my offer, Ms. Cooper. I hope it keeps you awake all night tonight, and every night hereafter until you give in and throw up your hands and knock on my door, begging me to let you in."

"In the meanwhile, why don't you open your presents."

"Ah, bribery. Try and divert me with material things."

I reached for the package under the tree and handed it to Jake. He unwrapped it slowly and dropped the paper next to him. "Where did you find them? Now *I'll* be up all night."

Three leather-bound volumes, all first editions of works he loved. Jake collected books, like I did, and was always searching out rare finds to add to his shelves. He handled the covers carefully, reading the names imprinted on the spines. "Faulkner, Hammett, Keats. Eclectic, and all favorites. What a perfect gift."

I slipped a smaller box out of the stocking with his name on it. "Something else?" This time he ripped at the red bow tied around the shiny white paper to reveal a black leather case. Inside was a pair of antique Edwardian cuff links, powder-blue enamel baked over eighteen-karat gold. "They're so handsome."

"I thought they'd show nicely when you're on air. When you're traveling without me and you wear them to do a story, I'll know you're thinking of me."

"Move in and you can stick them in my cuffs every morning yourself, just to make sure I do."

"You are hopelessly persistent." I poured another glass of champagne.

Jake walked to the tree and came back with the toy store package. "This one's for you."

I sat up and crossed my legs, undoing the green ribbon. When I got the box open, I lifted a giant stuffed teddy bear out and sat him next to me on the floor. I grinned. "Now why would I even need you when I've got a cuddly guy like this to come home to? I'm sure he's a much better listener than you are. No cross-examinations about my day, no complaints about the competition."

I turned to the bear and opened my mouth to speak. The words stuck in my throat when I saw what was gleaming on his furry chest. Pinned right where his heart should be was a magnificent sparkling diamond bird perched atop a large aquamarine stone. "That's just breathtaking, Jake." I threw my arms around his neck and hugged him to me.

"Let go of me and put it on."

"I'd rather let the bear wear it. That way I can look at it all the time."

"Bird on a rock. Your friend at the Schlumberger salon said

you've been eyeing it for years. Hold still." He unhooked it from the animal's plush stuffing and attached it to my pale silk pajama shirt. "That's why I had to get this outfit to go with the brooch."

I stood up and headed for the bedroom. "I've got to see how it looks. It's the most beautiful thing I've ever owned." Jake followed me in and watched me preen in front of the full-length mirror. "I'm never taking it off."

"Except when you go to work every day, and right at this very moment." He unbuttoned my top and laid it carefully across the chaise at the foot of the bed, the facets of my elegant bird catching every glimmer of light from the candles on the bedside tables. "That's how I want you to think of us, always. You're the exquisite, delicate bird, and you've always got me to land on, to be your bedrock. Merry Christmas, my angel."

We finished undressing and got under the covers, making love again before we drifted off in each other's arms.

Our internal alarm clocks each went off as usual at about six-thirty, as the morning sky was attempting to brighten. We ignored the signals and decided to sleep late, reveling in the fact that neither of us had a deadline or a decision to make the entire day. It was eleven o'clock by the time I was up and dressed and had brewed the first pot of coffee. After calling our families and friends, we bundled up in thermal underwear and heavy jackets and set out on a hike to Squibnocket Beach. For more than a mile, packed snow crunching beneath our boots, we walked along the ocean, hand in gloved hand, talking about things we had never explored with each other before.

Jake asked me questions about my relationship with Adam, and about my slow recovery from the nightmare of his death. He spoke about his broken engagement, when the woman he had dated for four years moved out and married one of his closest friends, tired of the instability of his life on the road and anxious to start a family.

The only people we passed were several of my neighbors,

walking dogs along the vast expanse of Atlantic beachfront. Back at the house, we converted the remains of our dinner into a lobster salad, and then spent the afternoon in front of the fireplace with our books. My Fitzgerald novel was constantly interrupted by Jake's discovery of something in his new Keats that he wanted to read aloud to me.

After a simple supper of chowder and some greens, we watched a DVD of *The Thirty-Nine Steps* and put ourselves to bed early. We were up before dawn, on a seven o'clock flight to Boston, connected to an eight-thirty shuttle back to La Guardia. Jake's car service picked us up in front of the terminal and we drove into Manhattan. I dropped him at the NBC studios at Rockefeller Center and we kissed good-bye.

"I'm expecting you at my apartment tonight. Till you get confirmation that your window has been replaced and that your pistol-packing victim isn't waiting by the front door, we're doing a test run of my proposition. See you later."

The driver took me down to Hogan Place and let me off in front of the entrance. It was after ten, and the place seemed like a ghost town. Only a skeleton staff would be at work today and tomorrow, and I expected to be able to get a lot done.

Laura had taken the day off, so I signed for the packet myself when the FedEx deliveryman appeared with an overnight letter from the New Jersey telephone company.

I opened the envelope to study the jumble of digits that comprised the incoming and outgoing calls made to and from Lola Dakota's temporary shelter at her sister Lily's. It could take hours for a detective, using a reverse directory, to put the numbers together with the subscriber to whose home or office the calls had been placed. Each was coded with the date, hour, and minute the connection was made, as well as its duration.

I scanned the pages until I found the day, one week earlier, of Lola's murder. I ran my finger down the rows of figures. There had been dozens of calls in the morning, when people had been coming and going to arrange the faked homicide performance. Then the activity had slowed to a standstill.

Lily had heard Lola make the call presumably to be picked up by a cab company. And then Lily had medicated herself and gone to bed.

I stopped at 1:36 P.M. A single call, made to a local Jersey number from Lily's home. Maybe I wouldn't need a detective to help decipher and track the telephone connection. The number looked familiar. What if Lily hadn't called a stranger to transport her safely to Manhattan, but had reached out for a friend instead?

I dialed the exchange and waited while the phone rang three times.

An operator answered. "Office of the District Attorney, may I help you?"

I swallowed hard. "Perhaps you can. I'm not sure if I dialed the right number. Is this Mr. Sinnelesi's office?"

"It's his office. But it's not his direct line."

"The extension I dialed," I said, looking down at the printed record, "is 8484. Can you tell me whose number that is?"

"Who are you trying to reach, ma'am?"

The last person to see Lola Dakota alive, I thought to myself. I stammered. "I, uh, I've got a message to call this number. I just can't make out the name my secretary took down."

"Oh, okay. This is Bartholomew Frankel's office. He's the executive assistant district attorney, Mr. Sinnelesi's number two man. Mr. Frankel stepped away for a bit. Shall I put you through to his secretary?"

17

"You saved me from a miserable afternoon with my mother." Mike had been at his desk in the squad when I called, and instantly agreed that we should drive out to Sinnelesi's office to confront Bart Frankel with our new information. The secretary had assured me he would be around all afternoon, so we were soon on our way through the Holland Tunnel.

"Mom's been begging me to help her plan her funeral. Pick out the coffin, go to—"

"Has she been ill?" I had known his mother for years and had no idea that anything was wrong. Perhaps that's why Mike had been delayed at the hospital on Monday morning.

"Fit as a horse. But at Midnight Mass on Christmas Eve, she

got me to promise I would take her to get everything arranged. Peace of mind and all that. She's so excited you'd think she was going to Disney World with John Elway, for chrissakes. Told her I was breaking the date 'cause of you. That's the only way I could get a reprieve."

"Tell her that when we solve this one, we'll both come out and take her to lunch. . . . Does it bother you as much as it does me that Frankel's the guy who got Lola's call?"

"Hey, if the escort was strictly professional, they would have had detectives taking her out of Lily's home and making sure she got inside her apartment safely. Your big guns in the Manhattan DA's office do witness escort and protection? I can just see Battaglia asking Pat McKinney to run somebody uptown to Harlem. Not a chance. You know Frankel?"

"I've only met him once, when Sinnelesi sent a delegation to talk to us about helping them stage this shooting of Lola. Anne Reininger was doing a very professional job with the investigation. She had some really good ideas about wiring an undercover cop and proving the case just through incriminating admissions from Kralovic. But the district attorney thought this sting would be great press for him, just in time for his reelection campaign. Battaglia and I disagreed. The plan was over-the-top hokey, dangerous, and unnecessary. Frankel came to our office to try to get me to change my mind."

"Any sense of what he's like?"

"I heard he's a law school buddy of Sinnelesi's, so he's probably the same age. About fifty. They were at NYU together. Frankel started with the Brooklyn district attorney, right out of school—"

"Which means he was rejected by your office, no doubt."

"He did six or seven years there, before my time. Then went into private practice, doing criminal defense work in New Jersey. When Sinnelesi was elected, he brought Bart in as his right-hand man. He really runs the shop."

"Did Lola ever mention him to you?"

"No. But we really weren't in contact often once Jersey got involved in the case. And when Bart came to see me with Anne, he was just acting like a supervisor. I never imagined he had any hands-on connection to the case."

"Hands *on*? How about private parts *in*? Can't wait to hear his explanation for this."

We parked behind the civic center and found our way up to Sinnelesi's office a bit after one o'clock. The receptionist was startled to see visitors on this quiet, postholiday afternoon.

"We're here for Mr. Frankel," Mike announced.

"Is he expecting you?"

Mike jerked his head in my direction. "She's an old friend of Bart's. Passing through town. I think we'd just like to surprise him."

"How nice," she said, smiling in my direction. "I'm sure he'll be pleased. He called to say he'd be stopping for a sandwich on his way back here, so he should be in any minute."

I took off my coat and hung it on the rack in the waiting room. "What the hell is that frigging glob you got stuck on your suit?" Mike was staring at the gift Jake had given me for Christmas.

"Well, I didn't stop at the apartment, and I was afraid to leave it in my office with the suitcase."

Self-consciously, I unpinned the bird and wrapped it in my handkerchief, putting it inside my shoulder bag.

"Guess Mr. NBC went to the well for that one. Don't let me cramp your style, blondie. You could probably wipe out the entire national debt of Sri Lanka if you—"

"Alex? How nice to see you."

Bart Frankel came through the front door and approached me to shake hands. I introduced him to Mike. "Are you here to meet with the district attorney?"

"No, Bart. We want to speak with you."

A large brown paper bag in one hand, Frankel pushed open the entrance to his wing with the other. "Come on in. I still can't get over what happened to Lola. Such a tragedy." He ushered us into his corner suite, removing his backpack and his coat. This prosecutor's small modern office complex in a suburban corporate park was far more gracious and comfortable than ours. Two chairs faced Frankel's desk. Mike and I seated ourselves while he unwrapped his lunch and put it to the side.

I couldn't help but notice that he was chewing gum.

"Can I order something in for you?"

"No, thanks."

"What can you tell me about how the investigation is going?" He took a tissue, swiveled in his chair, removed the gum, and threw it in his wastebasket. Mike gave me a thumbs-up.

"It's actually going really well, Bart. Faster than I expected. We've had some lucky breaks."

"What do you mean?" He glanced back and forth between Mike's stone face and mine. He laughed nervously, or so it seemed to me. "I get it. Need to know. Tell me and you'll have to shoot me." He nodded his head up and down. "Maybe it's sour grapes 'cause Battaglia wouldn't let you buy into our sting plan. Well, he was right, Alex. Tell him from me, off the record, that once again he made the right choice. Vinny's getting lots of heat from everybody. Starting with Lola's family. The dancing Dakotas, he calls them. A whole chorus line of whining siblings, waiting for their fifteen minutes of fame. That's what their mama primed them for." Bart was talking nonstop, tapping the fingers of both hands on his desktop.

"I got the governor on my back, too. She's big on domestic violence and all that political garbage. Then we got victims' rights groups. You name it, we got it. And you know the drill, Alex. When the shit hits the fan, the number one man is always unavailable for comment. Mr. Sinnelesi had to leave town. Family emergency down in Boca. Vinny, I tell him—Vinny, first I take a huge pay cut to come work for you and do public service, instead of making a real living for me and my family. Now I got to have my balls on the chopping block, too?"

"You wanna come up for air, Mr. Frankel, or you wanna just babble on?"

"Sorry, Mike. It's Mike, isn't it? Exactly what can I help you with?"

I answered, trying to set a pace for the conversation. "I hadn't spoken with Lola in months, as I think I told you when you and Anne Reininger came to my office. I'd really like to get a sense of what her life was like those last six weeks. How she was spending her time, who she was in touch with, what your contact was with her."

"Me? *My* contact with Lola?"

"Hey, who do you think she's talking to? You got somebody under your desk we can't see?"

"No, it's just, I mean —well, Anne's the prosecutor assigned to the case. I had to meet with Lola on a few occasions, just to oversee what was happening with the sting. Anne's the one who spoke to her almost every day. She can answer your questions."

"I'd like to begin with you, as long as we're here. Why don't you give us an idea of how many times you met with her? Where and when."

Frankel thought for a moment and opened his large red desk calendar. "All of my business appointments are logged in this. Let me just see." He opened the book about midway, to June, and began to flip through the pages. "I guess the first time I met Lola was in the early fall. September twenty-third, to be exact. Anne brought her up to me to introduce us. High-profile case and all that. Vinny likes me to keep an eye on things."

The intercom buzzed. "Excuse me, Mr. Frankel. I've got your daughter on line two. She wants to know if she can use the car tonight after you get home. Would you like to speak with her now?"

"Hold my calls, will you? Tell her yes, and try not to interrupt us till I'm through here, okay?"

"How many meetings after that?"

"Skimming through here, it looks like six, at the most."

"Where were they?"

"That was the only one in my office. The other times I went down to the second floor, to Anne's bureau. Family Violence Unit."

"Did you ever meet with her anywhere else, outside the office?"

"Yes. I was at her sister's house—Lily's—the day we staged the shooting. We went over, Anne and I, with the detectives just to make sure we approved the setup and to stroke the rest of the family. Pump Lola up."

Frankel was on his feet now, adjusting the blinds on his window as the sunlight bounced its glare off the icy surface of the parked cars in the lot below.

"Must have been a very tense morning. Were you there when the scam went down?"

He did the "me" thing again. "Me?"

"Yeah."

"No, I did what I had to do and got out of there. Had stuff to work on back at the office."

"What stuff?"

"Had to meet with one of the guys on a home-invasion case. Had to help him draft a bill of particulars."

"Got that in your big red book?" Mike asked.

"Got what?"

"Your meeting on the case you just told us about."

"That, um, that came up kind of unexpectedly. It's probably not in here." Frankel patted the cover of the book.

"Mind if I take a look through those entries?"

"I just told you, I doubt that one's in here."

"I mean the references to Lola. Mind if I jot down those dates?"

Frankel opened the book to the first September date and passed it across to Chapman. "Help yourself, Detective."

Mike rested his notepad on the desk. He turned the pages and copied the dates and times of the Dakota-Reininger-Frankel appointments. When he got to the day of the shooting, he paused and read aloud: "'Thursday morning, December nineteenth. Nine A.M. Meet Reininger at Dakota scene. Sting preparation. Noon. Lunch with Vinny. Two P.M. In the field.'

"Strangest thing. When my partner uses that expression—'in the field'—it means he took the rest of his tour off to get laid. But then, we're just cops. What does it mean to you, Mr. Frankel? What kind of home invasion were you working on?"

"Who's in control of this operation, Alex, you or this rude—?"

"Mike and I want to know exactly the same information. How did you spend that afternoon?"

"I, uh, I must have gone . . . I guess I left here early. I probably did some holiday shopping."

"Like Ms. Cooper tells the street mopes that sit in her office and lie to her all day, 'probably' and 'I guess' and 'I must have' don't cut it. This ain't ancient history, Mr. Frankel. It's one week ago this very day. When you and Fat Vinny pushed back from the lunch table, where did you go and what did you do?"

"My daughter was coming home from college the next day. I went over to the mall to pick up a few gifts for my kids."

"What stores? I assume you can tell me what you bought and give me receipts for the things."

"You know, Detective, I'm the executive assistant district attorney for this county. You blow in here like you're auditioning for a bit part as a wise guy on *The Sopranos*. All bluff and bluster and bullshit, and I actually let you rattle me, like I have something to worry about. Well, you came to the wrong place this time. I supervised this investigation. I'm not the subject of it. Why don't you two just crawl back through the tunnel, or however you dragged yourselves here, and go solve your case like professionals, okay?"

"Did you drive Lola back to Manhattan with your own wheels, or did you use a government car to take her home?"

Frankel strode to the door of his office and opened it wide.

Mike got up from his chair as though to leave, then walked behind the desk. He leaned over and reached into the trash, removing from it the Kleenex-wrapped piece of gum that had been discarded when Frankel first brought us into the room. He held it up to the light and admired it as though it were a trophy.

"What the f—?"

"I'm sorry. Would you prefer that I have the office sealed off while Ms. Cooper gets us a search warrant to take your droppings? You a Wrigley's man? Or would you suggest we compare your underwear to the things we found in Lola's apartment? I'd say those size-forty shorts would fit him pretty well, don't you think, blondie?"

Frankel walked over to Chapman and grabbed the tissue from his hand without meeting any resistance. "You two must have lost your minds."

He was like an animal trapped in his own lair. He was patently unhappy with our presence, but afraid that we would walk out without telling him what we knew. Then he put his hand to his eyes and shook his head. "Or maybe I have."

He walked to the windowsill and sat on its edge. "Lola was desperately lonely. She was looking for somebody to cling to, some kind of safety net. I took her out a few times. Never here, in New Jersey, where anyone could see us. In the city, up near the college. I'm not married, if that's what you're thinking. I've been divorced for a couple of years."

"That wasn't my first thought," I said. "I actually wondered how you could get involved with a victim while her case was pending in your office."

"My shrink wants to know the same thing." He sat at his desk and again his fingers tapped steadily against the wooden top. "I had thought about calling you, Alex. I just couldn't pick up the phone to do it. I realize that it's selfish, but if I get myself in the middle of all this, I obviously have to walk out the door here. Give up my job. Make waves for the district attorney."

I was waiting for him to invoke his right to counsel. Like most lawyers, he was loath to do it, figuring—I was certain—that he was smarter than any young prosecutor and the average cop, alone or in combination. I was trying to stay calm, wondering how Frankel could explain being with Lola in her apartment last Thursday afternoon, and how much we should consider him a suspect in her death.

He retraced his steps to his September meeting with Lola and filled in more of the blanks. She had called him again, he said, in October, and invited him to a presentation she was making at an academic convention at the New York Hilton. Her speech was magnificent, Frankel told us, and despite all the professional prohibitions, he began to come into the city to see her from time to time, becoming intimate with her before Thanksgiving.

"Does Vinny know?"

"He'd break my neck. I suspect this could cost him a few votes in the next election, and that's the bottom line."

Chapman worked him a bit more, and then I tried to move things along to the day of the murder. "After Lola called you, what happened that afternoon?"

"I was the only one who knew she was going to leave her sister's house. Lily was driving her crazy. The histrionics, the crying, the busybody nature of her personality. We had all we could do—Anne did, really—to keep Lola there long enough to execute the plan. I had promised to drive her home afterward. She didn't want detectives sitting around her apartment. She was tired of being watched and waited on. She just wanted to go home and get back to work."

"So she called you here at the office."

He looked at me quizzically. "Surveillance?"

"Even easier. Telephone records."

"I went back to Lily's neighborhood and waited around the corner. Lola was in great spirits. Felt she'd helped us nail Ivan, and that she would begin to regain a bit of control over her life.

We drove into town and I took her up to Riverside Drive. She had some things she wanted to do at home, and then she was going to meet me, at seven o'clock, for dinner at a Chinese place on Amsterdam Avenue. She never showed up. I called and called, and when I finally decided to drive back to the apartment to see what the problem was, cops were swarming all over the place. The last time I saw her was when I let her out of my car in front of her building."

We were all silent. Frankel had taken us halfway there, but I didn't believe that he was telling the truth about how he left Lola. I was thinking of the semen-stained sheets, and I'm sure Mike was, too.

"Where did you go? How'd you spend the rest of the afternoon?"

Frankel was fidgeting again. "Let me think a minute. Um, I—I drove down to, um—there are a couple of bookstores on Broadway. I wandered in and out of those. I had some coffee and read a newspaper."

Mike took the pencil he'd been writing with and snapped it in half. "I hate it when people lie to me."

"I don't remember exactly what I did that afternoon. But you don't want me to say I don't remember, so I'm telling you what I would have done. I was wandering around Columbia, I was walking in and out of shops, trying to keep warm and pass the time. It had no significance at the moment because I had no idea anything was wrong. I was just killing time—"

"Or Lola."

"Don't be a horse's ass, Detective. Don't sit in *my* office and even presume to treat me like I did something wrong." His voice was raised now, shrill and strident. "I never went inside Lola Dakota's apartment last Thursday." Frankel spit each word at us, slowly and angrily.

"Then how come there's seminal fluid all over the sheets on her sofa bed? And how come if you just spit over at me one more time, I'm gonna have enough of your goddamn body fluid from this slobbering saliva all over the new tie my aunt Bridget gave me for Christmas to let the lab match it up before your kid gets home with the car tonight."

"*If* there's semen on those sheets, and *if* it happens to be mine, Detective . . . let me stop right there. That's a really big 'if,' 'cause Lola and I did not exactly have what I would call an exclusive relationship."

"Maybe we can narrow it down a bit. Coop, how much you wanna bet that Mr. Frankel here has a pack of gum, white wrapper with that distinctive green arrow, right in his pants pocket?"

"I'm not betting against you, Mr. Chapman."

"What's the point of that?" Bart was furious.

"We've got DNA from the sheets, and DNA from the gum. You know where the bed linens were, and the two of us happen to know exactly where we found your chewed-up ball of saliva. Now all you have to do is remember how many places you were when you tossed your gum. Was it in Lola's bedroom? In the kitchen? For a guy with a regular habit like yours, it's gonna be hard to single out every stick you got rid of. Leave out an important stop, and I'll nail your ass to the wall. The easiest thing for you to do is just to retrace your steps for us, honestly this time. We know damn well that you're leaving something out."

"Well, I sure as hell wasn't in the elevator shaft when she was murdered. Alex, please. You've got to believe that I was never, *never* inside Lola's building the day she was killed. Of course I won't deny that we'd been intimate. But whatever you found on the sheets must be there from two or three weeks ago. We slipped away from Lily's one afternoon, and I took Lola to run some of the errands she needed to get done around school. Then we stopped by at her apartment and yes, we made love. She never spent another night there, so she obviously didn't have any time to do the laundry.

"And the gum? Yeah, I chew gum all the time. It's probably in every wastebasket in the apartment. It's a nervous habit. Started when I gave up cigarettes, and now I do it all the time."

Chapman fisted both hands and leaned his knuckles on the desk, bending toward Frankel. "If you didn't go into Lola's building that day, where else did you go? Help me. Tell me one other stop you made that I can verify."

Bart twisted and squirmed. Mike tried to nudge him in the right direction. "Start with the campus. Did you go anywhere near the college?"

"Columbia?"

"Or King's."

"I'm not familiar with King's. Didn't exist in my day. So I walked around Columbia a bit. But it was too cold. I got in my car and drove down Broadway. Manhattan has a bunch of these great little mystery bookstores. Four or five of them, all over town. It took me a while to find one. Just took a book into a coffee shop and read for a while. I told you that before, and it's true. I'll check at home and see if I can find a receipt."

Both of us knew, from the gum that Mike had spotted in the trash basket, that Bart had made a stop in Lola's office. I wondered if he had done that because she had asked him to pick something up, or if he had gone there on his own. Why wouldn't he give that to us? Why did he continue to lie about it? And what else did it mean he was lying about?

"Was there a reason Lola didn't want you to come upstairs with her?" I asked.

Bart reached into his pocket and stripped the wrapper off another stick of Wrigley's spearmint.

"Not really." He rolled his head in a circle and pressed his hand against the back of his neck. "I mean, what we had originally planned was to spend a few hours there. But when we pulled up in front of the building, one of her friends was on his way inside. We just decided that I should get lost for a few hours and come back later. Lola didn't want anyone asking questions, didn't want anything to happen to screw up the case. Like for Ivan to find out she was sleeping with a prosecutor. Shit, was I stupid."

"How the hell would Ivan find that out, just 'cause you were driving her home?"

"And staying overnight? He had eyes everywhere. Lola was paranoid. Thought he was paying people to find out information. Just figured it would get back to Ivan if we were caught together. She told me to stay loose and she'd give me a call later that afternoon on my cell phone." He looked pained. "The call that never came."

"And the friend, the guy who was going in when you pulled up to the building? What's his name?"

"Her friend, not mine. I never saw the guy before in my life. I think he teaches with her. Black guy with dreads and a kind of wild-looking beard."

Lavery, I thought. "Claude? Claude Lavery?"

"Yeah. That's the guy. Held the door for her and they walked in. I never saw her again after that."

18

Chapman was itching to get out of Frankel's office. Bart followed us past the receptionist's desk and into the hallway. "What do you think, Alex, do I have to tell Vinny about this?"

"Hey, schmuck. Get real. You're now a permanent part of my files on the case, and we're not even out of the box. Coop and me have a few dozen questions for you we haven't even thought of yet. We haven't talked about Ivan, we haven't asked you about the work Lola was doing, we haven't asked whether you know anything about a load of cash she was hiding. Or about drugs."

Mike gave up on the elevator and tugged on the strap of my bag as he turned to trot down the three flights of stairs to the exit. "Next stop for you is my office. Pick a day. Make it easy for yourself, Counselor. And try telling Vinny the truth. Might be a new thing for you. Or, you can tell him you're in the field. That seems to have worked for you before."

"Let's try and schedule an appointment for the beginning of the week, Bart," I said. "You know how this is going to break, so why don't you tell the district attorney about it before Battaglia gives him a call?"

Frankel was leaning over the banister, calling down to us as quietly as he could. "Do you think I'm going to need a lawyer?"

"Line up a good proctologist first, Mr. Frankel. It's rough in those maximum-security pens."

Mike started the engine and we sat in the lot while it took its time warming up. "Born loser. Knew it the minute I saw him. Know how I could tell? Grown man with a backpack. There's just no excuse for it. Half of those twerps in your office use 'em, too. I get on the elevator at Hogan Place, one of those guys from Appeals gets in after me and turns around. Bam! I get smacked right in the puss with nine pounds of law books. By the time you get out of high school, you should figure out some other way to carry stuff around. What are you thinking about?"

"The position Frankel put himself in. That he'll be out of a job before New Year's. Whatever his involvement is in Lola's death, he was terribly indiscreet to be sleeping with her. And we'll have to tell Sinnelesi that he withheld evidence from us. Not to tell us that he had been with Lola after she left Lily's, and that he actually saw her go into her building with a witness who we didn't even know about before this? Irresponsible and unethical."

"There's some reason that Bart wouldn't give up the fact that he went to Lola Dakota's office," Mike said. "Before we have him back over to interview, let's be sure and examine the inventory of stuff that was there, and get the photos Hal Sherman took at the college. It's even creepier to think that he might have gone there *after* he found out she was dead.

"Want to swing by the county jail and see if Ivan has anything to tell us? Talk to him about his student snitch, Julian Gariano? See what kind of mood he's in?"

"I'd love to, but his lawyer called on Tuesday while I was up at your office. Said Anne Reininger gave him my name and number. Left me a message telling me who he was and how to get in touch with him. And that under no circumstances was anyone to attempt to speak with his client out of his presence. Does Ivan still bother you, too?"

"Sure does. It's too neat to assume he didn't have something to do with Lola's murder, when he had already gone to such lengths to get rid of his wife. Suppose he figured out or got tipped off that the hit men were part of a government sting operation? It's too late to remove his voice from the tapes and get out of trouble completely. But say he sets up some kind of defense that proves he— what do you call it in legalese?—that he had withdrawn from the plan and he just let these mopes go ahead with it to show what grandstanders they were.

"Meantime, he makes a backup plan to kill Lola. Paying some- one in the city to let him know when she's returned to Manhattan. Lola gets knocked off . . . splat, all over the bottom of the eleva- tor. So even if you don't believe it's an accident, Ivan the Terrible's got a rock-solid alibi for the rest of last Thursday, sitting behind bars, waiting to be arraigned in a Jersey courtroom. And Fat Vinny looks like the incompetent that he is."

People like to think of domestic violence as an issue of the underclass, as something that occurs in minority communities, among the poor and uneducated, as something personal that is not "our problem." Both Mike and I, just like every cop and prose- cutor in this country, have investigated and charged doctors, lawyers, judges, businessmen, and clergy with beating, raping, abusing, and murdering their spouses. I was not about to ignore Ivan Kralovic, who had already proved that he was at best abusive, and at worst a potential killer.

"Am I dropping you at your office?"

"Let me check my messages. It was slated to be a slow day. There's no point going there if I don't have to." I used my cell phone to dial into my voice mail. The mechanical voice told me that I had four new messages. I played them back and the first two were from assistants in the unit, telling me about the new cases that had come in over the holiday. The third call was from Sylvia Foote.

"Your pal Sylvia called an hour ago," I told Mike. "About Professor Lockhart, from the history department—"

"The guy who was, shall we say, 'tutoring' the law student we interviewed?"

"Yes. He's returning to town tomorrow afternoon. She left his number. He's agreed to speak to us over the weekend anytime we like. Sylvia says Lockhart is willing to cooperate. Was very fond of Lola. That's the gist of it. She's still looking for Grenier and Lavery." I hit the prompt to save the message so that I could retrieve Lockhart's number and call him when he reached New York.

Message four. Three twenty-six P.M. I looked at my watch. It had been only ten minutes since that message was recorded. *Hey, Alex. It's Teague. I'm up at Special Victims with a new complaining witness. Just reaching out to see whether anyone could interview her before she heads back out to L.A. tonight.*

The Special Victims Unit occupied space in the same office building to which Manhattan North Homicide had been transferred more than two years ago. Just above 125th Street, in an unlikely-looking brick structure that faced the elevated subway tracks on the West Side, the two squads were on the same busy corridor. I dialed the number and the civilian aide who answered passed me along to Teague Ryner, another bright young detective who often teamed with Mercer.

"Thanks for calling back so quickly. I was hoping you'd make a decision on this one before she hops on a plane. I don't want to make an arrest unless you think we've got something. Want me to give you the facts?"

"Sure."

"Girl's name is Corinne. Twenty-eight years old. Lives in Santa Monica, says she works in the music business. It all started after she had a few Brain Tumors—"

"Brain tumors? How awful. Is she—"

Teague laughed. "Not *that* kind. It's a drink. A pretty lethal one."

"What's in it?"

I had seen women's vulnerability increase dramatically after downing multiple Tequila Sunrises, Long Island Iced Teas, Sex on the Beach, and other creations that bartenders invented with every new season. They woke up in strangers' apartments, on the backseats of taxicabs, beneath trees in Riverside Park, and on sidewalks in midtown. "It's my right," they would often tell me, "to drink whatever I want, and as much of it as I want." Detectives, prosecutors, advocates, and jurors were supposed to deal with the aftermath. This was my first Brain Tumor.

"About six different liqueurs mixed together," Teague told me. "She can't remember how many of them she drank. In fact, that's the trouble. She can't remember much of anything."

"Did she drink them voluntarily? I mean, she's not claiming someone drugged her, is she?" Two different kinds of problems, under the law.

"Voluntarily? She was chugging them like they were root beer."

"Tell you what. I'm with Chapman, on our way back from an interview in New Jersey. Since he's got to go up to the squad, I'll just come with him to your office and we'll figure it out together." No point spoiling the end of another colleague's day, as long as I was working.

"I'll check with you before I leave, okay?" I said to Mike as he let me out in front of the building. I headed upstairs while he parked the car.

The day tour had just ended, and the teams working four to twelve had come on duty. Teague had caught the case in the morning, when the victim had called the police from the emergency room at New York Hospital to make an official report. Even though many of the cops took vacation leave during Christmas week, sexual assaults continued to occur at an alarming rate. Despite the drastic reduction in street-crime statistics, the volume of acquaintance-rape cases remained steady. Women were far more likely to be attacked by men who were known to them rather than strangers—not the public perception but a well-documented fact. And the alcohol that fueled so many of the holiday parties, at people's offices as well as their homes, led to an alarming number of new incidents.

"Hey, Sarge, how've you been?"

"We can hardly keep up with everything. What a wild week."

"Where's Teague?"

The sergeant led me to a small cubicle in the back of the squad room. Ryner and his witness were talking quietly, as he took notes while she recalled more events of the night before. "Corinne, this is Alexandra Cooper. She's the prosecutor who can answer your questions."

Before I could be seated, Corinne asked the first one. "What kind of case do you think I have? I mean, like, I really don't want to go through, like, all the hassle if nothing's going to happen to this guy."

"I'll try to give you an answer, but I'm going to have to get a lot more detail from you about everything that went on during the evening."

"Well, that's part of the problem. I don't remember much of the night. I met this guy at a party. He told me he's a vocalist. Sings with the Baby Namzoos."

"Who?" Whatever happened to rock and roll?

"They're kind of a hot group now." She could barely disguise her disdain for my ignorance. "Anyway, I started drinking with him. Next thing I know it's ten o'clock in the morning, and I wake up in his hotel room. Naked. There's no way I would have done that unless he forced me to be there."

"Did he have sex with you?"

"Why else would I be naked and in bed with him? He must have. That's what I went to the hospital to find out."

"I'm going to have to start at the beginning with you, Corinne." No one was going to be charged with rape in this jurisdiction because a woman *assumed* that a crime must have occurred. The doctor or nurse who examined Corinne may have been able to find evidence that recent intercourse took place, but they would be unlikely to know whether it was with or without her consent.

"Any medical findings of significance?" I asked Teague.

"Nothing."

"Lacerations, abrasions, discoloration, swelling?" He shook his head in the negative.

I elicited background information from Corinne about her education and employment. I questioned her about the medications she took regularly and her alcohol consumption habits.

"Have you ever had so much to drink before that you couldn't remember things the next day?"

"Yeah. It happens to me every now and then. I've had some blackouts, too. Not passing out completely, but just carrying on with my friends, and then having no memory of it the next day. My doctor tells me I'm not supposed to mix my antidepressants with liquor, but most of the time it doesn't really bother me. . . . I haven't had anything to eat since last night. Do you think you could send out for a sandwich for me?"

"No problem," Teague replied. "There's a sandwich shop that delivers, or there's a guy on the corner with a hot dog stand. I can run down and get one for you, whichever you'd prefer."

Corinne's face screwed up in disgust. "You mean those New York City hot dogs that sit in that dirty water in those pushcarts all day? I couldn't possibly eat that stuff."

No, but she could drink a six-pack of some liquid concoction without a clue about what was in it or how it would mix with her medication, and never even blink. Teague left the room to call in an order for Corinne and a few cups of coffee to keep us all going.

Corinne rested her head, cushioned on her crossed arms, on the table in front of her. "Would you like to tell me about the evening, or as much of it as you can remember?" I asked.

She had met Craig at the party at about midnight, and they were really getting along well together. After a few vodka and cranberry juice cocktails, they left to go to a bar somewhere in the East Nineties. That's where she had the Brain Tumors. Maybe three of them. Maybe five.

"Was he coming on to you at all?"

"Like, what do you mean?"

"Did he seem to be interested in you physically? Did he ever touch you or kiss you?"

"Oh, yeah. We were dancing, I remember that. The jukebox was playing music and I asked him to dance with me."

"Fast or slow?"

"Slow stuff, mostly. He was kissing me, you could say."

"Were you kissing each other?"

"Sure. But I know what you're gonna say. And that doesn't give him any right to have sex with me, especially if he didn't use a condom."

"Did you see anybody else that you know at the bar?"

"No. He's the one who decided where to go drinking. I didn't know another soul."

"How about the bartender? Were you talking to him?"

Corinne thought for a minute. "Yeah. After we'd been there for a while, most of the place kind of cleared out. He and Craig were having a long talk about something—movies, I think it was. They both liked the same kind of movies. Science fiction, stuff I don't know about."

"So there's a good chance, if Teague stops over there tonight, that the bartender can help put together some of the things you don't remember when it came time to leave the bar?"

"Like, what do you mean?"

"How you two were acting toward each other. He might recall some of your conversation, if you had any in his presence at the bar. How many drinks he served you and how drunk you were. Or what kind of physical interaction there was between you and Craig." It was often useful to remind a witness that other people we could talk to might actually be able to help us reconstruct some of the things she had been too wasted to think about clearly.

"You're really going to speak with that bartender?"

"Don't you want us to? After all, part of what you claim is that you didn't go to Craig's hotel room willingly, under your own steam."

She extended one arm out on the table in front of her and rested her head back down on it. "What if he tells you, like, that Craig and I were making out while we were in the bar?"

"That still doesn't give him the right to force you to have sex with him, or to take advantage of you if you weren't participating." I fed her back the line she had tried to use earlier to get me to act on her complaint. If Craig had engaged in a sexual act with her after she had passed out, we might be able to establish the occurrence of a crime.

"Yeah, well, what if the bartender tells you that we both went into the men's room for a while? What's that gonna do to my case?"

"That depends on what you tell me happened in the men's room, doesn't it?"

"You're gonna be all judgmental about it." Corinne focused her eyes on a spot on the ceiling, above my head, and looked even more sullen than she had when I arrived.

"I have no reason to be judgmental. You tell me what the facts are, I'll tell you whether we've got evidence that proves a crime was committed."

"But it's only my word against his?" She was whimpering now.

"That's all we need—your word—in any case. It used to be

different, twenty years ago. There had to be more proof than the story of the woman who brings the charge. But now, rape is like every other crime. Your testimony—your *credible* testimony—is what I present to the jury. Then you're cross-examined by Craig's lawyer. After that, Craig tells him everything he remembers."

I paused to let that fact sink in. "Corinne, what happened in the bathroom at the bar? Did you have sex with him?"

Her eyes returned to the spot on the ceiling. "Not sex. I gave him a blow job. I didn't let him touch me."

I had told her I did not have to make judgments about people. That didn't stop me from wondering about her definition of sexual acts. Maybe it was a generational thing, although she was only ten years younger than I. I had heard it enough times that I had learned to train the young lawyers in my unit never to accept a victim's characterization of the encounter when she said there was "no sex." Ask, I taught them, exactly which body parts made contact with the other person. Most of us make too many assumptions about what other people call sexual acts.

Now she was rubbing her eyes and yawning. "You know, Miss Cooper, I never wanted to call the police about this. It wasn't my idea. That woman at the hospital made me do it. The only reason I went to the emergency room was to get a morning-after pill. I mean, like what if he had sex with me, didn't use a condom, and I find out I'm pregnant?"

"Do you think that's what happened?"

This time she groaned. "I don't know. I just don't know what happened. Don't you get it? That's exactly what I told the doctor who examined me. And after he told me he couldn't see anything unusual, that's when the counselor told me that maybe I was raped."

"*Maybe?* We don't charge people with felonies, Corinne, 'cause 'maybe' they did something bad. I have to believe a serious crime was committed before I authorize the police to make an arrest. And I have to persuade a jury, beyond a reasonable doubt, that the person charged committed that crime. I can't ask them to guess. I can't ask them to fill in the blanks that you don't remember. If Craig had intercourse with you when you were unconscious, that's another thing—that's a crime. But nobody goes to state prison for twenty-five years because you got drunk and then don't like the way the night ended for you.

"And Teague and I will have to spend a lot of time trying to figure out which of those things is what actually happened."

"But how can you do that?"

"Maybe we won't be able to. But we'll start with the bartender. We'll see if there's a desk clerk at the hotel who saw you coming in with Craig. Maybe even a security surveillance tape that will show you walking with him. It might suggest whether or not you were in any distress—or instead, that you were laughing, having a good time. I'll get the records of all the charges from his bill. See if there was any room service, any minibar use, any pay-TV movies charged to Craig's room during the time you were—"

"Oh, jeez, let's just forget about it then." Now she was moving from apathy to anger.

"You don't have to do all that work. That's Teague's job. Did I remind you of something you had forgotten? Did you have more to drink in the hotel room? Get into bed with the guy to watch a movie?" It wouldn't be the first time.

"Where's the detective? Can I talk to him a minute? I mean, like I have a plane to catch."

"Teague and I are here because you wanted our help. We'll get you to the airport. Please try and answer my questions. One call to the hotel and we'll have some of this information anyway. It's all part of the record that goes on the guest's bill."

Corinne was fuming. She wouldn't look at me for almost a minute, and then she spoke.

"All right, so we had some more to drink. He ordered up a bottle of champagne. Is that against the law? I had a couple of sips of champagne."

Nice nightcap for a bunch of Brain Tumors. The chances were good that there would be a charge for an X-rated movie on Craig's bill, shortly after room service arrived with the chilled bucket of bubbly.

"How about the movie, Corinne?"

"It was so gross I couldn't even watch it after the first ten minutes. Like group sex in a hot tub or something. *He* was into that shit. Not me. Look, let's just forget about this. I don't think I have much of a case." She twisted her watch around on her wrist to see the time. "If I don't go now, I'll never make this flight." She stood up and opened the door.

"This morning, when you woke up, did you ask Craig what had happened?"

"Yeah, I asked him. He was like all surprised I didn't remember. He said we—um—we like made love. That he thought I was having a really good time. I just know I wouldn't have done that if I had been sober. Not without a condom."

"But you weren't sober, Corinne. That's what alcohol does, that's what drugs do to us. They change the way we act, they loosen us up. Sometimes we say and do things we wouldn't have done otherwise. Sometimes it makes us more vulnerable to many kinds of danger."

"Well, I'm just too hungover and tired to deal with this now. I didn't want him arrested. I just wanted to teach him a lesson anyway. Please, can I go home?"

Teague had paid the delivery boy and returned to the interview room with Corinne's sandwich. I left them alone so that he could try to soothe her and get her to go over the more complete version of her story, which she had neatly trimmed for him on the first telling. The hot coffee tasted good at the end of a long day, and I walked back to sit with the sergeant and talk about the rash of holiday assaults.

The door to the squad room opened and Mike Chapman burst through before I could finish the cup. "Yo, Sarge. Be sure you get blondie delivered right to the door of Walter Cronkite's apartment when she leaves here. The most trusted man in television can take care of her for the night. Gotta run."

I stood up, holding my finger in the air to signal that I'd be ready in a minute. "Teague doesn't need me anymore. I can—"

"Sorry, kid. Just got a call from the boss at the Nineteenth Precinct. Seems like little miss Annie Oakley made an attempt to get into your building through the garage. Tried to get one of the attendants to let her in with his key. Slipped him twenty bucks. I'm meeting the cops over at P. J. Bernstein's. See if we can pick her off the street before she starts target practice. You and lover boy are grounded for the night, understand?"

I didn't have time to protest. Mike turned to leave, but stuck his head back into the room. "And by the way, I checked with Freddie Figueroa, the detective who canvassed Lola's building the day after the murder. Remember Claude Lavery, 'Professor Ganja-R-Us,' Coop? The upstairs neighbor? On the DD5, all Figueroa had written for his interview with Lavery was that he was in his apartment, working on a research paper and listening to classical music. Didn't see or hear anything unusual on Thursday afternoon. Freddie asked Lavery if he knew the deceased. Said he did, but that he hadn't spoken to her in over a month."

19

Jake dropped me off at the Roosevelt Island tram station at Second Avenue and Fifty-ninth Street on his way to La Guardia in a cab at 8 A.M. Friday morning. He was back off to Washington to cover the end-of-the-year resignation of the secretary of agriculture. I climbed the three-tiered staircase and watched one of the two cable cars pull out of the station as the second arrived and unloaded its crew of daily commuters.

With a few minutes to kill, I called Mike and found him still at home.

"I assume that you would have phoned me last night if you had any luck finding my friend, Miss Denzig."

"We rode around the neighborhood for almost two hours. Nowhere to be seen."

"I'm on my way over to Bird Coler Hospital to do that hearing. Jake won't be home in time for dinner tonight. Why don't you see if you can lure Mercer into town for our Christmas celebration? I'll think of someplace lively to go, okay?"

"Let me see what's cooking. You still planning to take a scenic tour of the island when you're done?"

"Yes. Nan asked one of the students who stayed in town during the holidays to show me the dig site. I'm headed out there now, so I may poke around a bit before I come back. Can you still meet me after I finish at Coler?"

"I'll beep you if I can get there."

There were only seven other people going to the island at that hour on this cold December morning. Two of them had tennis rackets and were clearly headed for the bubble in the sports complex at the foot of the tram station. I wondered what the business of each of the others could be. The young conductor opened the doors of the car and we all boarded. There was a bench at each end, with four large poles to hang on to at various points on the floor, and straps with metal handles hanging from the roof's interior.

Like a cable car at a ski resort, the doors closed and the heavy tram lumbered off, rising on thick steel wires as it lifted off above the city streets. I could see the people in the automobiles that were cruising down the Fifty-ninth Street Bridge ramp. Powerful winds rocked my massive carriage and it shuddered mildly as its several sets of wheels rolled over the stanchion at the first tower.

In the sky beyond, I watched a steady stream of takeoffs and landings heading to and from the La Guardia Airport runways, and below that, three gray stacks belching smoke from some unidentifiable factory in Queens. The crossing took less than four minutes, and I snaked my way out behind the other passengers, who all seemed familiar with the routine. A bus waited at the exit path, and I fished a quarter out of my bag to pay the fare.

The second stop, just beyond the original Blackwell farm-house, would put me on Main Street. When I stepped down from the bus, I was struck at once by the feeling that I was in a small town, millions of miles from Manhattan. The streets were lined with cobblestones, and the handful of new high-rise buildings stood alongside the redbrick facade of the Chapel of the Good Shepherd, constructed more than a century earlier for island residents.

I walked north, following the winding street the equivalent of a handful of city blocks, to the lighthouse at the island's tip, just beyond the hospital. The sweeping view of Manhattan from that point was the most spectacular panorama I had ever seen.

It was after nine o'clock when I presented my identification to the security guard at the desk at Coler Hospital. He directed me to the psychiatric ward on the second floor, where I was met by a slender young woman in a white lab coat. "Miss Cooper? I'm Sandie Herron. I'm the physician in charge of this wing of the hospital. We've got one of the arts-and-crafts rooms cleared and set up for your hearing today."

"Fine. Would you have a private place for me to interview the victim?"

"Yes. That's what I'm here to help you with." She asked me to follow her down the hallway to her office. "You're going to need some help with Tina. It's difficult to understand her unless you've worked with her for a while."

"Will she talk with me?"

"You won't be able to get her to stop talking. Problem is that because her mental disability is so severe, I don't think you'll be able to understand her without help from me or one of my staff."

"What's her history?"

"Tina's thirty years old. She's spent most of her adult life here at the hospital. She has some congenital brain damage, as well as being bipolar. Her developmental level is about that of an eight-year-old's. She has dramatic mood swings, from extreme emotional highs to very profound depression. She's on a number of medications, including Depakote and Neurontin."

I was trying to take down everything Herron was saying. "Don't worry, I've had a copy of Tina's chart made for you. All of the meds are listed in that. The problem . . . may I call you Alex? The problem is that her speech and language are particularly immature. She's incapable of normal verbal communication, and a lot of what she tries to express is incomprehensible to an outsider's untrained ear."

"Have you ever testified at a preliminary hearing, Doctor?"

"About a patient's condition? A diagnosis or finding?"

"No. I think I'd like you to stay with me while I try to ask Tina to tell me what happened. If she isn't able to make it clear to me, or to the judge, I'd like you to act as an interpreter."

"That's fine. Why don't we bring her in and let you get started." Herron called the nurses' station and asked one of the attendants to bring Tina to her office. "One thing you need to understand, Alex, is that Tina exhibits an unusual preoccupation with sex. She's what we call on the ward a chronic public masturbator. We have a companion assigned to be with her most of the day, so she doesn't interact sexually with the other patients."

My luck to draw this complication at a preliminary hearing. The best I could hope for would be to get a good judge who would appreciate the issues here. My witness would be an unintelligible thirty-year-old, with all the sexual interest and curiosity appropriate for a woman that age, but with the mental capacity of a child. The law presumed that she was incapable of consenting to whatever sexual act had occurred.

This must have been an "up" day for Tina, who did not yet have a clue that she was about to appear in a court proceeding in front of a judge, a defense attorney, and her assailant. She walked in holding the hand of her attendant, neatly dressed in a clean white sweatshirt and khaki slacks. She smiled at me when we were introduced, and said something that sounded like "pleased to meet you."

For more than an hour, I struggled to get a narrative from the young woman. Her companion sat by her side, stroking her arm gently when my most basic questions seemed to confuse Tina. If I failed to understand a response, Dr. Herron told me what the patient had said. Whenever I mentioned Chester's name, Tina became visibly agitated.

Somehow, despite all the precautions that had been taken at the hospital, a male patient named Jose had encountered Tina in the hallway after breakfast one morning and had invited her into his room. She liked Jose and accompanied him willingly. Dr. Herron interrupted softly to mention that Jose was a paranoid schizophrenic, with some confusion about his sexual orientation. Tina told us that Jose was always kind to her, and she had sex with him because she thought she was screaming. Her mouth widened and her tongue protruded as she tried to get it to move around the word "screaming" a second time.

"Screaming? Why were you—?"

"No, no, Alex. Tina said she thought she was dreaming when she did it." The patient smiled as Dr. Herron corrected me. "Tina's aware that we don't approve of her . . . well—she usually tries to account for her activity by saying she didn't think it was really happening. That she just imagined it or dreamed about it, isn't that right, Tina?"

She nodded her head in agreement with Herron. It was obvious to me that I would not be able to conduct the hearing unless the judge allowed me to use the doctor as an interpreter. "What happened after that?"

Tina explained that Jose left her to go to the bathroom. That's when Chester came in and found her in the room. He asked if he could get into bed and make love to her. She was scared because she knew that he had a terrible temper, but she told him it was okay.

"Were you afraid of Chester?" No answer.

"Did he say anything to threaten you?" I was wondering if I

could raise the level of the felony crime, if Chester had used any force.

Tina answered clearly when she said, "No."

"Jose came back to the room, Alex. When he saw Chester in bed with Tina, he went to get one of the nurses. That's the reason we know for sure that intercourse occurred. The nurse actually witnessed it."

"Fine. I can spare Tina having to testify at the hearing if I can use the nurse as a witness."

"I'm afraid she went back home to Montana for Christmas."

"What's Chester's ability to understand right from wrong?"

"He certainly knows the difference, and he knows that what he did with Tina was wrong. His psychiatrist can give you all that. His problem has to do with control of his temper and the explosive outbursts from which he suffers. Chester's twenty years old. He's been in and out of hospitals for most of his life, but was homeless at the time of his last arrest."

"What was the charge?"

"He beat up an old man who tried to stop him from getting on a bus without paying."

I continued to prepare Tina for the preliminary hearing, which had to be held before the end of the week in order to keep Chester in on bail. The hospital authorities wanted him removed from their facility, while our purpose would be to have him hospitalized in a prison psych ward during the pretrial period. I did not want to see him released, on the street, with no home to go to and no one to supervise the taking of his antipsychotic medication.

"Excuse me, Dr. Herron?" We all looked up as another nurse entered the room. "There's a call from a judge's clerk who's downstairs. He wants to know when this hearing is going to start."

It was after twelve. "I need another half hour, at least. Why don't we say one o'clock?"

"That's good for me, too, Alex. Tell them where we're setting up, and that we'll be ready at one. And let's be sure Tina has some lunch before you get going. She really slows down with all those meds unless she eats at regular intervals."

"There's a message for you, Ms. Cooper. Detective Chapman said he can meet you after the hearing, unless you call to tell him otherwise."

An hour later, I entered the arts-and-crafts center of the psych ward. Much like the walls of a kindergarten class, this room was lined with pictures, crayoned and painted by the patients, all of whom were adults. A makeshift judicial bench had been fashioned out of several of the tables, and the stark black of the judge's robes was in sharp contrast to the brightly colored, childlike illustrations that would be our background for this sad proceeding.

"Ms. Cooper? I was expecting Assistant District Attorney Dashfer to be here today."

"And I was expecting Judge Hayes, Your Honor." We each forced a smile.

The judge was probably as crestfallen as I appeared to be. I had mistakenly relied on the tentative schedule distributed earlier for the week's arraignment part, not figuring on holiday substitutions. Instead of Roger Hayes, one of the smartest and most sensitive jurists in our jurisdiction, I had been saddled with Bentley Vexter. I knew this would prove to be a more difficult experience for Tina, with a judge not long on patience or understanding.

My adversary was a young lawyer from the Legal Aid Society. He had met his client for the first time just minutes ago, when he arrived at the hospital. They conferred briefly while we waited for Sandie Herron to come to the room.

"Are the People ready to proceed?"

"Yes, Your Honor."

"Call your first witness." He held the criminal court complaint up to his nose and lifted his glasses to examine the typed accusation.

"I would like to make an application to the court before I do that."

The judge put the glasses back in place and met my statement with a frown. "We've wasted half a day out here while you got your witness ready for this. What is it now?"

I launched into a description of Tina's condition, both physical and mental, while she and Dr. Herron waited in the corridor. "The request I'm making is that the court allow the victim's physician to appear with her in the courtroom, to serve as a facilitator, should that become necessary during the taking of testimony."

"I'm going to have to object to that, Your Honor."

"Hold it a minute, Mr. Shirker. What, this woman doesn't speak the language? What kind of interpreter do you need? Nobody told my clerk we—"

"Not a foreign language interpreter, sir." I repeated the nature of Tina's difficulties and explained Dr. Herron's relationship with her.

"Objection."

"On what grounds, Counselor?" It was clear the judge had no idea whether he should grant my somewhat unusual request, so he was hoping the defense attorney would provide him with a legal basis to make Tina's task more arduous.

Mr. Shirker had nothing more than a gut feeling and a knee-jerk reaction. "Um, uh—due process, Your Honor."

"He's right, Ms. Cooper. This is a very peculiar step you're asking me to take."

"The fact that it is unconventional doesn't mean that it doesn't have a valid purpose in a legal proceeding. Our courts are supposed to be accessible to everyone. The fact that this witness has a severe impairment should not deprive her of her day in—"

The judge held his arm straight out in front of him to stop me. Then he lowered it, pointing his finger at the official stenographer. "We're off-the-record here, understand?"

I stood up to object. Vexter was most pernicious when he could clean up the official language of his hearings. His finger pointed back at me, telling me not to dare to stop him. "Look, Alex. You got a retard here who doesn't mind a roll in the hay. She hops into bed with Jose, so who's to say Chester can't have a date, too?"

"I'd like all of this to be *on* the record, Judge. I'd like the opportunity to respond to it." I wanted an official transcript reflecting his ignorance in black-and-white print that an appellate court and a judiciary committee could examine. Vexter's views were as limited as his intelligence.

The stenographer's hands were poised over her machine. She was waiting for the judge to give her the signal to resume working, while glancing back at me with a shrug of her shoulders, knowing that she was helpless to do as I asked. Vexter was in charge of the courtroom.

Vexter put his glasses on the tip of his nose and motioned to me and my adversary with his forefinger. "Why don't you approach the bench?"

"No, thank you, sir. I want all of this on the record. My witness is developmentally disabled, with severe mental and physical handicaps. But she knows what happened to her and she is entitled to tell her story in this forum."

Chester Rubiera was digging his fingers into the palm of his hand as he watched the goings-on around him. I expected him to draw blood at any moment.

"And I'm telling you that this whole thing is a waste of the court's goddamn time."

"Is that what you and Mr. Shirker mean by due process, Your Honor? Would you like me to talk about the law on this issue, or doesn't that particularly interest you?" Vexter knew as much about rules of evidence as I knew about NASA.

"You got cases on this?"

Catherine had sent the file on the matter to Jake's apartment. She had researched the issue and I had read the opinions last night. I nodded to the judge and started to cite opinions. "There's a Second Department case, *In the Matter of Luz P.*" I handed copies of the decision to the court officer to give to the judge and my adversary. "And the *People Against Dorothy Miller.*" I described the facts and holdings as the stenographer urged me to slow down.

"Yeah, I knew that," Vexter said, tossing the pages aside without reading them.

"The unaided testimony of this witness is likely to be meaningless without our ability to have Dr. Herron interpret her responses. Counsel is welcome to cross-examine and ask whatever appropriate questions he chooses. As previous courts have ruled, this is simply a pragmatic question, not a legal or scientific one."

The three of us continued to argue while the defendant became more irritated, and my witness no doubt grew more anxious out in the hallway. When the judge finally reversed himself and let us go forward, Dr. Herron guided Tina in and sat beside her. The patient's pleasant smile faded when she saw Chester sitting on the opposite side of the long worktable. She clung to Herron's hand and wriggled in her seat.

For the better part of the next two hours, we went through the encounter between Chester and Tina, with Herron clarifying the language whenever Tina's verbal utterances were incomprehensible. By the end of the cross-examination, the patient had exhausted herself by the combination of her concentration on the retelling of the story, and her apprehension about being close to Chester.

When Vexter ruled that there was sufficient evidence to hold the matter for the action of the grand jury, he released Tina from the room and dealt with the business of finding an appropriate facility in which to secure the defendant, away from Coler Hospital.

At four-fifteen, I thanked the doctor and retraced my steps to the lobby of the building, where Chapman was waiting. "Proud of yourself, blondie? Chester the Molester moving on to a better place? Can't believe they actually got a psychobabble disorder named for a bad disposition."

"Yeah. 'Intermittent explosive disorder'—temper tantrums that the perp's unable to control."

"And a medication that works for them?"

I nodded.

"Get a double dose and I'll keep it in my desk drawer, to have on hand for those days you lose it with me. C'mon, that student who was supposed to meet you had to leave for the day. One of the guys from the one-fourteen is going to cruise us around for ten minutes. Will that do?"

We went outside, where the sky was already darkening and the wind had picked up force. A blue and white RMP—radio motor patrol car—sat in front of the hospital. The two uniformed cops in the front seat looked less than thrilled to be chauffeuring us around the quiet little island.

They pointed out the landmarks as we wound our way south, past the remains of the Octagon, the apartment houses, the meditation steps, the observation pier. Near the southern tip, we came flat up against the heavy metal fencing that blocked off the ruins of the Smallpox Hospital.

"Can we get in there to see it?"

The driver flashed his annoyance at his partner, who answered more politely. "Nothing to see, really. You can't go inside the building 'cause it's all crumbled and full of falling blocks of granite. And broken glass. And then there's the rats."

I got the point. "Can we just drive up closer so I can take a look?"

With some hesitation, the driver started the car again and drove us to the locked fence. He got out of the RMP, inserted his card in the automated locking device, and watched as the gate slid open. He stepped back into the car and drove slowly through the entrance. In the wintry darkness of the late afternoon, I could barely make out the shapes of the large boulders on the darkened landscape. "You won't see much, and I can't let you out to walk around. Last guy I took in needed a tetanus shot from tripping and cutting himself open on some old can or bottle."

"What are these huge rocks?"

"The walls of the old City Penitentiary. That's what it all was, once. Came down in the 1940s. It's just been sitting here ever since. Kids used to really get hurt on this stuff. That's why they finally fenced it off."

He drove south until he stopped at the abandoned ruin of the Smallpox Hospital. Chapman and I stepped out of the car and walked to the waist-high wooden fence that kept trespassers at bay.

"Isn't it glorious?" The facade looked like an old castle, the dark gray stone porch of the entry now draped in icicles and bare of all the ivy that cascaded down its sides in summer. Through its paneless window frames, the enormous bright red neon letters of the bottling factory's Pepsi-Cola sign lighted the black sky above the river. On the Manhattan side, the glitter of the United Nations complex sparkled with the outline of its distinctive shape.

"This all that's here?" I could see Mike's breath forming the words in the chilled air.

The driver of the RMP nodded in response.

"Now you've seen it, kid. Let's hoof it back to the mainland. Must be like a girl thing. The place doesn't do anything for me. Mercer's gonna meet us at your place at seven-thirty."

The cops dropped us at the station and we waited with two other passengers until the cable car landed and disgorged its returning commuters.

Mike and I stood in the front of the tram, hanging on to the overhead straps, as the red behemoth lurched from its berth and lifted toward the first tower. For just a few moments we were below the roadway of the Fifty-ninth Street Bridge, and then we reached the height that put us almost at eye level with the huge girders that spanned the river. The wind was fiercer now, and I could feel the play in the tension of the steel wires.

Mike turned to say something to me when a burst of shots resounded on the side of the moving cab. They pinged and smacked against the steel sidings and the thick glass of the upper body of the tram. Before the second volley was fired off, and without a word between us, Mike had tackled me to the ground and covered my body with his own.

The window had shattered as the hail of gunfire continued, a second round and then a third. The car swayed and frigid air rushed in to fill the small heated space of the wounded tram. The remaining two minutes of the crossing seemed endless, and my mind flashed to those desperate moments almost five months earlier when Mercer had taken a bullet meant for me.

My face was pressed against the muddy tiled floor of the cab. I could hardly breathe from the combination of terror and the weight of Mike's body flattened against my back. I closed my eyes to keep the glass particles from blowing into them, and heard the sound of Mike's gun scraping against the floor of the tram as he positioned it alongside my ear to cover the opening of the door as we docked.

20

Startled commuters awaiting the short ride home gasped at the spectacle of the four of us, crawling on the bottom of the cable car, and a gun in the hand of Mike Chapman, who had been unable to reach into his pocket to display his badge.

"I'm a cop. It's okay," he said. He stood up and went to check on the older couple who had been sitting on the bench in the rear of the tram before they had dropped to the floor. "You two all right? I'm a police officer."

The elderly woman was clutching her chest and began to cry as Mike helped her to her feet. "He's got a heart condition," she said, pointing at her husband. "Is he—?"

Mike was assisting her husband onto the bench and restoring

the cane to his hand. "You wanna call for an ambulance?" he shouted to no one in particular, as the trembling man assured Mike that he was fine.

A bystander said that someone had already called 911 after the first shots were heard.

"How's your wife?" the old gent asked, pointing to me. I was standing up, brushing the slivers of glass off my knees and trying to maintain my composure.

"Nothing a six-pack of Dewar's won't fix in a minute. She takes a flop like that every couple of days, just to keep me on my toes." Mike was doing his best to defuse the situation, to keep everyone calm until he could sort out what fears were appropriate.

Within minutes, six cops bounded up the steps to the departure platform. Two of them recognized me and one of them had known Mike for years. They helped the older couple make their way down the staircase to an ambulance, and put me in the back of one of the patrol cars. One cop stayed with me to take the details for a police report, while Mike and the others examined the inside of the cab.

By the time Mike got back to the car, the uniformed sergeant had arrived and introduced himself to me. "They're doing stops at both ends of the bridge, Mike. What do you think it was?"

"I left 'em up there for Crime Scene to photo, but it's pellets of some kind. Meant to kill somebody? I doubt it. But you could send a loud message that way. Could be somebody just goofing around with a shotgun, could be somebody looking to break windows and scare the shit out of people, could be somebody thinks you're running a shooting gallery in the Nineteenth. I'll leave it to you to figure out."

"There's been a dingbat on the loose after Miss Cooper, hasn't there? Saw a scratch on it back at the house."

"Yeah, but this was definitely not a handgun. Besides, nobody knew it was going to be us on that tram. Maybe it's just some loose cannon, warming up for New Year's Eve."

I thought of Lola Dakota. Was I getting to be as paranoid as she had been? "Remember the kid who hanged himself last weekend? Lola wasn't so crazy. He *was* selling information to Kralovic about where she was and what she was doing. Maybe someone snitched that I was out on the island today, and this attack really was aimed at you and me."

"She's just out on a day pass, Sarge. I'm taking her back to Bellevue right now." Mike stepped out of the car to talk with the sergeant before he left, then slid back onto the seat beside me, closing the door behind him. "You want people to think you're nuts? That was just some carful of kids from Long Island being frisky on the ride home after an outing in the Big Apple. Don't start seeing your cases in every odd thing that happens."

He was running his fingers through his thick black hair, a sure sign that he was more upset than he was willing to acknowledge. Mike didn't believe this was random mischief any more than I did. "They'll beep me if their search turns up any goofballs with shotguns. My guess is that whoever did it was off the bridge before the nine-one-one call went through."

A couple of the cops returned to the patrol car and asked where we wanted to be dropped off.

"Let's go to my place to meet Mercer." This unexpected event had chewed up more than an hour of our time. "I'd like to put on some sliver-free, clean clothes for dinner, okay? Wash my face and hands."

"Dab some perfume on, too, Coop. You didn't smell so sweet when I was breathing down your neck."

Mercer was already waiting in the lobby of my building. The doorman stopped me as I crossed to the seating area to greet him. "Miss Cooper? The super asked me to tell you, if I saw you, that your window still hasn't been replaced. The glazier they use is on vacation, so it can't be fixed until January second. Is that okay?"

I didn't have much of an alternative. "As soon as they can get it done, I'd appreciate it."

On the way upstairs in the elevator, we told the story of our harrowing tram ride. Perhaps it was a result of his own recent attack, but when I left them in the living room to go change, Mercer was insisting to Mike that we make the cops work to identify the shooters.

Despite the tarp on the empty window frame, the apartment was as cold as the inside of a refrigerator. I changed into a casual outfit, packed some more clothes to take to Jake's place for the weekend, and returned to find Mercer and Mike pouring drinks in the den, the pocket doors closed in an effort to keep out the cold.

"Here's to our own little Christmas. Looks like it'll be the last one for this trio without significant others, spouses, offspring. Chokes me all up inside." Mike lifted his glass and we clinked together. "Too bad you didn't have your hardware on your chest today. This thing Jake gave her, Mercer? It must be like kryptonite. Probably could have melted that buckshot on the spot. We can't top it, blondie, but we have some trinkets—"

Mike interrupted himself and hit the television remote to eliminate the mute function. Alex Trebek announced that the *Final Jeopardy!* category was an audio question, and the topic was the Oscars. "How much, guys?"

Mercer and I smiled at each other. There were categories in which we didn't stand a chance against Mike, but we could both hold our own at the movies. "Fifty bucks."

"I'm in," I said to Mercer.

Mike was reluctant. "Probably some dumbass song from a Disney flick. Make it twenty."

Mercer held his ground and Mike yielded.

"Here's the music," Trebek said. The introduction to the song played, and the Main Ingredient did the opening lines of "Everybody Plays the Fool." Mercer took my hand and started to dance with me as Trebek gave the clue.

"Tonight's answer is, the Oscar-winning actor whose father was the lead singer in this group."

Mike protested as Mercer and I danced around him. "That's a really misleading category. What did the guy win the award for?"

Mercer and I answered at the same time. "Supporting actor."

"We'll split the pot on this one, Ms. Cooper, okay?"

Mike, like the three contestants, did not know the right question. "That's not cricket. You two know more about Motown than I know about the Civil War."

Mercer told Trebek that the question was "'Who is Cuba Gooding Junior?' Now," he continued, turning to Mike, "Mr. Chapman, show us the money." We each took twenty-five from Chapman and began to open our presents.

"For you, Detective Wallace," I said, passing a wrapped package to him. He ripped at the paper and smiled when he lifted the cover off the box to reveal a photograph in an antique sterling-silver frame. I had asked the mayor to inscribe the picture of himself with Mercer and his father taken at City Hall, when Mercer had received an award for his work on a prominent art dealer's murder. It had been taken the week he had gotten out of a wheelchair and was walking without assistance, and the expression on Spencer's face told the whole story.

I gave Mike his gifts. First was a complete set of Alfred Hitchcock videos accompanied by gift certificates for two tickets to his local movie theater good every month of the coming year.

For each, I had sketched an IOU for a plane ticket to the Vineyard, with dinners at the Outermost and the Beach Plum Inns, so we could all go up for a long weekend in the spring.

They had a bag full of surprises for me, including a little red voodoo doll, with a set of pins, labeled with Pat McKinney's name. They had wrapped a complete collection of Smokey Robinson CDs and had somehow managed to get Derek Jeter and Andy Pettitte to sign a note inviting me to the dugout after the opening game at Yankee Stadium in the spring, for which we all had tickets.

The last box was a tiny one, wrapped in shiny gold foil with white ribbon, with a card that read, *For our favorite partner.*

Inside was a pair of cuff links. Each was a miniature blue and gold NYPD detective shield, one bearing Mike's number and the other Mercer's. I took the navy silk knots out of the French-cuffed shirt I was wearing with my blazer and jeans and replaced them with their gift.

Mercer drove us across town to West Forty-ninth Street, where I had reserved an eight-thirty table at Baldoria's. The bouncer held open the door and we were greeted inside by Frank. Since the chic downtown offshoot of Rao's had opened last year, it was one of the hottest tables in town. The great buzz, the classy brown and white decor, the same superb jukebox selections, and the outstanding food combined to make the place an instant success.

Bo Dietl was at the bar. He had retired from the police department after solving the Palm Sunday Massacre in Brooklyn several years back, but he was a dogged private investigator who seemed to keep tabs on every crime that went down in Manhattan.

"Buy them a round," he told the bartender. He had Mike corralled in a bear hug as he got off his stool to offer it to me. "What are you drinking?"

"Make it doubles all around. We had a rocky ride this afternoon." The story of the tram shooting became more embellished with each telling. Bo was chewing on his cigar as Mike described how he knocked me to the ground and had to cover my mouth because I was screaming so frantically.

"I didn't scream. I was so terrified, I think the words froze in my throat."

Bo asked what we were working on and Mike explained where we were in the Dakota case. "Did you remember to call Professor Lockhart this afternoon?" he was reminded to ask, turning to me.

"Yes, from the hospital, when the hearing was over. He lives just north of the city, in White Plains. If we drive up there tomorrow morning, he'll be happy to talk with us."

Bo kept looking over my shoulder, at the table closest to the end of the bar. "Guess the case they had in Jersey is falling apart."

"Not that I'm aware of—"

"Hey, Alex. The Bo reads the newspapers, y'know." He had a Bob Doleish way of talking about himself in the third person. "That guy, sitting with the broad with all the hair poofed up on top of her head? That's Ivan Kralovic, isn't it?"

My head snapped in the direction Bo's cigar was pointing. The face of the man in the booth was obscured by an upswept bouffant hairdo, but the retired detective kept talking. "Heard it in the car on the radio when I was on my way over here. Sinnelesi's number two man was putting the wood to the dead professor. Sleeping with her in the middle of the investigation. I'm telling you, it would take a prosecutor to be that friggin' stupid. Sorry, Alex. Kralovic's lawyer made a bail application this afternoon. Seems the defense team had known about the affair for weeks. The judge was ripped about it, and granted the application today. Looks like old Ivan knew where to get his first good meal."

I could see Kralovic clearly now as he leaned in to cut the thick veal chop on the plate in front of him. Ivan's mourning period for Lola had ended.

21

"We'll be back another time," I said, kissing Frank good-bye and trailing out of the restaurant behind Mercer and Mike. "It's not the food, it's the company." The last thing I needed was Kralovic telling his lawyer I tried to talk to him when I ran into him at dinner.

"I had a real craving for Peking duck, anyway," Mike said, opening the rear door of Mercer's car to let me in. We drove across town to Shun Lee Palace, and I stopped in the phone booth to try to reach Paul Battaglia to tell him what had happened.

After eight rings, I remembered that he was out of town until New Year's Day. Reluctantly, I dialed Pat McKinney's home number. "Thanks, Alex. I actually knew a few hours ago. Sinnelesi called me when he couldn't find the boss."

It would have been courteous, not to mention useful, for McKinney to have beeped me to tell me about Kralovic's release on bail. I hated having to learn it from an outside source, late on a Friday evening when it was impossible to get accurate details. "Did he tell you anything else?"

"Yeah, he fired Bart Frankel today. It'll be all over the papers tomorrow morning. Ivan's lawyer made a pretty compelling argument to the judge this afternoon that his client only went along with the sting because he knew in advance exactly what was happening, and wanted to be able to argue entrapment to the court."

"You mean entrapment as a defense to hiring someone to kill his wife?"

"Yeah. He's saying the tapes will prove the whole operation was Sinnelesi's idea. They're going to argue that Kralovic had himself wired up for months, every time he met with or spoke to the undercovers. And that if the two sets of tapes aren't the same, he'll prove the New Jersey prosecutor was corrupt and simply out to get him."

It had never occurred to me that Lola's husband might have any kind of viable defense to the charge of trying to kill her. But Sinnelesi's reputation was not beyond question, as Battaglia's was. Perhaps Paul's nose had been even more accurate than usual in detecting a good reason not to participate in the Jersey plan. If our counterparts across the Hudson had been unable to nail Kralovic squarely for his penny-stock fraud, then maybe they had stretched procedure and undermined the attempted murder case.

All that was certain is that Ivan the Terrible had exactly what he had wanted. Lola was dead, and the evidence pointing to him as the prime mover in her killing was looking muddier and muddier.

We settled in for the meal. The little bit of appetite that remained after the tram ride had evaporated with our sighting of Kralovic dining at an elegant restaurant. I watched Mike and Mercer go through steamed dumplings and chicken soong and a deliciously crispy duck, but I even refused my fortune cookie for fear that its prophecy would depress me.

They had dropped me at Jake's apartment by eleven. I called him at the Watergate Hotel to let him know that I had been delivered home safely. Unable to sleep, I drew a steaming-hot bath and tried to escape with the latest issues of *In Style* and *Architectural Digest*. When they failed to make me sleepy, I immersed myself in an interminable *New Yorker* piece on a lost Tibetan temple that had been rediscovered by a group of British trekkers. Midway through the story I was ready to turn out the light.

Mike was waiting for me outside the building at eight-fifteen. We stopped for coffee on our way north to Westchester County, to the suburban home where Professor Lockhart was staying. The car stops on the Fifty-ninth Street Bridge the night before had been unsuccessful, and the ballistics lab confirmed that the pellets had come from some kind of shotgun, not a pistol. I tried to buy into Mike's theory that it was simply pranksters with an early burst of holiday fireworks.

It was almost nine-thirty when I rang the bell at the neo-Victorian home on a quiet dead-end street in White Plains. The sandy-haired man who opened the door to us looked no older than Mike. He had fine, chiseled features and an athletic build. "I'm Skip Lockhart. Why don't you come inside and warm up?"

The large living room was filled with antique furniture and decorated in a very formal style. There were pictures on all the tabletops, which I tried to scan as he led us into a study.

"Thanks for coming up here. I'm kind of stuck for the next week."

"We just assumed that you lived here."

"It's my parents' home, actually. They've gone out to Scotts-dale to visit my sister for the week, and I promised I'd come up here after Christmas to keep an eye on my grandfather, who lives with them. He's ninety, and as much as he thinks he can take care of himself, we need to keep an eye on him. I was a friend of Lola's. Anything I can do to be helpful, I'd like to try."

"Where's home?"

"In the city."

"Near campus? Near Lola's apartment?"

"A few blocks away."

Lockhart told us that he was thirty-eight years old, single, and an assistant professor of American history at King's College. He had known Lola for five or six years, and had never been romantically involved with her. Yes, he admitted that he had dated several students at the school, despite the fact that it was against the administrative guidelines. But he had never known Charlotte Voight and never given any thought to her disappearance.

"How much time did you spend with Dakota, on campus or off?"

"Very little, until she got me involved in the Blackwells Island project."

"What was your interest in that?"

"Two things, really," Lockhart answered, sitting back in his leather armchair and crossing one leg over the other knee. "Obviously, being a student of Americana, I'm quite familiar with the history of the area. An astounding number of well-known people have spent time there, and as a social phenomenon, it's a great resource for teaching students how we've dealt with society's outcasts throughout time."

He cleared his throat several times as he talked, looking us over and trying to get comfortable with us, it seemed to me.

"But I've always had a personal reason to be fascinated with that little strip of land. You see, my grandfather used to work on the island."

Mike was engaged now, both because of the investigation and because of his own love for historical nuggets. "What do you mean?"

"You probably know that the place was once covered by

institutions—hospitals, asylums, jailhouses. And the New York Penitentiary."

"We were over there yesterday. That building doesn't exist at all anymore, does it? Just a pile of rubble and rocks."

"You're right. It used to stand directly to the north of the Smallpox Hospital, but it was demolished before the Second World War. It was the gloomiest place on the island, which is saying quite a lot. Unless you've made a study of it, as I have, there'd be no reason for you to know about the terrible scandal that took place there shortly before it was closed."

"What kind of scandal?"

"During the Tammany Hall days, the prison was a cesspool of corruption and graft. The place was actually dominated by mob members who were inmates. You'd have to see photographs to believe the way they lived."

"You mean how awful it was?"

"Not for the top dogs. They had quite a luxurious lifestyle, with personal pets and private gardens, food and liquor that was smuggled in to them. A few even dealt drugs inside."

"That piece of it hasn't changed too much," Chapman said.

"Finally, when Fiorello La Guardia was elected to the mayoralty and Tammany Hall fell, he named a new commissioner of correction. A gentleman named Austin MacCormick. My grandfather was a young lawyer at the time, hired out of your office, Miss Cooper."

Lockhart leaned over and handed me one of the old photographs from the side table. "He wasn't even thirty years old. MacCormick hired him to work on the cleanup of the penitentiary. He and his cronies planned a huge surprise raid of the prison—a very successful one, which ended up shutting it down. It was quite a big deal. Gramps still has all the clippings to prove it."

Lockhart stood to adjust the thermostat in the room and check on the heat.

"Did Lola Dakota ever meet your grandfather?"

"Meet him? I thought she was going to elope with him." He laughed as he said it. "Once she found out that he had actually spent time on the island, there was no keeping her away from this house. And it was a godsend for my folks to have someone who took a real interest in the old guy, who could listen to his stories day in and day out."

"What did they talk about?"

"Everything he could remember. She listened to him describe the raid itself, she looked at his photo albums and read his diaries. In fact, I think she may still have had some of the volumes. I suppose someone will sort that all out and get them back to us. Seems rather irrelevant in light of what happened to Lola."

I made a note to look for the diaries among the inventory of Lola's books and papers.

"Were you there for those conversations?"

"Two or three times, at the outset. But I grew up on these stories and I've heard them all my life. I don't suppose there was anything he told her that I didn't already know. She'd just take the train up here, have lunch with my grandfather, spell my mother for a couple of hours. I don't think any great revelations came of it, Miss Cooper."

"Can you think of any reason, any motive for someone to kill Lola?"

"Is Ivan too obvious a choice? I've only met him a couple of times, but I know she was very frightened of him. There are plenty of students who hold her responsible for their not making the dean's list or bringing down their averages, but I don't think we had any homicidal maniacs among them."

"Did you ever accuse her of being a gold digger or a treasure seeker?"

Lockhart blushed. "That's what I get for being out of town when all this started. You've clearly covered some territory." He looked down at his Top-Siders and back up at Chapman. "Not in a literal sense. She wasn't after Ivan's money—if he really had any. It's just that she would latch onto people and use them for whatever she could suck out of them. Then she'd just discard them when they couldn't give her anything else. It wasn't a nice thing to watch."

"What do you know about Claude Lavery?"

Lockhart was slow to answer. "More than I ever wanted to. I can't tell you I objected to his activities at the college. I can't say he was selling drugs to kids, exactly, but he introduced so many of them to a culture in which there was a general acceptance of substance abuse. There are so many rumors about his misappropriation of funds—well, it just makes me furious. We've been struggling awfully hard to get King's off the ground, and Lavery did everything he could to allow intellectuals at the better schools to think we were just all about street jive."

"What do you know about the missing money?"

"Not a thing. I'm on a tenure track myself, trying to keep my hands clean and mind my own business."

"Lavery and Lola?"

"I didn't meddle with it. They were pals. Nothing intimate, of course. She was working on something else with him, and I just put up a Chinese wall between us."

"Would you mind if we talked with your grandfather, as long as we're here?" I asked.

"Not at all. I'm sure he'd be delighted, too. Hope you don't have to be anywhere very soon. You get him going on the Mac-Cormick raid and he'll bend your ear off."

Lockhart stood up to lead us out of the room, then turned back, biting the corner of his lip.

"Something wrong?"

"I doubt he'll realize that Lola is dead. I've told him about it, naturally, and I've read him the newspaper stories. It's just that he's got a bit of a problem with his memory. Long-term, it's quite remarkable. Doesn't forget a thing. But ask him what I gave him for breakfast, or the fact that Lola was murdered last week, and he won't know a thing about it. Some of the doctors believe it's an early stage of Alzheimer's, while others assume it's just part of his aging process."

Mike and I followed the young professor through the length of the rambling house, beyond the enormous kitchen to a cheerful solarium, where Lockhart's grandfather was sitting on a chintz sofa, washed in the sunlight that was streaming through the glass-walled room.

"Gramps, these are some people who are trying to help Lola. They'd like to talk to you."

"Lola? What's wrong with Lola?" The tall, lean man with an elegant mane of white hair raised himself to his feet and shook hands with Mike. "Orlyn Lockhart, sir. Who might you be?"

"I'm Michael Chapman. I'm a New York City detective. This is Alexandra Cooper. She works in the district attorney's office."

He checked behind himself to be sure the sofa cushion was in place, and as he lowered himself down, his grandson reached an arm out to steady his descent. "Did young Orlyn tell you I used to work there myself?"

"He certainly did." I smiled at Skip, who held up three fingers to indicate to me that he was the third Orlyn Lockhart.

"What service do you perform there? Are you a secretary?"

"No, sir. I'm an assistant district attorney in Mr. Battaglia's office. I run the Sex Crimes Prosecution Unit there."

"Still can't get used to the fact that women practice in the criminal courts." The old gent was shaking his head back and forth. "Wouldn't have seen one anywhere near the well of the courtroom in my day. Not a lawyer, not even allowed to serve on the jury. Where'd you go to school?"

"University of Virginia."

"Mr. Jefferson's university? My alma mater, too, young lady. They've come to let women in these days? I'm shocked. The whole damn school was men only back then, and a great place. Came out and went right to work in the best law office in the country. New

York County district attorney. Joab Banton—I was one of Banton's boys. Blame all these women in the courtroom on Kate Hepburn. She started the whole damn thing with her movies. And wearing pants, no less. Who's the DA now? It's not still Dewey, is it?"

Not since 1941, when he left to run for election as the governor of New York, before two unsuccessful attempts at the presidency. "No, sir. Paul Battaglia." I was beginning to question how reliable a conversation with this man could be.

"Where's Lola?" The man's eyes were alive with interest, the fine light blue color coated with a thin layer of glaucoma-like haze.

Mike mumbled under his breath. "On ice."

"You say you were with Lola?"

"I told you they were Lola's friends, Gramps." Skip tried again to explain our connection to Lola without mentioning her death. The old man didn't get it. As they talked I could see the yellowed front page of the New York *Herald Tribune,* framed on the table at his elbow, with its banner headlines proclaiming the top news story of January 24, 1934: GANGSTER RULE OF ISLAND SMASHED BY MACCORMICK. "Worst Prison in World Recaptured from Control of Prison Mob Bosses."

The lead article, with its photograph of MacCormick and the young, good-looking former prosecutor at his side, appeared just above the news that the notorious John Dillinger had been taken into custody in Tucson, Arizona.

I seated myself on an ottoman facing Orlyn Lockhart, our knees practically touching as we spoke. "Someone tried to hurt Lola, so we thought we should find out why. We're talking to all her friends."

"Seems to *me* you should talk to her enemies. That's what I would have done."

Mike winked at me as he sat next to Skip's grandfather. "Score that one for Banton's boys, blondie. Bet he never lost his touch."

"What did Lola like to talk about with you? Can you tell me?"

He kept it all in the present tense. "We don't have to wait for her. She's heard most of my tales. Loves to hear me talk about the island."

The telephone rang and Skip stood up to walk to the kitchen. "Will you call me if you would like something to drink or eat? Gramps, you okay? I've got some phoning to do."

Orlyn kept talking right over Skip's announcement. "Biggest thugs in New York, and they were the ones running the penitentiary—from inside, no less. It started with Boss Tweed, back before I was born. You know he stole millions from the City of New York, and when they finally caught up with him, they sentenced him to twelve years on Blackwells Island.

"Want to know how he was treated? Tweed was given a furnished apartment in the penitentiary. Never locked. Had his own library and even a private secretary who came in to do his work. Wore his own suits and fancy clothes. Even had his lady friends in to visit. Died there before he could serve out his sentence."

"How did you get involved?"

"I'd done my prosecutorial work in the Rackets Bureau, trying to bust organized criminals who were taking over the town. Did I hear you say you're a detective, young man?"

Mike explained his assignment to Lockhart. At the same time, I tried to remember what my father had told me about the workings of neurons and the degeneration of brain tissue, how some contemporary memories become completely inaccessible but events deep in the past could be as distinct as if they had occurred the day before.

"Perhaps you've heard stories about the island in my day?" he asked.

"Not really."

"First thing they did, turn of the last century, was change its name. Not to Roosevelt, mind you. That didn't happen until after the Second World War. But for a brief time they called it Welfare Island.

"Most people thought Blackwells was cursed. The city closed down most of the hospitals and moved the sick and insane to more benign places. All shut down, except for the penitentiary. Ever hear of Dutch Schultz?"

"Sure," Mike answered. "Arthur Flegenheimer. Legendary mobster. Controlled a lot of business in the city."

Orlyn Lockhart zoned out on me. He had found a responsive audience in Mike and was playing to him. "I put his right-hand man away." He was tapping his forefinger against his chest. "I tried the case myself. Joseph Reggio. Know that name, too?"

"Harlem racketeer. Probably the number two guy in the mob at the time."

"Convicted him of extortion, ran the beer and soda water trade. Word got back to us, down at the district attorney's office, that Reggio had set himself up in prison like a king. He'd bribed all the authorities to get the inmates in the jail's clinic moved out to the general population. Reggio took over and made that infirmary his home. Dressed in silk robes and used lavender cologne. Cultivated a nice garden, kept a pet cow to get his own milk. Dined on the finest steaks and wines in his own apartment."

"In the *penitentiary*?"

"Two of them, there were, took over the prison hospital. Reggio ran his men, and the Irish hoodlums were led by a guy called Edward Cleary. That's the guy who kept his German shepherd with him in his room. Named it Screw Hater. 'Screws' are what they used to call the guards. Both of these toughs kept homing pigeons with them. Actual cotes of birds that carried notes—and probably narcotics—in and out of the jail."

"These two mobsters swaggered around while the regular crooks waited on them like slaves. Sad part is that the men who really needed medical treatment were just dumped into the general population. All the boys with social diseases—that's what we used to call it back then—they were mixing freely with the

healthy ones. The whole place was a sea of misery. Full of degen-
erates. Faded tigers."

"Excuse me?"

"Didn't you ever read Dickens, young lady? When he visited
New York, he asked to be taken to see old Blackwells."

I thought I had plowed through most of him in my undergraduate days, but the phrase didn't sound at all familiar. Perhaps that explained why Dickens's sketch was on Lola Dakota's
bulletin board. Just one more notable figure who had connected
with this island that so fascinated her. Now what we still needed
to know was why Charlotte Voight's picture was there.

Lockhart was mumbling on about Dickens's visit to the prison,
inmates dressed in the black-and-buff garb that the Englishman
likened to faded tigers.

"Tell me about the raid," Mike said. Skip came back into the
room with chamomile tea for his grandfather and mugs of coffee
for us. He put them on the table, smiling at Mike's enthusiasm for
the tales he had heard so many times and walking back to the
kitchen. "Did you actually go along?"

"Go along, sir? MacCormick and I led the whole thing ourselves. I handpicked the detectives and wardens to come with us,
but we led the very charge into the pens. First one to fall was a
deputy warden who'd been on the take the whole time. Placed him
right under arrest."

"I'd like to have been at your side," Mike said, egging him on.

"MacCormick had this planned to the minute. Closed down the
prison switchboard so no one could call out while the raid was on.
He dispatched the first men to the hospital ward to drag out Reggio
and Cleary." Lockhart was chortling as he sipped his tea. "Guess he
was afraid to let us get at each other. So he had them taken out of
their luxurious quarters and thrown into solitary confinement."

"But you, did you go into the prison itself?"

"My boy, I can still smell it today. Most of the prisoners had
been turned into dope fiends."

"After they went inside the walls?"

"Reggio and Cleary were running a drug smuggling business in the jailhouse. That's how they got all their lackeys to keep them in style, and segregated. First thing I saw were rows of men, shivering on benches, pleading with us to let them take their drugs. Most of them were covered with needle scars, all up and down their arms. Word spread that Commissioner MacCormick was walking through the three-tiered cell block himself."

"Never happen today. They'd just show for the photo op."

"All of a sudden we heard lots of clanging and things being thrown about. I went running to see what it was. Turns out prisoners were throwing their weapons, and their drug paraphernalia, out from between their bars. Nobody wanted to be caught with contraband in their cells. I leaned over and picked up some blackened spoons, what they cooked the drugs in. Spikes they used to shoot up. Whole sets of hypodermics. Cloths soaked in a heroin solution."

"Did you find what you expected?"

"Worse than that. Far worse. Drugs of every sort. And then the weapons started coming. We took out meat cleavers, hatchets, stilettos, butcher knives. I've got pictures, missy, front page of every newspaper in the country. Skip'll show you my scrapbooks.

"These gorillas had a real pecking order. The two at the top had their henchmen. There were at least twenty-five of them who kept the lowlifes in line, living in the worst conditions, waiting on Reggio and Cleary, and doing it all to get narcotics. Meanwhile, the goon squad who helped the bosses lived off the fat of the land. Taken off by van every day to work at the warden's home and eat pretty well themselves."

"Did you actually see where Reggio lived?"

"You wouldn't believe the sight. Hell, I wouldn't have, unless I'd been there in the flesh. After he'd been taken out, MacCormick and I went up to see his lavish digs, just to find out whether the reports we'd gotten had been exaggerated. Hah! Not a bit. He had a large suite of rooms in the old hospital wing, all laid out with his finery. A maroon cashmere lounging robe was spread across the foot of his bed, with two pairs of shoes, shoe trees neatly in them, lined up underneath."

Lockhart was shaking his head and wringing his hands as though he were right in the middle of the scene he was describing.

"There was a locker below the window and I got one of the boys to break it open. Inside there were a dozen boxes of expensive cigars, bars of perfumed soap, monogrammed stationery, face cream, kid gloves, linen handkerchiefs." He shook his head. "Here I thought I'd condemned him to purgatory when he was sentenced to jail, and he was living far better than most folks I knew. That was before I saw his kitchen and his garden."

"His own kitchen?"

"Well, Reggio and Cleary shared a private one. The men downstairs were eating slop and gruel, just like the old days. These guys had gallons of fresh milk, crates of cranberries, fresh meat, pickled herrings, bags of potatoes. They had a pretty nice stash of liquor, too.

"Cleary, his room was a little less refined. Where Reggio had a crucifix over the bed and rosary beads beside it, Cleary had a dagger stuck in the wall over his head. I guess we'd interrupted him. There was an unplayed hand of pinochle on the table, some device up on the rafters that was concocting a home brew, and an empty pint bottle of whiskey. Screw Hater, the dog, was sitting next to the bed, trembling till we took him down and fed him one of his master's steaks. Then there was a little lounging area next to it where Cleary and his thugs spent the day, when he didn't choose to be out wandering the grounds."

"What grounds?"

"Behind the penitentiary. Reggio paid the other inmates to build him a garden. That's where he kept his milking cow and his pet goat. Beautiful spot it was, looking back over to Manhattan. He'd set up park benches and exquisite flowers, though they weren't in bloom that day. And he controlled who could enter the place. Kept the riffraff out.

"The pigeon cote was up in the roof above Cleary's room. Each of them had about two hundred birds, cooing themselves up a storm. MacCormick truly thought that's how they got messages in and out. Hell, it wouldn't have made a bit of difference. Once they'd bought the wardens, bribed them with all the mob money that Dutch Schultz could muster, they carried anything they wanted in and out the front door of the joint. Easy as that."

"So it must have been a great day for you." Mike had picked up the framed clipping and was reading the text of the story. "I've closed down a lot of joints in my time, Mr. Lockhart, but not quite the way you did. I'm impressed."

"Shut it tight. Demolished the entire building. A fortress, it was, and now it's just a pile of old stones." He pushed himself up and walked to the window at the side of the house, looking for signs of movement in the driveway. "Where's my Lola? Always brings me licorice. Those little bits of black licorice. She likes the part about the man who was killed."

"In the raid?"

"Only one hurt in the whole damn thing. Could have cost me my job."

"Why does Lola like that part?" I asked.

"Ask Lola." He shuffled back to his seat and eased himself down.

"One of the mobsters was killed?" Mike wanted to know.

"No, no. A gentleman. One of the cosseted prisoners who lived there like a lord. Paid Reggio a fortune to be mollycoddled in his own private prison aerie. That's probably why Lola liked him. He was a real gentleman. I knew him too, before he wound up in the penitentiary."

"Who was he?"

"Freeland Jennings, Detective. Wasn't half bad. Do they still talk about him?"

Mike and I exchanged glances. Neither of us had ever heard the name.

"Talk about the stooges like Dutch Schultz and Edward Cleary and everyone knows the tales, but nobody remembers the men who built the city. Freeland Jennings was a merchant, a friend of Pierre Cartier's. Cartier put him into the diamond trade and Jennings made himself a fortune. Spent half his life on ocean liners, crossing back and forth to London and Antwerp. But he was a great philanthropist, mind you. Helped Vanderbilt pay for the new opera house. Gave money to the public library and created the historical society."

"How'd he wind up inside the walls of the penitentiary?"

"Shot his wife. And I have to say, young lady"—Lockhart fixed his gaze on me and wagged his finger—"I have to say that it's a case I myself would never have prosecuted. Ariana, she was. Jennings married a foreigner. Clever, good-looking girl who had just about anything you could want. He showered her with jewels, of course, and showed her off everywhere. She'd have never been in the *Social Register,* being Italian and all, if she hadn't married Freeland. I used to play cards with him once a week, over at the University Club. Saw him just two days before the murder.

"Ariana became restless while he was abroad so much. Took up with a lover, a real rogue. It wasn't unheard of in my time, but most people kept quiet about it. Not Ariana—she flaunted it so's it was all over town. Took him to Jennings's box at the Metropolitan Opera, danced with him in public, some even say he was the father of her child."

The old man was tiring now. He'd been talking with great animation and was slowly losing steam in the process.

"It's names I have trouble remembering. Not the ones I put in jail, or the fellows I knew well, but some of these other characters. Forgive me. Anyway, Jennings was called back unexpectedly from Europe one time, and I guess he'd just had one embarrassment too many. Ariana wasn't home to greet him, but when he went out that evening, he ran into her with her beau, just strolling through the Grand Army Plaza. He made the assumption that they were just coming out of the Plaza Hotel after a rendezvous. Words were exchanged between the two men—I'm not exactly clear on what was said. But Ariana defended her lover. Right there on the street, nice people parading all around and minding their own business.

"Plain and simple, Jennings pulled a pistol and threatened his rival. The man taunted him—called him all kinds of names. Insulted his manhood. Freeland just went berserk and fired the gun. But he killed Ariana instead of her lover. Shot her once through the chest."

Lockhart thought about it for a minute. "Justifiable, is what *I* would have argued. 'Twas Ariana the cause of the whole damn mess. If she hadn't been such a loose woman—well . . . In any event, he was convicted of manslaughter."

Views about spousal murder had not changed very much over time. It was neither a new phenomenon nor a well-understood one. But that might have been enough of a reason for Lola's interest in the Freeland Jennings saga.

"And he was sentenced to the penitentiary?"

"Very same one, of course. And those convicts who weren't protected by the mob did some hard labor. Quarrying island stone and things that weren't fit for a gentleman to do. Fortunately for him, Freeland had the means to pay Reggio and Cleary for a finer lifestyle.

"That was actually their downfall. It was Freeland who complained to me about the narcotics problem. Wrote me a letter and explained to me how everything was for sale on the island. Liked his jailhouse apartment fine, he did, under the circumstances. Had a small turret in the prison, looking right out across the East River to his home on Manhattan. Paid dearly for it. He was allowed to keep some cases of wine with him and all his favorite clothes. Had a radio and headset so he could stay current on the news."

Lockhart's voice was giving out a bit. I leaned closer to hear him. "Freeland just couldn't tolerate the addiction, and what was happening to the lowest class of prisoners. Felt all those drugs coming in were making the situation dangerous for everyone. They were a scurvy bunch, desperate and violent."

"Was he killed when your cops went in with MacCormick? Did he resist—"

"Thank goodness, we had nothing to do with it. It was the thugs that got him. One of them rammed a shiv right between his ribs. Went like a stuck pig."

"Was it because he squealed about the narcotics in the penitentiary?"

Orlyn Lockhart paused. He rubbed his right eye with his hand and seemed exasperated when he spoke to me. "You're just as impatient as she is. It's Freeland's diamonds you want, just like Lola. Do you believe they're buried on Blackwells Island, too?"

22

The old man wanted to tell the story his way.

"MacCormick was right. He knew that Freeland Jennings was my friend, so he didn't think I ought to be anywhere near his quarters during the raid. As soon as my deputies seized Reggio and Cleary, their hoodlums scattered pretty quickly. Mind you, the mob lieutenants weren't even under lock and key at the time. There were a couple of dozen of them scrambling around, knowing they were about to get shipped up the river for real. These were their last moments of freedom before their corrupt world collapsed.

"Two of the most vicious broke into Jennings's apartment and cornered him there. He wasn't part of the rackets, of course, so he wasn't one of their own. They'd been treating him special only because he was paying the two top dogs for his privileges."

"They wanted his money, I guess."

"They wanted everything he had. And so a legend had grown up around my old acquaintance." He glanced back over at me. "This is the part you girls like. Story goes that what Joseph Reggio had demanded from Freeland Jennings was diamonds. Sparkling pieces of ice that could be smuggled out with ease. Forget about needing a pocket or pouch to hold them. You might actually come across an honest warden who would search in those things. Why, these'd fit inside a shoe without anybody noticing. Sneaked out in the folds of a hem when a lady visitor passed through. The most perfect currency for an imprisoned privateer."

"Did Jennings really keep diamonds in the penitentiary?"

"Well, he certainly hinted to me that he had. Did what he needed to do to stay alive."

"Did he have them right in his room?"

"This is the stuff of legends, now, son. I'm telling you what the boys told Commissioner MacCormick and me, not what I saw for myself. They said Jennings was the wily type and didn't trust any of these goons around him. Most he ever kept in his apartment were two or three gems, 'cause one of them went a long way at that time. It would have been a lot easier to hide a small stone than it was to try to conceal a stack of bills or enough gold to keep Reggio happy.

"But there were other places on the island, see, to keep his jewels."

"I realize they had the run of the penitentiary, Mr. Lockhart," Mike said, "but not access to the rest of the land beyond the jail walls."

"Ah, but you're forgetting what most of the prisoners did every day."

"Some of them had to work as caretakers in the other hospitals and asylums," I offered, still chilled by that startling fact.

"But most of them, missy, were doing hard labor. The island abounded with rich deposits of stone. Desirable building material, granite and gneiss. Most of the convicts were sent out in their striped uniforms to spend their days excavating the rock.

"And some of Reggio's men believed that Jennings had bought the services of a laborer to dig him a secure place in one of the quarries. A concealed lair in which he could secrete his cache of precious gems. That way, he didn't have to be afraid that if the thugs found everything he had in his room and robbed him of it, he'd lose his means to pay Reggio."

"So someone would smuggle the diamonds in to Mr. Jennings, and he'd use them as he needed them?"

"I suspect it was his lawyer who brought in the jewels. You know, since ancient times, there's been a universal method of carrying loose stones. You just fold them into a paper pouch, smaller than the palm of one's hand, and you can pretty much go anywhere you want, unmolested."

Lockhart was right. To this day, throughout the diamond district in midtown Manhattan and in the gem trade all over the world, the most incredibly valuable stones were carried this way—wrapped only in a thin slip of paper—in the pockets of pants and jackets of the most unlikely-looking couriers.

"Were any found during the raid?"

"Just two. Saw them myself, right in the warden's office, when one of the detectives carried them in to us. There was a rose-colored one, about the size of a pigeon's egg, sewed right into the cuff of a pair of pants. And then a crystal-clear diamond with more brilliance than the brightest star I've ever seen. It was just a small one, and it was stuffed in a tiny slit inside the leather cover of Freeland's mother's Bible that he kept next to the bed." He laughed to himself. "Guess it wouldn't occur to the thugs to look in the Lord's book.

"Problem was that one of Reggio's men—believe his name might have been Kennelly, but can't be sure—thought he could strong-arm Jennings right at the start of the raid. Knew it was his only chance to get the diamonds, and so he stormed the apartment with a cohort and demanded the gems." Lockhart was flagging now, and something had made him sad. "Blame myself, in some ways, for the fact that he died."

"How so?"

"If there really were other diamonds, well—the reason poor Freeland didn't yield to the bastards was because he thought he'd be perfectly safe during the raid."

"He knew that you and MacCormick were coming?"

"Let me say this, young man. I never betrayed a confidence of the commissioner's, but I was the one to whom Jennings was sending the letters. I certainly wanted to give his lawyer an assurance that we had heeded his message."

Lockhart stiffened in his chair and bored his eyes into Chapman's. "I wanted Jennings to understand that we believed the stories he was sending out. We should have made him safe the instant we got in. I argued with MacCormick about it, but he was all consumed with nailing the door shut on Reggio and Cleary. Just didn't figure that anything could go so very wrong."

"What happened to Jennings?"

"Kennelly and some other tough started roughing him about. They knew he had been assigned a couple of laborers to do his dirty work, but if he had actually trusted one of them to go out and bury his gems, my friend wasn't talking." He shook his head from side to side. "Might even have been smug about it because he was confident I'd be coming along.

"Whatever it was, Jennings was up against men who didn't know how to play by the rules. When they threatened him with a meat cleaver from Reggio's private kitchen, so the story goes, he picked up a sharpened knife he kept next to his bed. Beside the Bible, actually. He tried to use it to repel Kennelly, but he was no match for that animal. The two of them overpowered poor Jennings and one of them shoved the knife right between his ribs. Killed him instantly."

"And the diamonds?"

"My detectives were on these two fellows pretty quickly. Mind you, at the time, no one knew the men were in Jennings's room to find jewels. That's the story that other prisoners began to tell long after the dust settled. They both were examined quite thoroughly since we were all looking for contraband and drugs, small things that could be concealed. No jewels, my dear."

"Was the island searched?"

"By the time these stories surfaced, the penitentiary had long been abandoned and the quarries on the island had been mined of their riches. People have scoured it and fools will continue to do so well after I'm gone, if you ask me.

"Course, if I didn't have this tale to tell, probably wouldn't get a single visitor anymore. That's why Lola comes." He lifted his left arm and squinted to see the time. "She's late."

"Was Lola looking for Jennings's diamonds?"

"She may guess that I'm stupid and senile, but if Lola thinks I believe there's any other reason she's been here to visit me, she's mistaken. She's been all through my diaries, too. I suspect she's looking for clues that she thinks I've forgotten by now. Probably knows more about all my lady friends and some of the crooks I represented in my practice than she does about any buried treasure"—he smiled broadly now—"but if it keeps her coming back here to chat with me, she's welcome to them. Hell, I've answered to more important people than Lola about that."

"What do you mean?"

"Old MacCormick himself called me on the carpet many years after the raid. Thought I was living mighty high on the hog and had heard all the rumors by then. Looked me straight in the eye and asked whether Jennings had paid me off before the raid, or had I known where his stash was hidden. Even the mayor bought me a drink one night. Fiorella La Guardia. Over at the 21 Club it was. Had to know about the diamonds, he said, and whether I thought they were really there."

"What did—?"

"And Jennings's son. He was going off to Europe to fight. Middle of the Second World War. I call him Jennings's son, but all I know for sure is that his mother was Ariana. Hard to figure whether Freeland had been cuckolded by that tart before the kid was born. The boy had run through most of his old man's money and felt the diamonds were his due. He wasn't just curious. He accused me of stealing the damn things out from under my dead friend. Angry with me, he was. But it didn't make any difference. Never saw him again after that."

"Did you ever look for the diamonds yourself?"

"I only set foot on the island once, the day of the raid. No reason to go back, in my book."

"Did Lola talk to you about the deadhouse?"

He snapped his head to look at me. "You damn well must be her friend. What is it? Where is it? Damned if I ever heard that word before she sat at my feet going at me. Doesn't mean a thing to me, young lady."

"May we come back and visit you sometime, Mr. Lockhart?" Mike was on his feet, hand on the shoulder of the old guy so he didn't feel the need to stand up with us.

"Certainly, certainly you must. Come to the party next week. Skip's having a little holiday party at the house." His eyes brightened and he looked up at me. "You'll bring me some licorice, will you? And you, miss, you'll send my best to Mr. Hogan?"

Frank Hogan had been one of America's great prosecutors, before Bob Morgenthau and Paul Battaglia. He had died in 1974 after twenty-eight years as Manhattan's district attorney. I wondered anew how much of what Orlyn Lockhart had been telling us was fact, and how much was lost in the confusion of time past. Perhaps I could get some articles from the microfiche newspaper files at the New York Public Library and research the story of Freeland Jennings and the penitentiary raid.

We made our way back through the kitchen, where the professor was working on his laptop computer. He looked up as we entered the room. "Thanks for listening to my grandfather. You've just spelled me for an hour and I've gotten some work done."

Chapman was annoyed. "When I asked you about whether you'd ever called Ms. Dakota a gold digger, you jerked me around. Seems pretty obvious to me that you know she's been nagging the old man about buried treasure. You gonna tell me you haven't been party to her diamond excavations?"

Skip Lockhart stood up to face Mike. "Look, half of the stuff the guy's talking about is just nonsense he makes up, I'm sure of it. He likes to have an audience, and quite frankly, it's worn most of the family pretty thin over the years."

"But it's his story that interested you in the Blackwells project in the first place."

"Sure it is. But that's on an intellectual level. The raid really happened. The prison conditions that he probably described to you are quite accurate. I've researched all that. But my grandfather doesn't know any more about missing diamonds than you do."

"Except that he actually eyeballed two gemstones the very day of the raid. That gives some credence to the whole story, doesn't it? When will you be back in your office in the city?"

"Next Thursday, January second."

"Expect me. Early and often. And I'll want to see the reports of all your trips over to the island with Lola Dakota—and anything else that might relate to the project. Have them ready. And a list of the students who've worked on the dig with both of you."

My beeper began to vibrate as I buttoned my coat and walked out the door. I shuddered once against the cold and then a second time when I recognized Pat McKinney's home number. I opened the car door and dialed my cell phone.

"So what do you do for excitement when you and Chapman aren't making people's lives miserable?"

"That does seem to account for an inordinate amount of our

time, Pat." It was clear he was about to unload some kind of bad news on me. "Want me to think about it and get back to you?"

"I figured if you had nothing better to do today you could get yourself back over to New Jersey, to the medical center near Hackensack. Bart Frankel's car was rear-ended early this morning by a Mack truck. The truck won."

23

"If we got three choices, the only one I can rule out is suicide. Pretty hard to count on killing yourself by letting the car behind you run you off the road. Ain't always a sure thing."

It was early Saturday afternoon and the detective from Sinnelesi's office, Tony Parisi, was talking to us in the visitors' lounge at the hospital.

"Between an accident and a homicide attempt, what's your guess?"

"Tough to prove it's anything but an accident. Old shitcan of a car moving along on Route Seventeen, and a trucker comes barreling down behind it at one of those treacherous curves in the road. The driver gets distracted, hits a patch of ice, and slams on the brakes too late. Schmuck behind him just whacks him off the road into a row of trees. Splinter pie, man.

"And let me tell you, Bart was really distracted. When the news got out after that bail application yesterday and Kralovic was released, Bart was ready to crawl into a hole. If the old will to live has anything to do with getting him off the life-support machine, he ain't gonna make it. He's toast."

"What do you know about the truck?"

"Not even sure that's what it was. Hit-and-run is all we know. Somebody wanted him out of that lane real bad and then didn't even stop to see what happened. Shit, if Vinny Sinnelesi was in town, I'd put my money on him. He'll be royally pissed if Bart blew the Kralovic case for him."

"Don't you think he'll live?" I asked tentatively.

"Not a prayer. Just hooked him up so his kids could say good-bye to a warm body. They're in with him now. His lawyer claims he did one of those living wills. 'Don't crank me up again once the pump shuts off.' I'd say, you want to make sure it's curtains for Bart? You two grim reapers walk in the room and hand him one of your bona fide New York County subpoenas. *Finito*."

At least I didn't have to be paranoid that Pat McKinney was the only person who blamed me for Bart Frankel's condition. Mike ran his fingers through his dark hair, clearly troubled. He started to speak. "What—?"

"Don't even ask what you think you can do for him, Chapman. We'll be taking care of this one all on our own. You know we got real cops here in Jersey, too?"

"Yeah, but you haven't solved a friggin' case since the Lindbergh baby was kidnapped."

"Bart's one of ours, whether you liked him or not. Poor slob was thinking with his penis instead of his brain. Gettin' in bed with that Dakota dame was a stupid thing to do, but you got a long way to go to convince me he'd whack a broad or throw a case."

"Tony, I appreciate your feelings for Bart. And I understand why you're unhappy with us. But there was information he had that we needed." I was trying to dance around the fact that the prosecutor had not told us the truth. This detective had no cause to know it, and I did not want to broadcast the fact, given Bart's medical condition.

While it was possible to believe he had dropped Lola off at her building's entrance as he had claimed, it seemed hard to deny that he had then gone on to her office at King's College. He may even have taken something of significance from her desk. Something, I had hoped, that would lead us to the reason for her murder.

"Look, you got no jurisdiction here, Miss Cooper. And besides that, I don't think nobody that knew Bart even wants you on this end of the tunnel."

"Alex is being polite, pal. She isn't telling you the half of it. Executive Assistant District Attorney Bart Frankel looked the two of us in the eye and lied to us."

Parisi was unmoved.

"He fibbed about things that happened the very afternoon that Lola was killed. Not just the fact that he was sleeping with her. Where he was at the moment she died, what he was doing. He even held back for an entire week the name of the guy she walked into the building with."

Parisi bit his lip, not wanting to trust Chapman. "What do you want from me?"

"I want the chance to go to *his* office, the way he went through Lo—"

"Are you nuts or what? Don't even finish that sentence. I'm gonna take you two over to Sinnelesi's office while his main man is sucking on an air tube in a hospital bed, sneak you inside, maybe get my balls cut off in the process if anybody catches me, just 'cause you think you're gonna find something you can use to sink Bart in this even worse? Not happening, baby."

"We'll be fast. You can stay with us the whole time."

"And who's gonna hire a gone-to-seed former investigator for Vinny Sinnelesi when I get thrown out on my ass? Chapman, you've pulled a lot of crap in your day, but you ain't calling the shots on this one."

"Just for once, why don't you do something useful for society?"

"Screw you. I recycle."

"Tony, when we were up at Lily's house—Lola's sister—she told us that she had signed a power of attorney so that Vinny could go into Lola's office and remove her belongings. All of them. Who actually went and did that? Was it Bart?"

Parisi fidgeted.

"You're looking at this with blinders on. Buy into my facts for a minute. Bart went to the campus the day Lola was killed, maybe already knowing she was dead. He was searching for something. Alex and I can prove that. If he found what he wanted that day, or if he went back for it with legal authority to do so a few days later, maybe he got what he was after.

"And just suppose, for one minute, that what he discovered in Lola's office is what got him followed this morning. Got him killed."

"Suppose *you* start thinking that if there's any truth to what you're saying, I'm gonna be able to figure it out myself. It's what they pay me the big bucks to do." Parisi had given us all the time he was going to waste, so he turned on his heel and headed for the door.

"Tony, you know what to look for, right? You'll recognize all the players? Charlotte Voight, Skip Lockhart, Sylvia Foote, Freeland Jennings, the Blackwells project . . ."

Chapman was calling up every name he had heard in the past eight days, aware that none of them would ring a bell with the New Jersey detective. There was no reason for Parisi to have known them, but it worked perfectly to nag at his insecurity. His footsteps slowed.

"Twenty minutes, Tony. Just you and me. Blondie waits in the car."

My opportunity to participate in the search had just been sacrificed to the greater cause: male bonding.

"I must have a death wish. I'll meet you over at the office. Park a block away and leave her there." Parisi dismissed me with a heaving sigh and a look back over his shoulder. "Give me a ten-minute lead and I'll let you in the back door. Deal's off if any of the lawyers are in there working."

Mike checked his watch. "Saturday afternoon at three o'clock when it's eighteen degrees outside and we're in the middle of the holiday weekend? In Battaglia's office, even the cockroaches wouldn't be behind their desks."

He nudged me out of the waiting area. I walked to the nurses' station to inquire again about Bart Frankel's condition. A new face behind the desk asked me if I was family and I shook my head in the negative. "There's nothing I can tell you." Her grim expression spoke volumes.

We made the short drive to the prosecutor's office and this time, instead of using the rear parking lot, Mike stopped in front of the pizza shop at the far corner. He left the ignition on so that I could have the benefits of the heat and the radio.

"You mind?"

"I always knew I'd be the first thing to go. Come back with something good and I'll forgive you."

It was close to half an hour later when Mike returned to the car. The wind blew in with him as he opened the door and got back into the driver's seat. "I wouldn't say we hit the jackpot, but we got a few things to work with. This stuff would have sat in Sinnelesi's drawer till you started sprouting gray hair underneath that peroxide before anybody would have told us about it.

"First of all, Bart Frankel was—as a tribute to modern medicine, I'll say is—up to his ass in debt. Left his private practice, which wasn't exactly a thriving one, to come back to public service when the Fat Man called him. Paying a huge amount of alimony 'cause his ex has a serious medical problem. Three kids, two in college and one getting ready to go. And a slight penchant for the horses. The Meadowlands was his second home. Gambling debts running close to a quarter of a million."

Hard to do on a prosecutor's salary.

"What do you know about penny stocks, Coop? I mean the kinds that are bad schemes."

"The basics, why?"

"Explain 'em to me. I Xeroxed a file that was on top of Bart's desk, but I don't know anything about that business."

"They're generally really cheap stocks in small, sometimes dubious companies. A lot of them have involved investment scams. There are salesmen who make cold calls by telephone, just reading from a script. The guys behind the scam pump up the shares by fake trades and false publicity. When the stock soars, the promoters generally cash in and leave the other investors holding worthless shares."

"Ever hear of"—Mike looked down at the tab on the manila folder—"Jersey First Securities?"

"No."

"Seems like Sinnelesi's been investigating the company. The two partners behind the business are about to declare bankruptcy, and it looks like the note on the file quotes the feds as saying this was a 'continuing massive fraud.' And one of the penny-meisters is—"

"Ivan Kralovic, of course."

"So it would seem. And who lost lots of nickels and dimes betting on Ivan's pot?"

"Bart?"

"So when Vinny gets back from the sunny south, maybe he can explain to you why he'd let Bart anywhere near this investigation. Hold on to the file. Now, exhibit number two. Here's a photocopy of a little envelope," Mike said, holding up an image of a tiny white packet that looked no longer than three inches. "You recognize the penmanship?"

I did. It was Dakota's.

"Can't say I'm as familiar with it as you are, but when I saw the little Post-it attached with the initials L.D., I took a wild guess."

I looked at the single word printed on the front by Lola: "Blackwells."

"I lifted the flap and guess what slipped into my hand?"

I shook my head at Mike, puzzled.

"A little gold key. No markings, no numbers."

"Was there anything else with this?"

"Nope. It was buried under a few personal notes in his top drawer. Now all we have to do is find out what it fits into. Get one of your clones started on a warrant."

He revved up the engine and made a U-turn on the quiet street. "And last but not least, we're going to meet Dr. Claude Lavery."

"Now? Is he back? Why—"

"Because that's who Bart Frankel was on his way to see this morning when he was so rudely interrupted."

24

"Tony Parisi told you about Lavery?"

"No, he called over to Bart's house. I almost had him convinced after a once-over of Bart's office that he should walk me through his home to see if we could find anything. You know that if Bart's life was as screwed up as it sounds, he's probably got stuff there that we should be looking at. Anyway, one of his kids had taken a break from the hospital vigil and answered the phone, which put the kibosh on that idea for the moment."

I couldn't imagine what this was like for Bart's three children.

"But when Tony asked the daughter why her dad had left the house so early this morning, she said that a man had called him last night and Bart had told her that he had to go into the city to see him. There was a pad next to the telephone that had Lavery's name and number written on it."

"Not bad for a quick sweep through the office."

"Hey, easier than if I had to search your place for anything of value. You got four extra pairs of shoes under the desk, different-height heels for every occasion. Drawers filled with panty hose, nail polish, perfume, and Extra-Strength Tylenol. Somebody bumps you off and the first thing Battaglia has to do is run a tag sale to get rid of your beauty supplies."

Mike was enthused now. He had new directions in which to proceed and pieces of the puzzle to try to fit into place. "How do you even begin to figure out the significance of a key? And how do you know what door it fits?"

"Start with the fact that it's labeled 'Blackwells.'"

"Yeah, but there aren't a lot of buildings still standing on the island from those days. And the remnants that are there don't have doors."

"So it's something connected to the project, probably."

"I think even two hours' exposure to New Jersey has damaged your brain. No kidding, Coop. Like I needed your help to figure that one out."

"Were any of the things taken from Lola's office, after Lily gave Sinnelesi permission, listed and inventoried so we have a record of them?"

"Nope. Would it surprise you to learn that Bart Frankel picked two of his squad cops, drove over himself, and just sort of packed up the whole bundle to be sorted out at his convenience? In the privacy of his office. Somehow that stinks as bad as the rest of what he was doing."

"Where is the stuff now?"

"Parisi doesn't know. He'll have to find the guys who went with Bart and see what closet they dumped everything into."

"Sooner rather than later. We've got to see what he found."

"Give me credit for something, Coop. I do believe I've lit that fire under Parisi's ass."

"You think Lola knew, when she got into bed with Bart, that he had lost all his money in one of Ivan's deals?"

"Hard to imagine that it wouldn't have come up in conversation. Gave them both a reason to hate the guy. And it gave Bart an extra incentive to go after Ivan."

I thought for several minutes. "That's one way to look at it. But there's a darker side to that. Suppose Ivan's about to get jammed up by Sinnelesi's office. The number two man is up to his ears in debt, and Ivan knows why. What if he tried to buy his way out of the whole thing—two cases at the same time? I mean, how could Bart have screwed up Lola's undercover sting so badly? Bad enough that Ivan's back on the street. You'd have to try awfully hard to step on yourself that way."

Mike was with me. "So you go as far as having Bart getting paid off by Ivan. Bart maybe even delivering Lola right into the killer's hands. Dropping her off at her front door. *Ciao,* baby, see you later. Then he drives off into the sunset, stopping by the campus to pick up the key—the key to . . . ? That's sort of where the plan gets parked with me."

"I'm not saying that's what I think happened. I just know I'm praying for Bart's recovery for all the wrong reasons. I'd love him to answer some questions for us."

On the ride back to the city we thought aloud about all the possible links among Ivan's fraud investigation, the domestic violence complaints, and Lola's death.

The scene in front of 417 Riverside Drive was a much calmer one than the one the night of the murder. Mike rang the bell in the vestibule next to Lavery's name and within a minute, through the intercom, a voice said, "Yes?"

Mike muffled his mouth with his hand and spoke a single word: "Bart." "Bart" was a few hours late, but still welcome enough for Lavery to buzz us into the lobby. We entered together and walked to the elevator.

When we reached the sixteenth floor, the door to Lavery's apartment was ajar. I could hear someone speaking on the telephone, so I pushed it wider and Mike came inside behind me. The man whom we assumed to be Lavery was standing with his back to us. His conversation was ending, and he thanked his caller before he hung up and turned around, startled to see us.

"I'm Mike Chapman. NYPD Homicide," Mike said, flipping his gold shield out of its case. "This is Alexandra Cooper. Manhattan DA's Office. We've been—"

"Not exactly who I was expecting when I let you in, Detective." Lavery walked to the doorway behind us and stuck his head out in the hallway. "Is Bart coming along, too?"

I could sense that if Lavery did not yet know about Bart's accident, Mike wasn't going to tell him. "He's had a rough day. I doubt he's gonna make it."

Lavery was clearly puzzled. He walked to the CD player on the bookshelf along the far wall and lowered the volume. If Chapman had been expecting Bob Marley and the Wailers, with Lavery smoking weed through a wooden pipe, he must have been disappointed. A Beethoven adagio provided the soft background to our conversation. Lavery had apparently been sitting at a desk in front of his park-view window, working longhand on some piece of writing. He was dressed in African garb and still had his hair done in dreadlocks.

"Bart's been a friend of ours for a long time. He decided, after you two spoke on the phone, that he really didn't want to meet with you alone. He thinks it would be better if you say what you want to say to the two of us."

Lavery's expression gave nothing away, but he seemed too smart to trust the situation. Or the cop who was giving him the once-over.

He folded his arms across his chest and looked at me. "Aren't you the woman handling the investigation into Lola Dakota's death? I recognize your name from the news stories." His voice was a deep baritone, and he spoke in a measured cadence.

"Yes, we're both working on that case."

"Lola was a dear friend of mine. And a great supporter, in what have been some difficult days for me." He turned away to walk to a living area, motioning us to follow. "I suppose you've heard about that?" He asked it in the form of a question, not quite sure what to think.

"Yeah, we know a bit about it."

"Lola has stood by me from the outset. Taken my part with the administration. I shall miss her friendship terribly."

"Actually, that's what we'd like to talk to you about. We've been trying to reach you—"

"Would you mind if I called Bart, Detective? I'd prefer to—"

"Bart's out of the picture, Mr. Lavery. For the time—"

"Doctor. It's *Doctor* Lavery." He lowered himself into an armchair and we sat opposite him.

"You got a stethoscope, a prescription pad, and a license to practice medicine, then I'll call you 'doctor.' Every other ologist who writes a dissertation on some useless theoretical load of crap is just plain old 'mister' to me."

"Professor . . ." I tried to start anew.

"Ah, the diplomat on the team."

"Yeah, the Madeleine Albright of the Manhattan District Attorney's Office. She wants to know the same thing I do. Bart was kind of surprised when you called. He didn't know you were back in New York."

"I arrived home last evening. Around eleven o'clock."

"We've been trying to interview all of Ms. Dakota's associates and friends. I hope you don't mind if we ask a few questions?" I tried smiling at him. "They're quite routine."

"If it will assist you in finding the beast who did this, I'm pleased to help."

"When did you leave town, Professor? I mean, where were you coming from last evening?"

"I flew to visit friends during Christmas week. Went to St. Thomas, in the Caribbean."

"When did you leave town exactly?"

"On December twenty-first, I've still got the ticket right here. I can show it to you, if that's necessary."

"That's two days after Lola was killed. Last Saturday, am I right?"

"I guess it was. I debated about staying for her funeral in New Jersey on Monday, but my friends were expecting me and I didn't think there was anything I could do to be useful. Many of our colleagues didn't share Lola's feelings about my work."

"The guys from my squad canvassed the building on Friday. Miss Cooper and I have read those reports. I understand you were here in the apartment on the afternoon of the murder."

"Yes, I talked to the police. Of course, I have no idea what time it was when all this happened to Lola."

"Don't worry about that. Why don't you just tell us what you were doing that day?"

"Thursday the nineteenth . . . let me think a moment. Most days, I work from my home instead of the office over at King's. As you must be aware, I've been suspended from the college while they examine this glitch with my grant."

A several-hundred-thousand-dollar glitch, I thought to myself.

"I seem to recall going out in the morning to pick up some things I needed for the trip. The drugstore, the bank, the film shop. That sort of thing. It was snowing, and I remember coming home to work on a study that I've had to write up for the government. Never went outside again. I sat right at this table and kept looking across as the snow covered the bare limbs of the trees in Riverside Park, thinking over and over again that I'd be swimming in turquoise waters in a matter of days.

"Frivolous thoughts, really, when I heard later what had been going on down below. With Lola, I mean. I didn't hear the slightest bit of disturbance. I think that's what will always torment me."

Lavery seemed to be sincerely troubled.

"No loud voices arguing? No screams? No sounds of a struggle?"

"Exactly what does a struggle sound like, Detective?"

Mike was stumped. There had been no furniture overturned in Lola's apartment, no bruising to suggest a prolonged attack by her assailant. Just a wool scarf that had been pulled too tight for too long around her neck. It had caused her to be unable to breathe, and perhaps unable to scream as well.

"I have this tendency, you see, to sit here at my writing table, absorbed in my work no matter what kind of commotion is going on around me or outside on the street. It's a trait that has served me quite well in my career. And when I'm here at home, I've always got music playing. Sometimes a bit too loud, but then these old buildings were really built solid. They absorb the noise pretty well. Every now and then," Lavery said with a slight grin, "after a particularly booming crescendo, my friend Lola would bang on the pipes that ran up through her living room into mine.

"But the day she died," he said, somber again, "I can't say I heard anything at all."

"How well did you know Ms. Dakota?"

"Quite well, both professionally and socially. We were in different disciplines, of course, but she was a bit of a maverick, as I am, and she was interested in my approach to the urban drug problem. Away from the school, we spent some time together, too."

"Did you ever date?"

"Nothing like that. But we could sit up till the middle of the night, arguing about solutions for the homeless or the mentally ill. There was no off switch to Lola. She was always thinking and working and doing."

"Had you seen much of her in the days before her death?"

He took a long time to answer. "I have become so engulfed in my own legal entanglements, unfortunately, that I've tended to push most of my friends out of the way. I'm trying to recall the last time Lola and I had a good, long go-at-it together."

"How about a short one? How about a sighting?"

"I know I saw her the week of Thanksgiving. I remember coming in with a lot of groceries and stopping by to talk with her for a while on my way upstairs. Have a drink. Then she was off to her sister's home, and—I simply can't summon up any other time that I saw her."

Was he lying to us, or had Bart Frankel been mistaken when he told us he had left Lola at the door because she saw Lavery going into the building?

Chapman had nothing to lose at this point. "The day she died, like half an hour before she was killed, did you happen to run into her, right at the front door of the building?"

Lavery was biting the inside of his cheek, looking perplexed. "I may have gone down to the lobby once in the afternoon to get the mail, but after I came back from my errand that morning I'm absolutely certain I never went back outside. Where would you have heard something like that?"

"How do you know Bart Frankel?"

"He was in charge of her case, Ms. Cooper. He had come to the apartment once or twice to bring Lola papers to sign. I think that's what she told me. And to help prepare her for their plan to build the case against her husband, Mr. Kerlovic."

"Kralovic."

"I didn't know the man. I'm not really sure what his name was. One time, I ran into Lola with Bart Frankel at a restaurant in the neighborhood. I guess she had come to rely on him in these last difficult weeks."

"How come you called Bart last night and asked him to meet with you?"

Now he was growing more wary. "Well, Detective, either Bart told you the answer to that question when he asked you to come here, or you've pulled one over on me." He walked to his desk and picked up the receiver, looking at a number on the piece of paper next to the phone. "Shall I just call him and clear this up?"

Mike stood up, too. "No, but Bart did tell us he saw you walk into this building, holding the door open for Lola, about half an hour before she was killed."

"And *I'm* telling you that statement is not true, Mr. Chapman." Lavery started to dial.

"We'll have to resolve this some other way, Mr. Lavery. All you're gonna get is a machine. Or maybe one of Bart's kids. He's in the hospital. His car ran off the road this morning on his way here to see you."

Lavery replaced the receiver. "Was he hurt badly?"

"Probably won't make it."

The professor winced and sat down at his desk.

"You wanna explain to us why you called him to come talk to you? Tell us what you were planning on telling him?"

He looked up at Chapman to answer. "I didn't have anything to say to him."

"But you called him. Even his daughter can confirm that."

"I got back from my trip last night and among the messages on my answering machine was one to call Bart Frankel. He reminded me what his connection to Lola had been, and he left his home phone number in New Jersey."

By the end of next week, telephone records might again resolve the issue for us, but at the moment I did not know whether to believe him.

"Did he say what he wanted?"

I sensed that Lavery thought he had regained the upper hand. His tone was cool once more, and almost arrogant as he talked to us. "Not at all. Just that he needed to see me. I assumed it was about Lola's case."

"He was taken off that investigation. He's—"

"And I've been out of the country, Detective. Staying at a beach house in the islands with no television and with newspapers that arrived about three days after they hit the stands in Miami. So I don't have the faintest idea what's been going on up here. Why was he taken off the case? Would you like to bring me up-to-date?"

Mike ignored his question. "Did Lola talk to you about the Blackwells project?"

"Of course she did. It had consumed her these past few months. We're a relatively small faculty, Detective, compared to those at large universities like Harvard and Yale. I'd had my enemies when I first came over to King's, but we've generally tried to work it out among ourselves. When I was hired, the head of the anthropology department didn't want me working under his watch."

"Winston Shreve?"

"Precisely. But then Lola went to work on Shreve, on my behalf. I wouldn't say he's my close friend, but he accepted me within his division and has been rather kind to me lately, with all the troubles I've had. And Grenier, he's in charge of the biology division. He was a bit more anxious to have me.

"Now, if you're spending any time with those three—Dakota, Shreve, and Grenier—you can be sure the subject of Blackwells will come up," he said. "That's what they've spent most of their time working on for the better part of the year. And Lockhart. I'd say he's their fourth Musketeer."

"Have you had anything to do with the project yourself?"

"I live in the present, Ms. Cooper. Oh, they talk to me about what they're doing, and they ask me plenty of questions about it."

"Like what?"

"I think when Lola first found out about the drug trade in the old penitentiary, three-quarters of a century ago, she was amazed at the scale of the problem. But it was quite a famous scandal, and of course, I'm familiar with the history of the drug culture in this city. So I was able to explain to her what the drugs of choice were in those days and how widespread the narcotics business was— even inside American penal institutions."

"And Grenier, what was his relationship with Lola?"

"I bet you've had a hard time getting him to come to the table, haven't you?" Lavery wasn't wrong. I was hoping that by Monday we would have word from Sylvia Foote that the biology professor was back and available to us.

"Why do you say that?"

"Because Thomas Grenier is a selfish son of a bitch and it would be quite out of character if he was any use in a matter like this."

"We've been told that Grenier was actually willing to bring you into his department, when Shreve and the others weren't all that interested in having you in anthropology."

"That's true, Detective. But not because he had any belief in what I was doing. He saw it as a business proposition. It put dollar signs in front of his eyes, not mortarboards."

Both Mike and I were lost. "I never knew that money was so much of an issue in academia," I said.

"Then I would guess that you've never met Thomas Grenier. And you have no idea what the Internet has done to the college campus. Not in the classroom alone, but as universities have tried to cash in on the commercial market."

"Would you mind telling us what you mean?"

"It used to be, Ms. Cooper, that the idea of an academic making money from his research was not acceptable at any university. I'm not talking about *my* situation, if that's what you're thinking. There has always been a perception that we scholars are outside the marketplace, and we've long benefited from that. We've been giving away our knowledge for generations. Now many of the large institutions are looking to get a fair return on their intellectual capital. Turn it into financial capital, like the rest of the world."

"And the Internet?"

"It's a gold mine. It provides a much larger payback, and a much faster one, too. There's a lot of competition in the dot-com community, and administrators everywhere are trying to foster various opportunities to let faculty members increase their income—through the expanded use of their research—and let the universities themselves share in the bounty. That's the big score. I'm surprised you haven't read about this. Front page of *The Times* a short while ago. Grenier was a key player."

"I just do the sports page, comics, horoscope, and 'Dear Abby.' Tell me about it."

"Columbia University has sort of led the field in this business. The vice provost there has promoted the efforts of some of his professors to joint-venture with Internet start-ups. They've partnered with an on-line company to do a human nutrition study. And made money by mating with that junk-bond character, Michael Milken, in a curriculum of serious college courses. They've already made millions from that."

"What's the flap?"

"Well, under the old rules, Mr. Chapman, we professors owned the rights to any books and articles that were published. The institution itself owned the patents from our research, and we were lucky to get a quarter of the revenue. Columbia started a new policy last year. It allows the university to retain rights to Internet projects that are supported by Columbia's funds, or make substantial use of its labor, but professors can get a greater share in the revenue."

"And Grenier's role?"

"A lot of these Internet companies with a significant amount of venture capital have been sniffing around the campuses. Biology is one of the fields in which they figure they can buy a lot of research rather cheaply. And turn it into gold. Grenier was sort of pushed out of the department at Columbia. Couldn't get along with some of the favorites there. A bit too heavy-handed. He came here and is trying to get the same kind of interest revved up on the King's College campus.

"These biotech companies are all looking for major drug studies. Think of the return on an investment when you have some brilliant graduate student, not costing you a dime in salary, toiling over his laboratory test tubes all day. Guided by a professor whose income is just a fraction of what the corporate executives make."

"What's the problem?"

"A major conflict with the new president here, Paolo Recantati. He'd like to have firmer control over decisions on what type of research the college should support. He's a purist. He thinks there can be terrible fallout when the faculty or the college has a stake in the financial result of its work."

"Did Lola and Thomas Grenier get along?"

"Until she found out that he was trying to use me. That he had not been very candid about why he was interested in me. It turned out not to be for the reasons he expressed to the administration."

Long-term studies of health problems connected to substance abuse, if I remembered what Sylvia Foote had told us. Lavery chuckled. "Lola turned on Grenier like a rattlesnake on its prey. Ready to strike in a flash. If he said something was black, Lola said it was white. You know what I mean, I'm sure."

"When was that?"

"Early this fall, a few months back."

"What is it he really wanted from you?"

Lavery laughed more heartily. "What do you know about Viagra, Detective?"

"Not enough."

"Viagra's main ingredient comes from the poppy. The same seedpod that brings you opium and heroin. It works by increasing the blood flow directly to the penis. But it's had some disastrous side effects, as you're probably aware. It doesn't mix well with other medications.

"So a lot of pharmaceutical companies have been searching for a better fix, a healthier solution to an age-old problem. And nobody on the faculty knows the poppy as well as I do, in the professional sense. Grenier had made a deal with one of the large drug companies to lead the research team. He simply neglected to cut me in on any of the potential profit."

"Did you two have a falling-out?"

"We didn't come to blows with each other, but it hasn't been pretty. I don't like being taken advantage of."

"Where did Lola stand in this?"

"With me, Detective. I can't say she has any personal regard for Grenier."

"But they still worked together on the Blackwells business?"

"I'm not sure the sandbox was big enough for both of them, but she tried to make do."

"Did you know about the legend of Freeland Jennings's diamonds?"

Lavery pushed away from the desk and laughed again. "Of course I did. That's one of the things Lola and I used to argue about late into the night. Do this dig for whatever historical purposes interest you, I used to tell her. There's a lot of sorry history of this city on that island—a storehouse of human misery. But don't be wasting your energy on some far-fetched tale that may not even have been true."

"Is that what kept Thomas Grenier and Lola Dakota together?"

"Don't be ridiculous. The man is a scientist. He thought that Lola was foolish to have believed the diamonds were still in the ground. His interest in the island is strictly scientific."

"What's in it for him?"

"Grenier again expects to profit from the work the students will be doing when they study the Smallpox Hospital. There's enormous debate in the field of medical ethics about whether or not the smallpox virus should be completely eradicated when the disease is conquered worldwide. Since you need the actual virus to make the vaccine, does one save a small amount of it against the day that some form of the pox reappears in the world? And who is the keeper of the deadly virus? Whom do we trust not to engage in germ warfare?"

"And obviously, some biotech company would support this project, hoping that a study of all the plagues treated on Blackwells Island a century ago would be useful to scientists making determinations about the future," I reasoned.

"Exactly. It's hard to think of any other finite stretch of land, isolated from the population, which institutionalized, treated, and buried so many of society's untouchables. That's why Grenier loves it there."

"Does this venture of his have a name?"

Lavery paused for a few moments and then shook his head. "I should know it, but it's not coming to me right now. You'll have to ask him yourself. Some fairly gruesome pox-related thing. Lola used to joke and call it deadhouse dot com."

"Deadhouse?"

"That's how Lola referred to the island."

"Do you know why?" It appeared that the phrase was not as mysterious as it had seemed when we first encountered the word on a piece of paper in her apartment.

"You know that a lot of the interns who worked on the project refused to be involved with the plans at that old smallpox hospital? They're enthralled with the insane asylum and the penitentiary, but that abandoned hospital spooks the best of them. Many of those who aren't science majors believe that they might dig up things that are still germ infested, that contagion lurks even now in some of the objects that were buried a century ago. They simply don't want anything to do with all that deadly history."

"Did you ever go with her to Blackwells—I mean, to Roosevelt Island?"

"Only three or four times. She walked me through the area they call the Octagon, with that magnificent staircase. And of course we had to see the remains of the hospital. I'd always wondered what it was, from this side of the water."

"Would you mind, Professor, if I asked you about the accusations concerning the misappropriation of the grant money?" It seemed unusual that Lola would be such an advocate for Lavery, under the circumstances that Sylvia Foote had described.

His mood changed again and he stiffened. "I have an attorney, Ms. Cooper, and I've been instructed not to discuss this matter with anyone out of his presence."

Chapman veered off in another direction. "You know anything about this kid Julian Gariano? The one who hanged himself last weekend?"

It was hard to discern whether Lavery had a good poker face or truly had never crossed paths with the campus drug dealer. "Gariano? The name doesn't sound familiar to me. Was he a King's student? It must have happened after I left for the Caribbean."

"One more thing, Professor. There's a young woman who was a junior at the college last year. I don't believe she was in any of your classes, but I understand she had a problem with drugs, and I thought perhaps you might have heard something about her disappearance. Her name is Voight. Charlotte Voight."

"I had heard that she had dropped out, although I didn't know her either. The administration always circulates a notice to the faculty if something unusual happens or if a student withdraws from classes without an official leave. These kids are often going through a tough time, and one of us might be a lifeline to them. Dropping out is nothing new for college students, is it?"

Lavery stopped speaking for a moment, then looked up at me. "But Charlotte Voight is back around, isn't she?"

Perhaps Lavery had information we didn't. "That's news to us. Any clue where she is?"

"No, I have no idea. But the last time I talked to Lola, that's what she told me. That she knew where the Voight girl was, and that she was going to see her."

25

Each time I thought we were about to take a step or two forward, we were thrown back five or six. Mike had pushed Lavery hard on when it was that Lola Dakota had told him she was going to see the missing girl. If the professor was being truthful, he had not seen his neighbor for almost one month. But if Bart had been honest, then Lavery might have heard that news from Lola within an hour of her death.

Either way, the effort before us grew larger rather than focused. Had Charlotte Voight returned to the King's College campus a few days before Christmas, ready to attempt to reenter school for the new semester? Did her reappearance have anything to do with the suicide of her former lover, Julian Gariano, who had supplied her with drugs? And who else other than Lola knew where the girl was?

There were significant discrepancies between the story told to us by Bart Frankel and the facts as reported by Claude Lavery. Each of them was undoubtedly lying about something. Lavery seemed to paint a flawed picture of each of his colleagues while underscoring the feuding world of academic politics. And why wouldn't Lavery admit that he had seen and spoken with Lola Dakota when she had returned to the building just a short time before she was killed?

"We've got to sit down on Monday morning and map out all these connections. I'm so tired and emotionally drained at this point. It's lucky that no one from Special Victims beeped me these last two days." The clock on the dashboard of Mike's car was slow, but it was already close to seven o'clock in the evening as we headed downtown from Lavery's apartment. "The last thing I need is a handful of new complaints."

"It's Fleet Week, isn't it?"

"Yes, and I'm delighted that everybody's so well behaved this season. That's usually good for five or six cases." From time to time, when a special event like the Fourth of July or New Year's called for it, a large contingent of warships would gather in New York's ports and harbor. There were festivities aboard as well as up and down the Hudson River. But sometimes, when the sailors who had been at sea for long stretches reached Gotham City, the parties got out of control.

"Maybe the guys don't even bother coming ashore anymore. Maybe 'don't ask, don't tell' is working better than anybody thinks."

"And maybe I'll just keep my fingers crossed for a quiet evening. Jake's supposed to be back from D.C. by now. We'll probably run up to Butterfield 81 for a steak. Why don't you hang out with us?"

"'Cause I've got a date. I'm gonna drop you off and go over to her place for dinner."

"And she is . . . ?"

"A good cook."

"That's all you're telling me?"

"I'm not ready to go public." He grinned at me. "You're worse than my mother."

"Well, you've been much too secretive about what you're up to. Makes me suspect something more serious is going on. I hate to say the *i* word, but I'm beginning to believe that you're actually involved with someone. Especially after that heart-to-heart talk you had with me on our way home from Mercer's house."

"You'll be the first to know, blondie."

Mike dropped me at the entrance to Jake's building and the doorman helped me out of the car. "Mr. Tyler just came in himself a few minutes ago, ma'am. Asked if I'd seen you this evening."

"Thanks, Richard." I took the elevator upstairs and slipped my key in the lock. Jake was on the StairMaster in his den, a set of headphones linking him to yet another cycle of news on the television in front of him. He didn't see me come in. I took off my coat and gloves and sat in the leather chair behind him, waiting until he finished his exercise and stepped off the machine.

"I'm not so bad to come home to, am I?" he asked, walking over to kiss me on the nose. "Have you and Chapman solved this one yet? I've given you a week."

"My brain is spinning. Can we talk about *your* day?"

"I'll take a quick shower and then we can head out for dinner, okay?"

Despite the cold wind, we walked uptown to the restaurant, passing storefronts with their Christmas decorations and, now, all the signs for postholiday sales. We settled into a quiet corner banquette, and the dark, handsome decor of the room suited my mood. I was brooding about the week's events and the gloom that had enveloped this season that I so loved. Jake devoured his steak while I swiped a few of his perfect *pommes frites* to go along with my soup and salad, and we sipped a wonderful Burgundy.

By the time we were ready to go home, the temperature had dropped precipitously and we hailed a cab on Lexington Avenue to take us to the apartment. Once inside, I undressed and got into bed alongside Jake. I fell asleep with the lights still on and Jake still flipping the channels. When a nightmare awakened me at 3 A.M., I cradled myself against his body and tried to push out of my mind the autopsy photographs of Lola Dakota.

I had already bathed and dressed by the time he opened his eyes on Sunday morning. The coffee beans were ground and brewed, and I had taken the newspaper in from the doormat. Jake went into the kitchen and opened the refrigerator door.

"Scrambled? Sunny-side up? Omelette?"

"One egg over easy."

He looked over my shoulder at the paper. "Why do you start with the obituaries? Looking for business? Or are you just reading it, as my father used to say, to make sure your own name isn't in it?"

I put the section aside and set the table for breakfast. We lingered in the dining room for more than an hour, Jake working the Sunday crossword puzzle while I was determined to finish the tougher Saturday maze.

"What shall we do today?"

"How about the Frick? They've got an exhibition of Velázquez paintings. We can walk over there, spend an hour or two, and then come home and I can do some paperwork on the case."

"Are you all set for New Year's Eve? I mean, this won't get in the way, will it?"

"I expect it'll be fine." Joan Stafford was giving a dinner party for five couples in Washington. We were going to take a late afternoon shuttle down on Tuesday and spend the night with Joan and Jim, coming back early the next morning now that Mercer and Vickee had included us in their wedding plans.

This was the one holiday I hated. There was such an artificial air about the forced gaiety, and my favorite way of celebrating had always been to stay at home with friends. Joan was a superb hostess, and the idea of laughing and relaxing with her in front of a great fire, dining at her elegant table, then climbing the stairs to curl up for the night in the guest room of her Georgetown town house seemed a delightful way to welcome in another year.

"There's a winter storm warning for tomorrow evening. I guess we can always take the Metroliner."

I was rinsing the dishes when the phone rang for the first time. Jake came back into the kitchen and put his arms around me, embracing me from behind and pressing his mouth against the top of my head. "That was Mike, darling."

"I've been waiting for this call." Tears had already formed and I fought them back.

"Bart Frankel died. They disconnected the life support this morning." He tried to turn me around to face him, but I stood at the sink, staring out the window at the gray day while the hot water ran over my hands. "I just want to hold you for a minute, Alex."

I shook my head.

"You're going to have to let me in one of these days." Jake rubbed his hand across my back. "Mike said to tell you he's got the search warrant for Frankel's office. He's on his way to New Jersey to get it signed so he can pick up the evidence this afternoon." He was massaging my neck with his right hand, his left still holding my waist. "This isn't your fault."

I didn't blame myself for Bart's death, but I was pained by the unfortunate chain of events that had been created from the moment Lola placed herself in the hands of Vinny Sinnelesi. She had just wanted to extricate herself from the violent relationship with Ivan Kralovic, but instead had become a pawn in the prosecutor's efforts to stage a sensational vote-getting stunt. So often I had heard Paul Battaglia remind his senior staff that you can't play politics with people's lives. I admired his wisdom.

Bart had clearly been in greater turmoil than anyone knew. Now he had died under circumstances that were at best mysterious, with his reputation tarnished and his debts substantial. And the children, I suddenly remembered, squeezing my eyes shut. There were three children who had to cope with both loss and disgrace.

I leaned over the sink, cupping my hands and filling them with steaming water, holding them against my eyes. "Let's take a walk, okay?"

I held on to Jake's arm as we made our way uptown to the small museum at the corner of Fifth Avenue and Seventieth Street. I tried to explain my feelings, speaking as the frost grabbed at my breath and formed rings that rose in the icy air. The need to explore the lives of the people whose tragedies came our way took us to intimate places I had no more desire to enter than the deceased would have had to let me in. For me, it was impossible to do this work with a clinical remove. I could evaluate evidence dispassionately, and I could make judgments about witness credibility with precision, but there was an emotional pull that nagged at my heart with every life that was lost.

We strolled through the stunning exhibit, on loan from the Prado in Madrid. When we had seen our fill of royal portraits, we reclaimed our things from the cloakroom and walked around the corner to Madison Avenue for a cup of hot chocolate. We had almost reached home when my beeper went off.

I saw the complaint-room number and stopped in the doorway to take out my cell phone. The supervisor answered and I identified myself. "It's Alexandra Cooper. What's up?"

"There's a woman looking for you. Her name is Sylvia Foote. Says she's a lawyer for King's College. Claims she even has your home number but can't find you anywhere, so I thought you wouldn't mind the beep."

"Not at all." I had given Sylvia all my contact numbers before the window was broken at my apartment, and had forgotten to check my machine in two days. I could have kicked myself. "Did she say how long she's been trying to get me?"

"Just an hour or two. She left a number." I recognized her office phone. "While I have you, Alex, can I ask you something about a case that just came in?"

"Sure."

"Cops in Central Park made an arrest this morning around ten o'clock. Locked up a guy in one of the bathrooms for public lewdness and endangering the welfare of a child. Turns out he's a commercial pilot for an international carrier. Supposed to fly to Geneva at six tonight."

"Glad to know he's resting up for the long night ahead of him."

"Yeah, the cop told me his penis was on autopilot till they nabbed him. Anyway, the lawyer for the airline is down here kicking and screaming. Wants the case jumped ahead of all the other docketed matters so the Red Baron can be out of here and make the six o'clock flight. They're European-based so there's no backup for him; if he's not out of jail in time, they'll have to put all the passengers on other flights. Can I do it?"

"Does he have a residence here? Any roots, any reason to return?"

"Nope."

"Anybody interview the victim yet?"

"Only the cop. Says the kid is terrific, and that there's an adult witness, too. Strong case."

"Don't go through any hoops for the pilot. I hate to inconvenience all those people, but I imagine he won't be in very good shape to rocket that spaceship back home to Switzerland. A day in the pens and a few hours in the courtroom—"

"Not to mention that the press got hold of it already. Mickey Diamond's down here trying to get a photo for the *Post* to go with his headline story about the pilot and his juvenile joystick. Diamond's usual good taste."

"Just let it take its normal course. And ask for some reasonable bail. If they reroute him to the Far East, we won't ever see this guy again."

I put my phone back in my shoulder bag. "Let's go home. I'll give Sylvia Foote a call." We went back to the apartment and Jake hung our coats, then followed me into the den while I returned Sylvia's message.

"I'm terribly sorry to hunt you down on a Sunday afternoon, Alex, but I knew you'd be displeased if I didn't respond to the requests you and Detective Chapman made."

"That's very gracious of you, Sylvia. I didn't expect you to give up your holiday weekend to get those things done."

"I'd like very much to clear this all up before we start a new year. I hadn't any plans for the day anyway. Now, I found out a few hours ago that Claude Lavery is back in—"

"Yes, Sylvia. We actually dropped by to see him yesterday afternoon."

"Oh." Her voice dropped and the enthusiasm she had mustered went with it. "I don't suppose you'll accept the fact that I *am* trying to cooperate with you. I came over to the school a while ago to write up some reports and I ran into Thomas Grenier, the biologist you've wanted to meet. So we've got almost everyone you need now, haven't we? I gave Grenier the detective's number and told him to call there on Monday."

"Where is he now? Right now?"

"I believe that he's in with the president."

"In Recantati's office?"

"Yes. They've been arguing with each other for the last ten minutes. I can hear them all the way down the hall."

"Can you hold them there for me? Ask them to stay until I get there?"

"Today?"

"Yes, Sylvia. I can hop in a cab and be there in twenty minutes." There was no point waiting until tomorrow to pin down Grenier. At the rate things were happening in the case, I would need all the time available to schedule interviews and examine any files that we might be able to get from Sinnelesi's office. Something had sparked the interest of a few of Lola's colleagues to have them back in the college building when I had not expected to find them there.

Sylvia was clearly annoyed. "They're grown men, Alex. I can't hold them here. I suppose if they want to talk to you, they'll wait."

"Well, will you tell them I'm coming?"

"Of course. I'll be here."

I turned around to look at Jake. "Do you mind terribly if I scoot up to the college for an hour or two?"

"I was just getting hooked on the domesticity of this scene. Reams of newspapers to read, sweat suits and slippers, me cooking, you doing the dishes, The Temptations singing 'My Girl.' I was even beginning to fantasize that one of my secret-recipe spicy Bloody Marys could lead to an afternoon nap that might turn into enough of a personal workout that I wouldn't have to get back on that damn machine for my daily exercise."

I went over and sat on his lap, my arms around his neck. "You do understand, don't you?"

"Absolutely. Want company? You're like a fish out of water without Mike and Mercer."

"Not necessary. I'm only going to the administration building. Recantati walked out on us the other day, so I'd love a few minutes with him, away from the presence of my not-so-gentle grand inquisitor, the ever-tactful Detective Chapman. And this Grenier guy has been completely unavailable to us until this very moment. Maybe that's just because of the holiday, but we do need to speak to him." I kissed his mouth and he kissed me back, deeply and lovingly.

"When you put it that way, I can't object to a thing you do. And the faster you get out of here to do it, the sooner you'll be back." Jake raised his knees to bump me off his lap and patted me on my bottom. "Dinner at home tonight."

"Radical idea." I was brushing my hair and putting on lipstick. "You're not expecting any help from me, are you?"

"Hey, I was thrilled to see you set up the Christmas tree stand the same way I do. Hot water in the pot to let the sap flow out. That's devotion, Alex. I was even set to invite you to move in with me before I was certain you could boil water."

"Just luck that you've got a whistling teapot. I'm not entirely sure how to know when it's boiling otherwise." I not only loved Jake's companionship, but also the fact that he never griped about my inability to cook anything more complicated than an English muffin.

"Eight o'clock. I picked up some salmon on my way in last night. I've got a delicious recipe stuck in the back of a cookbook somewhere. That'll keep me busy till you get home."

The doorman helped me hail a taxi and I huddled in the back of it while I tried to explain to the driver, whose Urdu was incomprehensible to me, that Claremont Avenue was a block west of Broadway, near the campus of Columbia University.

A security guard stared at my face to match it to the photograph on my DA's identification card. Grudgingly, he admitted me to the building and I ran up the staircase to Sylvia Foote's office. The usual crusty expression on her face summed up her attitude about my arrival.

"They're not pleased about your coming here today. Neither one of them. But it did stop them from screeching at each other." She slammed her door shut behind us as she pointed me down to President Recantati's suite of rooms.

"What were they arguing about?"

She flashed another sour look at me. "What we're all on a short tether about. Lola Dakota. Nobody wants to be dragged into this mess."

"You're her colleagues and—"

"That doesn't mean that we wanted to be involved with her dirty laundry."

Foote knocked when she reached his office. "Come in."

Recantati had appeared so mild-mannered when Mike and I

first met him the day after Lola's death. Now he scowled to see me, as much because of what we had asked him as for the fact that I knew at least one thing about him that he wished to keep a secret.

"Thomas, this is Ms. Cooper, from the Manhattan District Attorney's Office."

"Good afternoon. I'm Thomas Grenier."

The biology professor was slightly built but rather wiry-looking. He had thinning dark hair and glasses that sat tightly on the bridge of his nose. He was no more anxious to shake my hand than was Recantati.

Foote turned to walk out of the room. I had one more question for her, which I wanted both of the men to hear. "Before you go, Sylvia, I was wondering if you had any recent contact with Charlotte Voight?"

"What?"

"A call that she wanted to register for class in the new semester, perhaps? Have any of the faculty or students heard from her, that she's back in town?"

Foote and Recantati exchanged glances. "Not a word. Why do you ask?"

"Her name came up in an interview we did yesterday. I just wondered whether anyone mentioned to you that they had seen her recently."

"I told you I'd let you know if I did. It's almost five o'clock, Alex. If you don't need me here, I'm going home." She pulled the door shut behind her and left the three of us standing in Recantati's office. He asked Grenier to step out into the anteroom while he had a few words alone with me, and I sat in the chair facing his large desk.

"Ms. Cooper, first I'd like to apologize for my walking out on you during our interview the other day. It must have created a terrible impression of me and I'm simply mortified—"

His voice broke off and he stopped talking.

"Nobody enjoys talking to the police, Professor."

"I don't really understand all about DNA and what kind of evidence it leaves behind. Thomas knows a lot more than I do. I learned from talking to him that a person can simply touch things—doorknobs and drinking glasses—and it can leave enough skin cells behind to develop a DNA pattern."

"That's quite true." There was enough genetic material in the skin cells that were sloughed off in just minutes of normal contact that it was becoming possible to solve even *non*violent crimes, like burglary, with the use of this technology.

I tried to put Recantati more at ease. "In England, they use DNA to solve property crimes, like car thefts. Detectives figured out that in order to jump-start a car, the thief usually touches some place on the steering column. So the Brits just wipe that part of the car down once they've recovered it, and put the profile in their computers. They solve cases they never used to be able to any other way. No blood or semen necessary."

He wasn't listening to my evidence-collection lecture. He was trying to find a way to convince me that he had never had a sexual relationship with Lola Dakota. "I don't want to deal with Detective Chapman anymore. But I'd like *you* to believe me, Ms. Cooper. I was not—I was never involved with Professor Dakota. She was a friend, she was a colleague"—he hesitated before he went on—"and she was also guaranteed to be trouble. I don't look for trouble."

"But you had spent time in her apartment, right? That's why you think we might have something with your DNA on it."

"I, uh—no, never alone. I had been to Lola's apartment, but only for coffee, or when she had a few of us in for cocktails. That's not what I'm concerned about.

"My position here is tentative. I'm just here in the role of acting president. And if I don't get the permanent appointment, then I'd like to be able to go back to my job at Princeton. Without a scandal. They won't take me back if there's any scandal."

"Then, I don't understand your concern."

"Ms. Cooper, I saw your Crime Scene Unit men when they came to Lola's office the day after the murder. I don't know what they're capable of determining with DNA, but they were processing the room for fingerprints, too. I've been a nervous wreck, that's why I walked out on you and the detective."

"Why? What are you afraid of?"

"The morning after Professor Dakota was killed I, uh—I went into her office. I didn't take anything, I swear to you. But I went in there quite early, before anyone else was in the building."

"How did you get in? Why—"

"I'm the president of the college, for the time being. When I asked the janitor to open her door for me, he would never have refused. I . . . um, I touched everything. I was a bit frantic. And then your policeman noticed that things seemed out of place, and the other men were called in to do all that scientific processing. I've just been beside myself."

"But *why* did you go in?"

He lowered his voice even more and bent his head in the direction of the door. "That's just it. I had been reluctant to tell you until I could talk to Thomas face-to-face. He's just back from the West Coast this morning, on the red-eye."

Why was he being so evasive?

"My wife called me from our home in Princeton at about one o'clock in the morning. I'm talking about the night after Lola was killed. She said that Thomas Grenier had called there from California, looking for me. Said he didn't have my number at the apartment in the city, which is just a sublet, so the phone isn't listed in my name. It all sounded so logical, I—I—I . . ."

"What did he tell her?"

"Thomas told her that it was urgent that she get a message to me. That I *must* get into Lola's office before the police did. That there was something in her desk that would, um, well—that it could prove to be an embarrassment to the college if anyone found it.

"Not illegal. Not anything that would be a crime for me to remove. I would never, never have participated in any such thing. But to avoid a scandal—"

"What kind of scandal?"

"We had several going already, Ms. Cooper. I didn't know what he was referring to at the time. He just told Elena—that's my wife—Grenier told her that he'd explain it all to me when he got back to New York. That I was just to take the envelope and slip it under *his* door."

"And that's what you did?"

"That's what I tried to do." He shook his head from side to side. "I stayed up half the night worrying about it, then got here at the crack of dawn. Actually, and perhaps this just goes to my own naïveté—or, well, ignorance—it never occurred to me that the police would have any need to come to see Lola's office. I, uh, I've never had anything to do with a murder investigation. When I got that call from Elena, we all assumed that Ivan had killed Lola, and the school would have no reason to be involved."

Recantati was talking so quickly I thought he was going to run out of breath.

"I must have been in there for an hour. I started looking over her desk, neatly and calmly. When I couldn't find the envelope that Thomas had referred to, I practically panicked. I went through everything I could think of until I began to hear voices and footsteps in the corridor. I slipped out and went back up to my office."

Recantati rocked back and forth in his swiveling desk chair. "This will be the end of me with Sylvia Foote. She's so nauseatingly sanctimonious. And I was just doing what Thomas Grenier suggested to hold on to my job. It seemed perfectly harmless at the time. Besides that, I never found the damn thing."

"What kind of envelope was it?"

"A small one, very small. It had something to do with the project they were working on. The word 'Blackwells' was written on the front of it."

With the help of Mike's good instincts and a valid search warrant, I hoped that little envelope would be on my desk by the time I got there in the morning. When Recantati and Grenier were arguing before I arrived, it must have been about this.

"Did you and Grenier speak again during the week?"

"No, no. Not until today. He never called back, and I had no idea where in California he was staying. Since I 'failed' at his mission," Recantati said sarcastically, "I thought I'd just wait and tell him about it when I saw him. After I met you people last Friday, I knew I wasn't going back into Lola's office for a second try."

"I assume you were talking to Professor Grenier before I came in just now." I wanted to hear what the biologist had told Recantati before I interviewed him myself. "Did he explain to you why he wanted you to get the envelope, and what was in it that might possibly cause trouble for the school?"

"That's just it, Ms. Cooper. I'm afraid I snapped at Thomas, rather than talking with him. You see, he denies knowing anything about an envelope or a problem involving the Blackwells project. Thomas Grenier claims that he never made that telephone call to my wife."

26

"Shall I wait while you talk to Professor Grenier?"

"I'd prefer to speak with him alone, as we've done with each of you. Perhaps he and I can go down to his office, so I don't inconvenience you any longer. Will you be here at the college during this week?"

"The next two days. In fact, Sylvia and I were discussing the idea of rounding up some of the faculty tomorrow afternoon and having our own meeting about these events."

"I can't tell you how to run your institution, sir, but I hope you don't intend to conduct a private roundtable discussion about Lola Dakota's murder. If that's your plan, the detective and I would like to be present."

Recantati seemed hesitant to challenge any of Sylvia Foote's suggestions. "I, uh, I'll have to check with Sylvia. We were thinking more of housekeeping matters. Making sure that everyone knows we want them to assist you in any way they can." He bowed his head. "I'm so ashamed of the fact that I might have done something to make your job harder. I probably ought to tell them all what I did."

"Please don't, Professor. For the moment, I take it only Grenier is aware of this. Am I right, or have you told anyone else?"

"He's the only one."

Grenier and the person who had actually made the telephone call, if there was such a person. "Let's leave it that way. I'd appreciate it if you let me know if you do decide to get a group of the faculty together.

"One other thing. What have you done with the books that were in Professor Dakota's office? Where are they now?"

"Her sister sent someone to pick up most of her personal effects—her papers and photographs, the knickknacks on her desk and the frames on her wall. But she didn't seem interested in Lola's books. Most of those have been packed away in boxes until we get word from the police that they're not needed for the investigation. Those things related to the Blackwells project will be distributed to other members of the faculty who are part of the team, and some of her research volumes will go to the library, of course."

"May I look through those cartons while I'm here?"

"Is that—? Well . . ."

"Is it legal? Yes, it's fine. I'll make a formal record of anything I take."

"I'll explain to Grenier where we've stored them, and he can take you there when you and he are finished. It's just down the hall from his room."

Recantati stepped out to the anteroom to give Grenier a few words of instruction, and then I followed the biologist to his office one flight above.

In contrast to the stark decor of Recantati's temporary space, this was garnished with awards and diplomas, a series of lithographs of Edward Jenner vaccinating his experimental population of village folk in England, and a collection of cobalt-blue antique apothecary jars. They were lined up in alphabetical order, with the one labeled "Arsenic" closest to my chair. A large model of the double helix, with its ladderlike strands of DNA in bright primary colors, sat before me on the desk. Grenier expanded and closed it like an accordion while I described my position and the nature of our investigation. I had used the same exhibit in many of my training lectures on the subject of genetic fingerprinting.

"Whatever Lola wants, eh? Lola gets." The biology professor smiled as he spoke the words of the song.

"I don't think she wanted dead, Professor."

"No," he said slowly, stretching out the single syllable. "But how she would have delighted in being the cause of all this intrigue. I think what she would have liked best is the air of suspicion that's been created here and the pointing of fingers at those of us who crossed her. If every one of us whom she disliked could be suspects for even a nanosecond, I think Lola would have left us behind without a second thought."

"Your concern for her is touching."

"Anything else would be pure charade, as you've probably heard. I once made the mistake of singing that song from *Damn Yankees* to her, the one about whatever Lola wants. I was jabbing at her, mocking her way of wheedling whatever she wanted out of the administration. Unfortunately she countered with the end of the refrain—'and little man, little Lola wants *you.*'" He pushed his glasses back against the bridge of his nose and squinted at me. "I hated being called a little man. She knew that. And she delighted in teasing me about not being able to get me. I'm gay, you see. Open, unashamed, perfectly content to take her humor. It was the 'little' business that used to drive me crazy.

"But she had a mean streak a mile long. And when she thought I had tried to deceive Dr. Lavery, she came after me like a man-eating shark."

"Would you tell me what that was all about?"

The helix twisted and turned in his hands. "I'm dead tired, Ms. Cooper. The flight in was extremely turbulent and I was awake the entire night. May we do this another time?"

"It would be helpful if I could get started now. The discussion you were just having with Professor Recantati, about the telephone call that was made to his home last week—?"

"I didn't make the damn call. I don't know anything about it. And quite frankly, the idea of that man going through the desk drawers of any one of us is frightening. Sylvia Foote probably cracked her big whip and Paolo jumped through the hoop for her. Just like her to want to know everything that each one of us is up to, and to use the acting president to do her bidding."

"How would you describe your relationship with Lola Dakota?"

The yawn he feigned to gain a few seconds to think about his answer was in direct contrast to the lively fidgeting of his bony hands. "Sorry, I'm so tired I can hardly think. Lola?

"We had gotten along just fine, most of the time. I assume that you've done your homework and know about the matter we were working on together?"

"On Roosevelt Island, the Blackwells project? Yes, I've learned a bit about it."

"We both shared a love for a particular building."

"The Smallpox Hospital?"

"Yes. Quite the most magnificent structure in New York City, in my view. And for me, of course, this program offered a rather dramatic study of the history of disease, as well as links to the future, like the potential of using these eradicated viruses for germ warfare. I'll have my hands full for years to come."

"And Lola's interest?"

"It started, appropriately enough, with her discipline—political science and the history of urban institutions. But the old island romanced her, Ms. Cooper."

"Interesting choice of words."

"Well, that ruin is a stunningly romantic building, don't you think?"

"I do, actually. But what do you mean about Lola?"

"For me, it's intellectually valuable to understand how all the infected populations of a large city were isolated in a single location. Typhus, cholera, ship fever. And then this glorious hospital, designed by one of America's greatest architects as though to disguise the fact that it was dedicated to the deadly smallpox.

"The city still has records of who these patients were, how they were treated, and how many—I should say how few—were cured and returned to their homes. I'm interested in documenting that information and using my students to put it together for the first time."

"What about Lola?"

"A lot of our interests overlapped—same records, same patients. For her studies of the culture, it was intriguing that the charity patients—mostly impoverished immigrants—were kept in a ward on the lower floors. The rich who were infected were banished to the same facility, but to private rooms on the upper floor. For *my* work, that's of no importance. But Lola liked that kind of cultural detail. She constructed entire fantasies about the people who passed through here."

"And Freeland Jennings's diamonds?"

"Hogwash, as far as I'm concerned. Those stories involved the penitentiary, not the hospital. Lola walked in both worlds, but my business was only with the medical aspects of the island."

"And you do have a business interest in the project, then?"

The helix was spinning wildly in Grenier's hands. "You've been listening to Claude Lavery. What we intend to do with this medical knowledge is to let society benefit from it. Hardly an evil motive, is it, Ms. Cooper? There are still places in this world where these diseases have not been wiped out. There still exist strains of these plagues that are resistant to current kinds of medication." The tone of his voice became more strident. "I guess you think I'm just supposed to let someone else profit from this when it's perfectly legal for me to do so myself?"

"But surely, Professor Lavery is also entitled—"

"We're into entitlements now, are we, Madam Prosecutor? Look, everyone's out there on that island digging around for a particular reason. Are you going to be the one to decide someone is more or less selfish than I am, more or less altruistic? Let's not be ridiculous.

"Recantati tells me he's going to get us all together tomorrow to discuss the late lamented Lola Dakota—Lavery, Shreve, Lockhart, Foote. Join us, Ms. Cooper. Come see the seamier side of academia."

"I'm hoping to be there. Professor Grenier, I wonder if you can tell me if there's an office, or a room, that's used as a base for the Blackwells project? Someplace that serves as a central headquarters for the work you've all been doing?" Someplace that needs a key to enter, I thought to myself.

"King's College is small enough and our offices are close together in this building, so there has not been a need for a dedicated space over here. And for the moment, until something comes of it, we've just got a rented room with a secretary as the sole staffer, which is over on Roosevelt Island, on Main Street. It's just a studio apartment that we're using until we need something larger to store any objects that we might find in the dig."

"Who has keys to that room?"

He yawned again. "We all do. Even a number of the students. No secrets in there, if that's what you're thinking. Just a desk, a phone, a few filing cabinets. You're welcome to go visit it anytime you like. What are you looking for?"

I wish I knew. "Something related to Blackwells that one might keep locked up."

Grenier placed the double helix on the corner of his desk. "One of Lola's little secrets, no doubt. I'll sleep on it, Ms. Cooper. Maybe one of my charming colleagues knows the answer." He rose to his feet. "I understand I'm to show you the packing boxes with her books?"

"That would be helpful." We walked a short distance from his office. The door was unlocked and he flipped on the light switch. Cardboard cartons lined the bare walls.

"Paolo says they've all been moved in here while I was away. Looking for something special?"

"Not really." *Not that I need to tell you.*

"He says there's an inventory taped to the wall over near the window. See it?"

I looked over the cartons and nodded to him.

"Can you let yourself out?"

"Yes, thanks."

Grenier said good night and I started to browse through the descriptions of the books. It was an eclectic collection, everything from Chernow's brilliant biographies of the titans of business through Wallace's definitive study of Gotham; nineteenth-century geological surveys to reports of the Department of Correction from the early twentieth century; stories of immigrants from every part of the world and tales of urban America. I couldn't imagine disliking anyone who had such a love of books and had preserved so many of them with such care.

My finger ran up and down the pages that were hanging on the wall above the boxes. I found the reference I had been looking for, listed with the items in carton eighteen.

The only noise in the empty corridor was the thud of the book crates as I unstacked and stacked them again to get to the one I wanted. The label on its top flap was marked "Blackwells Project— Penitentiary." I dragged it off to the side and sat on the floor to explore its contents.

The top volumes were years of annual reports from the Board of

Health, which supervised those prisoners who served as "nurses" in the other institutions. Below those were records of the Department of Correction, leading up to MacCormick's raid, which closed the penitentiary permanently. I piled up a few copies of each series and jotted down a note about which ones I was taking with me.

Three-quarters of the way down in the package was a set of matching black leather albums, their grainy finish frayed at the edges. The bottom right corner of each bore the stamped gold initials O.L. I opened the cover of the one on top and saw the elegant penmanship of the then-young man who had documented his life with such care.

I lifted the six volumes of Orlyn Lockhart's diaries from the box and added them to my stack of organizational reports. Now I could hear footsteps coming closer and resounding in the darkened corridor outside the small room. I stood to gather my night's reading material and put on my coat to leave.

When I opened the door I stood face-to-face with the night custodian. "Just coming to get you, miss. I'm supposed to lock up the main door at seven o'clock. Heat gets shut way low. The president asked me to be sure you got out okay."

I thanked him and we walked together down the staircase to the front door. The wind came howling off the river behind my back as I turned up to 116th Street and swept me up to Broadway in its wake. The air was heavy with moisture and the sky was an even shade of dark gray, clouds covering the tops of the tall buildings in the distance. It took me almost ten minutes and several blocks of walking south to find a taxi to take me back to Jake's.

"Smells heavenly." I dropped my books on the table in the entryway and walked into the kitchen, where he was putting a salad together.

"Worth the trip?"

"Definitely." I described the conversations and the two meetings.

"Mike called. Said he's got what you sent him for and he'll see you in the morning."

The table was already set and the candles were lighted. I went inside to slip into leggings and a warm sweater when the chef advised me that dinner would be ready in half an hour.

Back in the living room, I picked up the first volume of Lockhart's diaries. It was dated 1933, when he was still a prosecutor in the Manhattan District Attorney's Office. I read aloud to Jake, amused by the description of the work in those days. I browsed through the opening pages of the next three books, landing on the one that concerned the raid.

Jake had opened a report by the commissioner of correction and was reading selectively from it to me. "'January 11, 1934. The problem of the female offender is growing, due to her emancipation and tendency toward greater sexual freedom.' Are you listening?"

"Sorry. I'm looking for the part about Freeland Jennings." I skimmed quickly through Lockhart's recounting of the raid, and his personal pain when he learned of the death of his friend. There was no mention of diamonds or precious jewels, and I recalled that Lockhart had said those stories didn't surface until much later on.

"Slow down. You can read till your heart's content after dinner."

I came to the description of Jennings's fancy living quarters in the penitentiary. Then the entries stopped for several days. The narrative resumed after the funeral.

I should like to have something of Jennings's to keep for myself, something to remind me both of him and of this daring raid we conducted to weed out the evil on the island. The belonging that most intrigues me is his miniature secret garden, a detailed replica of all of the great buildings of Blackwells constructed in the last century.

It seems that Freeland befriended an indigent prisoner, a stonemason from Italy—same region as Ariana, actually—who was sentenced to the penitentiary because he was a grave robber. Broke into mausoleums and took precious objects that decorated private family crypts. A petty criminal but a gifted artisan nonetheless. He created a meticulous tabletop copy of the island which my own friend kept in his prison room. An exceptional piece of artwork, really. Shows every edifice, every tree, and practically every rock on the whole place. I shall ask Commissioner MacCormick if I may claim the model as my souvenir of our endeavor.

Freeland wrote to me concerning his garden once. Said he would tell me more about it when I came to visit. He said it held the secret to his survival on the island.

27

"I've got to call Skip Lockhart."

"It's almost eight-fifteen. Can it wait until after dinner?"

I read the section about Jennings's secret model to Jake. "Maybe this miniature tableau of the island has something to do with Lola's murder. Why hasn't anyone mentioned it to me? Just five minutes and I'll be ready."

Jake looked annoyed. "Dinner will be on the table in three. Care to join me?"

I went into the den and opened one of my files. I dialed the number Skip Lockhart had given us for his apartment in Manhattan and got the answering machine. "It's Alexandra Cooper. Could you please call me first thing tomorrow morning? It's about your grandfather's diaries." There was no point being coy about this. I assumed he had read the volumes before letting Lola get her hands on them. "I'd like to talk to you about the model of Blackwells that Freeland Jennings kept in his jail cell."

Then I tried the Lockhart number in White Plains. A woman answered and when I told her who I was, she told me that Skip had gone back into town. "Would it be possible for me to have a few words with your father-in-law?"

"I'm sorry, dear. He ate his dinner at six o'clock and I'm afraid he's sound asleep now. Why don't you try him again tomorrow?"

I called Sylvia Foote's machine at the office to leave her a message, too. "It's Alex. I'm expecting to hear from you in the morning about the faculty meeting you may be planning later in the day. I'd like to be there for part of it, to explain to the group exactly what's going on and what I might need from them." As casually as I could, I dropped in an additional request. "And when you speak to them, Sylvia, tell them I'm interested in talking to them about the Lockhart diaries. You know, the ones kept by Skip's grandfather. And what any of them know about the model of his secret garden on Blackwells. Thanks a lot."

The old volumes had been kept in Lola Dakota's office, without any particular safeguarding. Even now, no one had claimed them or spirited them away. I assumed that any of the people with a particular interest in the project had already scoured the books for information anyway, and that there were likely to be dozens of photocopies floating around.

I didn't think the mention of the diaries would trigger any unusual response, but I was curious to see whether my inquiry about the miniature model of the island fueled a reaction.

Jake was seated at the dinner table when I returned to join him. The salmon and baby asparagus awaited me, and he had already begun eating. He was annoyed, and rightly so. Now, I wish I had put off those calls until after the meal, as he had suggested.

"I apologize. I'm sorry for getting so carried away with this investigation. Why don't you tell me about the rest of your afternoon. Any calls?"

"Joan called about New Year's Eve. Wants to know if you can bring some of that great caviar you served at her birthday party. I reminded her that we had to fly back first thing in the morning for Mercer's wedding. I lined up most of my plans for next week. Nothing as exciting as what you're in the middle of."

He was cool and removed now. Not the right moment to remind him that prepositions weren't good words with which to end sentences. I could usually tease him about grammar whenever he made an on-air slip.

"I'm going to have to pick up some things from my apartment after work tomorrow. I'll need an outfit for Joan's dinner and my travel kit."

"We're not even going to be away for twenty-four hours." Jake realized he was snapping at me and tried to bring it down a notch. "If Mike can't drive you by there after work, we can meet at my office and I'll take you over." We were both thinking about Shirley Denzig and whether she was still lurking in the neighborhood.

I reached over and put my hand on top of his, and he loosened up as we both ate and chatted. It was my fault that the fish was dry and overdone, so I finished all of it, so as not to be berated for that, too.

"Go ahead inside. I'll clean up." The job was quick and easy, and ten minutes later I joined him in the living room, where he was reading briefing papers for his next day's assignments. I sat on the far end of the sofa and entangled my legs in his while I carefully read the 1935 volume of the Lockhart diaries from cover to cover.

At 10:35 the phone rang.

"How've you been?" he asked the caller. Usually he mouthed to me the name of the person he was speaking to, if I could not recognize who it was from the context of the conversation. This time he did not.

"No, I don't remember ever meeting him. I've heard of him, of course. I think Tom did a feature piece about his firm, if I'm not mistaken."

The other party spoke.

"You're kidding." Jake sat bolt upright, both feet on the floor. "When?"

Presumably an answer.

"In Montauk? Where is he now? Where are the kids?"

Another brief reply.

"What makes you think it was murder?"

I put down the book and stared at Jake, who was looking straight ahead.

"Just hold on a minute, will you? I want to go into the den." He turned to me. "Darling, would you mind if I take this one inside?" He didn't wait for an answer. "Just hang it up for me when you hear me get on, okay?"

He walked toward the den and I held the receiver until I heard him ask if his caller was still there. She answered, "Yes."

For almost fifteen minutes while they talked, I sat in the living room and fumed. Less than a week ago Jake had invited me to move into his home. I had done so reluctantly, encouraged by the circumstances inside and outside my own apartment. The intimacies that had begun to make me savor our days and nights together were fragile enough to be shattered by one conversation he refused to have in my presence.

I got up to pour myself a drink.

"Don't I get one, too?" he asked as he came back into the living room.

"Sorry. I didn't know when you'd be off the phone." I returned to the bar and fixed him a scotch. The mood shift had been completed. Now I was cool and abrupt to Jake and he was fired up with the adrenaline rush created by an exclusive piece of breaking news.

He sensed my pout immediately. "You're not jealous, are you?"

"Of whom? I don't even know who called." He didn't offer to tell me her name.

"She's just an old friend. A paralegal at one of the big white-shoe firms."

"I wouldn't care if it was Gwyneth Paltrow or Emma Thompson. I am just stunned that there is something you can't talk about in my presence." I steered away from the sofa and sat in an arm-chair across the room. "You go through this whole big deal about *me* needing to let you more into my life and *me* needing to open up to you. You try to convince me that I should move in with you, and then the first time you get a serious telephone call you fly out of the room because there's a conversation that I'm not permitted to be privy to."

"There's your preposition, darling."

"I'm not amused, Jake. You can be damn sure"—I got up and walked in a circle around the chair as I talked—"*damn* sure that I'm not ever about to live with someone who takes private calls in a separate room. And especially when I hear the word 'murder.' Now, do you want to tell me what that was about?"

He leaned forward and rested his forearms on his thighs, his glass in one hand. He was smiling as he looked over at me. "Am I talking to my lover, or am I talking to a prosecutor?"

"When you say 'murder' and 'kids' in the space of a few min-utes, I regret to inform you—*darling*—that I am a prosecutor."

He sat back. "That's the problem. My sources are privileged. I got this information in confidence, so don't ask me anything I can't tell you." He was too anxious to repeat the story not to go on. "She was working—"

"She?"

"The source. My friend. She was called in to assist a partner who had a business appointment with a client. Emergency meet-ing on a Sunday evening because the client's a stock analyst, spe-cializing in foreign securities. He was supposed to be off to

Europe in the morning. Very well-known guy in the financial community."

"What's his name?"

Jake looked at me. "Can't do that."

He paused. "They sit through half an hour of the meeting, then the senior partner takes a break to go to the men's room. Client follows him in and, standing next to him at the urinal, tells him that he killed his wife on Saturday and—"

Mike Chapman would have had an appropriate comment about the guy's timing, but the moment and its humor were lost on me. "In Manhattan?"

"They live here, but this happened somewhere between New York City and their beach home on Long Island. Nassau or Suffolk County, Madam Prosecutor. Not your jurisdiction."

He couldn't possibly think that I would fail to be appalled about a homicide that had occurred outside the confines of the city limits of my legal responsibility. "And the kids? What's the part about children?"

Jake paused slightly before answering. "This guy actually put his wife's remains in the trunk of his car. Then he got the two kids and drove upstate to dump the body."

"*Where?*"

"Where what?"

"Where is that woman's body right at this very moment? And where the hell are the children?"

"They're fine. She assures me that they're perfectly okay."

"And you're not going to tell me who this victim is and whether she's lying out in the woods or dumped in a lake or—?"

"Look, my informant's in a tough position, Alex. This is their client and the information he's giving them is privileged. They're trying to do the right thing and deal with getting him surrendered before he leaves the country, but right now he's resisting that idea. When there's more that I can tell you—"

The phone rang again and Jake answered. "Hey, that's fine. No problem. You can call me any hour of the night with a story like this. In the meantime, why don't we plan on lunch tomorrow? You can give me all the details then."

His caller clearly liked the idea.

"Michael's. Fifty-fifth Street between Fifth and Sixth, at twelve-thirty. There's a great table in an alcove in the front. Very private. No overheards. I'll call in the morning and reserve it."

She had a suggestion for Jake.

"No, you're not disturbing anything. Sure, if you get something else, call right back." He hung up and turned back to me. "You can't solve all the world's problems, Alex."

"I'd like to think that even if I were not a prosecutor, this story would be so upsetting that it would make me get off my ass and do something about it. I can't understand how you can sit there and probably just think about whether you can scoop the other networks with some lurid personal detail about this woman's murder. I can't understand why calling the police isn't the first thing you do."

The phone rang again and this time, without asking my permission, Jake held up a finger as if to suggest that I wait a few minutes till he returned from the den to finish our conversation. He trotted off to the other room to take his call alone.

I walked to the window and looked out at the murky night sky. Three minutes of that did nothing to calm me. I picked up my cell phone, Jake's spare set of keys, the forty-seven dollars cash I had left until I hit the ATM in the morning, and I stuffed them in my shoulder bag. I had to get out of the apartment before my temper exploded. And I needed to find out who the dead woman might be.

Jake was still in the den when I put on my coat and walked out to the elevator.

I pushed the revolving door open before the doorman could get to his feet and reach out for it. A fine layer of sleet was falling as I turned the corner and tried to find a coffee shop where I could make some calls to local precincts to see whether any relatives or friends had reported a missing female in the past twenty-four hours.

After going three blocks, it was apparent that nothing in the area was open after eleven o'clock on a Sunday evening. Although I was less than five minutes from my own apartment, I knew it was foolish to go there. I did not want to risk an encounter with the unstable, stalking complainant, Shirley Denzig, and I had not received word that the window had been repaired.

I reached inside my coat and lifted my beeper when I felt it vibrating on my waistband. I held it up under the streetlight and saw it display Jake's number. I replaced it, tightened the collar of my coat, raised it against the sleet, and crossed the street.

If I walked another few blocks north, I would reach the Nineteenth Precinct station house on Sixty-seventh Street. If I went east instead, I could get to Mike's building just as quickly. He knew every homicide detective in a fifty-mile radius of the city. We could sit in his tiny studio apartment, which he had long ago nicknamed The Coffin, making calls all night if need be until we figured out who this killer was and locked him up before he fled the country.

I picked up my pace as I headed east to York Avenue. A coat of ice was forming on the sidewalks and streets and I took care not to slip as I walked briskly along. The only people outside were those who needed to be there. Dog walkers out for the last effort of the evening, hospital workers heading for the midnight shift at Cornell Medical Center, and the occasional homeless person huddled in a storefront or alleyway.

When I reached the entrance to the old tenement that stood dwarfed amid the surrounding high-rise condos and upscale restaurants, I opened the outer door, shook the drops off my sleeves, and looked for the buzzer to Mike's apartment. It was marked with the number of his gold detective's shield rather than his name. As the beeper on my waistband went off a second time, I continued to ignore it and pressed the doorbell.

The several seconds it took for Mike's voice to come over the intercom seemed like an hour.

"Yeah?"

"I've got a problem. It's Alex. Buzz me in?"

The brass handle yielded to my grip as the signal to unlock it sounded in the small lobby. I grabbed at the banister in the dingy hallway and jogged up the staircase, flight after flight, to the fifth floor of the narrow building. I was huffing and puffing when I got to the landing and stopped to catch my breath.

I could hear Mike unlatch the dead bolt. He cracked the door about a foot wide and stood in the opening, his chest bare and a towel wrapped around him and knotted at his waist.

"Sorry, it never occurred to me you'd be asleep at this hour." I walked toward the door, expecting him to let me in. "Don't be modest, Mikey. I won't rip it off you. That could be the first thing I've had to laugh about all evening."

I reached my arm out to push at the door. I assumed he thought I'd want him to get dressed before I came into the small room. He held his ground as he gave me a once-over, as though looking from head to toe for an injury. "You okay?"

"Cold and wet. And furious. You've got to help me."

I brushed past him and stepped over the threshold as he started to speak. "Alex, just give me a minute to—"

I gasped as I stood beside him. There was a woman asleep in his bed, and I cringed as I realized how rude I had been to burst in and impose on his friendship so abruptly.

I put my right hand up in front of my face and tried to whisper an apology. "I'm mortified," I said, fighting off tears and backing out of the doorway. "It was so inconsiderate of me to rush up here without calling."

He grabbed for my wrist as I pulled away and turned toward the staircase. "Alex, don't be ridiculous. I just want to—"

"I'll call you in the morning," I said over my shoulder. "Don't worry. I'm on my way to Jake's. I'm fine." I was flying down the steps, calling up to him from two flights below. There was no way I'd go back to Jake's apartment now, but I didn't want Mike to worry about me heading for my own place. I ignored Mike's shouts to me to slow down and stop, and instead was planning the most direct route to the station house to get someone in the squad to help me.

There was very little traffic on the slick street so I dismissed the traffic light and dashed across York Avenue, moving west. If Mike had been dressed, I knew he would have been chasing me by now, so I broke into a trot and started running, in case he even thought about putting clothes on to follow me.

My mind was short-circuiting with irrelevancies. What would he do when he called Jake's apartment in five minutes and learned that I hadn't returned there? Maybe I should just suck up what had happened and go back to confront Jake, call the police in his presence. But if he objected to my doing so, I would be forced to walk out on him again anyway. Who was the woman in Mike's apartment, I wondered, and why had he been so closemouthed about her? And how sorry I felt for her to have this madwoman burst in on her in her boyfriend's home at a most unsuitable time for a house call.

I stood on the corner of First Avenue to wait for a bus to pass, panting as I came to a halt. Maybe she slept through the whole thing, I thought to myself. And what would he say to explain the situation to her if she had not?

I reached the curb on the far side of the street and practically lost my balance as I stepped on a slippery patch of black ice. Calm down, I tried to urge myself. Just a few blocks more and I could sit in the detectives' squad room making my calls, warm and secure.

Footsteps smacked at the pavement off in the distance behind me. Some other fool was out on this miserable night. I spun around to make sure that it was not Chapman coming after me, but saw only the dark figure of a man crossing the avenue against the traffic. If it were Mike, he would have called out to me by this point, and I assured myself that I would have stopped and explained to him the reason for my untimely visit.

I started loping along again, wiping the freezing rain from my eyelids and ducking my head to avoid the wind.

The running steps grew closer to me now and I turned again. This time the man was almost upon me and I could see him clearly. His face resembled the sketch of the young assailant who had been attacking women in this neighborhood for the past two months. My heart beat wildly as I tried to think of a way to get out of his path. Second Avenue was a long sprint from the middle of the block, but the brownstone buildings on either side of the quiet street required keys to get inside their front doors.

I accelerated and ran into the middle of the roadway, racing toward the busier thoroughfare ahead that would be bound to have taxi and bus traffic. Before I could reach the corner, the man had lapped me from the back. His muscular arms stabbed my shoulder blades and he tried to clutch at my mouth, muttering at me in a soft accented voice, repeatedly telling me to shut up.

I fell to the ground and my knees smashed against the concrete. My gloved hands flapped out in front of me and broke my fall. In a flash, my attacker ripped the strap of my bag off my arm and ran toward the avenue as I lay sprawled on the icy street.

28

"Hey, Quick Draw, wanna put out an APB for me?"

I was sitting inside the Nineteenth Precinct squad commander's office, shielded from the detectives' desks by the clouded glass window on the door, when I heard Chapman's voice, at top volume, calling across the room to Walter DeGraw.

"I'm looking for a dumb blonde. Big-time bad judgment written all over her. Put it out on the wires in case any of your guys see her skating around the city streets on the midnight tour. About five feet ten inches, too skinny for my taste, too stubborn to ask a cop for help, too vain to shed tears and run her mascara, too stupid to put a hat on her head in a snowstorm so her blonde hair's looking a little bedraggled from the sleet. But great wheels. And well dressed. They find her alive, she's likely to kill me if I didn't add those things. You seen her around or I oughtta try the psych ward down at Bellevue?"

DeGraw pushed open the door and Chapman reached out his arm to balance himself against the frame of it and stare down at me. I was sitting in the lieutenant's armchair, holding a steaming mug of coffee in both hands to warm them up, and wearing a turtleneck sweater that one of the guys had taken from his locker to put over my wet clothes.

"For a smart broad, sometimes you got the brains of a pigeon."

DeGraw started to excuse himself and get out of the room.

"Don't go, Walter," I implored him. He had begun to type the complaint report and the sooner I finished giving him the details, the faster I could get out of the cold station house.

Chapman stepped into the room and squatted in front of me. He placed his palms against my knees and realized when I jerked reflexively away from him that I had hurt them in my fall. He pried the coffee cup away from my clutches and pressed my hands between his own, rubbing them together gently but firmly.

"What's this all about, kid?"

I shook my head, not wanting to tell the whole story here and now, and DeGraw shuffled nervously, knowing that he was in the middle of something more personal. A uniformed cop knocked on the door, which was still ajar.

"Excuse me, Detective DeGraw? The desk sergeant sent me up." He was clutching my shoulder bag. "My partner found this on the sidewalk, about two blocks south of where she was hit. Nothing in it. Sarge wants to know if you can identify it, Counselor."

"There wasn't much in it anyway. Yes, it's mine."

DeGraw called over his shoulder to another detective in the squad room. "Hey, Guido. Wanna bring me a voucher for Ms. Cooper's bag?"

Now we were five, crowded into the tiny office, filling out police forms and documenting my thickheadedness.

"Word's out on the street, Coop. Even the perp knew it wasn't worth wasting his time to make you do it."

Don't bite, I urged myself. He's trying to make me laugh but I wasn't in the mood.

Chapman's grip on my hands was comforting, and it felt good to be with people who would care about finding the murdered woman Jake had been called about.

"What word?" Guido asked, suckered into Chapman's bait. "Make her do what?"

"The guy who mugged her's the one who's been chasing women around up here. Making them perform oral sodomy. But he didn't even slow down his pace for Cooper. Just took the money and ran. Must have heard she's no good at blow—"

"Why don't you back off, Chapman?" Lieutenant Grier had returned from his meal and walked upstairs to see what was causing such a late-night commotion. "There's a Mr. Tyler on the phone, Alex. Says he's a friend. Wants to know if he can come over here."

"Tell him no, please. Tell him I'll call him tomorrow." I pulled my hands away from Chapman and he stood up. I pressed my damp hair down and pulled the dangling strings of it behind my ears. "I don't know how he knew where I'd be. You either."

"You ran out of my place like a bat out of hell. Said you were going to Jake's. I waited five minutes and called him to make sure you got there." The men were listening to our conversation with interest, forgetting they had other things to do. "When he told me you'd had a fight and it had something to do with a missing woman, I just called over here, figuring that you had come to me to get information from the police. Next place you'd probably go was the precinct. I phoned and got Walter, who told me he had a hallucinating homeless woman, who looked like a vaguely familiar water-logged prosecutor, dragging in a few minutes back with her tail between her legs. Told me what happened to you. Never dreamed you'd march in here as an aided case instead of an amateur dick."

"I'm not an aided case. I don't need an ambulance." I pulled my hands back and lowered them to my lap.

"Listen, Coop, you got less than forty-eight hours to turn your karma around before the New Year starts. Understand?"

Lieutenant Grier had walked away and returned from his own desk with a bottle of Glenfiddich. He chased the uniformed cop back downstairs, poured us each a shot into drinking glasses, and apologized to the three detectives as he served them in paper cups. "Happy New Year, everybody."

I drank the warm scotch and the rich single-malt stung as it went down my throat.

"Want to tell us about the call Jake got?" Mike asked.

I wasn't sure everyone in the room needed to hear the conversation.

"She gets real moody whenever she gets jealous, Loo," Chapman said, taking off his jacket and sitting on the edge of the desk. "Threw a tantrum 'cause she caught me with another broad. There probably isn't any missing woman at all. Just Coop trying to get my attention back."

"'Missing' isn't the operative word, Lieutenant. 'Murdered' is a bit more accurate." Maybe I had overreacted when I saw that Mike had been in bed with a woman. I had run down the stairs without waiting for an introduction or an explanation, and now I was trying to convince myself that it was not jealousy that had sent me reeling back out to the treacherously icy street.

"See the extremes she goes to when the green monster rears its ugly head? The lights were out, the candles were lit, my clothes were tidily stacked on a chair, and for once in a blue moon I'm in bed with a—"

"We ain't all that interested in your wishful thinking, Chapman. Guido, Walter—why don't you go out and finish up what you need to do with the paperwork on Ms. Cooper's mugging." The two old-timers reluctantly picked up their cups and reports and shuffled off to the larger squad room. "Alex, you want to tell us what set off this whole thing?" Grier asked, closing the door behind him.

I explained to Lieutenant Grier who Jake Tyler was and why he had a professional obligation to protect his sources.

"Yeah, but not even to tell *you*? It don't make sense to me."

"Believe me, Loo. I understand the principle, but it doesn't make any sense to me, either. There's no question that the information Jake got from the legal assistant who called him is that their client had killed his wife—"

"In Manhattan?"

"I'm not sure, Mike."

"Where, then?"

"Maybe Suffolk County. Jake said something about a summerhouse on Long Island."

The lieutenant had less patience than I had expected. "Give me a place to start, Alex. There's five counties in the city and fifty-seven more in the rest of the state. You expect me to call every single one of them?"

He took a slug of his neat scotch and paced the floor. "What else do you know about these people? How old are they? How many children are we talking about? What does she do for—"

"I told you everything I know, Loo, and I realize it isn't much to go on. I just thought if we checked with a few of the precincts, maybe someone would have reported that a colleague hadn't shown up for work, or a sister didn't make it to a family birthday party, or that the baby-sitter was alarmed 'cause the kids were gone."

He looked at his watch as Mike walked behind me and stood at my back, rubbing my neck and shoulders. "More likely people would think the whole family's away for the weekend. I'll have the guys call around, but I wouldn't expect to hear nothing until tomorrow."

"Mind if we stay here awhile and use your phones?" Mike asked.

"Suit yourself. Seems like a shot in the dark to me." He walked out of the room.

"That's what you want to do, isn't it?"

I leaned forward, pushing the bottle out of my way, and rested my head on the desktop. "I just can't bear the thought that a woman's body is somewhere out there, exposed to this storm, while some member of my esteemed profession—for the right price—is probably arranging for the killer to get out of the jurisdiction."

"They can't do *that*, can they?"

"Not supposed to. But while the lawyer gets all his ducks in a row, hoping to bargain for a deal before the surrender, who knows where a financier with international connections will wind up?"

Mike refreshed his drink and sat opposite me, trying to make eye contact. "You and Jake going to be all right?"

I was silent.

"He hasn't got a choice in this, does he, Coop? He did what he had to do. You guys are good together."

"Looks like I'm the one who has a choice to make. It never occurred to me that he'd have to cover criminal cases until this happened. I'm not about to sit on the floor of the closet with the door closed and my hands over my ears when the phone rings and somebody confesses to homicide in the middle of the night."

"You want to come back up to my—?"

"I called David Mitchell as soon as I got here. He and Renee were still awake. David promised to take a spare key down to the doorman. I've slept on their couch dozens of times." Mike knew my neighbor, a prominent psychiatrist who had become a close friend over the years. He and his fiancée lived down the hall from me, and I had often spent the night, sharing the sofa with their dog, Prozac. "A wet nose snuggled up against my neck might be just what I need."

Chapman was dialing the phone as I spoke. "Mike Chapman, Manhattan North Homicide here. Who's this?" He paused to listen. "You got any missing persons reports in the last forty-eight hours? Yeah, I'll hold." A minute passed. "Fifteen-year-old run-away. Left home Thursday after a three-week correspondence with some guy she met on the Internet—"

I shook my head in the negative.

"—and a female black, topless dancer from a joint on Pine Street, last seen getting into a car with a Japanese businessman two nights ago. DWA oughtta be a crime, Sarge. Thanks."

Driving While Asian was one of Chapman's favorite legislative proposals for an amendment to the Penal Law. He could never resist running his mouth at a politically incorrect target.

"Nothing unusual in the First, blondie. You keep thinking about how to put your love life back on track and I'll—"

"I'm not thinking. I don't want to think anymore."

"I'm on the case." He dialed again, working from the list of precinct numbers in the department telephone book in the top drawer of the desk. From the lower end of Manhattan moving north, Mike called squad after squad. At some, the phone rang interminably and he never got a response. At most, the answers were predictable. The occasional missing adolescent, the husband not back from a weekend jaunt with his pals, the family of a men-tally handicapped adult who had wandered away from a voca-tional training program and hadn't been seen since Friday.

I walked out among the maze of old wooden desks and found the rest room. By the time I came back, Mike was waiting for a detective to check the blotter in the Twenty-fourth Precinct, on the Upper West Side. I lifted my empty purse from the metal tray of the out box and looked in the zippered compartment, knowing the cash was gone.

"Hope you had the good sense to take your Christmas present when you blew out of Jake's place. We could hock that heap of glass and run off to the Keys, live the rest of our lives down there without ever working again. I could go bonefishing all day and you could drink margaritas and listen to Jimmy Buffett. D'you bring it?"

I smiled and shook my head. It was Mike's way of making sure that my pin hadn't been stolen in the mugging, knowing I would be too embarrassed to want to tell him.

"Boa constrictor? West Eighty-third Street? No thanks." He hung up and checked the number for the Twenty-sixth Precinct, talking as he dialed. "Woman moved into a sublet last week. In the middle of the night, an eight-foot boa comes slithering up on the pillow next to her, trying to give her a kiss. Last guy who lived in the place raised 'em. Seems he left one behind as a housewarming gift. Speckled band and all that . . ."

"Who's this? Yo, Monty, it's Chapman. Looking for a missing broad." The guy who answered asked a few questions of Mike. "No, schmuck. If I knew who or where then she wouldn't be missing very long, would she?" Chapman listened. "Why'd they go up to King's College at this hour of the morning?" After a moment he placed the receiver back on the cradle.

"Time for forty winks, blondie. I'll look for your damsel in distress tomorrow. Somebody broke into the administration building at your favorite school after they locked up tonight. Must have gotten spooked in the middle of the getaway. Cartons of books were piled up next to the back door. The thief only made off with a few of them. They're the boxes marked with Lola Dakota's name on them."

29

Renee and I caught up over morning coffee. I had finally fallen asleep about 3 A.M., and had not even heard David slip out to walk the dog at seven o'clock. I borrowed her bathrobe and the spare key to my apartment. It was too cold to shower there, with the window still not repaired, but I needed a set of my thin silk thermal underwear to put on beneath my charcoal-gray pantsuit. For once the weatherman's prediction seemed to be on target, and just the news reports of the impending snowstorm chilled me again.

At eight-thirty I went downstairs to wait for Mike. All of the Christmas tips had been distributed to the building staff in the preceding weeks, and they remained unusually responsive to opening car doors, helping women with baby strollers into elevators, and ferrying packages from the entrance to the elevator banks. Poinsettias fringed the tables and glass windows of the marble-trimmed lobby, and everyone except for me seemed especially cheerful as they set out to work on this last week of the year.

"How's my little Nanook doing this morning?"

I had left my coat in the apartment and opted to wear my ski parka over the long johns and business suit. "Overkill, you think?" I asked Mike as I opened the car door.

"Not if you're planning to spend the night in an igloo. You get any sleep?"

"Took a steaming-hot shower and went out like a light. Listen, I really want to apologize for showing up on your doorstep last night. It was rude of me not—"

"Yeah, it was."

I turned to look at Mike's face, to see whether he was kidding. There was no smile. "I mean, it just wasn't like you at all. I didn't know who the hell was ringing the buzzer at that hour on a Sunday night. I just figured most people would have called first. You're the last person I expected to hear when I answered the intercom."

"But—"

"But what? You always get so grouchy when I show up in the middle of one of your romantic interludes, like it's gonna be the last time you'll ever get laid."

"How was I supposed to know I'd be interrupting a domestic vignette in your dark little lair if you never talk about your social life these days? I'm trying to apologize to you, if you let me get a word in. And to, to . . . ? Does she have a name, Detective?"

Mike concentrated on the slippery road surface as he steered the car onto the FDR Drive.

"Maybe I'll just refer to your guest as 'her.' That okay with you?" I barreled off a list of questions about the nameless figure in the bed. "Did I spoil your evening with her? Are you going to tell me how you met her? Have you given any thought to when you're going to bring her out of the closet and let your friends—"

"Valerie."

"That wasn't too tough, was it? Valerie. Nice name. Okay, tell me about Valerie, Mr. Chapman. Am I moving too fast for you? I'm trying to start with the easy things."

"She's an architect. Only woman partner in a pretty sizable firm. Does design work for large urban projects, everything from creating new sites adjacent to Battery Park City to planning the Miami Heat sports complex."

I guess the answer surprised me. I paused long enough between questions for Mike to sense my reaction.

"You were expecting a barmaid? Or maybe a peanut vendor from Yankee Stadium?"

I blushed as I protested, "I, uh, I wasn't expecting anything in particular." I had seen Mike through a number of casual relationships over the years, usually with women who had a lifestyle as uprooted as his—journalists, flight attendants, actresses—and rarely grounded at a serious stage in their professions.

"Thirty-two years old. Went to UCLA, majored in medieval history. She can sit up all night talking to me about the rule of Saint Benedict and reciting lines from Havelock the Dane. Don't imagine it would turn *you* on, blondie, but it works like magic on me."

"She sounds—"

"Got so hooked on Gothic architecture—flying buttresses and Rayonnant design—she went on for her graduate degree at Stanford. Don't even toy with me on the subject, kid. I'll be murder on those *Jeopardy!* questions now."

"I'd love to—"

"Don't be patronizing with me. She's every bit as intelligent as your frigging pals."

"What are you getting so damn defensive about? I'm trying to tell you that I'd like to get to know her, to spend time with her."

"Jacobsen."

I slapped my hand on the dashboard. "That's what you're being so weird about." I laughed. "She's Jewish, too?"

"Like you're the only one I'm supposed to find interesting?"

"Like I'm delighted that you stepped out of your narrow-minded little world and—"

"You're only barking at me like this because you *are* jealous. I was right last night. You can't get beyond having me at your disposal, twenty-four-seven, then jerking me around when you set off on a jaunt with one of your fancy beaux."

"I can't believe that's the way you would characterize our friendship. There's nothing in the world I wouldn't do for you, and I know you've demonstrated that over and over again for me. Why wouldn't I want you to be happy?"

There was not a single reason for Mike to be sniping at me. I leaned back in the seat and pushed myself again to explore my feelings about our relationship. There was no question that I had never expected him to be seriously involved with someone who was not Catholic, and I had often wondered, despite his obvious intelligence, whether he was threatened by women of substantial professional accomplishment. Maybe we had both struggled against our mutual attraction from time to time. I hated the idea that I might be envious of his lover.

I shook off my concern and smiled over at Mike, hoping to soothe him with an effort at a joke. "What you don't realize is how flattering I find this whole thing."

"Right."

"Accomplished, interesting, smart, Jewish. Pat McKinney might even think I'm the one who opened your eyes to a different kind of woman."

Instead of responding with a clever dig, Mike snarled, "Val's nothing like you."

"Don't be such a Grinch. You know I'm just kidding about—"

"She's not lucky, Coop. You're the luckiest girl I know, and Val is way overdue for a heavy dose of the good fortune you've been dealt." I had not seen Mike this intense since Mercer's shooting. There was no relieving his edge.

I didn't know in which direction to move the conversation. Every angle I started with met a dead end. I stared out the window as the wipers swished the soft flakes from side to side and waited for Mike to take this where he wanted.

We were in the underpass beneath the United Nations Building now, stuck in the middle lane behind three cars that had piled up in a fender bender. When Mike spoke, I couldn't see his face because of the darkness in the short tunnel.

"I guess Sloan-Kettering isn't the best place in the world to pick up a girl."

The superb cancer facility occupied a city block on York Avenue, midway between Mike's apartment and my own. Many of my friends had been treated and saved by the phenomenal medical staff that served its patient population. I looked at the shadow of Mike's profile while he talked to me.

"After Mercer was hit, I made it a point to donate blood, to replace all the pints that had been used in his surgery. All the guys did it. I decided to go to Sloan-Kettering. Just seemed like the best place to give. First time I was there, in the blood center, I saw her. She was resting on one of the recliners, like she was at the beach. Had a bright blue silk scarf tied around her head, knotted at the nape of her neck, with a big smile on her face while she chatted with the nurse. Just the most luminous skin I'd ever seen.

"We only talked for about fifteen minutes that day. She had to give some of her own blood to be tested for a kind of experimental treatment. She was finishing her juice, getting ready to leave, and they were prepping me to start. Long enough for me to find out what her name was and where she worked."

Mike maneuvered out from behind the stuck cars and into the right-hand lane, crawling back out onto the wet highway. "She wouldn't see me for more than a month. I hadn't realized that there was no hair under her scarf, and she was afraid to tell me. Afraid I wouldn't want to take the next step."

I thought back to my glimpse of the woman in Mike's bed. I had only seen the slender outline of her body beneath the sheet, and the short-cropped brunette hair against the pillow. "What kind of cancer does she have?"

"I'm using the past tense. Had. Val *had* breast cancer. A very aggressive kind, no family history. They did a mastectomy last year and some radical chemotherapy. She's healthy now."

He paused and looked away from me, out toward the river. "I'm betting on her, Coop."

"Of course you should be. You've got a whole built-in cheering section, for chrissakes. Why wouldn't you think Mercer and Vickee and Jake and I can't be part of this?"

He didn't answer me aloud but nodded his head in assent. Perhaps it had more to do with Mike exposing his own vulnerability to us than keeping Val away from his friends.

"How about next weekend, Jake and I can do a dinner party?"

Mike took his eyes off the road, looked over at me, and chuckled.

"See, I knew I could make you smile. Jake can cook, I'll do the dishes."

"You'll like her. You two can go on and on about Chaucer and Malory and the *Cursor Mundi*—all that Middle English literature you guys thrive on." The familiar grin was gone now. "She just gets tired easily. We'll make the first one an early night, if you don't mind."

I cursed myself for my glibness about Mike's mysterious woman. I knew and appreciated the blessings of good health and good genes. Last night, while Val was cradled safely in the arms of the man who adored her, I was tramping around the darkened streets of Manhattan in a petulant tantrum, thinking I could enlist Mike's aid like Guinevere summoning her knights. Why wasn't I content to stay at home and talk things through with Jake?

Mike let me out in front of the courthouse and I stopped to buy coffee for both of us before going upstairs to my office. There was a voice mail from Laura telling me that she wouldn't be in today from Staten Island because of the bad weather, and two messages from Jake, asking me to call. The earlier one was solicitous in tone, the second was stern and somber. I ignored both.

This would be a quiet week, with many assistants taking vacation leave during the court hiatus between Christmas and New Year's.

Sylvia Foote was the first to call, confirming the meeting she had set for one o'clock and asking whether I had heard about last night's burglary. Police were once again working their way through the King's College building, even as Foote's animosity toward me once again increased.

Mike walked in as I hung up the phone. He picked up the receiver and dialed Information, asking for Michael's restaurant. The automated voice connected him directly, at the additional cost of thirty cents to the district attorney.

"Good morning. This is Jake Tyler, NBC News. I called last night to book a table for lunch."

"He wanted that private table in the alcove, under the window," I reminded Mike in a whisper.

"That's right, that nice one up front. I won't be needing it after all. I'd appreciate it if you cancel my reservation." He hung up, then took off his trench coat and threw it on a chair. "Make you feel better? At least when he shows up with his secret source, they won't be holding a special place for him."

Mike picked up the phone when it rang again. "Hey, Jake." He looked at me for guidance.

I mouthed the word "no" as clearly as I could.

"Nope. Haven't seen her yet. Think she spent the night with David and Renee. You really put her in some kind of snit, man. Nothing that about three dozen yellow roses and the sight of you on your knees in the slush can't correct. Oh, and the whereabouts of that broad who got whacked this weekend. Call back when you got that, Jake. I'll tell her to give you a buzz when she gets down here."

He pressed the plastic button to end the call and stood with the receiver in his hand as the phone immediately rang again. "Ms. Cooper's office and she *really* doesn't want to talk to an asshole like you." Mike paused. "Whoops, sorry, Your Honor. I'm new here. Thought you were just another crank caller for the lovely prosecutor."

Mike passed the call to me. "Yes, sir, I do recognize the name. No, I think she's away for the week but I'll be right down. Yes, I'll handle it myself." I gave the phone back to Mike. "Make yourself useful. I've got to go down to AP3. There's a bit of a crisis on one of our old cases and the assistant has the week off."

I slipped the chain with my identification badge around my neck and went to the staircase to wind my way over to the elevator bank that descended to the misdemeanor courtrooms on the fourth floor of the building. My deputy, Sarah Brenner, had been on maternity leave since her baby was born in the middle of the summer, and it wouldn't be soon enough until she returned to the unit. It was impossible to stem the daily flow of incoming mayhem, even in the midst of an ongoing murder investigation.

I entered the rear of All-Purpose Part 3 through the double-swinging doors, and scanned the rows of benches for Juan Modesto. I couldn't spot him anywhere. Judge Fink had asked me to speak with the clerk, and the court officer guarding the entrance to the well of the courtroom unhooked the metal chain and let me through.

When I approached the clerk's desk, she motioned me to lean in so that she could speak to me without disturbing the judge during his plea negotiations with a defendant on a buy-and-bust case.

"Are you familiar with this one?"

"Pretty well," I said, trying to pull up the facts from my memory. "Modesto beat and raped his girlfriend. He's out on bail, pending the indictment. She's been uncooperative, claims he's been threatening her to drop charges or he'll kidnap the baby and take him back to the Dominican Republic. The judge issued an order of protection last time the case was on. I think we asked for an adjournment to late in January, figuring we might be able to change her mind after the holidays.

"Sorry, I didn't have instructions down here today. I honestly didn't know the case was on the calendar."

"It's not. Check this one out. You know what your victim looks like?"

"Yes. I've met her a couple of times." I had spent the better part of an afternoon with her at the beginning of the month, trying to convince her to prosecute. Together with my young colleague who was assigned to the matter, I had reminded her that Modesto's assaults were occurring with greater frequency and causing more serious injury.

"Why don't you take a slow walk back down the aisle. Second row, end seat on your left. Tell me who you think is hiding beneath the wig, sunglasses, and lady's overcoat?"

I made a cautious circle around the busy room, pretending to be in search of a witness, before returning to the clerk's desk. "It's not my victim, if that's what you mean."

"The judge just wanted to be sure. He thinks it's Juan Modesto himself. Marched right up to me, told me she was Lavinia Cabrinas, and that she wanted to ask Judge Fink to drop all the charges against Modesto and vacate the order of protection. We thought the five o'clock shadow and the falsetto voice were a little off for Ms. Cabrinas, so I told 'her' to have a seat. The judge just wants you to confirm it before we call the case."

I turned to check the audience again. "Not even close. I've seen lots of guys beat the rap, but never this way."

"Why don't you wait over here, behind me."

When the plea on the drug possession case was completed, the clerk nodded to the judge, who directed a recall on the Modesto matter, adding it to the day's calendar. The defendant moved to the railing behind the well and repeated his request, in his prissiest imitation of a soft-spoken Latina.

Four court officers surrounded him as Neal Fink, a no-nonsense jurist, ordered him to take off his glasses, which he did without hesitation. The next request was to remove his wig. Modesto froze, and again the judge told him to take off his hairpiece. When he refused to acknowledge the direction a fourth time, the judge told the officers to lift the jumble of black acrylic from the petitioner's head. Two held his arms while the others tugged at the phony curls, pulling them free from the bobby pins that had secured the wig to Modesto's own greasy pompadour.

"Your bail is revoked, Mr. Modesto. Put him in, gentlemen. You are remanded without bail, sir. Miss Cooper, I expect you'll be ready to advance this matter and move to the grand jury most expeditiously. And that you'll be adding the charges of hindering prosecuting and obstructing governmental administration. Can you get this done by the end of the week?"

"We'll do our best, Your Honor."

The last thing I needed now was any diversion from the Dakota investigation. Especially another domestic violence victim willing to give her man a break, ignoring the acute danger of her situation and the lengths to which he would go to escape prosecution.

Mike was playing solitaire at Laura's desk when I came back upstairs. "Battaglia's looking for you. He sounds completely pissed off. Sinnelesi called to complain about the stuff you had taken out of Bart Frankel's office. Battaglia wants a complete accounting of it. Says he's shocked you did that search warrant without running it past the front office first. Bad position to put him in with another elected official. You know the drill. You oughtta go on over and cool him down. I suggested maybe he should put you over his knee."

"Bet he passed on that one."

"Told me I could take the first shot, actually."

"This is one time he'll have to wait for me. No politics slowing down this train."

I opened the Dakota file folder to the sheet of information with all the case names and telephone numbers and dialed the Lockhart home in White Plains. Skip's mother passed me on to the grandfather, who was no doubt in his favorite chair in the solarium.

"Mr. Lockhart? It's Alexandra Cooper."

"He just left, Miss Cooper."

"Who just left?"

"Skip. That's who you're looking for, isn't it?"

"No, sir. I had a few more questions for you."

"What did you do to rile up the boy, Miss Cooper?"

"I haven't seen Skip today, or talked with him. I'm calling because when we met with you I hadn't read your diaries. I didn't know anything about Freeland Jennings's secret garden. But I was looking through your books last evening, and I'm interested in learning what became of Jennings's model of Blackwells. Do you still have it, Mr. Lockhart?"

"Don't be telling me you had nothing to do with firing up my grandson. He practically tore through the whole place today looking for that damn thing."

I took a breath. "Did Skip find it? Did he take it with him?"

"You know where it is?"

"I believed that you had it, sir."

"Skip's mad as a hornet with me. I told him to talk to Lola about it. Can't recall exactly the last time I saw it, but Lola knows. She's got it, maybe. Skip's coming back later to look through the garage. I'll tell him you were asking about it."

Back to square one. "Thanks, Mr. Lockhart. Sorry to trouble you."

I dialed Sylvia Foote's number again. "Check with your professors. Any of them have cars?" I thought for a moment about the weather. "Four-wheel drive? I think we should take a quick trip to

White Plains this afternoon. Perhaps if all of us are together with the Lockharts, senior and junior, we can make some headway. I'd like to start the meeting in your office and make a run up to see if the old man is hiding more than he's telling any of us."

"But—"

"I'll explain when we get there. I think a field trip might help, Sylvia."

Maybe my phone message to Sylvia last evening, when I was reading the Lockhart diaries, had been a mistake. I thought it might alert the small group of faculty members that we were onto something that one of them might have concealed from us, but I had only meant to rattle the cages in preparation for our meeting today. I didn't want anyone making an end run around us.

Mike's feet were propped on Laura's desk when I hung up the phone and came out to intercept the kid from the mailroom who was distributing the Monday delivery.

"What have you got for me, Gilbert?"

"Just the usual, Miss C."

I sorted through the envelopes to see whether any subpoenaed information had been returned in the late-morning mail. The thicker-than-usual batch, rubber-banded together, consisted mainly of printed greeting cards from sleazy law firms and private investigators, complete with the tacky little calendars and wallet-size laminated business cards that served as clear reminders of whom *not* to call in case of emergency.

Halfway through the pack, I pulled out a legal-size envelope with a return address scrawled in sloppy handwriting that was practically illegible. I squinted and looked again, then read the name to Mike. "Bart Frankel. Postmarked Saturday morning."

"Where from, blondie? Heaven or hell?"

"What a weird feeling, to get this today. He's not even buried yet."

"Think Shirley MacLaine. Think Dionne Warwick. Open the frigging thing, will you?"

I held the envelope in my fingertips by one corner, and used the letter opener on Laura's desk to slit a hole along the top. I withdrew the small slip of paper from inside and read the yellow Post-it that Bart had attached to the longer white page.

Alex—Everything in my life is out of control. I never meant to lie about any of it to you. I'll try and make it right next week, when we sit down at your office. Had a scare tonight. Thought I was followed to my home. I'm putting this in the mail when I walk the dog later. It's the paper I took from Lola's desk the day she was killed. I swear to you I had nothing to do with her murder. B. Frankel.

I lifted the note and looked at the enclosure. It was a hand-drawn map of Blackwells Island—circa 1925—meticulously crafted and perfectly scaled to dimension. Every building, every tree, every bench, and every boulder was assigned a number. On the bottom of the page was the signature of Freeland Jennings.

30

"Looks like the weatherman may give us a break."

It had taken us nearly an hour to drive from the courthouse to King's College. The radio continued to promise a winter storm, but was delaying its arrival until nightfall, and the wet flakes that deposited themselves limply on the windshield did not seem to be sticking.

Like any college community at Christmas break, the area around 116th Street and Broadway felt like a ghost town. The Barnard, Columbia, and King's students had scattered to their homes and families, and the normally lively sidewalks and footpaths were bare of young adults and earnest academics.

At one-fifteen, we knocked on the door of Sylvia Foote's office and were invited in. I glanced around the conference table, taking an informal inventory of the assembled guests. She ushered us to our seats, and I squeezed in between Chapman and Acting President Recantati. As I placed my pocketbook on the floor behind me, my pager beeped loudly.

"Excuse me, please. I'll turn it off." I removed it and checked the number, worried that Battaglia might be tracking me down, annoyed that I had blown him off when he had requested that I come in to talk to him. Relieved to see that it was only Jake, beeping me for the third time since we had left downtown, I clicked the mechanism off and tossed it inside my bag.

"Unhappy boss?" Mike asked.

"Unhappy boyfriend."

Mike, in the meanwhile, was checking off the faces present against his list of names: Sylvia Foote, Paolo Recantati, Winston Shreve, Nan Rothschild, Skip Lockhart, and Thomas Grenier.

"As an aficionado of the detective story, Mr. Chapman, it appears to me that you've come here expecting one of us to stand up and announce that he—or she—is, in fact, Professor Plum, who killed Lola Dakota in the library with the lead pipe." It was Grenier who tried to break the ice with a bit of facetious humor.

"This isn't a board game." Mike glared at the biology professor, whom he was meeting for the first time. "But if any one of you wants to save us some effort, I'd welcome the admission."

"Are we waiting for Claude Lavery?" Grenier asked Foote, striking a more serious tone.

She turned to Mike. "Professor Lavery won't be coming. He called an hour ago to say that since we've severed him from college affairs while he's under investigation for the grant impropriety, he doesn't feel obligated to participate."

I watched pairs of eyes find each other across the table, silently affirming alliances.

Winston Shreve, the anthropologist, looked back at me.

"Perhaps that message you asked Sylvia to deliver to us last night unsettled him. About the diaries and the so-called secret garden."

"Why him in particular?"

"Claude Lavery and Lola Dakota confided in each other. They were neighbors, good friends." It was Paolo Recantati who picked up Shreve's lead. "I can't believe he didn't come here today. It's either arrogance, or it's exactly what Winston is suggesting. Claude won't discuss what he knows in front of the rest of us."

Sylvia Foote tried to regain control of her herd. "I thought it would be useful for those of us who worked with Lola to sit down together as a group and examine her professional circumstances. Most of us, of course, believe her death relates to her complicated personal situation. But perhaps if Miss Cooper and Mr. Chapman get a better sense of what was going on here at the college, they'll understand why we feel this way."

And they'll get out of our hair, she seemed to imply.

Sylvia asked Nan Rothschild to begin the conversation. If the severe general counsel meant to set herself a smooth sail, then she had chosen well. As the quiet anthropologist began her description of the Blackwells project, I tried to focus on her words and keep my imagination from divining the real dynamic between the two successful women, Rothschild and Dakota. Had I been too quick to eliminate Nan's interests and possible motives simply because I had known her as a casual acquaintance from the ballet studio?

Mike was making notes, and I jotted a reminder to myself to ask him whether he thought the tension between the female professors was something to explore.

Nan started with how the working teams came to be formed, then moved along to the technical aspects of the dig, which I found fascinating now, in light of the stories of old Mr. Lockhart. Wouldn't the high-tech equipment used by the interns and volunteers have uncovered any of the legendary treasures that had been concealed on the island? It didn't seem clear, though, that the team had actually done any work on the southern tip, where the prison had once stood.

Nan then turned the narrative over to Winston Shreve. With frequent punctuation by Lockhart and Grenier, Shreve led us through a much more congenial version of the academic staff relationships than we had been treated to during the one-on-one interviews. Any hopes that this gathering would help us disappeared by the end of the first hour.

I could tell that Mike wanted to take the meeting in another direction. While his pen jiggled up and down between the first two fingers of his right hand, he was brushing back his hair with the left.

"Let me ask you this, Ms. Foote. Is there any additional discipline the college could impose on Claude Lavery while his matter is pending a decision? Any other action to take against him?"

"I'm not sure I understand, Detective. What are you suggesting?"

"Suppose he lied. Supposed he lied about what Ms. Cooper here might call a material fact."

"Related to what?"

"To Dakota. Lola Dakota."

"Why don't you tell us the fact?" Recantati asked, trying, perhaps, to reclaim the position he had undermined by entering Lola's office after her death.

Mike looked over at me to see whether I agreed that we should reveal information, hoping to gain something in return. The slight nod of my head told him that I did.

"We've got a witness, an eyewitness," Mike began. He obviously didn't want to tell the assembled group that Bart Frankel was dead. "This guy observed Lola Dakota walking into her apartment building within an hour of her death."

No one spoke.

"Claude Lavery held the door open for Lola and walked inside with her."

Again, I tried to identify the allies. Recantati's eyes darted from Foote to Rothschild, Lockhart sought a reaction from Shreve, Grenier fixed on Mike Chapman.

"Problem for me is that when I interviewed Lavery, he denied seeing Dakota. Never mentioned it. Told me the last time he saw Dakota was around Thanksgiving, three weeks or so before she was killed."

"There's no reason to assume Claude's the one who's lying, Detective." Sylvia Foote was quick to take the supportive role. "It depends, doesn't it, on how reliable your eyewitness is. Someone who knew both of them? Some passerby who might be mistaken?"

"Solid as a rock," Mike answered, neglecting to add that he'd be as difficult as a rock to cross-examine at this point, too. "No mistake. I'm asking you to assume for the moment that Claude Lavery outright lied about something as important as that. Why? Does it put him in any worse situation with the college, or does it tell me something I need to know for my investigation?"

Eyelids raised, brows furrowed. I didn't know what Mike was digging for, but I was certain that this message was designed to get back to Lavery as soon as the meeting broke up. Stirring the pot, the lieutenant liked to call it. Seeing whether anyone could be flushed out or who would turn against whom.

"I thought from the outset that it was strange that Claude didn't report hearing any noise, living directly upstairs from Lola." Thomas Grenier wanted to get that off his chest. Nan Rothschild frowned, and I inferred from her expression that she disapproved of his candor.

"I'm a bit surprised, actually," said Shreve. "I don't know why Lavery said that to you. The morning after Lola's death—before he left for vacation—I called Claude to talk about her, about how sad it was. I sort of assumed he'd know more details, being a neighbor and all that. I *know* he told me that he had gone up in the elevator with her that same day. I'm positive about that. Maybe we can speak with him—"

"That's my job, Professor. I'd appreciate it if you let me do the interviews."

"If your question, Mr. Chapman, is whether Lavery faced administrative action of any other kind, then the answer is no. We'd leave that portion of the case up to you."

"You want to tell us, Mr. Lockhart, what you learned from your grandfather this morning, when you went there to ask him about Freeland Jennings's legacy? You find anything in the attic?"

The young instructor blushed as his colleagues all turned to follow Mike's jab. "I, uh, I had forgotten all about that model until Sylvia's message. Of course I tried to see if it was still at the house. Obviously, I would have brought it back here to the meeting. That's what Miss Cooper wanted to know about, wasn't it?

"I'm planning to drive back up to White Plains after this meeting. Sit down and try to have a lucid conversation with my grandfather, if you all think that would help." Skip Lockhart looked at the faces around the table.

"Maybe Ms. Foote told you, buddy. We're going to keep you company." Mike circled his hand in the air, drawing the group in the room into an imaginary ring.

"I'm game," Shreve said. "We're all interested in this, Skip."

"Well, we can't just pile in on him. The excitement would be too much." Lockhart fidgeted in his chair.

"We don't all have to talk to him at once," Shreve went on. "The detective and you can do the interview. We can wait in another room, so we can brainstorm if he remembers anything. After all, we've got a pretty good collective knowledge of Lola and her habits."

The phone rang and Sylvia answered it. "Just a minute. I'll have him pick up an extension." She motioned to Mike, who stepped out of the room.

"I don't think I need to go," Recantati said. "None of this has anything to do with me."

"Well then, Sylvia," Shreve said, "you can ride up in my car if you like. I've always wanted to meet your grandfather, Skip. Lola told me about his fascinating stories. I assume Miss Cooper and the detective will go together?"

"Yes, we'll meet you there."

Skip seemed reluctant. He had little choice but to offer to drive Nan Rothschild and Thomas Grenier with him.

The door opened and Mike waved me out to the secretary's anteroom. "You mind grabbing a ride with one of them and trying to charm the pants off Grandpa?"

I started to ask him why but turned my head as I noticed that both Winston Shreve and Skip Lockhart had followed me out, looking for paper on the desk behind me to write directions.

"Listen up, blondie. You put the Rand McNally in a safe place, right?"

I was distracted again as Lockhart dropped his pen on the floor. "What?"

"The map."

I nodded that I had.

He looked at his watch and noted that it was almost three o'clock. "I can be in White Plains in an hour. I just got to swing over the bridge to Newark and take a peek in the Hertz parking lot by the airport."

The two professors reentered Sylvia Foote's office.

"How come?"

I was pleased to see his trademark grin. "Tony Parisi called. He's working round the clock on Bart Frankel's unexpected demise. Found out that one of the private investigators Ivan Kralovic had been using on Lola the last year may have a connection to Saturday morning's 'accident.'"

"What kind of connection?"

"A very direct one, apparently. Enough to make Parisi tell me the Jersey prosecutors think they can put the cuffs on Ivan the Terrible and lock him up before he has to shovel the snow out of his driveway tomorrow. Looks like the PI rented a van at the airport on Friday and brought it back in yesterday afternoon, claiming he'd had a fender bender on the turnpike."

"Any damage?"

"There's a big dent on the right front fender and it's covered with chipped paint and what looks like blood, so he's having it tested. Wants you to check the jerk's bank account for deposits from Kralovic when you get a free minute. And he wants me to eyeball it before they haul it off for repair."

31

I returned to Sylvia's office as the group was breaking up. "Mike has to make a slight detour," I explained to the academics. "Another case. He'll meet us in White Plains, if I can ride with you and Professor Shreve."

Sylvia deferred to Shreve, who confirmed that he had plenty of room. Nan was calling her husband to explain why she would not be back in the city until six or seven this evening as Sylvia and I walked down the hall to use the rest room.

On our way back, I noticed the lanky figure of a young man silhouetted against the wall beyond her door. "Efrem?" she asked.

"Yes, ma'am."

"Alex, this is the young man I told you about, Efrem Zavislan.

He's one of Lola's brightest students. He called Nan this morning to ask her a question about the dig, and when I learned he was still in town, I thought you might want to meet him. Lola entrusted her most important research projects to Efrem. Everything all right? Any reason you didn't go home to Colorado for the break?"

"My folks came east to see my grandparents, so we're all in town. Miss Foote said you might have questions about Professor Dakota that I can answer," he said, turning to me.

Skip Lockhart came out of Sylvia's office with Winston Shreve, each buttoning his coat and lifting his collar against the brewing storm outside. "What's up, Efrem?"

"Nothing, Professor Lockhart. Just wanted to see if there was any progress in finding the guy who killed Professor Dakota."

"You're not working out on the island in this weather, are you?" asked Shreve.

"All closed down for a few weeks. Most of us weren't in the mood anyway."

"We'll be back in a few minutes with the cars. I'm parked in the garage over on Broadway. Sylvia, can I bring you a cup of coffee for the road? Miss Cooper?"

"Thank you, Winston," Sylvia answered. "How about some hot chocolate for me? Extra milk, if you would. Alex, coffee?"

"I've had enough caffeine to keep me wired for weeks. Chocolate sounds good."

I waited for the men to walk away before stepping aside with Efrem. "Do you mind, Sylvia, if I just have a few minutes with him?"

I led the student around the corner for a bit of privacy. Although I guessed he was not more than twenty years old, he towered over me, and seemed possessed of a maturity that most of the others I had met these past ten days lacked. He was eager to talk about Dakota, clearly sharing her passion for scholarship, and for the Blackwells project.

"Do you know anything about the miniature model of the

island that one of the prisoners built for Freeland Jennings when he was in the penitentiary?"

Efrem's hands came out of his jeans pockets and he began to speak with great animation. "Have you seen it? It's amazing."

I wanted to keep our voices down. No need to alert the others that this kid might actually know the whereabouts of the mysterious piece. "No. But the police and I are quite interested in taking a look at it. Do you know where it is now?"

"Well, no. I mean, Professor Dakota had it. She let me see it a couple of times, but that was months ago."

"Where was it when you saw it?"

"At her office, right in this building. But she moved it out of here a while back."

"To?"

"I don't know. She told me she had to find another place for it. No room in her office."

"Do you know why it was so important?"

He looked puzzled. "I'm not sure it was. Least, not that she ever told me. I just thought it was beautiful. Made with such painstaking devotion, accurate to the most minute detail."

Lola may have liked this kid a lot, but she didn't seem to have trusted anyone with the importance of her discovery.

"Would it help you guys if I poked around the island some more? There's lots of places to hide things over there. Places nobody goes to or looks in."

"I don't want you doing anything to get in trouble at school. How about you let the detectives do it with you?"

"Yeah, that's fine. You want me to take you around there tomorrow?"

"I don't want to screw up the visit with your family." I checked the time. "I'm going to see the detective I'm working with in another hour or so. Why don't you give him a call later on tonight and we can work out a way to do this together? Any day that it's convenient for you will work for us." I took out one of my business cards and wrote Mike's beeper number on the back. "In the meantime, just give some thought to where you think she would have stored the model for safekeeping, okay?"

If we weren't able to jog Orlyn Lockhart's memory, then maybe Mike and I could more thoroughly interrogate Efrem later tonight. I thanked him for coming by and rejoined the disgruntled-looking characters who were marching down the staircase to the lobby. This was not a good day for a ride in the country.

Lockhart pulled up in front of the building and honked his horn. Thomas Grenier held Nan by the arm and walked her to his SUV, closing the back door after he helped her inside, and then settling himself in the passenger seat.

Recantati waited several minutes with Sylvia and me until Winston Shreve arrived in a gray minivan. He slid back the door and I hoisted myself into the rear. Recantati boosted Sylvia up by the elbow and Shreve held her bag while she buckled up the seat belt, telling Recantati she would call him in the morning. He whispered something to her that I was unable to hear, then shut the door and walked away as the engine started up.

"Turn up the heat, Winston," she ordered with her usual display of charm. He angled the rearview mirror into place, and I could catch the corner of his smile as he then adjusted the temperature controls on the dashboard.

There was a steaming container of cocoa in the cup holder of each of our armrests. Shreve opened his and sipped at the hot drink.

"You know the way, do you?" Sylvia asked.

"Yes, Sylvia. Skip's given me directions," he said, holding up a slip of paper. "It's right off the Saw Mill River Parkway. Won't take long to get there. I just want to drink a bit of this before I start driving. Otherwise it will spill all over us."

"Good idea."

We uncapped the lids and I blew on the chocolate, warming my hands as I took a swallow. "Detective Chapman and I were up there the other day. The house is easy to find. I grew up not too far away."

"In White Plains?"

"No, in Harrison." I sipped a few more times before Shreve pulled away from the curb, making the westbound turn to head over to Riverside Drive and the entrance to the West Side Highway. "Spent a lot of time there. I was a competitive swimmer in high school and they were our archrivals. Next town over."

"Just get us up there and back before this snow starts piling in," Sylvia said.

The liquid sloshed around the rim of the cardboard cup as Shreve accelerated past the yield sign, and I took another big gulp of hot chocolate, wiping the drops off my parka.

We were passing under the cloverleaf roadway that led up to the George Washington Bridge, following the signs to Westchester County, when I heard Sylvia make a gurgling sound. Her neck snapped forward and her chin dangled against her chest.

I reached for the headrest behind her seat to pull myself forward and yelled for Shreve to stop the car. "Are you all right, Sylvia?" is what I tried to say, but my tongue twisted around the words and they slurred as they came out.

My arms felt like leaden weights as I unbuckled my seat belt, pushed the strap out of the way, and attempted to reach toward Winston Shreve. Snowflakes swirled outside at a dizzying speed, blurring into one as I slid off the seat and onto the floor of the van.

32

My first sensation was of the cold, biting and urgent, piercing every pore of my body. The stinging pain that grated on my wrist and ankles was caused by bindings of some kind, although I could not see them as I lay facedown in the darkened space. A soft piece of cloth covered my mouth, tied behind my scalp.

Wind shrieked above my head and still the blur of white flakes fell around me. I was inside some structure, flattened against the remains of a wooden floorboard that had been partially destroyed by years of exposure to the elements. Whatever it had been, the draft and snow told me there was now no roof covering the walls.

I heard no sounds of a human presence. No inhalation or exhalation of breath. No footsteps. No words.

I shifted my weight and turned my body onto its side. Still, no response from anyone to the rustling sound made by my own movement.

Even this slight change of position charged the flashes of light that raced inside my brain, and the pounding waves of dizziness and nausea returned. I had been in my office, I remembered that. I was talking with Mike Chapman, and I was pretty certain that had happened. But now the crests and swells of wobbly images flooded my head again and I was sure of nothing.

Thoughts would not come clearly and my eyes closed, ceding to whatever it was that had overpowered all my senses.

I don't know for how long I lost consciousness this second time, but when I was able to see again, the inky surroundings were identical. I was dressed in my ski parka, and the lapel of a gray suit stuck out above the zipper. I pushed to order my thoughts, trying to recall when I had dressed this way to leave my home. There was a moth-eaten old plaid blanket stretched out down the length of my body, heavy now from the wet snow that it had absorbed.

My hands were gloved and boots were still on my feet. I could feel them. Only my face was exposed to the pelting drops of ice. I rolled it back onto the flooring. Think, I told myself over and over again. Think where you were today and who you were with. Think where you were going that brought you to this godforsaken place. But the neurons were short-circuiting and something had poisoned my brain's ability to connect the dots. All I knew for certain was that I was cold.

I drifted off again and wakened later still. Now I could see a brick wall a few feet away from my head, the side of whatever building I was in. I arched my back and saw, two or three feet above the floorboards, the empty frame of a window. Get to that, I directed myself. Get to that and find out where you are.

Turning back onto my side, I started to wriggle my feet, making sure I could control their movement. I bent my knees and drew them up toward my waist. Slowly, like some primitive, reptilian apoda, I extended my legs as far as possible and edged my body forward toward the wall. Repeating the motion eight or nine times, I worked myself across the splintered floor until my head touched the crumbling rows of brick.

I rested there for several minutes before trying to slide my body into an upright position. Sitting up would bring back the dizziness, since the oxygen would flow away from my brain. Expect that, I reminded myself. Mental and physical processes were all operating in slow motion. Don't fight it, I said, forming the words with my mouth.

Inch by inch, I righted my body and twisted to lean my back against the wall. It felt sturdier than its uneven surface appeared, and I knew it could support my weight. My head pounded as I forced it to remain erect. I settled there for several more minutes, adjusting my eyes to the darkness around me.

Something moved within the walls of my enclosure. I blinked and tried to clear my vision, tensing for the arrival of my captor. But these were scratching sounds, sharp and rapid, playing off the icy surface of the floor.

Rats. Two or three of them, chasing each other through an open portal and out the gaping hole where glass once fitted in a window.

For the first time, I had a reassuring thought. Large rodents terrified me, but I was relieved to think the odds were good that I was still somewhere in New York City.

Now I saw the outline of the building walls. The window beside me was on the ground level, but it looked as though there were two tiers of empty frames on flights above—three stories in all, though the flooring was missing from all but the foundation. The four sides, without a roof, seemed to be the entirety of the structure. Too small to be an institution, but too grim to have been a private home.

I dragged myself closer to the smooth orange brick that

marked the window jamb closest to me. My left ear ached anew as the wind howled past. Straining my neck to look out the rough stone archway, I saw sharp icicles jutting down from every overhanging surface.

Cutting through the storm's gray haze was the glare of huge red neon letters. Read the words, I charged myself. Over my shoulder, the rats danced again, in and out of the asymmetrical cavities at the far end of the building.

I concentrated on the giant script sign, which was like trying to make out the object inside the dome when a snow globe has been turned upside down.

Pepsi-Cola. I read it four or five times to convince myself those were the words.

Why did I know that graphic? A huge red advertisement that I had seen more times than I could ever count, I thought. Focus on it, I urged myself. Make the pieces come together. The district attorney's office, my home, the skyline, the city. Make each image relate to another. Every night when I left the office and headed uptown on the FDR Drive, I saw the *Pepsi-Cola* sign, several stories high, shining across the East River from its enormous perch along the Queens side of the water.

I twisted farther to the left, an icy stalagmite gnawing at my chin as I tried to widen my view. Yes, there were the four great smokestacks of Big Allis, belching dense clouds into the night sky, blowing back at nature's offering.

So this must be the island in the middle of the river. Not Roosevelt, not the one I had visited several days ago. But Blackwells. Some gutted shell of a nineteenth-century building that had been abandoned and was waiting to be explored by scholars and students, historians and treasure seekers.

Now I began to reconstruct the puzzle. I remembered being at my office with Chapman. I had a clear recollection of our ride uptown to the King's College meeting with Sylvia Foote. But then everything turned hazy, and I couldn't figure whether I had sustained an injury to my head or ingested something that affected my memory.

It was difficult to move because of my restraints, but it was impossible for me to remain still. With my hands bracing my body behind my back, I pushed away from the window and propelled myself in the opposite direction, toward what looked like the gabled opening of the building entrance.

Wrenching myself back onto my knees, I tried to read an inscription that had mostly faded from a plaque on the wall. The bottom corner credited the Bible, and from what was left of the letters it looked like Hosea. Something about ransoming someone from the power of the grave and redeeming him from death. I didn't know the biblical context but I cherished the thought.

In the dim light, I could make out larger letters carved above the plaque into the terra-cotta panel that bordered the archway: STRECKER MEMORIAL LABORATORY.

I sank back to the floor as though I had been punched in the gut. This was the morgue.

What had Nan told us about it? One of the first pathology laboratories built in America, she had said. This must have been the place to which all the bodies on Blackwells Island had been taken. Why was I here? Who had bound me and left me in this frigid shell?

I could hear the screech of rats again, sprinting closer to the entryway. I half crawled, half pulled myself to the far side of the door, fearing that the filthy animals would find me in their path.

Another window sucked in frigid air from the night sky and I slithered past it, trying to get to one of the building's corners for a bit more shelter. My feet were tied so tightly together that I was unable to raise myself and stand on them. My back bumped against the contour of a wooden cabinet and I came to a stop. The top and edges had rotted completely and come loose from the support, jutting out into the room and making my passage more difficult.

I rested for a minute then pushed forward around this antique chamber, but my jacket snagged on a rusted metal strip that I had not seen, ripping a tear down the length of the sleeve.

I backpedaled to free the fabric and saw for the first time what had snared me. The mouths of the cabinets were agape as I turned to disengage my arm from the metal spike. Side by side were three drawers of morgue trays, each mounted in double rows, the wood decayed but the metal still intact.

The steel grooves were fixed in place, some rolled back into the drawers and others hanging partway into the room. This is where every plague-ridden patient on Blackwells had been stored, studied, and dissected.

As my bound hands ripped away, I jerked forward and bumped my head against the middle set of drawers. On the bottom tray I could see the profile of a small body, wrapped in a blanket of the same plaid design that had covered me. I was swept by another wave of nausea.

Beside the feet, closest to me, was a slim leather-bound book. I leaned my arms toward it and pulled it out onto the floor.

As quickly as I could, I pushed myself away from the gruesome cabinet, kicking the book before me with my knee. It spun around and I tipped back the cover, revealing the title page of the volume of García Lorca's poems, and the small print of the owner's name in the top corner.

I was here alone in the morgue with Charlotte Voight.

33

By the time Winston Shreve stepped through the old doorway, I had dragged myself back into the farthest corner of the deteriorated laboratory—away from the remains of Charlotte Voight, away from the rats, and away from the man who had kidnapped me.

He was dressed for the occasion—with a ski jacket, jeans, and heavy boots—and now I remembered I had seen him at the college, in Sylvia Foote's office during the afternoon, when he had worn a blazer and slacks. I still had no memory of how I had left the administration building and what had happened.

I shuddered when he spotted me in the dark recess into which I had crawled, but I had been shivering with cold for hours.

Shreve's tread crunched on the packed snow as he walked

toward me, stopping to pick up the blanket that had fallen off my body as I'd moved myself around the room. He kneeled in front of me and replaced it around my shoulders.

"I'm not a killer. That's the first thing you've got to understand."

My eyes must have expressed my terror. He spoke to me again.

"I'm not going to hurt you, Alex. I've brought you here because I need your help tonight. I'm not a killer."

It was difficult to believe him with Charlotte's body between me and the front door.

"You've got something I need, I think, and we're going to have to trust each other for a while." He reached behind me and removed the binding from around my wrists. I could see that it was a man's necktie.

"I'm going to remove the gag from your mouth, too. Maybe that will help convince you that I'm not going to do anything extreme." He undid the knot in the handkerchief and then used it to wipe some of the moisture off my forehead and cheeks. I noted that his tools had been those of an amateur—spare pieces of clothing—rather than ropes and duct tape, and tried to draw hope from that fact.

I moved my jaw around, opening and closing my mouth. It was sore and stiff from the restraint. I was unconvinced by his removing the gag. Now that I knew my whereabouts, I assumed that there was not a living soul within a mile of us. Water surrounded us on three sides, and there was a wasteland of debris to the north that was gated off from the population of Roosevelt Island by metal fencing and razor wire. Even without the bluster of the fierce wind, there was no one to hear me scream.

I found my voice. "Is that Charlotte Voight?"

The anthropologist was standing in front of me, and he turned to look at the cabinet of steel morgue trays before he answered. "Yes. But I didn't kill her." He repeated his denial, slowly but firmly, as though it made a difference if I believed him.

"I was infatuated with Charlotte. There was nothing I would ever have done to hurt her."

I thought back to the students we had interviewed and their rumors about affairs between faculty members and undergraduates. It should have been obvious to me that Winston Shreve would be a likely offender. Hadn't he told us when we questioned him that his ex-wife, Giselle, had been one of his students when he taught in Paris? How typical to have repeated the pattern. He was probably a classic case of arrested development, fixated on twenty-year-old students and consummating that original love affair over and over again.

"This is one way you can help me, Alex," he said, squatting again and lifting the blanket off my shoulders to cover my head as well. "As a prosecutor, I mean. I can explain this to you and then you can tell them that I am innocent."

If he was waiting for a response, he got none.

"Charlotte and I had been having a relationship for months. Oh, there were boys now and then whom she got involved with, but she was as enamored of me, I think, as I was of her. She was nothing at all like most of the kids. She thought like a woman, not a child."

How many times had he used that bullshit line on some unsuspecting adolescent?

"I brought her over to the island to get her involved in the project. She didn't have much interest in the work here, but she loved the place itself. Not the new part," he said, waving his arm in the direction of the residential half of the island. "She liked my stories about the past, about the history. And she loved walking through the ruins."

Of course Charlotte Voight would have liked it here. She was an outcast herself, isolated from whatever home and family she had come to New York to escape, and alienated from many of the kids her age at the college. This, the centuries-old island of outcasts, had worked its spell on her, too.

"During last winter, there were many nights Charlotte had come to my apartment. It's easy to be disapproving, but I was a hell of a lot safer company than the hoodlums who were trying to keep her doped up all the time. But then, one night last April, she wanted to come here, to the island.

"It was a beautiful spring evening. She thought it would be romantic to make love out in the open, looking back at the city."

"That sounds more like *your* idea." It sounded exactly like what Shreve had told Mike and me he had done when Lola Dakota first introduced him to Roosevelt Island. "A romantic evening on a blanket in front of the ruins, watching the tall ships and the fireworks, drinking wine, looking back over at River House, where your father grew up."

Why could I remember last week's interviews so well and have no idea about what had hit me today?

"It hardly matters whose idea it was at this point, does it? The unfortunate part is that I couldn't get Charlotte to give up the drugs, no matter how hard I tried. She'd been using them back home in South America since she was thirteen, experimenting with anything that anyone offered to her. So on her way to meet me, she stopped to score some pills. But I didn't know it at the time, you've got to understand that."

"We spoke with her friends. She never got to Julian's. Is that what you mean, pills from what they called the 'lab'?"

Shreve sat in the window frame to answer me. "When Charlotte said she was going to the lab, *this* is what she meant."

How stupid of me. Strecker Memorial Laboratory. The pathology lab.

"Ghoulish, you'll say. But that was Charlotte's humor. She wanted to get high and wander around the lab and the old hospital. See what ghosts she could conjure. These things didn't scare or repulse her as they do most young people. She thought it was almost mystical, like a connection to another generation, another period of time."

"And that night?"

"We drove over here together. I've got a master key, of course, to get inside the gates. I'd brought a couple of bottles of wine. Charlotte got to explore all the hideaways she'd wanted to see, and we lay on the blanket for hours, looking at the constellations and talking about her life. But she became agitated, the more she drank. Got up and started climbing around the old buildings. I was afraid she was going to fall and hurt herself. I tried to slow her down, but she was euphoric, acting like she was hallucinating.

"That's when I realized she must have been taking pills, in addition to the alcohol."

"Did you ask her what?"

"Of course I did. She was behaving so irrationally that it was obviously something that had reacted badly with the alcohol. Ecstasy, she told me. Lots of Ecstasy."

Lessen her inhibitions. Enhance her sexual experience. Create a false euphoria. Turn an evening at the lab with Winston Shreve into a psychedelic delight.

I asked my question softly. "What happened to her?"

"A seizure of some sort. First she had a panic attack. I tried to grab her and convince her to get in the car so I could take her to a doctor. But she screamed at me and ran farther away. I chased after her, but she was breathless and agitated. I wasn't aware, at first, that it was some kind of overdose, but that must have been what happened. She was flailing wildly, twitching and shaking uncontrollably. And then she just collapsed in my arms."

"Didn't you try to get her to a hospital?"

"Charlotte was dead. What good would that have done? She'd had a massive paroxysm."

I'd seen cases like that related to my work. Kids who overdosed with what they considered a harmless drug at nightclubs and rave parties. Dead before the ambulance arrived. "I know that can happen, Mr. Shreve. Why didn't you call the police? Get help?"

"At the time, I didn't understand why she died. Now I've read about the drugs and realize they can be deadly, but I had no idea of that the night Charlotte OD'ed. I, I guess I just panicked. I saw my entire career wiped out. I sat on the far side of that wall," he said, and pointed to the entryway, "holding Charlotte's body in my arms, and I knew that everything I had worked for in my professional life had been destroyed."

"So you just left her here?" I looked around at the decaying rubble of the young girl's tomb.

Shreve was unhappy to be challenged. "I never planned to do that. I needed the night to think. I needed to figure out how I could walk into a medical center on a spring morning with this beautiful child in my arms and tell them that a terrible accident had occurred. I needed to find a way to explain her death to Sylvia Foote and the people at the college who believed in me."

All he was concerned with was his own predicament.

"This was, after all, a morgue," he went on. "I put my blanket around Charlotte, and I carried her inside here and put her down for the night." I filled in the blanks: on a rust-covered metal morgue tray in a rat-infested skeleton of a building, for the next eight months.

"And you never came back?"

"I thought I'd have a plan by the next morning, that I'd drive back over and—. And I couldn't do it, I couldn't bring myself to come back over here to see her. I knew that occasionally there would be workmen in this area, and I expected one of them to find the body long before now.

"In fact, I *wanted* them to find the body. But this part of the island spooks everyone. I never expected it would be this long before she could be taken out of here. If they autopsied Charlotte, everyone would know she wasn't murdered. Don't you think they can still tell that, I mean about the toxicology and how she died? There have been other cases like this in the city, haven't there?"

"Other deaths like that, yes." Other bodies left to rot by a brilliant self-centered anthropology professor? I doubt it.

"This building is actually designated to be converted into an equipment station for the new subway line. It will be renovated soon. Then they can give Charlotte a proper burial."

Had he lost his mind completely, that he could walk away from here and leave the girl behind another time?

I was certain, now, that I had left the administration building in the company of Sylvia Foote when this afternoon's meeting broke up. I forced myself to look in the direction of Charlotte's body, to see whether any of the other trays were occupied. The snow fell steadily and the shadows made it impossible for me to see.

"Sylvia Foote? Is she here, too, Mr. Shreve?" I thought of all my battles with her over the years and all the times I had wished her misery. "Is she dead?"

He pushed himself up from his windowsill seat and brushed his hands together to clean off his gloves. "Not at all, Alex. Sylvia's my alibi for this evening. I've spent hours with her at the hospital, since late this afternoon. Took her there myself, right into the emergency room. Stayed with her while they examined her and pumped her stomach. I was at Sylvia's side the whole time. Treated her with kid gloves until she was out of the woods and the resident cleared her to be admitted for the night, just to be safe.

"Some dreadful attack of food poisoning. Must have been something she drank."

34

"We're going to take a short walk," Shreve said, working to undo the knot on the piece of fabric that bound my ankles. "Perhaps it will calm you to get you away from Charlotte."

He placed his hand around my elbow and hoisted me onto my feet. The blanket slipped to the ground and he bent to lift it, then replaced the hood of my parka over my matted hair. I tried to steady myself without touching him for support, but my legs were numb from the combination of the cold and the hours of immobility.

Shreve guided my tentative steps past the cabinet of morgue trays and the frozen body of the young student toward the entrance arch and out of the ruined building.

A hundred yards away, to the south, stood the massive remains of the Smallpox Hospital. He led me that way on the slick footpaths, both of us bowing our heads against the ferocious gusts of wind that kicked up off the East River. When I lifted my eyes from time to time to check our course, I could see the crenellated parapets of the eerie giant looming before us.

I chided myself for the scores of times I had looked across from the FDR Drive at the elegant outline of this Gothic masterpiece and imagined it as a place of romance and intrigue. Now this hell-hole where thousands of souls had perished before me might become my snowy tomb. What had Mike said to me on our drive to work? The luckiest girl he knew? The thought was almost enough to make me smile.

Wooden posts, like elongated stilts, supported the rear walls of the ancient granite structure. Shreve stepped around them, leaving our footsteps to be covered again by falling snow. When he stepped inside a doorway, he withdrew from his pocket a small flashlight and turned it on to ease his way through the littered flooring of the abandoned rooms. The light from the tiny plastic instrument was too dim and too concentrated to be seen across the river. Besides, I knew it would be masked completely by the floodlights that were focused on the great facade of the hospital from the ground outside, the ones that had made it possible for me to admire Renwick's skeleton as I drove home most nights.

As with the Strecker Laboratory, there was no roof left covering this building. Although abandoned for the better part of a century, its crumbling interior was clearly familiar to Shreve. Without hesitation, he led me through a maze of half-walled spaces that had once been patients' rooms.

Nan Rothschild had not exaggerated her description of how abruptly the city had abandoned these haunted properties. Old bedsteads were still in place, pairs of primitive crutches were scattered on the splintered floorboards, and glass-fronted cabinets with broken windowpanes held empty bottles on their dilapidated shelves.

We had crossed through what I assumed had once been the formal central hall of the hospital and continued on to a room in the very corner of the building. For the first time in hours, the precipitation seemed to have stopped. I looked up and saw, instead, that someone had fashioned a makeshift ceiling out of a thin layer of plywood.

Shreve moved forward and my eyes followed the track made by his light. Here was an alcove that had been transformed into a sort of shelter in this outpost of exposed ruins. On the floor in the corner was a slim mattress from one of the old hospital beds. Not even two inches thick, the mattress had faded ticking that barely showed from decades of wear and exposure. A small table sat beneath the long stretch of open space that had once been a window, and assorted pieces of rubble had been carried in to prop up the boards overhead.

"Sit there," Shreve said, pointing to a wooden seat with a high back that had once been a wheelchair. He eased me onto the slats, which tilted backward and tottered as he knelt to retie my ankles. He stood behind me and reached around to place the handkerchief in my mouth again, tying it in back.

He walked out through the threshold of this small chamber and disappeared into the blackness of the adjacent rooms. What was he up to now? I wondered. Chills raced through my joints, my head still pounded, and my empty stomach ached and growled at me in the quiet of the very late night.

I stiffened my neck, shook off an array of grim thoughts, and pulled myself upright. Glancing out between the stone blocks, mitred at the top to form a pointed window frame, I could see from this direction the glitter of Manhattan's skyline muted by the endless flakes of falling snow. Straining my eyes, I could make out the spire of River House directly across the water from my corner seat.

Shreve must have made a call from his cell phone and left me alone so I would not overhear his conversation. But his voice echoed from within the thick gray walls of the neighboring area and I heard him ask for Detective Wallace. Why would he know anything about Mercer?

"Mr. Wallace? Winston Shreve here. Professor Shreve." Something about having just returned to his apartment and finding a message on his answering machine from Wallace. I had no idea what time it was now, whether it was still late Monday evening or the early hours of Tuesday morning, the very last day of the year.

Of course, if I had been missing for any period of time, even Mercer would have been brought in from home in the effort to find me.

Shreve, in his most professorial manner, was telling him that he didn't mind repeating something he had told Detective Chapman earlier in the evening. "The two ladies got into my car in front of the school and I headed onto the West Side Highway to go up to Westchester. Sylvia was complaining of nausea and dizziness. We thought perhaps it was something she had eaten for lunch that was making her sick. We'd just gone over that bridge into Riverdale when she sort of fainted, I guess you'd say."

Wallace must have asked a couple of questions and Shreve mumbled more answers that were inaudible to me. Flashbacks were coming to me now, just as drugged victims described as they emerged from the haze. I remembered being in the minivan and drinking the cocoa that the professor had bought for us.

"No, no. It was Ms. Cooper's idea. She suggested I get off and turn around. We drove immediately back to Columbia Presbyterian Hospital. Ms. Cooper knew where the emergency room was. Said she'd been there many times to see victims. I didn't want to waste time looking for a place to park, so she waited in the car and I carried Sylvia inside.

"Then when the doctor made the decision to admit her, I went back out to tell Ms. Cooper that I wasn't going to leave the hospital until I knew that Ms. Foote would be all right."

Wallace had questions. I rooted for him to break this goddamn alibi.

"Yes, Detective, Alex insisted on coming inside and waiting with me. I called the Lockhart house and told Skip's mother that we'd encountered a problem and wouldn't be able to keep the meeting after all. Alex came into the waiting room and—"

Shreve must have turned around and faced the other direction. It was more difficult to hear him but it sounded as though he was explaining how I'd passed the time while Sylvia was being treated by the medical team.

Whatever Shreve had drugged us with, I had no memory of the hours after the session in Sylvia's office broke up. It must have had amnesiac qualities. Is it possible that I actually had been inside the emergency room waiting area at Columbia Presbyterian? And if not, what a clever ruse. That place was a perpetual zoo. An endless procession of gunshot wounds, stabbings, car accidents, drug overdoses, women in labor, and miscellaneous misery of every sort. Most admissions were accompanied by strings of relatives and friends—whining, wheedling, bawling, and generally filling every inch of the enormous holding tank in which they waited for news of a loved one's condition.

The wind carried Shreve's words back to me. He must have shifted position again.

"For hours, Detective. She was there for hours. Watching television a bit, like everyone else. Making some phone calls."

Wallace was trying to figure out when I had left the hospital.

"Must have been close to nine o'clock. Yes, yes, of course. It was after they told us that Sylvia was awake and responding, but that they were going to keep her overnight for observation. I didn't want to leave without seeing her myself, but Ms. Cooper seemed impatient at that point. Told me she'd just grab a cab out on Broadway and get herself downtown."

Shreve hesitated before he threw in the next suggestion. "Seemed to be in a bad mood, Mr. Wallace. Something about a row with her boyfriend. Her beeper had been going off repeatedly and she paid it no attention. Rather willful, I'd say."

No one would argue with him on that point.

Shreve hadn't missed a detail. How stupid of me to have announced aloud to Mike that I had an unhappy boyfriend when my beeper had gone off at the beginning of the meeting in Sylvia's office.

"You mean come into the station house? Right now? But I've just told you everything that I know about—"

Break his balls, Mercer. Shreve'll never make it through a face-to-face encounter with you.

"Certainly, Mr. Wallace. No, no, thanks, I don't need a ride."

Shreve's footsteps crunched again on the packed snow as he walked closer to my little sanctuary and bent his head to come in under the plywood covering. He ungagged me and stood in front of me to explain that he was going to leave for a short while.

"What did you give me to knock me out? What did you do to Sylvia?"

"You needn't worry. Nothing with long-term effects. Just a sedative to make sure I could get you here and get her out of the way."

"A lot of a sedative. I can't remember anything."

Shreve smiled. "Gamma-hydroxybutyrate."

"GHB?" I knew it better than most. A colorless, odorless, taste-less designer drug, and I had quickly ingested it in my hot choco-late in a matter of minutes. Most ironic of all is that it was making the rounds as a date-rape drug, being slipped into drinks of unsus-pecting women to render them unconscious for several hours.

"Amazing what you can buy on the Internet. I didn't know any-thing about these drugs until Charlotte died, but it's all there on the Web."

He wasn't exaggerating. Earlier in the year, a joint task force of city detectives and DEA agents had run a sting in which they bought two gallons of GHB from a Web site called www.DreamOn.com for several thousand dollars. It was simple to do.

"But surely the doctors will find traces of it when they test

Sylvia." I didn't believe that he had really taken her to the hospital and was trying to challenge him to admit that.

"You should know better than that, Ms. Cooper. The ER admission is for a seventy-year-old woman who became ill after lunch while sitting in a car with a college professor and a prominent prosecutor. Why in the world would *anyone* suspect something like a date-rape drug to be the cause? They just pumped her stomach and were thankful when she came round. Keep her in overnight and she'll be released in the morning."

Shreve was right once again. Unlike cocaine and heroin, which leave trace material in the bloodstream for days, GHB doesn't even show up in blood. And it's evacuated from the urine within twenty-four hours of ingestion. No one would even think to look for it in Sylvia's case, and they would be likely to credit this brief physical disturbance in an elderly woman to a bad reaction to something in her last meal.

"I'm taking the tram over to talk to the police. I should be back in less than two hours."

That meant it could not be much later than midnight. The tram shut down at 2 A.M., and he was planning to return before it stopped operating.

Shreve wasn't telling me any more details about how he had gotten me here, but I was beginning to understand it. After Sylvia and I passed out, eagerly gulping down our potions, he must have driven across town and come onto the island with his van. It would already have been dark when he let himself into the deserted southern end and deposited my body in the Strecker Lab before taking Sylvia back to Columbia Presbyterian Hospital.

He would then have spent four or five hours making himself visible to the nurses and doctors in the waiting area, inquiring solicitously about his dear colleague. In the meantime, inches of snow would have completely obliterated the tire tracks that had taken me to the old morgue, and I would have been sleeping off the toxin that had felled me.

He must have redeposited his car safely in his garage so that it would be dry and warm if the police decided to examine it, and then returned by tram to begin his encounter with me. He obviously hadn't counted on a mandatory midnight visit to the detective squad.

"Don't worry, Ms. Cooper. I *am* coming back for you. You don't have to die, you know. If that were my intention, it would have happened already. As I said before, you can help me out of all this." Although Shreve had removed the gag, he left me tied in place. He had not wanted me to scream in the background while he had been on the telephone, but now there was no one to hear me.

"I just need to calm your colleagues," he went on. "Chapman's brought in this other fellow called Wallace. They're worried that they haven't heard from you."

"I can tell you an easy way to relax Chapman about me," I said to him softly.

Shreve looked back at me quizzically.

"I mean if that would get you back here faster so you'll let me go." I wasn't taking odds on the fact that he truly might release me at the end of this ordeal, but I was hoping to send a signal to my friends.

"What would you suggest, Ms. Cooper?"

I twisted in my seat and the old wooden slats creaked in response. "We watch *Jeopardy!* almost every night."

"You watch what?"

"It's a game show, on television. Do you know it?" Shreve had PBS written all over him and he stared at me blankly. I explained the final question to him and he laughed at me in disbelief.

I racked my brain for ideas, trying to make this work. I reminded him that Mike had known about Petra and discussed it with Shreve when we first met him. "You, uh . . . you could tell him we were watching the show together while we were waiting at the hospital for word about Sylvia. You could tell him that I insisted on watching the last question."

He was beginning to think about the idea.

"There'd be no other way for you to know that about me, and about Detective Chapman, unless you and I had been together at seven-thirty tonight. You know, we were just chatting and I was telling you about these silly bets we make against each other." I was trying not to sound too much as though I was pleading with him, but everything about me was on edge. "He'll be convinced I was all right while the two of us were together."

For God's sake let him go along with me on this one.

I took the next step. "I'll make up something for you. Mike was obviously much too busy to have been watching television tonight. He was probably talking to old Orlyn Lockhart, or had left White Plains on his way back to the city when the show was on. Just make it some category he doesn't know very well."

I furrowed my brow and pretended to come up with a question. "Like feminist stuff. Tell him—I know, tell him that the last answer was the name of the first woman doctor in America. And if you add that it stumped me, too, he'll buy right into it."

Please do exactly what I'm telling you and please let Chapman recall that we were together last week when that very subject came up: Who was Elizabeth Blackwell? I needed Chapman to remember that and then Chapman would know that Shreve was lying through his teeth. And with any luck he would also realize that I was somewhere on Blackwells Island.

"We'll see whether that helps things, Ms. Cooper. Then when I come back, I want you to think about how cooperative you're going to be about helping me find the diamonds that are buried on the island."

I was stunned. Winston Shreve believed that the diamonds were really still here? And what did he think I knew about how to find them?

"We'll talk about Lola later. Perhaps you're not even aware of the information you have," he said. I hadn't even thought about Lola Dakota since regaining consciousness. Shreve must be after something I had come across in the investigation. But what?

"I've got a legitimate right to those diamonds, Ms. Cooper. Not like those other fortune hunters. They belonged to my grandfather."

"Your grandfather?"

"Yes, Ms. Cooper. There were men like Orlyn Lockhart who were, shall we say, the gatekeepers of the island at the time. And then there were the men who spent their time here on the inside. The patients in this hospital, doomed as they were. And just a hundred yards away, the prisoners in the penitentiary.

"Freeland Jennings, Ms. Cooper. Freeland Jennings was my grandfather."

35

"Really, Ms. Cooper, you don't believe that all of us who grub around in the groves of academe have purely intellectual motives? Each of the scholars you've met has a selfish goal, whether it stems from the Blackwells project or his or her own special interests. Grenier stands to make a fortune from the drug companies for his research, Lavery's success would solve all his problems with the scandal, Lockhart gets on a fast track for tenure—" He interrupted himself when he mentioned that name.

"Do you have any idea how sick it made me to hear Skip pontificate about his grandfather leading the raid on the corrupt scum of the penitentiary? My grandfather died in that raid. My family was destroyed by those events."

"Did Professor Lockhart know that Freeland Jennings was your grandfather?"

"He's blinded by his own greed. And I had no intention of telling him, anyway. It just would have made him and the others more intent on their own ends."

"I'm not sure I understand the connection either," I said. In fact, I couldn't make sense of anything any longer. Dizziness had yielded to simple exhaustion, and the cold was numbing.

"My grandmother was Ariana, Freeland Jennings's beautiful young wife. The *eye*-talian, as Orlyn Lockhart used to say. After my grandfather was convicted of killing Ariana, his sister took my father in. He was only seven years old. But once Granddad was murdered during the raid on the island, that sister and the rest of the Jennings family put my father in an orphanage."

He paused. "They weren't quite sure whether Freeland was really his father, after all. So why bother to split that lovely Jennings' fortune with a possible bastard? No one protested when it was decided to send the child out West. Out of sight, out of mind. Out of the will."

"And that's what became of your father?"

"That was the plan. But in the end, Ariana's lover took him off their hands. You see, it was the Church orphanage that was making all the arrangements to send the boy out West—very common in those days. Brandon Shreve apparently had reason to believe that he might be the father. Either that, or he loved Ariana enough to want to keep her child." He hesitated, then said what we both were thinking. "I suppose your DNA technology would answer all this for us today. But not in those times.

"So Brandon Shreve just gave the Church double the money the Jennings family had offered to lose every trace of the child, and both sides were happy. Shreve adopted my father and, of course, changed his name."

"But the boy remembered, didn't he?"

"Vividly. He talked to me about it all the time. Shreve was a good father, but my father's first seven years as a Jennings had instilled in him an interest in the Jennings birthright. Those diamonds were meant to be his, Ms. Cooper. Now they're meant to be mine.

"So I'm going to leave you for just a little while. If the snow breaks off, it's not a bad view. It's the same vista my grandfather had from his room in the penitentiary—straight across the water to his home in the River House. I'll be sure to give your regards to the gendarmes."

Shreve led himself out with the tiny flashlight and I was once again surrounded by darkness in my frigid quarters. Outside and on the ground just below the window frame, a spotlight beamed up at the brilliant architectural detail of the building's trim. If I could concentrate its aim just thirty feet lower, someone far away might be able to see the ghostly outline of a desperate woman and come to save me.

Dreaming about rescue didn't help. I tugged at my ties and squirmed to loosen the knots around my ankles. I told myself to slow down and make the attempts one at a time. I was far too rattled and weak to take on both tasks at once.

My efforts to work myself free were unsuccessful. I slumped against the back of the chair and closed my eyes. Think, I commanded myself. Do anything but give in to the paralyzing cold. Think. All I could think was why we should have smelled a rat in Winston Shreve.

Just looking at his résumé, Mike and I should have known the Blackwells project didn't suit his professional interests. This man had devoted his academic career to classic historical sites and digs on ancient civilizations like Petra and Lutetia. This little strip of land was too modern and too devoid of cultural importance to pique his interest.

And wasn't it Lola Dakota who had told him about the diamonds? She knew he was Freeland Jennings's descendant. She must have known. That night, so many years ago, when Lola brought him out to the island and made love to him while they watched the fireworks, they, too, had looked back at the fabled apartment building. What had he said to Mike and me in describing that romantic scene?—"Where my father lived before I was born"—not too far from the view that his grandfather had in the jail cell.

My weariness was fueled by my growing anger at myself. I wondered if Mike would remember the fit Shreve had thrown when we said that we'd be getting a tour of the island. How he had insisted that *he* wanted to be the one to bring the two of us here. What better control could a killer have? I could picture his demeanor and attitude. He would have let us in the security gate and driven us within spitting distance of the hospital and laboratory, cautioning us against the dangers of falling granite and broken glass. For the sake of our safety. All the time, he would have known that Charlotte Voight's body was under our noses.

It was probably Winston Shreve who had called Paolo Recantati's wife and pretended to be Professor Grenier. Shreve was smart enough to know that Recantati was thoroughly insecure about the growing scandal at the college. He could have been easily prodded into retrieving an envelope from Dakota's office— especially if such a harmless action could make all the trouble fade away. And Mrs. Recantati hadn't met any of them, so she wouldn't have known the difference between Shreve's voice and Grenier's.

For the first hour after regaining consciousness I had wanted to believe Winston Shreve. I wanted to believe that I would be safe and could trust him. He hadn't killed Charlotte Voight. But what crueler fate could he have masterminded than to leave her body in this desolate place?

And what about Lola Dakota? Why had Lola Dakota died? Her death, unlike Charlotte's, was not an accident.

And then I remembered what Claude Lavery had told us. He had tried to convince us that he had not seen Lola since almost a month before her death. From Bart, we knew otherwise. But Claude was firm in his recollection that the last thing Lola had told him was that she knew where Charlotte Voight was, and that she was going to see the girl.

That statement had raised in Mike and me the false hope that Charlotte was still alive. Now my brain fought the sedatives that had slowed its normal processing and focused on the logical sequence of events.

If Bart had been right, then Lavery and Lola had encountered each other on their way into the building. Lavery was already facing a jail sentence from the feds. He didn't need to become a scapegoat in the murder investigation, the last person to see Lola Dakota alive.

But suppose she trusted him enough to tell him what she had finally figured out? That she knew where the Voight girl was, and she was going to see her, to find her. Like me, Lavery had assumed that meant that Charlotte was alive. Lola knew better. Did she confront Shreve with that fact, between the time she got to her apartment and the time she tried to leave, less than one hour later? Did she threaten to go out to the island to prove her theory? And was it Shreve who prevented her from doing that?

Now I was squirming again. Feet first, exerting every remaining ounce of my energy against the restraints. I couldn't tell if they truly felt looser or whether I just wanted to believe that they did.

I stopped to rest. Wind rushed in the oversize hole that had once been a window. It found every crevice around me, blowing in the sides of my parka's hood to sting my ears and whooshing up my sleeves to test the strength of my thermal underwear.

Homeless people survived this every winter night, I told myself. Older men and women, infirm and insane, were at this very moment hunkered down in cardboard boxes and storefront doorways all over the city streets and sidewalks. You can make it, little voices whispered to me. People know you're missing and they're looking for you. How many empty morgue trays were there on either side of Charlotte? What did I have to do so that I didn't wind up in one of them, waiting for the spring thaw?

I heard the footsteps packing down the thick snow before I saw the narrow sliver of light. Winston Shreve was back, carrying with him a six-foot-long piece of thick rope.

36

Shreve talked to me but I could not take my eyes off the rope. He crouched in front of me to remove my bindings, and they seemed like doll's clothes compared with the powerful weapon he had just dropped onto the fraying, stained mattress pad.

"That's only if things go terribly wrong, Ms. Cooper. Don't let it scare you."

I see. So far, things are right on schedule. Going really well. What had I unleashed when I'd stormed out of Jake's apartment on Sunday night? I shut my eyes tight and willed myself back on his living room sofa, thinking about how good it would feel to have him caress me and make love to me. What could go more terribly wrong than the events of the past twenty-four hours?

I played with my wrists and ankles, trying to limber them. My feet tingled from the deadening effect of pins and needles, from hours of restricted circulation.

Shreve had a plastic bag from some twenty-four-hour deli that he must have passed on his way back to the Second Avenue tram. He unwrapped sandwich halves from their aluminum foil and took the lids off two large Styrofoam cups of coffee.

"Here, perfectly safe." He took several sips from the container to show me that it had not been doctored. I drank the lukewarm liquid and it heated a few of the cold-restricted inches of my throat as I downed it. Maybe I didn't care if it was drugged. Sleep might be better than whatever I was facing in this urban igloo. I finished the entire container in three minutes. Something—either the caffeine or Shreve's return—had jolted me to full attention.

He passed the foil to me but I refused the sandwich. My hunger had been intense for hours, yet now I was gripped again by nausea and unable to look at solid food.

"What do you know about my grandfather's miniature garden of the island, Ms. Cooper?"

I didn't speak.

"You'll feel better if you put something in your stomach. You're going to fight me, aren't you?" He helped himself to some turkey while I watched in silence. "Trying to drag this out until daylight?"

I knew that Mike and Mercer would never have let Shreve walk out of the station house without putting a tail on him, especially once he came up with the phony line about the *Jeopardy!* question. If I could stall for a bit, I was certain that the homicide squad would find me.

"What did Detective Chapman say?"

"I'm sorry. I should have started with that. Mr. Chapman was nowhere to be seen tonight."

My right hand flew to my face to cover my mouth and I gnawed on the damp glove leather to mask my emotion. It wasn't possible that Mike hadn't been there to intercept the one clue I thought might lead him to me.

"Something about following a lead on another part of the investigation in New Jersey. A different fellow took all the information. An African-American gentleman, Mr. Wallace. He's getting married tomorrow, on New Year's Day. Everyone was quite cheerful there, actually. Bottles of whiskey out, toasting him and his bride. A bit distracted from the business of finding you, I would say.

"Wallace seemed to know about this television game, too. Said that sounded just like you. Always watching the final question."

Dammit. He was right. The information would have been reassuring to Mercer. The idea that I would have watched the quiz show in the hospital waiting room would have made perfect sense to him, and he had not been with Mike and me when the question about Elizabeth Blackwell had been aired last week. It would not set off any alarms in his mind. Would he even think to tell Mike about it when they next spoke?

"I believe Mr. Wallace understood my concern about your walking out of the emergency room at nine o'clock or so to find a taxicab by yourself. He said that neighborhood is plagued with drug dealers and youth gangs. I hope they double their efforts there to look for you. Seems they found an elderly woman in an alley just a few hours ago, beaten to a pulp by some young hoodlums, just to rob her of seven dollars and a crucifix on a gold chain. Brought her to the same emergency room where you and I waited for Sylvia."

Shreve paused. "And then another detective reminded Mr. Wallace that some woman had been harassing you as well. Some lady with a gun." He shook his head in mock dismay, and I thought how easily the detectives could be off on a red herring now, combing the East Seventies for my unhappy stalker.

I sank deeper into my frosted terror. What if Mike wasn't worried about me at all? What if he and Valerie were home together, enjoying each other's company like a normal couple? Maybe he'd gotten fed up with my repeated rituals of independence, believing that I'd walked out of Sylvia Foote's hospital scene just as I'd run away from Jake's conversation with an informant and run again from Mike's scene of domestic intimacy. Maybe I deserved to be marooned in an abandoned ruin with a killer.

"The miniature model that my grandfather had built, Ms. Cooper. You seem to be as interested in it as I am. Shall we talk?"

Shreve had let me live so far because he thought I either knew something about the model's whereabouts or the key to its treasures. Now he was determined to get the answers.

"You've tried to convince me that you're not a killer, Professor. That Charlotte Voight was responsible for her own death." He looked at me but didn't speak. "But Lola Dakota is dead, too. And if you're going to tell me that was also an accident, then we've got nothing to discuss."

"It wasn't a murder, Ms. Cooper. Nothing was premeditated. I didn't go there to kill her."

Most lawyers didn't know the distinction between premeditation and intention, so why should Winston Shreve? He didn't have to plot the murder of his friend Lola before he went to see her that day, he simply had to form the intent to kill her in the moments before he executed the plan. Maybe it was a genetic thing, inherited from his grandfather.

All I knew is that I didn't want to be another notation in his agenda of women who had met their demise accidentally.

"In fact, it was Claude Lavery who caused her death."

"I don't believe that." As soon as I snapped those words at Shreve, I didn't know why I had said them. I was overwhelmed with confusion—from the sedatives, the situation, and the snow.

"I spoke to Lola often while she was out in New Jersey at her sister's house." He was standing again, swinging his arms as though to keep warm. "Both of us had been certain that the old laboratory—"

"Strecker?"

"Yes, that the Strecker building was the deadhouse. It's an old Scottish word meaning a morgue, or a place where dead bodies are kept."

How fitting that it has kept in character after all these years, I thought, not daring to imagine the condition of Charlotte Voight's remains.

"While Lola was hiding out at her sister's house she was also researching the island, using a lot of primary source material that student volunteers had come up with while assigned to the Blackwells project. Things they had found in the municipal archives, records from the Department of Health and Hospitals. Papers no one had touched for the better part of a century. Documents that explained exactly what the deadhouse was."

"And it wasn't the laboratory?" Could there have been a more ghastly place than Strecker?

"Its purpose was plain. It was just a theater for autopsies and a lab to examine the specimens. But there wasn't enough room to keep the bodies from all the plague-ridden institutions on Blackwells Island.

"Deadhouses were the wooden shacks they built all along the waterfront. Places to store and stack the corpses until they could be taken back home for burial."

The first sight from the Manhattan side of the water that patients bound for the island would see. The reason that some of them jumped into the deadly current to chance escape rather than a sure sentence of death by contagion. Deadhouses.

"Weren't they destroyed?"

"Moved, actually. Torn down and hauled to the other coast of Blackwells, to face the factories and mills on the Queens side of the river. No patients were shipped in from that direction, so the buildings were simply reerected out of sight of the arriving population. To give the patients hope, Ms. Cooper, to give them something to believe in."

Exactly what I needed at the moment. Something to make me believe that I could get off the island alive, too.

"But what did the deadhouses have to do with your grandfather?"

"It took Lola to figure that out. There was Freeland Jennings, a realist if one ever existed, stuck in a penitentiary with all of those lower-class criminals, most of them immigrants, full of their primitive superstitions. All of the papers make reference to the fact that none of the laborers would go anywhere near the wooden deadhouses."

"Those hospitals had all been closed years before your grandfather was sentenced to prison."

"Yes, but the buildings still stood there, much as you see them today. The Smallpox Hospital, Strecker, the Octagon Tower, and even the row of grim little shacks that had housed the dead. Freeland wrote about the circumstances in the letters he sent to his sister—the same one who was taking care of my father. First, his months of observations of the other inmates and their coarse manners and odd habits. Then his fascination with the way these seemingly fearless street thugs would avoid, like a ritual, the haunted remnants of all the places that had sheltered the terminally ill.

"It didn't take him long to figure out a safe place to hide his diamonds, the jewels he considered his lifeline."

"Under the deadhouses." I thought of the map Bart Frankel had mailed to me shortly before he died, and how it diagrammed every inch of the island, signed by Freeland Jennings.

"Luigi Bennino was the prisoner who created my grandfather's model of the island. And it was Luigi he hired to dig the hiding places for his gems. No one would think to go where all that disease and pestilence might still lurk. Even today, lots of our students and faculty won't go near this building, fearful that they'll unearth some encapsulated germs that still bear their lethal poison."

"Bennino was an uneducated peasant, too. Why wasn't he just as superstitious about contamination?"

"Don't forget his crime, Ms. Cooper. He was a grave robber. Young Luigi had clearly overcome his concern about contact with the dear departed long before he reached Blackwells Island. He was the perfect henchman for my grandfather's needs.

"It's just that Freeland had learned never to put all his trust in another human being. And although it's kind of veiled in his correspondence, it would appear that he paid a second prisoner to double-cross Bennino and move the diamonds. Still in the deadhouses, but in entirely different locations in the ground."

"Another grave robber?" How fortunate for him to find two such thieves.

"No. A murderer. A man who had killed a prostitute down at the Five Points," Shreve said, referring to a once notorious area of the city where our courthouse now stood. "Freeland talks about him in the letters, a much too solicitous concern for the man who was dying of syphilis. One last charitable thing that Granddad could do for him, so that his family would have enough money for a proper burial. And so that he would take Freeland's secret with him, well rewarded for his trouble."

"So three men knew about the diamonds and where they were buried."

"And all three died on the rock, as it were. My grandfather's death in the raid could not possibly have been anticipated. He never had time to retrieve his fortune. That's why I'd like the map, Ms. Cooper. The map and the model of the island." Shreve sat in the frame of the window, hands on his knees, and stared me in the eye.

"And Lola had them?"

"And Lola's dead."

"But if you hadn't killed her—"

His gloved hands slapped against his thighs as his temper flared. "Why would I have killed her without getting what I needed from her? It's Claude Lavery's fault that she's dead."

How could I evaluate what he was telling me? Maybe Chapman and I had given him an opportunity to blame Lavery by telling the group of professors that Lavery had been seen going into Lola's building with her the day she died. Maybe Shreve hadn't known that until we gave the fact away. And now he was just using it to make me think he wasn't the killer. Or perhaps both of them were involved, and they were both responsible for her death. How could I know?

I was more tentative now, talking softly to Shreve, aware that he might keep me alive as long as he thought I could give him what he wanted.

What had I done with the map before Mike and I had dashed out of the office on the way to King's College? Is it possible that it had been less than twenty-four hours since all that had happened? I bit my lip and took myself back one day. I had given my paralegal the map to copy, telling her to lock the original in one of the file cabinets until Mike could voucher it. And I had given one of the copies to him, then folded the other to slip in the pocket of my gray slacks, to examine later that night when I got home. Had Shreve overheard Mike ask me, in Sylvia Foote's office, whether I had secured Jennings's blueprint of the island?

I looked down at my pants leg to make certain that I was still wearing that same suit. My pocketbook and case folder were either in Shreve's van or his apartment. Perhaps he had gone through them in search of the map or any references to it, but if he hadn't thought to search my clothing, he would not have found the map.

The adrenaline pumped again and I swallowed hard. Now I knew that what Shreve wanted was here under his nose, and if he found the small slip of paper, there would be no reason to maintain our dialogue. I would be as good as dead.

"But Lola was telling you all these things while she was at Lily's house, doing the research. What did you two have to fight about the day she was killed?"

"I didn't go to see her to argue about anything. I was excited, thrilled that she might have solved the puzzle about my grandfather's fortune. I wanted to see the map for myself."

"Did she have it?"

"She was mad that I had come to her apartment. She stalled and tried to put me off. Told me she didn't have it with her. Told me the prosecutor from New Jersey was going to be arriving shortly and that she'd call me the next day. Of course, I didn't know at the time that she wasn't kidding about the prosecutor. He actually was coming over." Shreve sneered. "Not for Lola, but for his money."

"What money?"

"Apparently the guy had all kinds of financial problems. Lola was doling out cash to him to keep him afloat. Probably to keep him coming back to bed with her, which wasn't necessarily a pleasant place to be."

"How do you know that? I mean, about the cash?"

"After she died, Claude Lavery told me. That's what drove the two of them apart. Lola knew that Claude took an unorthodox view of his grant money. She pleaded with him to let her borrow some of it, claiming she needed it for the Blackwells project. Claude called me last week and asked me to return the money. I had to tell him she hadn't used a nickel of it for the dig. Then I remembered what she'd told me about the prosecutor and his financial problems. The money must have all been going to the deadbeat boyfriend."

Lola's shoe boxes full of cash. She had put the squeeze on Lavery to share some of his stash, pretending it was for her professional needs, but she was using it to solve Bart Frankel's personal problems.

I leaned forward and tried to look sincere when I asked the next question. I didn't believe what I was saying, but I wanted Shreve to think I did. "So why did Claude kill Lola? Was it about the money?"

He took too long to answer. I shivered again and put my hand to my side, trying to feel the piece of paper through the layers of clothing. Was it there? I could not be sure.

"She had called me earlier in the week to tell me she would be home that afternoon. Not to worry about the news stories about Ivan's attempt on her life, if I should hear them. I stopped by the building—I was on the way to the college, actually. I tried her bell and she was home. Had just gotten there. She let me come up but was anxious to get rid of me."

"And Professor Lavery?"

A slight hesitation. Shreve wanted to tell a story that would weave Lavery into the murder, but he was not doing it convincingly. "Lola wouldn't let me in the door. Kept me in the hallway. Lavery was inside, although I didn't know it was him at the time. Lola told me that she was going over to the island."

"Then? Right then?"

"The next day. I wanted to go with her. She had no right to my grandfather's possessions."

The wind seemed less ferocious now, and my tone had lowered as well. "She had figured out about Charlotte, Mr. Shreve. Hadn't she? She was threatening to expose your—your accident." I tried not to choke on the last word. "She let you know that she'd just told Lavery that she'd figured out where Charlotte Voight was."

I remembered Lavery saying that to Mike and me, but Lavery had interpreted Lola's words to mean that Charlotte was still alive. Shreve, on the other hand, must have panicked about Charlotte's body being found just as he was about to locate his grandfather's fortune.

"Lola wanted something in exchange for the map, didn't she?"

"She had no right to any of those diamonds, Ms. Cooper. She was trying to blackmail me, just like she had coaxed Claude Lavery out of his grant money."

Shreve was standing now, poised in the doorway of the small room. "Lola slammed the door on me, but I wouldn't leave. She came out later, maybe five, maybe ten minutes. I asked where she was going but she wouldn't answer me. I knew she was going to the island. To Strecker, to find Charlotte. I tried to stop her but she pushed past me and got on the elevator."

"Just the two of you?"

"Claude. That's when Claude came out of her apartment. I was shocked to see him there. The elevator lurched and I grabbed at Lola to pull her off. All I got was her scarf, her long woolen scarf.

"But the doors closed and caught the ends of the scarf as the cab started to move. I yelled at Claude to push the buttons and I pried the sides apart with my hands. There was Lola, completely blue in the face, flailing her arms and trying to fight for air or to catch her breath to scream. She thought I had done it on purpose."

Perhaps that part was true. He had painted such a vivid picture of Lola, almost hanged to death by a piece of clothing caught in the elevator doors. A soft piece of woolen material, on top of the thick fabric of a winter coat collar, that would not even leave ligature marks.

"But she was still alive then?"

"Oh, yes. She couldn't speak, she couldn't loosen the scarf. 'It was an *accident*,' I said to her. I reached for the coat to undo it and she recoiled.

"That's when she started to scream."

I imagined that she did, also having figured that Shreve had somehow been responsible for Charlotte Voight's disappearance. I would have been shouting what I wanted to say to his face right at that moment. *Murderer!*

He stumbled now, stuttering instead of delivering a clear narrative. "It was Claude who did it. He wanted her to stop screaming, to make her be quiet."

It made no sense to me for Claude to want to kill Lola. But I had given Shreve the opening to insert an accomplice into his recreation of the events.

"Claude grabbed at the scarf and pulled it tighter. He dragged her off the elevator and onto the floor of the hallway. He was calling her names, he was—"

It's not a fast death, strangulation. Not like a gunshot wound to the head or a knife in the chest. No doubt it had been hastened in this instance by the fact that she was almost hanged by the jaws of the elevator door. She was already weakened and had a compromised airway, so it would not have taken much effort to finish her off.

Shreve searched for words and actions to attribute to Lavery, but I knew better now.

"She, she didn't scream very loud. I, uh, I tried to pull Claude back but he wouldn't let go. He was so mad at her." He lowered his head and tried to add convincing facts. "That's when he told me that Lola had been blackmailing him for cash from his grant money."

"And Lola's body?"

"I wanted to call the police. I know you won't believe that, because of—" He broke off midsentence and nodded his head to the side, in the direction of the Strecker building. Toward Charlotte Voight's body. "This time it was Claude who refused. He was about to be indicted by the federal authorities for fraud. He, uh, he told me to leave. That he would handle this himself. And I did, assuming he would take care of things in an appropriate way.

"I never imagined that he'd roll her body into the elevator shaft. I mean, Claude's the one who lives there. I wasn't even aware anything was wrong in the building, that the elevators sometimes stopped between floors. How could I have possibly known that?"

He had me for a moment. It made sense for Lavery to know that fact. But any fool who had visited the old building and been on the elevator when it malfunctioned could have known it, too. It happened with the three elevators in our office building every day of the week.

"You put that map in my hands, Ms. Cooper, and when you prosecute Professor Lavery, I'll come back from Paris and testify at the trial. Now, who has the map? In what safe place did you leave it this morning?"

37

"You *do* know the piece of paper I mean?"

I tried to force myself to focus. Once he knew how to get his hands on the map, there was no need to keep me alive. I thought of the paper in my pocket and my hand unconsciously moved to stroke my throat, thinking of Lola's fate and imagining the many uses of the thick length of rope Shreve had brought back with him. There were two other copies, and I had to make him think I was indispensable in getting them into his possession.

"I didn't know about the significance of the map when we came across it, of course. I never knew the story of your grandfather's diamonds until just the other day. But I do know how to get it for you."

He was calm now, and talking to me as he squatted next to the chair.

"Look, Ms. Cooper. I'm a French citizen. You get me this map, and I'll find Freeland's ransom, go back to my home abroad, and donate half the money to the college or any cause you name."

I listened. Surely he would know we could extradite him from France. Or was he that certain that he could talk his way out of a murder charge?

"We're talking about millions of dollars." My head dropped to avoid his gaze. "Ah, ever the earnest prosecutor. Once you help convince all the authorities how Charlotte died, I'll be home free. And you'll still have Claude to blame for Lola Dakota's death."

"You'll need me to get the map, Mr. Shreve. The original is in the safe in Paul Battaglia's office."

"Your team is too efficient not to have made some copies. I took the liberty of looking through your file—the one that was in my car—but no map."

"One copy." I sucked in some frigid air and prayed that what I was about to say would not put Mike in harm's way. "Detective Chapman has that copy. And I can help you get it from him."

"How can you do that?"

I would have to think of something specific by daybreak, less than an hour or so away. "Because he'll do whatever I ask him to do."

"No wonder you've got some problems with your boyfriend. Rather confident of that, aren't you?"

"Chapman's a very intelligent man, Mr. Shreve. If you let me call him and arrange for him to meet us, you can tell him exactly what you've told me about Charlotte Voight and Lola Dakota."

"Surrender?"

"If Charlotte's death was accidental, and Lavery killed Lola, then you've got nothing to worry about."

I needed to talk myself out of this black abyss and into the open areas outside the building where someone might actually be able to see us once the morning came.

"I'd rather get back home to the Sixth Arrondissement and let *you* break the news to the NYPD. Where's the Blackwells Island miniature that my grandfather had Bennino make, Ms. Cooper? Do you know that, too?"

I moved my head up and down, slowly trying to think of a possible answer.

"Was that a 'yes'?"

"Yes, I do." Shreve himself had given me the idea when he had talked about Lola's weeks in hiding. "It's at Lily's house, Lola's sister." Why hadn't I thought of that possibility in all the days since the murder? Lola must have taken a lot of things with her to occupy her during the weeks in New Jersey. She was too much of a workhorse not to have done so. If that's where she was when she figured out Jennings's deadhouse scheme, that's probably where the model was concealed.

I went on weaving my tale, which seemed to interest Winston Shreve. "There's a key to a trunk that's in Lily's garage. It's where Lola left the miniature when she came back to the city. Chapman has that key. I'm supposed to meet him at nine o'clock this morning to go with him to pick up the model."

"And all that charade about old man Lockhart and going up to listen to his story?"

"To try to determine who else knew about the map and the diamonds. If you let me call Chapman now, on your cell phone, I know he'll agree to meet with us." And I know he'll get the tech unit to trace the call immediately. They could do amazing things with satellite systems, even pinpointing the location of the caller in a matter of seconds.

"I wouldn't want to alarm him in the middle of the night. He might be busy."

Shreve was right. Mike might be much too involved with Valerie to be giving me a second thought.

I didn't want to end my life in this godforsaken ruin like one more of the outcasts sent here and left to die. Slowly, I raised my head to meet his eyes. "I've studied your grandfather's map, Mr. Shreve. I believe I could recognize the shapes of some of the areas, the pieces of land where the wooden sheds once stood, if I saw them. If you want to walk outside with me, I can try to help you find the rocks that correspond with the locations noted on the map."

"That's a good way to start, Ms. Cooper." He turned to look out the hollowed window frame. It was still dark, and the storm had subsided. The precipitation had stopped and large wet flakes of snow blew lazily upward from the ground instead of falling in sheets. "The positions on the map, were they numbered?"

"Yes, yes, they were numbered." The first time I said that word aloud I recalled another set of numbers. In the pocket of the black sweater that we'd found in Lola Dakota's apartment just hours after her murder was the slip of paper that we had removed. The paper that bore the words THE DEADHOUSE, followed by a list of numbers. They meant nothing to us at the time, and now I realized they must have been the key to the map that Lola had deciphered while holed up at her sister's home.

Lola had come back from New Jersey wearing that sweater, but removed it at some point before she walked out of her apartment for the last time. Shreve had gone to intercept her, looking for the map and the numbers that might correspond to it and lead him to the diamonds.

"The numbers, Ms. Cooper. Tell me how they were ordered."

"I honestly can't remember that. I know that the lower numbers started at the southern tip of the island. I, uh, I could probably show you where some of the areas that were highlighted on the map are, if I could actually see the terrain."

"Nice try, Ms. Cooper. That's hardly the way it was half a century ago."

"But some of it is exactly the same. I, I—when I saw the map, I didn't even realize what the outline of the Strecker building represented. But I know there were areas to the east of that, along the seawall, that were starred by Professor Dakota on her map." After Shreve's explanation this morning, it didn't take much else to figure out where the wooden sheds had been built, close to the morgue and out of view of patients arriving from Manhattan.

He was too smart to trust me entirely.

"You've got nothing to lose." I tried to say it casually, not to reveal how anxious I was to get out of this hellhole. "I can't get very far." Surrounded as we were on three sides by water that was so cold it would kill the strongest swimmer within minutes of submersion, even before the current could carry one away, and bounded on the fourth side by a razor-wire fence, Shreve could hardly disagree.

He picked up one of his neckties and rewound it around my hands, binding them in front of me—rather than behind—so I could move more easily. He carried the long piece of rope in his left hand, while lifting me to my feet with his right. "I'll call your bluff, Ms. Cooper. You've got a bit of time to see if you can find me a gem or two."

It took me several seconds on my feet before I was able to walk a few steps. The cold air had numbed them, and I was fearful of frostbite. That was a good thing, I reminded myself. It at least meant that I thought I was going to survive this ordeal if I was worried about losing a few toes.

Shreve led me through the shell of the building and out the rear door, the same way we had come in hours before. It was the only side of the structure that was not lit by floodlights, and so he knew he could guide me out to the shoreline without detection, in the event anyone had even thought to look for me in this unlikely place.

The city nightscape was more visible to me now. The gray-black sky had cleared to cobalt blue, in the final hour of predawn darkness on the last day of the year. Off in the distance on the Manhattan side, the Art Deco crown beneath the spire of the

Chrysler Building was bathed in the red and green lights of the holiday season. Closer to me, in Queens, the Citicorp tower dominated the skyline, standing behind the Domino Sugar, Silvercup, and *Daily News* signs that stood atop the company plants that fronted the river.

Below the neon lights and factory smokestacks, on the streets and piers, I could not make out a single human being across the water.

Holding my elbow, Shreve walked me to the edge of the river. Rats the size of piglets scampered up and over the boulders that edged the seawall. There were boat docks farther north, on the populated part of the island, but no vessel could come close to this granite border without smashing its hull against the rocks.

I turned back to look at the two ghostlike structures. On my left, parallel with the front wall of the old hospital, was a giant elm tree, bare of her leaves and coated with icicles.

"That tree is one of the markers on the map. Behind us"—I swiveled and pointed with my bound forefingers locked together—"is where the island widens and curves north."

Shreve looked at the shape of the wall, following my direction. I went on, "That had to be the strip on which the deadhouses were built. It's close to the morgue, but still out of sight." That much was logical. I tried to sound just as convincing as I continued to speak. "The map had foundations of four old wooden buildings. The first one was a bit north of that bend in the seawall, if I remember it correctly."

He moved away from me and took a few steps to the edge of the wall, taking care not to slip on the icy boulders. He braced himself with one leg on a piece of granite closest to the water, and I saw it wobble beneath his foot. It must have given him a scare, because I heard him curse beneath his breath and back away from the edge. He decided to explore the loose boulder and got down onto his knees. The rock lifted easily and although it was dark where we were standing, there did not appear to be any treasure hidden beneath it. He scraped a gloved hand against the frozen ground, but the dirt wouldn't yield to such a soft probe. I assume that years of neglect had caused the seawall to decay, too.

"I don't think any of the rocks that close to the edge were marked on the map," I cautioned. I wriggled my hands in the direction of a paved area that seemed to be composed of crumbling material. "This patch would have been under the base of one of the buildings," I suggested.

Again, Shreve dropped to his knees and began to dig his fingers into the crevices, moving anything loose out of his way but coming up empty. No long-buried treasure was going to be that close to the petrified surface of the land.

He was getting short with me now, figuring that I was leading him on a wild-goose chase to save my own neck. He pushed himself back to a standing position and picked up the rope from the ground beside him.

"It makes more sense if you just wait for me inside." Shreve took a step toward me and it was clear that he was ready to use the thick cable to restrain me. I knew he had less than an hour to decide whether it was safe to tie me up and leave me alive beside Charlotte Voight while he returned to Manhattan for the day, or if it was better to dispose of me in the icy current just ten feet away.

I slid my feet backward, one at a time, away from his outstretched arms. "Come on, Ms. Cooper," he said, extending the rope with one hand and trying to grab my wrists with the other. "I'll go over to the college and see what progress the police are making with your disappearance. Don't worry, I'll be here in the afternoon with something for you to eat, and another chance for you to cooperate."

I glided back in the direction of the footpath and Shreve tried to keep up with me, both of us slipping and sliding on the frosted rocks' glassy surface. I was not going back inside the morgue, to be a companion to the decomposed remains of Charlotte Voight.

"Don't be stupid, young lady. You've got nowhere to go."

"Take me with you," I pleaded, skating sideways as he fell on one knee and struggled to keep his balance.

As Shreve scrambled to get back on his feet, I could see over the top of his head that three police cars, red bubble lights flashing, were coming over the small bridge from Long Island City to the northern end, near Roosevelt Island's Main Street. My heartbeat quickened. Perhaps Mercer had given Mike the *Jeopardy!* message after all. Perhaps the motorcade was looking for me.

They were still miles away from this isolated strip of earth, and I needed to stall for as long as possible until they might find me.

I turned south, away from the ruins of Strecker, and headed for the southernmost tip of the island, the only point that could be seen from both Manhattan and Queens. It was treacherous going, and Shreve tried to overtake me as I balanced every tread on the slippery path. He was moving carefully, not racing, since it was as obvious to him as it was to me that I had no way to escape him.

When I was just several feet from the narrow end, I stopped and looked back at my pursuer. In the air, to my left, one of the giant red cabs of the tram had lumbered into view and was cruising down into its station. It was still too early for the system to be operating, and I prayed the movement meant that the police had pressed it into service. Shreve was bearing down on me and had not noticed the police cars or the tram that was traveling behind his back.

"I lied to you," I screamed out at him, my words blown off over the water by the fierce wind.

"What?" he answered, yelling back as he was still trying to make his way to me.

Off the very point of the island was a spit of rock, a huge boulder that was connected to the land by a series of smaller stones. Sometimes barely visible throughout the year, the stones now protruded through the water's surface because of the heavy buildup of snow and frost. Between and around them were patches of ice, thin coatings that endured defiantly during this cold spell against the constant pounding of the swift current.

Only a ten-foot-high beacon stood on the barren rock, useful in fog to guide ships around the island into the channels on either side.

"What did you say?" he shouted at me again as I scanned the horizon, hoping to see patrol cars careering onto the roadway that led to my lonely outpost.

He was not more than an arm's length away, and he paused to catch his breath, winding and twisting the rope like a rodeo rider about to snare a calf. He was confident, and I was terrified, trying to buy time as he closed in on me.

"I said I lied to you before."

He laughed aloud at me. "And exactly which part was a lie?"

I checked over my shoulder and back to the very edge of the seawall. As I stood on top of an ancient fragment of granite, I pushed my jacket aside and poked my bound hands around the edges of my pants pockets.

Shreve's face screwed into a puzzled expression as he watched me fumble.

I strained to hear beyond the howl of the wind but could not make out the noise of any sirens. Where could the cops be? What was taking them so long to find us?

I stepped one foot down onto a flat rock that jutted out of the black water and was the first link to the boulder less than ten feet away. When I was standing securely with two legs in place, I glanced back at Shreve and pulled the paper from my pocket.

"It's the map, Mr. Shreve. I lied when I told you I had time to make copies. This is the original. It arrived in yesterday's mail, just before we went up to the meeting in Sylvia's office. This is what you want, Professor. It's the only one there is."

The wind whipped at the paper and tried to snatch it from my hands and carry it away. I crammed it into the pocket of my parka, and continued on my hazardous journey.

It was *my* turn to be confident now. If I could navigate the seven or eight stones to get across to the large boulder, I would be safe. Shreve would not dare to follow me. The more than eighty pounds that separated what I guessed our weights to be would fracture the ice, should he attempt to step on it. And I could cling to the beacon, waiting out the sunrise, sure that the police were on their way to find me.

If I didn't make it, and I was keenly aware of that possibility, it would be an awful death. But faster, I assured myself, than anything Winston Shreve had in mind.

I hadn't counted on how badly he wanted to get his hands on the map.

I was on the fourth stone in the icy archipelago, straining to keep my feet from slipping, hindered by my inability to stretch out my arms and stabilize myself against the wind above and the slick surface below. Behind me, I heard the crackling noise of breaking ice.

I ignored the voice in my head that had been telling me not to look back. Shreve had followed my path and was on the first stone. He had stepped off to the second one, but his feet were longer than mine and the rocky incline could not hold his thick boots. His left leg had slid down and landed on the crust of ice, breaking it apart and allowing the black water to bubble through.

"Give me the goddamn map," he screamed at me. He had frozen in place, it seemed, now aware of the dangerous trail he had undertaken. "Give me the paper!"

The wind played with him, too, and his words were lost somewhere over the roiling water.

My next two obstacles were relatively flat and elongated. I moved across them easily and counted only three more on my course to the big rock.

A glance back and it was clear that Shreve was consumed by his desire to get to the map. He had made the decision to come after me. His feet held on the third step, and he paused there to figure how to make it safely onto the next one.

The great buildings of the United Nations were directly across to my right now. Lights were going on in some of the offices as the sky began to brighten. The city was coming to life. Someone would find me.

My foot reached out to anchor itself on the next rock, but it was peaked and ragged, with no flat area on which to step. I leaned forward and grabbed its crest with my clasped hands, stretching out the toe of my right foot to find a hold on the slippery cover. It seemed secure, and so I pulled myself forward, balancing my one hundred fifteen pounds on either side of the crest. As fast as I could free my hands and move again, I teetered forward to the adjacent perch, almost at my goal.

As I stood on the next-to-the-last rock, I was ready to launch myself to safety. I grabbed at the naked shrub that was poised on the ledge in front of me and tried to pull myself onto the slick boulder. But the ice beneath my left foot ruptured sharply and my entire leg was submerged in the frigid water. I clung desperately to the small gray stubble of the branch that was supporting me and kicked my quickly benumbed leg furiously to get it out of the icy river.

Slowly and agonizingly, I hoisted myself onto solid ground. Shreve's scream pierced the air and the wind slammed its sound against my head.

I opened my eyes and saw him grasping for my leg, which was dangling over the side of the great boulder. He was trying to get me to save him, I thought, not to hurt me, although it hardly mattered at that point. As he had reached out for me, he slid off the peaked rock and collapsed through the slim coating of ice.

"The rope!" I yelled at him. "Throw me the rope."

But the wicked current tugged at him and swept him away from the rocks. I pulled myself up to a standing position using the sturdiest branch of the small bush, but with my hands still tied I was unable to extend my reach near the drowning man.

Shreve screamed once more as he struggled to keep his head above the waves. The turbulent inky water had claimed him, and he was dragged downriver at ferocious speed. He shouted something again, gurgling insensibly as he was pulled down by the paralyzing force of the raging flow.

I lowered myself onto the ground, wet and frozen. I rested my head against a low stump and gave up waiting for salvation. The Pepsi-Cola sign flashed and there seemed to be early morning traffic racing along the FDR Drive.

The little red snub-nosed tugboat of the New York City Fire Department seemed to be making a beeline for my deserted boulder. I tried to tell myself its crew would see me here, with dawn breaking through the night sky. As it neared me, on its prow I thought I could make out the figures of Mike Chapman and Mercer Wallace, standing beside two uniformed firemen. Mercer must have repeated the story I fed to Shreve about the Blackwell *Jeopardy!* clue, and Mike had made the connection.

Cold, exhaustion, and hunger overwhelmed me.

I closed my eyes.

When I came to, the first thing I saw was the pure white counterpane on my hospital bed. I felt warm and comforted for the first time in days. Looped around the upper rim of the metal railing was an intravenous tube. The IV pole was next to my headboard, and I could see that the glucose solution was almost empty. I must have been badly dehydrated.

I looked at the clock on the bedside table and it said 11:42. The shades were drawn three-quarters of the way down, open enough to reveal that it was night.

I rolled from my side onto my back, wiggling my toes as I did so. I lifted each foot, one at a time, to reach my hands, and counted to make sure I had all my toes.

When I moved onto my other side, my cheek scraped against something hard. There, pinned against the corner of the pillow, was Jake's glittering little bird atop a rock.

Through the glass windows that separated my room from the nurses' station, I could see five people standing together. Jake Tyler and Mercer Wallace were leaning against the counter, watching Mike Chapman and laughing at him. He was gesturing with great animation, regaling two nurses with his war stories and adventures.

I knew it wouldn't take long for Mike and Mercer to coax me back to Blackwells, with the old map, to dig for diamonds with them. They would find my stalker, too. I was sure of that.

Outside the door to my room was another IV stand. Attached to it, hanging upside down, was a bottle of champagne. Tomorrow would begin a happier new year.

I smiled and closed my eyes.